SHADES OF
THE LINGERING

A NEW PSYCHOLOGICAL THRILLER

SONYA PRITCHARD

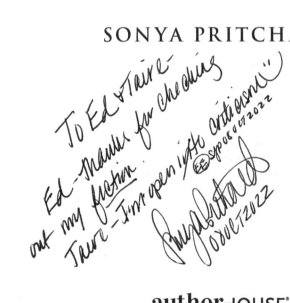

authorHOUSE®

AuthorHouse™
1663 Liberty Drive
Bloomington, IN 47403
www.authorhouse.com
Phone: 833-262-8899

Published by AuthorHouse 08/19/2022

ISBN: 978-1-6655-6775-6 (sc)
ISBN: 978-1-6655-6773-2 (hc)
ISBN: 978-1-6655-6774-9 (e)

Library of Congress Control Number: 2022915431

Print information available on the last page.

This book is printed on acid-free paper.

Cover design courtesy of Professor Nightmare Inc.

DEDICATION

This book is dedicated to my family and my friends.
You've listened to so many of my crazy ideas over the years....
and yet you're still there for me when I want to talk about another one.

Acknowledgements

So many people have shown their unwavering support during my 16-year journey to take this manuscript to print. A heartfelt thanks goes out to each and every one of you! You kept asking how it was going, never lost faith in me, and got as excited as I did when it was close to completion. Your support means the world to me. I love you all!

A few of you deserve special thanks.

First, I want to thank my daughter, Cayla, for helping me through the ups and downs, when I loved my book and when I hated it. You urged me on, and when I finally submitted it, you said you were proud of me. Those words meant so much, especially knowing how proud I am of you for all of the amazing things you've accomplished in your life so far. You've shown me, on so many occasions, that it is absolutely possible to make your dream a reality. You have always inspired me to remain true to my goal.

Second, I want to thank my mom. You were the first to read my earliest drafts, and you were patient through all of my revisions. The suggestions you offered along the way helped to make this a much better book. Thank you for always being there to talk things through when I got frustrated. Whether you know it or not, you've always shown me what one person can do when they set their mind to it. I've witnessed your endless energy and seen you create incredible things. To this day, you continue to amaze me.

Third, a huge thanks to John Denley, AKA Professor Nightmare, a fellow fan of all things spooky. Years ago, you listened to my ideas for this book, helped me brainstorm possible titles, and used this information to surprise me with a phenomenal cover design that I could use when I was ready. Every time I looked at it, I was inspired to keep going, to see it where it was meant to be. When I reached out years later and told you that the title had been taken, you willingly reworked the original design. I appreciate your collaboration on this project more than you can ever know, and I am so very proud to showcase your creative talent on the cover of my first novel.

Finally, I want to thank the team at AuthorHouse. Back in 2006, when I started the outline for this story, I had no idea what I was going to do with it or whether it was even possible to one day see it in print. You've helped me realize a lifelong dream. Thank you for your guidance and your expertise, and thank you for being there for authors like me who have always hoped to one day hold a book in our hands, a book containing words that once existed only in our minds.

Scientific discoveries can spring from various sources ... brilliant minds, one person's dream, and often, by pure chance ... if there is such a thing.

CONTENTS

Dedication...v
Acknowledgements...vii
Prologue...xiii

Chapter 1..1
Chapter 2..16
Chapter 3..23
Chapter 4..32
Chapter 5..44
Chapter 6..60
Chapter 7..64
Chapter 8..74
Chapter 9..77
Chapter 10..81
Chapter 11..90
Chapter 12..93
Chapter 13..101
Chapter 14..109
Chapter 15..116
Chapter 16..120
Chapter 17..122
Chapter 18..125
Chapter 19..127
Chapter 20..133
Chapter 21..139
Chapter 22..147

Chapter 23..154
Chapter 24 158
Chapter 25..180
Chapter 26..185
Chapter 27..199
Chapter 28..201
Chapter 29..204
Chapter 30..207
Chapter 31 209
Chapter 32..211
Chapter 33..224
Chapter 34..238
Chapter 35..241
Chapter 36..244
Chapter 37..249
Chapter 38..258
Chapter 39..260
Chapter 40 275
Chapter 41 282
Chapter 42..290
Chapter 43..299
Chapter 44 302

Epilogue...307

PROLOGUE

Dear reader:

Before we begin, let me introduce myself. My name is Nadia King, and like you, I've played a few different roles in my lifetime. The four most relevant to this story are granddaughter, daughter, scientist, and author. I've also had the rare chance of witnessing three levels of existence, but more to come on that.

As a constant student of this strange and sometimes hard-to-understand world we live in, I'm always listening, watching, and questioning. I've learned a good deal, especially in these past few years, but not nearly as much as my grandmother, Marianna Rose. I have a feeling that Gram Marie learned a lot more than most. Looking back, I wish I'd asked more questions while I had the chance, but don't we all?

I visited my Gram Marie in the hospital on the day she died. She reached for my hand as I slid into the seat beside her bed, but she only spoke after everyone else had left the room. Once we were alone, she offered one of her playful winks and gave my hand a little squeeze. Knowing it was hard for her to speak above a whisper, I leaned in close.

"There will come a time," she said, her voice scratchy, her tired eyes glistening in the harsh fluorescent light, "when you'll be able to look back at your life, with its twists and turns and odd coincidences, and see it for all that it really was. I should have told you more a long time ago, Nadia. I should have got you on your way a little quicker." She gave a raspy inhale. "It's too late for that now, though, but no matter. I trust you'll figure it out, and I'll see you on the other side. You come find me, you hear?" Two breaths after that, she was gone—gone from this level of existence, at least.

I sat there for a long time, not wanting to let go of her hand, not sure what to make of what she'd just said, but I understand now, and I think a part of my job in this crazy world is to get you, dear reader, "on your way a little quicker." If you've ever wondered whether some nonphysical part of our selves might linger in the world of the living even after our souls are left without a body to call home, then this book is for you. Someone like you will want to know what I've discovered.

Times are changing, and the changes are forcing us to adjust our perception. Hidden truths have been teasing us for ages. We've seen hints of them here and there, dangling like frayed threads just beyond our reach, but now is the time to start seeing them for what they really are, to quit denying that they exist. Our self-imposed blindness has to end.

Take a look back at your own life. Believe in the things you've questioned and listen to what I've found. I hope you enjoy the answers as much as I do.

Sincerely,
Nadia

If a man is offered a fact which goes against his instincts, he will scrutinize it closely, and unless the evidence is overwhelming, he will refuse to believe it. If, on the other hand, he is offered something which affords a reason for acting in accordance to his instincts, he will accept it even on the slightest evidence. The origin of myths is explained in this way.
—Bertrand Russell

It came as a whisper ...
Open your eyes.
What do you see?
Now close them, and make yourself believe me
when I tell you there is so much *more*.
Now open your eyes. Has anything changed?
Your answer should be ... everything.
—Remmington

From the Journal of Nadia King
Age Twenty-Five

My morning walk with the dog triggers this entry.

We were nearly home, a few steps from the front door, when Hera, my sleek and ever curious white Greyhound, turned around mid-stride. She craned her long, thin neck and lowered her muzzle to the ground and then backtracked to a spot a few feet away. When her nose came to rest over a small patch of clover near the edge of the sidewalk, she froze. Her nostrils flared as she pulled in some scent.

While I watched her, a thought occurred to me. *How often does a dog stop to do this?* We've seen it hundreds of times, and more often than not, we ourselves never smell anything out of the ordinary. We accept our human limitations and never question the scent's existence.

A canine's sense of smell is at least a thousand times more sensitive than our own thanks to basic anatomy. Dogs and humans possess the same olfactory receptors in the nose; it's just that canines have more than 220 million of them. Humans have about five million, so it's easy to see why Hera is much better at picking up a faint scent than I could ever hope to be.

A part of me wonders if there might be other things in this world that most of us don't notice due to a similar glitch in human anatomy. Auras and the passing energies that some call ghosts come to mind. What if some of us just have the right type, or the right number, of receptors to detect them? Given my past experiences, I have no other explanation.

A recent poll claims that 45 percent of Americans believe in ghosts, and 41 percent believe in psychic ability. What about the rest? Surely, they too must have experienced something during the course of their lives that made them question their disbelief. Surely, at least once, they must have glimpsed a fleeting shadow and wondered if it was more than just a figment of their imagination. They must have, at one point, read at least one of the documented accounts of psychic energy and given it some degree of credit.

I read an article this morning about an English physicist who spent his entire life in the company of these fleeting shadows. He believed they were the lingering energies of the deceased and proposed that a person could learn to transition between their world and ours while still alive, as if passing through this thin veil was no different than strolling through an open door. His name was Sir Anthony Bard, and he left an interesting note on the final page of his journal right before he disappeared:

> Doubters may claim that seeing is believing, but sometimes, as in the case of ghosts and the afterlife, one first needs to believe in order to finally see.

The journal, left open on his desk, was allegedly discovered by his wife shortly after she heard a "sharp crack" that came from inside his study. She was on her way to the kitchen with a pot of tea when the sound broke the silence. She claims that when she looked inside, her husband was gone.

"Vanished into thin air," were her exact words.

He hasn't been seen since.

Of course, there are doubters. Some even believe that this tiny woman, a teacher by trade, killed her husband and hid the body. Then there are people like me who are left wondering. We both want answers, but we each have different ideas of what those might be.

Sir Anthony Bard went looking for answers, unafraid of what he might find, and I think he might have been onto something. I'm just as curious as he was, but unlike him, I'm too afraid of the unknown to go poking around in it. I do believe in ghosts. I even envy those who willingly see them, but most of the time, I think I'd rather not see any more than I have already.

CHAPTER 1

The Present
Age Forty-One
Recurring Dreams

The moon shines bright and full in the sky, making the long row of dense summer trees cast thick shadows. They offer the promise of camouflage, which is why I stay close to them as I work my way around to the back of the house. Using the rear door makes more sense given the circumstances.

I stop under the last tree, huddle there in the dark, and steal one final glance over my shoulder into the alley behind me. No movement catches my eye, but the stillness provides little comfort. I know better than to let down my guard. Someone, or something, is following me, and even though I haven't actually seen it yet, I know it's there. I can smell it on the breeze, smoky at first, pungent. Whatever it is has been staying just out of my line of vision for most of my walk, but my gut instinct tells me it's getting braver as we near the house. I can feel it following more closely than it ever has in the past.

I study the open expanse of lawn that stretches out between me and the back patio. It spans no more than fifty feet, but even this seems too far, too long of a stretch to be out in the open, but there's nothing more I can do, and there's no time for hesitation. I push off and sprint toward the house. A barberry hedge lines the perimeter, and when I reach it, I press my back against the scratchy branches and look once again toward the alley. Still clear.

Three concrete steps on my left lead up to the raised patio, a place

1

where I used to spend endless summers reading books, playing with friends, and sipping lemonade from mugs filled to the brim with ice. Those were better days than this, but then again, things could be worse. At least the terrain is familiar. At least I know where I need to go. I'm almost there.

I climb the steps. The wet leaves that cover them feel cool against my bare feet. My shoes lie in a ditch a few miles back. I tossed them there, afraid that their incessant tapping against the road would keep me from hearing anything that might be shuffling along behind me. When I get to the top step, I regret that decision immediately.

Strewn across the surface of the patio are a million fragments of glass, each one catching the moonlight as if to taunt me. The sliding door stands no more than ten feet away, its frame now empty.

They think this will stop you. They think they've cornered you, but they're wrong. You can walk across the glass, Nadia. You know you can, and you know you won't get hurt if you do.

This thought doesn't come immediately. I stand there for a full minute worrying before I realize that this is just a dream, a very lucid dream. I remember that I'm the one controlling it, and then I look again at the glass and take a step.

Tiny shards crunch under my toes as I cross the patio, but there's no pain. When I get to the door, I slide through the opening and into the breakfast nook without a scratch. Glancing back through the shattered door, I see that the alley is still clear, but I can't stop myself from yanking the heavy draperies closed nonetheless. I know they won't keep anything out, but they at least block my view. Without the visual, I feel safer somehow, even with the darkness of the house pressing in around me.

A full moon guided me through the streets, but inside, my eyes struggle to grasp even a fragment of light. The kitchen, just beyond the breakfast nook, seems to be better lit, so I move in that direction. In the archway, my feet involuntarily stop me in my tracks. The kitchen is a room linked to many childhood memories, most of them good, others I'd rather forget. A distant streetlamp pushes light in through the small window above the sink, and as the trees sway in the wind outside, the angle of the incoming beam casts strange shadows. These shadows summon an unwelcomed thought. It's one of those memories that I don't want to recall just now, but my mind latches onto it and won't let go. Long faces. Empty eyes. Extended hands. Shadows that waited at the top of the basement stairs. I was just five years old when I first saw them. A french door separated us, but those rectangles of glass left nothing to the imagination.

All the better to see you with, my dear.

A shiver runs up my spine, and I shoot a nervous glance toward the far corner of the kitchen where that same french door leads to the basement. I don't want to go any closer, but I need to see it, need to know if it's open or closed. Instinctively, I reach out my hand and feel for the light switch on the far wall.

Don't do it, Nadia. Light will draw attention to where you've gone.

The thought actually makes me laugh out loud. My pursuers already know where to find me, and they've never needed light before. In fact, they actually prefer finding you in the dark. It's more frightening that way.

Still, I decide to drop my hand. My eyes are already beginning to adjust to the darkness. I can see the outline of the basement door, dark against the lighter-colored walls around it. I inch closer, and from about three feet away, I can make out the shape of the brass chain in the upper left-hand corner. I can't yet tell if it's latched or not. Two steps more do the trick. The wave of relief is immediate. From here, I can see that the door is closed and the chain is indeed latched. My childhood visitors will have to find another way in this time. I don't even check to see if they're standing in the dark cellarway beyond the door. I simply turn and continue on my way.

A swinging door leads into the dining room. It's propped open and secured in place with a chair, revealing a room that's even brighter than the kitchen. My path has been clearly laid out. Glass door shattered, dining room door left open, each room brighter than the previous. *Just follow the breadcrumbs*, I think. *This way, my pretty.*

As I squeeze past the chair, I take a moment to peek behind the door, not to look for shadows this time but just to see if the typewriter is still there. I find that it is, just like I knew it would be. Each time I visited Gram Marie as a kid, I'd drag the heavy brown case to the living room floor, flip up the lid to expose the bulky antique beast inside, then sit and type for hours, using one finger of each hand to punch at the keys. The old manual typewriter required more finger strength than my tiny hands could ever muster, but that never stopped me from using it. Gram Marie always said I'd be a writer, and here I am. The thought makes me smile.

My smile fades though as I begin to notice my surroundings.

Why is the furniture piled in the corners? Is that graffiti on the walls?

As I'm thinking this, the scraping sound comes again, the one I've heard intermittently on my way to the house. I cock an ear back in the direction of the breakfast nook and listen. There's only silence at first, but then, after a few seconds, a raspy voice floats toward me through the air as no more than a whisper. The words are garbled, but the voice is clearly recognizable. My heart skips a beat even though I know better than to think it's really my father. Rowan has warned me that they can disguise their voices, changing them to target the person they're trying to find. Her warning is secondary to another more important fact, however. The voice doesn't belong to my father because my father is dead.

A part of me wants to run, that little-girl part who vividly remembers the shadows in this house. It battles with the part of me that wants to stay and face what's coming. I've always been torn between these two options, but when the scraping noise comes again, the little girl wins. I scramble past the clutter and the graffiti, over the piles of papers that are stacked on the floor. I keep going until I reach the living room.

There, a bright sheet of moonlight spills in through the large picture window on the facing wall. It pools in the center of the floor, the glow making the room's disarray even more obvious. Nothing is where it should be. On my left, the couch has been pulled away from the wall and flipped onto its back. It lies on a diagonal, one of its arms jutting toward the center of the room. To my right, vases and picture frames have been brushed off the fireplace mantel and lie in broken mounds on the floor. Beside those, the pillows from the armchair and couch are heaped in a pile.

Nadia, you know what they're doing. They're trying to distract you. You just have to keep going. This is the little girl speaking. The grown-up in me fights back. *Rowan wants me to stay and face them, and so does my father. That's why I'm here.*

4

Beyond the living room's picture window, moonlight cascades across the field in the distance. Trees sway in time with the increasing wind. The enormous white-yellow disc of the moon looms over the trees, and with its overwhelming presence, nothing on the ground is concealed. I can see for miles, even beyond the edges of the field. *The scene would make a beautiful painting*, I think.

As soon as this thought crosses my mind, a figure steps into the frame, the thing I'd hoped the draperies in the breakfast nook would hide, one of the things I suspected might be lurking in the stairwell to the basement. In the bottom left-hand corner of the window, just on the other side of the glass stands a tall figure. I can make out the shape of a head and broad shoulders, but because the figure is backlit with moonlight, its features aren't clear. I have no way of knowing if it's facing the house or looking off into the distance. Hoping for the latter, and hoping I'm not too late, I inch backward, out of the circle of light, drop to my knees, and scurry behind the overturned couch.

I peer around its edge. The figure gives no indication as to whether it's seen me or not. I want to believe that it hasn't, but my heart knows the truth. It knows I'm here, and it knows of my curiosity as well as my fear, just as it always has. It's toying with me.

I look around to gather my bearings. To my left, I find a clear path of carpet leading to the stairs, which is exactly where I need to go. I crawl the distance, keeping one shoulder pressed against the couch. As I approach the other end, I can make out a vague shape near the bottom step. A completely unexpected smell of freshly hung linen hits my nose. It's a smell reminiscent of my childhood. It makes me think of Gram Marie. She always hung the sheets and pillowcases outside to dry, and when I pulled them over my head in the middle of a nightmare, I liked to pretend that the smell kept me safe, a force field of sorts, protection from the things that roamed the house. The shape, in fact, turns out to be a laundry basket, full to the brim with neatly folded clothes. It seems so out of place.

Just push it aside and keep moving, Nadia. They don't want you to go upstairs. They don't want you to see what's there, but you need to.

I push it aside and continue to crawl, feeling my knees press into the damp carpet on the stairs. Beyond the basket, the smells fall more in tune with the obvious decay of the house. The air is musty, thick with acrid hints of moisture and mold. Halfway to the top, my mind convinces me to pause, curious to know if the figure is still in the window. I grasp two of the stair balusters, one in each hand, and press my forehead against them, like a child trying to catch a glimpse of Santa. I peer down into the living room below. The window reveals an empty yard beyond. The figure is gone.

It's gone to find a way inside, I think. *It's coming for you.*

This is enough to make me stand and sprint up the remaining stairs. There seems to be far too many of them, but that's how it always is in dreams. My legs feel rubbery, and my right hand swings at my side, never losing its grip on the object it holds, the thing that caused me to come here in the first place. When I finally reach the second-floor landing, it's dark again. The curtains over the window at the top of the stairs have been drawn. I double over, hands on my knees, taking a minute to catch my breath and let my eyes readjust. As I stand there, a new sound comes, not a scraping or a whisper this time, but more of a quiet humming. It comes from near my feet and around me all at once, and while I can't immediately place the sound, it doesn't frighten me. When something soft brushes against my leg, I don't scream. This, I recognize.

My hands search blindly for the curtains on the window, and when my fingers find the damp fabric, I yank them aside and turn to face my company.

Moonlight spills over my shoulder and illuminates at least two dozen cats. They're everywhere, perched on the window seat, on the banister, and some even on the stairs that I just climbed, each one watching me with eyes that glint the bright yellow-green of fireflies. The big one, the one whose tail has wrapped around my leg, remains at my feet and yowls up at me. It's another distraction, I know this, but even so, I bend over to run a hand down his back. His fur is soft, and he lifts his chin so I can scratch underneath, making me think of Ares, who also loves to be scratched there. The humming is his purring. As I ruffle his fur, a hint of smokiness wafts up from it, as if the animal has been hanging around a campfire for days.

And why would he smell smoky, Nadia?

I continue stroking the cat, but when the scent changes, I pull back my hand and look toward the stairs. On my next inhale, there it is, the pungent smell from the alley, the smell that first accompanied my realization that I was being followed. It's the scent of flowers and something dead all at once, and it's growing stronger, leaving no doubt in my mind that whatever has been following me is now inside the house and getting closer.

Every one of the cats has its eyes on me. They don't seem to notice the scent, but cats are never particularly keen on smell, are they? Sight is their strength, even in the dark. I turn and glance down the hall behind me. The bedroom I used to sleep in as a child is at the far end of it. That's where I need to be.

Four of the largest cats follow as I turn and sprint down the ever-lengthening hallway, two of them weaving between my feet as if they mean to trip me. I hear one squeal as I accidentally tramp on a wayward paw, but I don't stop until I reach the bedroom door. I fling it open and rush inside, having every intention to slam it closed again before the cats can follow me in. To my surprise, though, when I turn, I find that they've stopped a few feet from the threshold. They don't seem to want to come any closer. Even when I open the door wide, they stay where they are, crouched in the hallway, staring up at me, tails twitching, like tigers watching their prey. I lean my head out into the hall and look toward the stairs. The cat I trampled sits a few yards back, licking its paw, a silhouette against the moonlight, like the figure beyond the picture window.

Why won't they come in?

Of course, we always assume that animals have some innate ability to detect the "wrongness" of a place, don't we? Back when I was a kid, my Gram Marie's cat, Phillipe, always refused to go into her basement. Based on what I saw there, I never blamed him.

I look behind me into the room. Darkness is all I can see.

Like every other goddamn room in this place, I think. *In or out, Nadia. Make up your mind and do it fast.*

That's when I see the cats turn and glance toward the stairs. Something back there has their attention now. This is enough to make up my mind.

I back into the room, ease the door shut, and press my shoulder blades into the wood. I slide down onto my haunches and pull my knees into my chest. It's coming.

Faint meows filter in under the door. Fur brushes up against the wood. I can hear more cats gathering, the yowls getting louder.

Get out of here, you stupid cats, I think. *Move away from the door. You're going to lead it right to me.*

Just then, the hall falls perfectly silent, as if I'd been imagining the sounds in the first place. Minutes tick by with no sound whatsoever. I place my ear against the door, straining to hear anything that might tell me what's happening on the other side, and then I shudder when I imagine my pursuer doing the same, its cold ear only the thickness of the wood away from my own but very capable of hearing my heavy breathing. I lean forward to check the thin strip of moonlight under the door, watching for any hint of a shadow. As I do this, I feel a draft caress the back of my neck.

Gooseflesh prickles my arms as another childhood memory springs to mind. Drafts like this are what woke me in the middle of the night when I slept in this room as a child. I never wanted to know what caused them back then, but Rowan would want me to know now. My father would want me to know. If Gram Marie were here, she'd tell me to close my eyes until the draft stops, so that's what I do. I close my eyes and wait.

It isn't long until a soft click interrupts the silence. My eyelids take on that pinkish glow that suggests a light has come on in the room. When I open my eyes, what I see confuses me.

In the center of the room is an operating table, a man stretched out on top of it. His face and body are covered by a drape of green cloth. I can only see the top of his head. A piece of his skull has been removed, and within that circle of white bone, a glistening mass of brain tissue has been exposed. The machines behind him beep in a perfect rhythm, promising that he's alive even though I see no heave to his chest. I watch the IV bag drip and then look past the table and the equipment. The room is immaculate, white, not anything like the bedroom I stayed in as a child with its warm colors and perfectly placed art on the walls. These walls are bare.

My eyes go back to the man on the table, mostly because something about him, something about this situation, strikes me as familiar. I reach out to remove the drape of cloth from his face, but just before my fingers can even touch it, the draft comes again. This time, it tousles my hair and scatters the leaves that litter the floor, leaves that hadn't been there a minute ago. As I watch the leaves swirl around my feet, a cold hand comes to rest on my shoulder. All at once, I hear the raspy whispering, smell the flowers, and note the thin film of sweat that has collected on my hands and face.

I've been found. I was curious enough to look under the drape, and now it's time.

I turn to face my pursuer, but before I can see his face, the room goes dark again, leaving me only with the lingering scent. *But the scent has changed again, hasn't it?* It's pleasant now, spicy, like cinnamon, but not really. This, too, I recognize. This is what I was meant to learn from the very beginning. Gram Marie was right.

The next thing I know, I'm sitting in my favorite chair in the library, clothes drenched in sweat. I scan the room, taking in the familiarity of the huge stone fireplace and my overflowing bookshelves. Ares, our fluffy gray cat, is curled up in an identical brown leather chair next to me.

The dreams come and go like this sometimes, vivid and frantic, crammed with scenes that switch from one to another in rapid succession, one having absolutely nothing to do with the next. The recurring patterns might seem odd to those who analyze them, but in fact, each scene is surprisingly symbolic of my life. More often than not, my dreams, like my paintings, are actually premonitions.

In recent years, I've learned how to gain control over my dreams. At this point, I can make choices and change them at will, rewind or fast-forward. Professionals in sleep analysis call this lucid dreaming, and I've become quite the expert at it, which is why I'm now a favorite subject of Jakob's at the University. The only thing I haven't been able to do is prevent the nightmares in the first place. If I could learn how to do that, I might feel like I'd accomplished something useful. Maybe then I could get a decent night's sleep.

The clock over the mantel claims it's 6:30 a.m. I must have come down in the middle of the night to get a drink of water and then fallen asleep in the chair as I often do. The fact that I don't remember this isn't surprising. I've always been a sleepwalker. On the floor, spread open near my feet, is yesterday's local newspaper. The headline, including my name, stares up at me in bold letters. Attention is apparently unavoidable when you're a small-town author whose first novel quickly becomes a best seller.

I reach down and grab one corner of the paper, roll it into a tube, and then tuck it under my arm. I carry it with me into the laundry room. There, I peel off my sweat-drenched pajamas and replace them with my favorite pair of jeans and a black T-shirt, both of which wait on top of the clothes basket, neatly folded. Given my previous dream, I'm eager to peek into the bedroom upstairs, the one at the end of the hall.

Ares pads up the stairs alongside me but keeps his distance as we navigate the upstairs hallway. He doesn't twirl between my legs like the other cats did. At the far end of the hall, the bedroom door is closed, the room beyond it quiet. I press an ear against one of the top panels, listening, unsure of whether I'm ready to go inside or not.

Ares stares up at me, unblinking, the little V of dark gray fur between his eyes giving him an angry sort of expression. He looks at me as if to say, "Well, what the hell else are you going to do at this point if you don't go in?"

He's right, of course, so I give the door a shove.

The old hinges creak as it opens, and in response to the noise, the man on the bed looks up from his book. A pair of reading glasses is balanced on the end of his suntanned nose. His long legs are stretched out in front of him, one ankle crossed over the other. Bright sunlight streams in through the windows behind him and bounces off the room's yellow walls.

The dogs are sprawled on the floor in front of the bed and don't move a muscle when I step inside. Only their eyes shift, regarding me. They're content where they are, happy with the company, and I don't blame them.

Ares, however, makes no move to enter the room. He's perfectly content in the hall. He sits just beyond the threshold, still as a statue, his eyes reflecting the morning light.

I look at the man and smile. He's exactly as I remember him, at least how I remember him before he got sick. Propped up against the headboard, leaning against a pile of pillows, he's finally wearing something other than his "power suit," which I've grown so accustomed to seeing him in. An oversized gray sweatshirt and comfortable jeans have replaced the business attire, and like me, he's without socks despite the chill in the room. No telltale signs remain of the cancer that hit him so hard, ravaging his body as it does to so many these days. The frailty that had been so evident during those long months of treatment have been exchanged for a remarkably healthy glow. The weight that he lost has been regained, and his dark hair is full again, except for that one spot on top, of course. It's nice to see him looking so healthy.

He smiles in my direction, as if he can read my mind, one far too busy flipping through old memories to even think of offering a hello. I think of how this one man has motivated me to do more than I ever would have attempted otherwise, how he seems to have unlimited resources at his disposal. With his help, and his connections, my dreams became possible.

Without saying a word, he shifts a few of the smaller decorative pillows out of the way to make room for me at the edge of the bed. I remain in the doorway, not sure if I'm ready to be that close just yet. It's his first visit under these new arrangements. Noting my hesitation, he doesn't press further. He knows me too well, knows that I'll come to him when I'm ready. I, on the other hand, don't seem to know him as well as I thought I did.

How could I have missed what was happening? How could I have been so blind?

He's had an ulterior motive all along. Men always do, yet I never saw it coming. What bothers me even more is the fact that we wasted so much time on formality when things could have been different so much sooner. But this is my own fault, isn't it? I was the one who put up defenses. Now that he's back, though, we'll have our second chance. Of course, this means that things will have to change at Amulet. Once people know he's been involved in the project, our research will be forced to take a different direction.

Amulet is my brainchild, an institute whose research has the potential to touch nearly every aspect of science as we know it today, an institute that teeters on the verge of making what, I believe, will be one of the greatest discoveries of our time. Until now, and for many different reasons, I've left most of the decisions up to one of my lead scientists, Dr. Jorg Sterling. To date, Amulet's fate hinges on the results of one final experiment, and it just so happens that my returning visitor is the only one who can provide the knowledge and the connections needed to finish our work. His role in the project has been kept a secret up until now, but those involved will have to be told something soon. Just not everything. And not everyone. At least not yet.

I glance at the clock on the nightstand. It's nearly seven o'clock, almost time to leave for work. I want nothing more than to talk about us, about him, about where he's been, but those things will have to wait. We don't have much time.

I move closer to the bed and drop the newspaper onto his lap. It flops open to the headline. He doesn't even look down. His eyes remain locked on mine, eyes so brown they're almost black.

"Thank you for the invite, Nadia," he says, his voice deep and calm.

The faintest hint of his cologne floats in the air between us. He smells of Old Spice, the scent like cinnamon, but not really. It's another distraction that I have to push aside for now. We need to discuss the paper. The headline is only there because of him.

I point at it. "This wasn't the plan, you know. My novel was supposed to get me out of the lab, not keep me in it. Now that things are going so well, though, Sterling is practically drooling over the idea of a breakthrough. We'll have to wrap up soon. I'm just not sure he's ready for what comes next."

My visitor lifts the paper, gives it a cursory glance, and then places it on the bed to his left. His eyes lock on mine again.

"Sterling has no choice but to be ready," he says, peering up at me over his glasses. "Which means you've got to be ready as well, Nadia. Let's face it, Sterling's not the only one who might have a problem with this discovery of yours. It's going to cause a little confusion for quite a few people out there."

I laugh. "A little confusion? That's putting it mildly, don't you think?"

He studies me. "Are you worried?"

"Of course, I'm worried."

He smiles. "Well, like I've told you a million times before, worrying is wasted energy, and you know it. There's no way out now." His eyes hold mine. "You should be looking forward to what comes next, not dreading it."

"I might be less worried if I thought Sterling was going to continue supporting the project once he knows the whole story. What if he denies any connection to Amulet once he finds out how much we've kept from him along the way? He could pull out, taking his research and his cells with him. Then what?"

He shakes his head. "There you go again with the worrying." He motions for me to sit next to him, patting his hand on the edge of the mattress. "Come here," he says.

Still hesitant, I perch on the edge of the bed. I study his face, noting the sharp jaw, the deep laugh lines that bracket each side of his mouth.

Have his eyes always been so dark?

"Nadia, listen to me," he says. "We've been through this before. All you can do is prepare and take each day as it comes. You haven't proven anything just yet. There's still work to be done. Before you worry yourself to death, collect your data. Get everything in order, and then, if you get the results you're expecting … that's when you can start to worry, but only about who you'll tell first."

I'm struck by something he's just said.

"What do you mean *if* we get the results we're expecting? Are you saying there's a chance this final experiment could fail?"

He reaches out and wraps both of his hands around mine. His palms are rough and warm. There's a hint of concern in his eyes.

"Nadia," he says, "I have complete confidence in you. That said, it's always possible that you'll run into a few unexpected bumps along the way. I have no doubt you'll find a way to make it work, though. Consider this," he says, giving my hands a squeeze. "Would you be talking to me right now if this isn't what you were meant to be doing?"

I look down at his hands and shrug.

He places a finger under my chin and lifts it so I have no choice but to look directly at him. "No, you wouldn't," he says. "So, stop questioning it, all right?"

When I nod, he smiles and falls back against the pillows behind him.

"So, we keep to the original plan?" he asks.

"I don't know about that," I say, and then I point to the paper. "You should look at the article. Sterling is telling people that Amulet is on the verge of finding a cure for stroke." I raise my eyebrows at him. "I think he might be in for a little surprise, don't you?"

He glances at the paper but doesn't pick it up.

"To be honest," I say, "I think it might be best if you make an appearance soon."

"Have you thought about how you'll explain my role in this to Sterling?" he asks. "Let's not forget who we're dealing with."

"He's been better lately," I offer. "Even Rowan agrees. I think when the time comes, he'll understand why we went about it the way we did."

He starts to say something, but when I see that it's 6:58 a.m., I place a hand on his knee. The alarm is about to go off.

"Let me take care of Sterling," I say. "How about you just promise not to disappear again? How's that? When you leave today, promise me you'll come back."

He grins, but when I go to stand, he grabs my hand.

"Keep me out of the picture as long as possible, all right? Make Sterling give you the credit you deserve. He needs to trust you, needs to believe in you. No matter what he decides to do, stay or go, I'll make sure he gets recognized for his part of the discovery, but as for your contributions to the project … just remember, those ideas were all yours, not mine. Understood?"

I look at the clock on the nightstand. 6:59 a.m.

"I've got to get ready for work now, but let's talk again soon. I want to try to catch Sterling first thing this morning and sort this out."

Before he can answer, the alarm blares. The dogs turn in my direction as I fumble with the button to shut it off. Attis, a boxy-headed black Labrador retriever, is closest to the bed. Nyx, our newest addition, is just beyond him, her brindle coat an array of tiger stripes in the colors of coffee and dark chocolate. She's the youngest of the bunch, an awkward six-month old Great Dane puppy with floppy ears and droopy eyes. Quake, a full-grown Harlequin Dane, has a more majestic look, dressed in black spots over a white background, ears neatly cropped. He weighs in at nearly 195 pounds of pure muscle and takes up the remainder of the floor.

On my way to the door, I bend over Quake and run a hand along his back.

"How about you go talk to Sterling for me?" I say. "I bet he'd listen to you."

Quake flops onto his side and groans, as if to say this is a terrible idea.

I glance at the other two. "Any other takers?"

They watch me with interest, but only because they're waiting for a different question. Ares, hovering in the hallway, is waiting for it too. I see Nyx's ears twitch in anticipation as I step closer to the door. Quake sits up.

"Who ... in ... here ..." I say, stretching out the words to tease them, "is ready ... to go ... outside?"

Before I even finish, the dogs are rushing past me, out into the upstairs hall.

CHAPTER 2

The Present
Age Forty-One
Monday

T
he dogs follow me down the wide curved staircase to the first floor. The cat, less patient, bolts past all of us, getting ahead to avoid the stampede.

At the bottom of the stairs, we make a right and go through the stone archway that opens into the kitchen. The smell of coffee hits me immediately. My daughter, Maeve, has made enough for both of us before heading off to class. A nearly full pot sits on the counter next to the fridge. She's even set out my favorite mug, along with the sugar bowl and a pitcher of her homemade oat milk. She must have filled the dogs' bowls too because they waste no time making their way over to them. Ares, on the other hand, waits at my feet, looking up at me. He likes to have his food poured while he watches, as if he wants to make sure you're doing it right. I grab the Tupperware of cat food from the cabinet and tip it over his bowl. He gives the food an assessing sniff and then begins to eat. As I watch him, I remember the cats in my dream.

Ares stops eating and blinks up at me, as if he senses my thoughts, as if he knows I need help remembering more of the details. His eyes are an iridescent green, bringing another spark of dream recognition. Before I can make any further progress with the recall, though, I feel Quake's hip press against mine. He and Nyx are notorious leaners. When they want attention, this is what they do. I turn in his direction and find his nose a few inches from my own.

"I suppose this means my coffee has to wait?" I ask. "Is that what you're telling me?"

He turns his head in the direction of the french doors that open out into the backyard. The other two dogs are already there, eagerly watching our conversation. Attis perks his ears and gives a muffled bark. I glance down at the cat who has gone back to eating and realize that any chance of further dream recall has been lost.

Quake leads me to the doors, and as soon as I open them, he bolts out onto the lawn. Nyx follows, close at his heels. The two of them hug the edge of the garden, staying neck and neck for a bit, but because her legs are so much shorter than his, it isn't long before he disappears around the corner of the house ahead of her. I watch until she sprints out of view, and then I look over at Attis. Like most Labs, he's in no hurry at all. He waddles outside onto the patio and stops at the edge of the slate, just beyond the wrought iron table and chairs. There, he lifts his boxy snout into the air, sniffs a few times in every direction, and then anchors his back feet in place and falls into a deep bow. His black coat gleams in the morning sun as he stretches, reminding me of a wet seal. I wonder if he's ever questioned why the other two are always in such a hurry. As if answering my thoughts, he turns to face me, gives his body a full shake, and then ambles off to join the others.

With the dogs gone, Ares strolls over and stops at my feet. The cat peers out into the yard, his ears pivoting like tiny satellite dishes. His long white whiskers jut out at odd angles. He reaches out one front paw, touches it to the cold slate, and then immediately flicks it in the air as if it's shocked him. Unimpressed, he turns back into the kitchen where he leaps up to his favorite perch in the bay window, squeezing in among the orchids. There, he falls onto his side, sets his tail in motion, and yawns, showing off a mouthful of jagged teeth.

Unlike Ares, I can never resist a perfect fall day, especially when I know bad weather is just around the corner. The sun is bright, and the air is crisp. My coffee can wait. I slide my feet into the old pair of green garden clogs that sit next to the door and slip on my robe, which is still hanging on the hook from the day before. Tying the belt, I step out onto the patio and take in the wide expanse of lawn that stretches out in every direction. Oaks and maples have been busy dropping red and gold leaves across its surface. The air smells of ripe apples. A huge basket of them sits under the bay window to my left, waiting to be taken to the local shelter. The trees in the back produce so many, it seems a shame to let them go to waste. This late-season harvest will likely be the last of the year.

Balanced on top of the pile is a small perfectly shaped one, only partially red. I reach for it, but I stop when I notice Ares watching me though the glass. He's crouched among the flowers now, the tip of his tail flicking back and forth, like a tiger waiting to pounce. His green eyes catch the sunlight, and the full recollection of my dream finally hits.

There were cats in the hallway, they wouldn't come into the room, but what was the rest?

A gust of wind spins a twister of leaves around my feet.

Leaves were scattered on the floor of the operating room. My grandmother's house. I was holding something in my hand as I ran up to the second floor. It was a newspaper.

I look at my watch. The paper would already be at the foot of the drive. With plenty of time to grab it before work, I start down the cobblestone path that leads to the top of the driveway. As I pass a cluster of mums and approach the corner of the house, a wave of gooseflesh prickles my arms and neck.

"Someone walking over your grave," my mother would say.

I shoot a quick glance over my shoulder, toward the low stone wall that sits just beyond the patio, and then I look back toward the driveway. In the distance, beyond the end of the cobblestone walkway and across a swath of grass, is the front door to the house. The yard is empty. Nothing seems out of the ordinary, but of course, I don't expect to see anything just yet. The sensory cascade, the official term for what's about to happen, has only just begun.

My Gram Marie used to call these cascades "the willies." I think she used the playful name to make it seem less scary for me as a child, but no matter what you called it, it meant that something was coming, something that wouldn't be revealed until the very end. That's just the way it works. This is how they start.

I stuff my hands deep into the pockets of the robe and feel the wind pick up around me as I wait for the rest. The familiar tingling in the pit of my stomach begins a few seconds later. When I was five, I used to tell Gram Marie it felt like I'd swallowed a cupful of grasshoppers. She'd laugh, but also nod. Gram Marie got the willies too.

When the fluttering in my stomach finally fades, the crickets take over. This is what I used to call the high-pitched ringing in my ears. An overwhelming sense of gravity pulls at my feet as the ringing grows louder, making them feel as if they're bound in lead boots and bolted to the ground. The pressure between my heels and the path feels almost magnetic. This part never bothered me, even as a child, but when the pressure begins to move upward, from my feet to my ears, this is when the discomfort always sets in. When the pressure reaches my chest, breathing becomes difficult. As a child, this part always made me cry. It's like the pressure you feel when you dive to the bottom of a very deep pool just to see if you can touch the bottom, the water pressing in until your eardrums feel like they're about to pop. Now I know the feeling will pass, that the cascade will run its course, and when it's over, I'll be shown what I'm meant to see. I think of Rowan, of the things she's been teaching me, of what she and Jakob would say if they were here.

Stay calm and wait for it, they'd both agree. *You know what to do.*

If my Gram Marie were here, she'd take me for ice cream to help me forget that the cascade had even started, to prevent me from seeing what I was meant to see at the end.

The cascades are back with a vengeance, happening now more than ever before, their intensity ten times as strong. I could blame the house, but I know better. It wasn't like this when we first moved in. I've been inviting this, and now it's time to pay attention.

From the Journal of Nadia King
Age Thirty-Nine

We've been living in the new house for a month, and something is happening. I don't know if it's the house, or if it's just my work with Rowan and Jakob that's causing it, but I'm sensing more and more every day. We've been working on the nightmares, and we're making some progress there, but I can never really relax. I'm always on alert here, always waiting for something. I've tried meditating again, but that's strange here too. It helped during the divorce, but now it just makes me more anxious. Back then, the hardest part was getting started. Now, stopping is the problem. It's like my mind gets stuck somewhere, like something wants my attention again, and once they have it, they won't let go. The loss of control reminds me too much of those times in front of the basement door at Gram Marie's. I think this afternoon's meditation might be my last.

Aaron and I actually found an old trunk full of art supplies while poking around in the attic this morning. We found brushes and oil paints. A few of the tubes are dried out, but most are fine. There are even a few canvases. Maybe painting can become my new way to relax.

We set up everything in the back room on the first floor, the one with all of the windows. Aaron thinks it's the perfect space for a studio since it gets natural light most of the day. He says he'll install track lighting next week for me, so I'll have enough light at night as well. I told him not to expect any masterpieces.

Aaron seems to like it here. He seems happy. I'm glad he agreed to come along. This morning, when a delivery came, he introduced himself as the caretaker. I was in the kitchen and had to smile when I heard it. He thinks we should start calling the house "the Baird" again, like they did when it was first built. He visited the local historical society last week and has been reading everything he can get his hands on about the property. He's even studying the old photos, trying to make the house look like it used to. He's been a huge help, but I hope he knows that isn't the only reason I asked him to move here onto the property with us. I hope he knows that I consider him one of my dearest friends. He listens, even when I sound a little crazy, which is more often than not these days, I'm afraid. Maeve enjoys having him here too. She even allowed him to pick the name for the stray kitten she found in the garden, a little fluffy gray thing. His name is Ares.

From the Journal of Nadia King
Age Thirty-Nine

We've been in the Baird for two months now, and Aaron has installed the track lighting in the studio. I've been spending far too many hours in there as a result. The good news is that I'm getting better.

I finished my first official painting today. It's of Ares in the bay window, a basket of apples below. This seems to be his favorite spot in the house, maybe because he can watch all of the birds and squirrels in the backyard from there. When Aaron saw the painting, he said he didn't believe that I've never painted before. I'm actually a little surprised myself. It's not half bad. He says he's going to hang it in the foyer. He says it will "liven up the place" until we have a chance to paint.

From the Journal of Nadia King
Age Thirty-Nine

Four months in the Baird now, and things keep getting stranger. I could try to justify my long hours in the studio by saying that painting just takes practice, or that it's just a new infatuation and that the novelty will eventually wear off, but I don't know if that's really it. It's gotten to the point where I'll drop everything to paint, as if there's some pressing need to capture an image before it leaves my mind. Sometimes I wake up in the middle of the night and head to the studio. Other times, I don't wake at all.

Last night, I woke up with a paintbrush in my hand, a painting half done in front of me, the image slightly disturbing. This new little trick has brought my sleepwalking to a whole new level, although I think there's more to it. I've begun to notice that my paintings, like my dreams these days, are more like premonitions. Take the shark I painted a few days ago, the one that was belly-up on the sand, the tip of its tail just out of the water. As I was working on it, I had no idea why a shark had come to mind. In fact, it seemed an odd choice of subjects until my uncle stopped by yesterday to see the house.

We were chatting over a cup of coffee in the kitchen when he pulled out his phone and thumbed his way through a series of photos. He and his wife had just gotten back from a trip, and he said he wanted to show me "something cool." When he handed me the phone, I didn't say a word. The photo showed a shark on a beach, belly-up, complete with the accompanying heart-shaped rock and yellow swim fins that were also in my painting. He and my aunt had come across it while walking up the beach. I handed the phone back to him and excused myself for a minute.

I went to my studio and just stared at the painting, wondering how it was possible. When I came back to the kitchen, I brought it with me, my own version of his photo on a twenty-by-twenty-four-inch canvas. When I held it up in front of him, he didn't look surprised. He simply looked at the photo on his phone, to the painting, and then back again. He said he didn't have an explanation, but thought Gram Marie could probably pose a few ideas if she was still alive. He said that his mother used to do this to him all the time. He'd come home after a late night out drinking with his friends and find a little sketch on the dining room table. The sketch would show him with the same friends sitting around a campfire, beer bottles in hand.

"Somehow, she just knew," he said.

I'd never heard this story, and I never knew this about Gram Marie.

CHAPTER 3

The Present
Age Forty-One
Monday

Sensory cascades are often the very things that drive me to my studio. The chills, the ringing in my ears, and the gravity in my heels are good indicators that a painting will follow, the subject usually determined by the cascade's reveal. Most of the time, as with the shark, the reason for the painting is obvious not long after it's done. Other times, I'm simply left wondering.

One of my more recent paintings is of a decorative urn, its curved outline surrounded by flowers, deep red amaryllis and delicate paperwhites. The urn carries a small nameplate on its base, but the inscription isn't clear. My brushstrokes simply hint at what could possibly be letters. Just before I woke up in front of the canvas, I'd been in the middle of a dream, one starring a five-year-old Nadia. She'd been crying, standing alone in a white room, her ears ringing. The cascades come in my dreams, as well. I worry about what this painting might mean. To know that amaryllis and paperwhites are two of my favorite flowers is a bit worrisome. I can only hope that their placement beside an urn with an indecipherable nameplate isn't a premonition of things to come anytime soon.

A few months after setting up the studio, Aaron and I were back up in the attic, digging through what was left and came across a few paintings done by the previous owner of the house, a woman named Jillian Stiles. According to her granddaughter, Stiles also had a knack for painting scenes with a predictive nature. She became well-known for this, and as a result, people traveled for miles to see her work. It wasn't uncommon for her visitors to stumble across a painting that held significant meaning for them. By the time Stiles died at age ninety-seven, she'd sold more than two thousand pieces, many of them to a handful of loyal customers.

"It's like she knew they were coming," her granddaughter said one day. "She'd paint a man in overalls next to an old blue Ford, set it up in the dining room to dry, and a week later, some little old woman would come to the house, see it, and end up taking the painting of her late husband home with her, sometimes pulling out of the driveway in the same old car."

Jillian's granddaughter still fields calls from collectors hoping to buy any remaining paintings. There are a few of them left in the attic, but I can't bring myself to part with them. I have a feeling they were left behind for a reason.

My paintings and hers are oddly similar. Stiles and I both use the same blending of color, the same sharp brushstrokes. Seeing my work alongside hers would make anyone think that I've simply copied her style, but that's just not the case. By the time Aaron and I found her paintings in the attic, I'd already completed a good number of my own. Even I was shocked by the resemblance.

The resemblance sometimes goes far beyond a similarity in style, though. One of Jillian's paintings in particular takes the eeriness to a whole new level. I've carried this one down from the attic on more than one occasion to have a closer look, leaning it up against the wall in the foyer, just below my first painting of Ares in the window. Seeing the two paintings together makes me wonder how it's even remotely possible. Even my own brain, geared for science, trained to make sense out of coincidence, can't seem to come up with an answer.

If I were to hang the two side by side, mine on the right, hers on the left, their interior edges would match up exactly. Together, they offer a wider wraparound view of the house as if seen on the surface of a gazing ball in a Victorian garden. In hers, a young woman stands on the cobblestone path just beyond the patio, her head turned so she's looking back in the direction of the house. In mine, you see the rest of the patio, the bay window, and the basket of apples just underneath. When I first saw the woman in Jillian's painting, I couldn't help but note the unmistakable resemblance to myself. Dark shoulder-length hair pulled back in a ponytail. Slim build. And even her white robe. The first time I saw the two paintings together, I didn't know what to think. I still don't.

As I stand on the cobblestone path, my ears ringing and my feet rooted to the earth, I think again of Jillian's painting. I feel the hairs on my arms stand on end and know that something is coming, something that Rowan has been preparing me for all along. I count away the seconds like I used to as a child, waiting for the pressure in my chest to ease, taking short and shallow breaths. When the pressure finally dissipates, I look again out into the yard. The dogs are still nowhere in sight. The stream behind the house can entertain them for hours, so they're probably there. I don't really want to be alone, but I know that's how it needs to be. That's the only way it can work. That's when we see things best. I tighten the belt on the robe and watch as a few leaves dance toward me across the grass.

"Don't be afraid," Rowan would say, if she was here. "You just have to focus and let the cascade guide you."

I think back to the years of bad dreams, how I've always run from my pursuers. I think of my visitor and of my work at Amulet. Rowan and Jakob are right. I've been afraid for far too long. Rowan's instructions are simple, nothing more than a slight twist on guided meditation, but then again, maybe that's what makes me nervous. The loss of control. I remind myself of the five-year old children in Jakob's paranormal study groups. I think of the little girl, Tina, of the things she's seen, in particular, and of her carefree attitude toward them.

If she can do this, so can I.

Birds chatter in the trees around me. I pull in a deep breath as I picture Rowan's easy smile, her simple instructions. On the exhale, and with my eyes closed, I visualize my breath escaping my mouth as a thin wisp of steam. With each successive breath, I do the same, allowing the wisps to collect into an imagined cloud that floats on the air in front of me. When a gust of wind comes in from my left, I imagine it carrying the cloud, my target image, with it and turn my body as if to follow its progress. According to Rowan, when the wind stops, I'll have turned far enough, and when I open my eyes, I'll be facing what I'm meant to see, the cascade's reveal.

When the wind eventually stills, I have second thoughts about opening my eyes. I'm still afraid of what might be there. I think of the things I saw as a child. I think of the man on the operating table.

You worry too much, I hear my visitor say. *You need to do this, Nadia. Open your eyes.*

When I finally do, the house is directly in front of me, the bay window lit from inside, the basket of apples just below. Ares is up on his back feet, pawing at the glass. My chest prickles with heat.

Déjà vu, I think. *You've seen this before, haven't you?*

The painting that hangs in the foyer is a near duplicate of the scene that faces me, and I stand there wrapped in the white robe, my dark hair pulled back in a ponytail, as if I'm posing for the painting done by Stiles. One difference is obvious, however. I was a novice at this game when I first painted the scene. Thinking I had a choice, I omitted a few key details, details that frightened the hell out of me at the time.

I'm being given a second chance to do it right, I think.

Ares continues to paw at the glass, surrounded by green leaves and multicolored orchids. My eyes aren't on the cat this time, though. It's the space *behind* Ares that holds my attention. Something about the shadows and the reflection of the plants in the glass make it look like several people are returning my gaze from inside. I cock my head, much like Attis does when he hears a sound that strikes him as funny, and when I do this, the leaves behind Ares begin to move.

Just a draft, I think, but quickly correct myself. *No, not this time, Nadia. This time, we don't make excuses. This time, we see it for what it really is.*

Once this conscious decision is made, I see one particular figure in the crowd lift his hand in a wave. This minor shift in perception is over in a matter of seconds, which is probably why most people dismiss it—or miss it completely. The leaves become leaves again, and Ares drops to his haunches on the other side of the glass.

The first time this happened, I wrote off the figures as my imagination, the result of being in a new house, of hearing one too many ghost stories in my day, but now I know better. I turn to face the yard, angling my back toward the window. I look out past the low stone wall, to the gravestones beyond. Yes, as with many old estates, the Baird came with its very own collection of these.

If one of the figures was my father, who were the other two?

I nearly turn around to look again, but I stop when I suddenly become aware of a lingering tickle at the nape of my neck, a nagging pressure at my temples. The sensation reminds me of a game we used to play as children.

The game was called Watcher, and it started by placing a stack of white index cards in a paper bag, one for each player. One of the cards was marked with an X, another with an O, and the rest were left blank. Each player, usually about ten of us, drew a single card to start. The person who drew the X had to hold it up. That person was the Victim, and they were immediately blindfolded and placed cross-legged in the middle of the floor. The rest of the players would then gather around the Victim in a circle, facing her. We'd hold up our own cards so that everyone could see who held the O. This player was the Watcher.

The Watcher had one job: to stare at the blindfolded Victim while the other players closed their eyes. Anyone new to the game was told that the Watcher's stare should be so intense that it could bore a hole right into the Victim's very soul. Blinking wasn't allowed.

The goal of the game was simple. The blindfolded Victim had to identify their Watcher. In other words, the Victim had to see if they could sense the stare. The Victim got three chances to point at their Watcher, and if they succeeded, the blindfold was removed and the game started over. If the Victim failed three times in a row (three strikes, and you're out, as the saying goes) they had to serve a Sentence. The Sentence was thirteen minutes alone in a dark room, preferably a dark basement, if it was available.

Needless to say, with my desperate fear of the dark, and even more desperate fear of basements, I quickly learned how to recognize the weight of a Watcher's stare. I mastered this skill, and as a result, I was never forced to serve a Sentence beyond the fifth grade.

As I gaze out into the yard beyond the patio, my back toward the window, I have no doubt that I'm being observed by something other than the cat. I'm sure I saw each of the three figures disperse, but based on this feeling, that simply isn't the case.

The events of the past week are coming together.

I'd like nothing better than to go to my studio and paint the scene, but I know that if I do, I'll be late for work. Plus, I still need to see the newspaper, so without even glancing back at the house, I resume my walk down the cobblestone path. With each step away from the house, the weight of the Watcher's stare weakens, and by the time I get to the top of the driveway, the strange sensation is completely gone. I reach into the pocket of my robe and pull out a small yellow notepad and pen, and then I scribble a few messy sentences on the top page, details of what I just saw. I know these details will fade as the day passes just as a dream tends to fade if you don't recall it shortly upon waking. I note the colors and the play of light in the window, how Ares had pawed at the glass, and most of all, the descriptions of the figures in the background, one of them all too familiar. My final note describes the sensation of being watched. With all of this down on paper, the urge to paint dissipates.

I keep these small yellow "idea notebooks" handy at all times. It's how I track the countless thoughts that course through my head like a whirlwind on any given day. Taking notes and talking to myself have become habits over the years, both tricks suggested by the therapist I visited regularly during my marriage.

"Get the thoughts out of your head. Either onto paper or out into the air," she used to say. "They'll occupy your mind all day, if you don't."

It's some of the best advice I've ever been given.

I stuff the notepad back into my pocket and glance toward the front door of the house before starting down the gravel drive. The holly bushes are getting tall and will need to be trimmed soon. If my father was still alive, he'd insist on coming over to do it for me. He loved to work outside. He'd probably insist that the gravel driveway needed a little work too. We'd had one back home, and he was meticulous about it. Each stone had to be smoothed evenly and raked just so. I notice the bare patches here and there as I make my way toward the front gate, knowing this would never do if he were alive. I'm still thinking of my father when I hear the crackle of sticks breaking in front of me. I look up to find Aaron at the far end of the drive, near the gate, already hard at work for the day. He squats near a quaint stone garden shed, partially hidden behind a wheelbarrow that's piled high with branches. His shock of unruly white hair gleams in the sun, long strands of it shifting around his head with the breeze. When he sees me, he pushes himself up to standing and waves an arm in the air.

"Mornin' sleepyhead," he yells, as I continue walking toward him. "If you're down here lookin' for the paper, I already took it up to the house. Grabbed it as soon as it came. Wanted to catch the news before I got started out here." He puts his hands on his hips. "Not sure you wanna catch that first page before you head off into work though. Best to save that one for later maybe. Gonna force some steam from your ears."

He tosses another pile of twigs into the wheelbarrow, and his gloves nearly go along for the ride. He gives the cuffs a quick tug while I make a mental note to stop at the garden shop on the way home to grab him a smaller pair.

Aaron moved onto the property at the same time as Maeve and me, not long after my first novel started selling like wildfire. The move was an adjustment for all of us, but especially for him. He'd been homeless before that. He and I met in the shelter where I used to work as a volunteer, and we became close friends almost immediately. He's always been one of those people who never wants to talk about his own problems but is always more than willing to listen to yours, and God knows I had plenty of problems back then. This is why I didn't hesitate when I finally had the chance to help him.

The Baird estate, about fifteen acres in total, is one of the oldest properties in the area. When I bought it, the ivy-covered manor house and scattered outbuildings were in a bad state of repair, to say the least. The carriage house near the front gate had been in much better shape, and I decided it would be perfect for Aaron, his chance for a new start.

"Thanks for doing all of this," I say, looking out at the tidy yard.

He waves a dismissive hand. "Anything for you, my dear. You know that. Now get goin' or you're gonna be late for work, and you can't be holding up progress. We're all waiting for those discoveries of yours, don't you know?"

He's referring to my work at Amulet. Despite the novel's success, a majority of my time is still spent in the lab. Aaron knows what we're working on, knows that we're close to making a fairly significant discovery, but I don't think he realizes just how close.

He uses a hand to shield his eyes from the sun and tips his head toward the house. "Paper's up there on the patio table, but like I said, you'd best leave that first page for later. Read it over a nice glass of wine tonight."

With that, he bends and tosses another handful of sticks into the wheelbarrow. I blow him a kiss before turning to leave. He pauses long enough to catch it theatrically.

Just as Aaron promised, the newspaper waits for me on the wrought iron table just outside the french doors. It sits there in its bright blue plastic bag, and as I stare at the splash of color, I wonder how I could have possibly missed it when I first stepped outside. The color stands out in stark contrast to the dark patina of the table. This, of course, makes me think of Rowan. According to her, all things happen for a reason. According to her, we only see what we're meant to see at any given time. If I'd seen the paper when I first stepped outside, I never would have gone down the path, and if I hadn't gone down the path, I never would have seen the figures in the window. So, maybe she's right.

I step up to the table and lift the sealed edge of the bag. The paper slides out and unfolds in front of me, exposing the article that Aaron had most likely been referring to, the one he suggested I avoid. My name appears in bold letters about halfway down the page. I shake my head as I skim the article.

"The community paper must be in desperate need of stories if they've chosen ours," I say out loud. Still shaking my head, I carry the paper inside.

Ares meets me just beyond the french doors and watches as I kick off the clogs and hang the robe back on its hook. I shoot a nervous glance around the kitchen and find it empty. I'm not sure if this sets my mind at ease or if it disappoints me, probably a little of both.

Do you suppose the shadows keep their distance because they know I'm still uneasy?

I make my way over to the center island with the paper and then look back at the cat. "I think we may need some caffeine to tackle this one, my furry friend."

I add coffee, sugar, and milk to my favorite mug, and then I move to my normal spot at the end of the island where I perch on a stool and spread the paper out in front of me. I pull out a second stool for Ares and tilt my head toward the seat.

"Care to join me, handsome?" I ask. My mother thinks I'm crazy for talking to the animals like I do, but that never stops me. I think they understand a lot more than we give them credit for.

Ares seems to consider the invitation for a second, and then he leaps up onto the stool. I give his head a scratch and then begin to read the article aloud so that he, and whoever else might be listening, can hear it. The first few lines are tabloid worthy and actually make me laugh out loud.

"Is It Science or Is It Fiction? Does Local Author Nadia King Have Ties to Groundbreaking Research at Amulet? Only one question comes to mind for most of us: How will we know what to believe?"

Apparently, I need to talk to Sterling about more than I originally thought.

CHAPTER 4

The Present
Age Forty-One
Monday

An hour later, I arrive on campus.

I snag the last spot in the parking garage and make my way across the street, the sun hot against my black blazer. I'm in a hurry, which must be obvious. A small congregation of students on the front steps to our building moves aside as I approach the revolving door. I nod a quick thank you in their direction as I push through.

Inside the lobby, I spy Erma. She's standing behind the main desk, nearly ten yards away, but even at that distance, her bright orange halo of curls seems to glow. I slow my pace immediately. Erma is the last person I want to deal with at the moment. She's a sweetheart, but she can talk your ear off when she wants to, which is most of the time. Thankfully, she looks busy, immersed in a large pile of folders stacked in front of her. Her head is down. I'd give anything to pass by unnoticed, but I know that Erma rarely misses a trick. Sure enough, as soon as the heel of my boot steps off the entryway mat and onto the tile floor, she looks up. A broad smile spreads across her face, and she flaps a hand wildly in the air.

"Oh, Nadia," she bellows. "There you are! I was just wondering when you'd get here!" Her voice echoes throughout the lobby, her New York accent as strong as ever, and several students standing near the water fountain turn their heads to look in our direction. Her hand drops to her plump hip, one currently squeezed into a pair of powder blue polyester pants. "And don't you look so nice today?"

I look the same as I ever do. Hair pulled back in a ponytail, black blazer, jeans, and boots. Nothing special. Erma is fishing. I thank her for the compliment once I'm close enough to speak at a normal volume, but I keep walking, hoping she'll notice my rush and let me pass without saying much more. Of course, she doesn't take the hint.

"It's been a little crazy here this morning already," she says. "I'm guessing you saw the paper?"

I shake a finger in her direction as if she's just reminded me of something important. "I did," I say, continuing past the desk, "and that's exactly why I'm in a bit of a rush, Erma. I have to run for now, but I'll catch you a little later, OK?"

Erma doesn't bite. She calls after me. "It's exciting, don't you think? All this news? The paper writing about us? Here … at Amulet? I already called my son, Andy, and I told him to go buy me a couple copies."

Not ever wanting to be rude to anyone, I stop in the middle of the lobby and take a few steps back to the desk. Sometimes, if you give Erma just a few seconds of undivided attention, she's good for the day. I lean in, rest my forearms on the counter, and ask about Andy and her grandkids. When she finally runs out of steam, I look at my watch.

"You haven't by any chance seen Sterling yet this morning, have you?"

Erma's bright red lips break into a smile. "I have, in fact. The big boss is in his office," she says, eyebrows raised. "He has a call soon … with the people from the paper. He asked me to make sure he wasn't interrupted, but if you want, I could go get him for you."

The glint in her eye tells me she'd be more than happy to put her nose in the middle of this, but that's the last thing I want.

I shake my head. "That's OK, Erma. I was just curious. I can wait until he's done. It looks like you have plenty to do already. That's a lot of files you've got there."

She looks down at the stack, and before she can say anything more, I resume my walk up the east wing corridor. She stays surprisingly silent behind me. At the end of the hall, I duck through a pair of green metal doors on my right and take the stairs up to the second floor.

The building that Amulet occupies suits our needs perfectly. Our laboratories, located on the first floor, take up the entire back portion of the west wing, beyond the lecture halls. Our offices, including Sterling's, line the second-floor hallway, each one of them practically large enough to live in. Floors three and four house labs not officially associated with our project—at least not yet. This would be changing soon, however, if all went well.

Sterling and I moved our work into this new facility right after renovations to the first floor were complete. I promised him a lab filled with new equipment if he agreed to the move, and that's exactly what he got. Our current team is made up of fewer than ten researchers, but thanks to the help of one consultant, my visitor from that morning, work has progressed with lightning speed.

On paper, Sterling leads the project, but Jakob Fairheart, a brilliant man, passionate scientist, and dear friend, is the real heart and soul of the whole operation. From the start, he's been the magnet that keeps our team together. Fortunately, he and I see eye to eye on most things, and his interest in my ideas is what prompted him to suggest my meeting Sterling in the first place. The labs on the third and fourth floors are his, and this building, known locally as "the University" has been the home to Jakob's project since its conception nearly thirty years ago, long before Amulet, and long before I knew either Jakob or Sterling.

Jakob's institute was founded here as an offshoot of his alma mater, the University of Edinburgh in Scotland, using private funds donated by a wealthy friend who just so happened to have faith in his project. Private funding is important for people like Jakob. His work isn't exactly mainstream science. Instead, its focus is on projects that most other scientists refuse to investigate, things like ESP, dream state analysis, psychokinesis, telepathy, and various other forms of paranormal phenomena. Despite the stigma attached to his field of research, Jakob has done remarkably well for himself. He's world-renowned for his work but far too humble to admit it. He's also a very well-respected and well-loved professor on campus.

Dr. Jorg Sterling, on the other hand, is another story. With endless publications to his name, he's a highly regarded neuroscientist in the field of animal cognition. His work with primates and sign language is well known, but while he may be well respected in his field, Sterling is more often feared than loved by his students.

In addition to leading the project at Amulet, Sterling also manages his primate lab across town. He doesn't believe in anything related to the paranormal, which is why ours and Jakob's labs currently function, and will continue to function, as completely separate entities as long as Sterling has the final say. Of course, Jakob knew of Sterling's opinions even before he introduced the two of us. He also knew that his friend would never willingly agree to be involved in any type of controversial side project, but that didn't stop Jakob from arranging it. Jakob knew how badly I needed access to one of Sterling's latest discoveries. So, from the outset of this strange collaboration, certain strategies were put in place to protect Sterling's reputation while also letting Jakob and me get exactly what we wanted. Privacy, and maybe even secrecy, were the main reasons for founding Amulet.

As it stands, Sterling has no idea what he's gotten himself into, at least not the full extent of it. He knows enough to keep him involved, but not much more. Is this unfair? Absolutely, but if we'd told Sterling our hypothesis in the beginning, he never would have agreed to the move. Jakob's creative wording was the only thing that allowed this collaboration to evolve. Jakob, for some unknown reason, has that kind of power over Sterling, a power that few people have the chance to enjoy.

Combining efforts is the only reasonable progression for the three of us in the future, especially based on the results of the past weeks' experiments. Sterling might refuse to admit this at the moment, but it's only a matter of time before he'll have to agree.

At the end of the second-floor hallway, Sterling's office door is closed. I tilt an ear toward it and listen for any indication that he might be on the phone with the "people from the paper," as Erma had put it.

I have no idea how the paper has gotten wind of our project or why they think it's worth covering, but that's what has happened, and this needs to be fixed soon. They can write about me and my novel all they want, it only helps with book sales, but they need to stay away from our research. Sharing any details while work is still in progress is a huge risk. The last thing any lab wants is for another team to get wind of their ideas and possibly run with them. In science, credit only goes to those who make the discovery first. Those who lose the race don't get recognized. Look at Darwin, his name perpetually tied to his theory of evolution. The same goes for Mendel and his advances in genetics, or Leeuwenhoek for his development of the microscope and subsequent discovery of single-celled organisms. We're so close at Amulet. I have no desire to share this discovery with anyone but Jakob and Sterling.

There's a muffled laugh from inside the office, and then the casters of Sterling's heavy office chair squeak as they roll across the floor. I can imagine him leaning back in his chair, one ankle crossed over the opposite knee. One hand is likely holding the phone to his ear, the fingers of his other hand raking through his thick salt-and-pepper hair. I've seen the stance a million times. Rowan likes to describe it as "very male, very dominant, and very Sterling."

As gently as I can, I place my hand on the doorknob and shoot one final glance down the empty hallway, still not 100 percent sure of my plan. I only hesitate for a second, though, before barging into Sterling's office without so much as a knock.

Sterling falls forward in his chair, his feet landing squarely on the floor in front of him. His hair is tousled from running his fingers through it, and he looks somewhat dumbfounded when he realizes who's standing over him. When I snatch the phone out of his hands, he doesn't resist. He doesn't have time.

I hold a finger to my lips. "Shh."

Sterling glares at me as I lift the phone to my ear but says nothing.

"Hello, this is Nadia King," I say, cheerily, as if I'd been requested on the call.

The woman's voice on the other end of the line falls silent as she makes the connection. It doesn't take her long to recover, though, and before I know it, she's rambling on about how much she loves my novel and about how she's considered writing one of her own. Without even missing a beat, she transitions into an impromptu interview.

"So, you must know that people are talking, Ms. King," she says, her voice smooth and professional. "You've acquired quite the audience with this novel of yours, as I'm sure you know. Even my husband, who doesn't typically care for ghost stories, was impressed. He's in research, as well. Says the science sounds convincingly real. And, well … let's be honest here, Ms. King, now that you're working with Dr. Sterling, I think a lot of people are beginning to wonder if this just might be the case. So, tell me, is it?"

She pauses, giving me a chance to respond, but I don't take the bait. A few seconds of silence pass, and when she realizes I don't intend to answer, she continues her spiel, seemingly unaffected.

"I'm sure your readers would love to know how Dr. Sterling's research is linked to your novel, Ms. King. That's the only part that isn't really clear, right? I mean, you must be dying to explain the connection."

I can hear papers shuffling in the background.

"Let's see," she hums. "My calendar tells me I can meet you tomorrow over lunch if that works for you. What do you say? A good story could be great publicity for your new book." A few more seconds of silence. "You are working on a second, right? Isn't that what I hear?"

I glance at Sterling. He sits there, arms folded over his chest, a miserable look on his face. Given that the woman on the phone has been doing all of the talking, I'm sure he's wondering what's being said.

"Honestly," I say into the phone, "I only interrupted the call to tell you that we'd prefer to avoid any further conversation right now. And despite what you might think, I'm not actually working *with* Professor Sterling. He's just been kind enough to let me dabble a bit. I miss the lab, that's all."

A smug grin spreads over Sterling's face.

"Oh, come on, Ms. King," the woman says. "Let's be real. If the work being done there has nothing to do with your book, then why is Sterling at the University? And why would you be calling your new lab Amulet? That is the name of the research facility in your novel, is it not?"

I'm not sure how she knows that we've been calling the new lab by this name, but she's right. Using the name Amulet hadn't been my idea, but I'd gone along with it, thinking there was no harm in doing so. Maybe I was wrong.

"After all," she says, "if you think about it, technically speaking, you could say that the work of both Dr. Jakob Fairheart and Dr. Jorg Sterling is focused on nonverbal communication, wouldn't you agree? I believe that was the running theme of your first novel, as well, was it not, Ms. King?"

She was right, in a way. Technically speaking, extrasensory perception and sign language do qualify as nonverbal communication, but equating the two is quite a stretch.

"I'm pretty sure Dr. Sterling would disagree with that statement," I say, looking at him.

Sterling cocks his head with curiosity.

I take the phone away from my ear. "What do you think, Dr. Sterling? Are you and Jakob working on the same type of thing?"

Sterling's face goes a deep red, and he reaches for the phone.

I hold up a finger, telling him to wait. It's time to end the call. Before hanging up, though, I offer a quick thank you just to leave the conversation on pleasant terms. After all, there's a good chance we might be talking to this same woman again sometime soon. As my mother likes to say, don't burn any bridges.

I drop the handset back into its base and turn to face Sterling. He sits there, arms folded across his chest, his icy blue eyes studying me through small dark-rimmed glasses. He's an attractive man, no doubt, well-built for his late fifties, clearly an athlete when he was younger, but unfortunately, he possesses the air of someone overly confident in himself. I know the type all too well. He reminds me a lot of my ex-husband. We've certainly had our fair share of arguments, and I'm more than prepared for another one at the moment. He, of all people, knows better than to speak to someone outside the lab about our work. I want to remind him of this, but I realize something isn't right. He looks angry, but he hasn't said a single word since I stepped into the office, which isn't like him at all.

"Are you OK?" I ask.

"I'm just peachy, Nadia," Sterling snorts. "Just fucking peachy."

And here he is. The Sterling we all know and love.

"So, that's what I get for being nice? For asking if you're OK?"

He shrugs.

"Forget I asked," I say, shaking my head. "But how about this, Sterling? Correct me if I'm wrong, but I could swear that our reason for forming Amulet was to isolate this project. To keep things quiet? Do you remember that conversation?"

Sterling glares back at me, blue eyes locked on mine, but he still doesn't say a word.

I shrug. "It's OK. You don't have to respond. We both know the answer anyway. What I don't understand is why or how this story ended up in the paper. Number one, it seems strange to me that something like this would even make the headlines. And number two, I never imagined you, of all people, taking our work public when you know how risky that is." I pull the newspaper out from under my arm and toss it onto the desk in front of him. "Is this where you were headed Friday when you left the lab early? To talk to this woman?"

Sterling doesn't even look at the paper.

"Are you serious, Nadia?" he asks, his voice agitated. "Why in the hell would I go to the press? I know better than you to keep this under wraps. I was on the phone with that woman just now to try to fix this fucking mess. How about you try to see my side of things for once here?"

I raise my eyebrows at him. "And just what is your side of things, Sterling? Please, enlighten me."

"You seem to forget that it was *my* work that prompted Jakob to get us together in the first place. I brought *you* onto *my* project. My biggest concern right now is making sure people understand that what we're doing here is credible science and not some kind of voodoo nonsense. They need to get it into their thick skulls that my research and Jakob's are two completely separate things," he says. "We may be in the same building now, but that doesn't mean our projects are connected in any way. They have absolutely nothing to do with each other and certainly nothing to do with that stupid-ass book of yours. I don't even know why people keep bringing that up." He leans forward. "My research and my name are on the line here, Nadia—and that's why I'm more than a little agitated right now. That's why I'm trying to fix things."

I take a step toward his desk. "You know, the last time I looked, Sterling, this was a team effort and all of our names were on the line.

Plus … if I'm not mistaken, you're a lot further along in your project than you ever would have been without my help. Jakob brought us together for a reason. You'd still be scrambling for funding if he hadn't stepped in when he did."

Sterling yanks off his glasses and tosses them on the desk. He jabs a finger in the air at me. "And you, my dear, would have nothing if you didn't have my cells, so, let's just face the facts. You need me. And, just so you know, I wasn't the one who started this fucking newspaper business. It was Tom who went to that nosy woman. I don't think he's too happy that you excluded him from the Amulet team when we made the move. Am I glad you made that call? Hell, yes. He's a fucking nutball, but his warped sense of reality is also the reason why it didn't surprise me when I heard what he told that woman."

It takes a minute for what he's said to register. I hadn't even suspected Tom. "What *Tom* told her?"

"Well, it certainly wasn't me," Sterling says, sitting back in his chair. "Have you read the articles? Does any of that sound like something I'd say?"

I had read them, and no, it didn't sound like Sterling at all. I'd only assumed it was him because he was always bragging about how big of a discovery our work was going to be.

"Nadia, he told this woman that our research is going to prove that we can communicate with the dead." He turns up his palms, acting as if this is the most ridiculous thing anyone has ever said. "Did you miss that part? And yet you wonder why I felt the need to talk to this woman today? I can't afford to have people thinking I work on any kind of supernatural bullshit. I've worked too hard all my life to have my reputation go down the tubes over something as idiotic as this."

Good old crazy Tom, I think. *He may be a nutball, but he certainly isn't stupid. And apparently, he doesn't miss a trick.*

"I talked to that same woman last week," Sterling says, "after the first article went out, in hopes of setting her straight. I only called her again today to ask her what the hell she thought she was doing. She literally twisted everything I said." He jams his glasses back onto his face, lifts the corner of the paper, and jabs an angry finger at the picture of my novel at the side of the page. "And again, why the fuck is this in here?" A vein on his temple bulges. "Some hometown girl writes a ghost story, and suddenly what she's doing is all the rage? What about me? I'm about to make a huge leap in medical research, but no one seems to care about that." He shoves the paper across the desk. "That woman on the phone wasn't the least bit curious about the work my team has put into this project from day one. Every ... single ... fucking ... question that woman threw out today revolved around you and your goddamn book."

"And you should be thankful for that," I say. "The fewer questions about our research right now, the better."

Of course, I can understand his frustration. Groundbreaking research is hard to come by. Sterling wants the recognition. I just want the truth.

"Look, Sterling," I say, lowering my voice, "I had no idea that Tom was involved in this, and honestly, I don't want to stand here yelling anymore. What's done is done. Can we just ignore these people for now and focus on what we need to do to wrap this up?"

He offers no response.

I raise my eyebrows. "Can we?"

He gives a reluctant tip of his head and sinks back into his chair.

I turn to walk away, but I suddenly feel the need to get one more thing off my chest. "You know," I say, turning back, "I'm really getting tired of you dumping on my novel, Sterling. People do like it whether you want to acknowledge that or not. And you know what? I bet there are a few people out there right now looking you up too, checking out your work just because of these newspaper articles, and that's actually good for us. Let them see what you've done so far, let them get excited about your work. Once we have the full story, they'll understand even more."

Sterling seems to consider this. He lays his glasses on the desk and presses his palms to his eyes. "Maybe I should just write the damn paper now. We have enough data. I could get the preliminary research published, and then they'd see." He gives me a serious look. "This is going to be big news once we get it all together, Nadia. You realize that, right?"

Sterling has no idea how big this is going to be. He thinks we have some new stem cell that might allow stroke victims to recover more quickly, but I think we have something much bigger than that.

"Let's get through a few more experiments, Sterling," I say, turning to leave. "A few more weeks or so is all we need. Don't jump ship yet. We're almost there."

I step out into the hall, but Sterling calls after me.

"Nadia ..."

I turn back and shake my head. "Let's talk tomorrow, Sterling. I have some other things to take care of right now. I'm sorry I blamed you for all of this."

My own office is just across the hall. Inside, I collapse into my desk chair and spin to face the windows that span the opposite wall. They offer a view of the courtyard below, one lined with huge sycamores and a scattering of old-fashioned iron benches, all of this surrounding an oblong pond. The courtyard reminds me of a playground that my daughter loved as a child. The only thing missing is the set of swings, the one piece of playground equipment that could occupy Maeve for hours at a time.

Years earlier, on my way home from work, I stopped at that same playground wanting just a few minutes to think. My father had just passed away, and I was still trying to process it. Those few minutes turned into hours, and it was during that time that I first envisioned Amulet and what it could be, at least in theory. I filled a notebook with ideas, but it wasn't until years later that those notes were put to good use. They actually became the story line for my first novel, the one in which Amulet made its first appearance, the one Tom had read, for sure. My fictional Amulet had indeed proven that contact with the dead was entirely possible. The real Amulet only came into being once my fictional tale began weaving itself into reality. *Oh, yes, we've definitely stumbled onto something very big.*

Outside my office window, two frantic squirrels jump between the limbs of the closest trees. I watch them, thinking about the most recent progression of events and start to worry.

What if Sterling's cells actually prove to be what I think they are? Would the similarities between the cells in my novel and those discovered at Amulet call the lab's data into question? Could my association with Sterling discredit his research?

I stand up and pace the room.

"You have to stop worrying about this, Nadia," I say out loud. "There's no turning back now. We're too close. You have to tell Sterling. There's no putting it off any longer."

I look at the stack of lab notebooks on my desk and consider the hours I've spent reviewing the data inside them. I look at the microscope perched on a table in the corner of the room. Black plastic boxes, each about the size of a textbook, are stacked neatly next to it, all of them filled with hundreds of slides, slices of brain tissue, primate and human.

The success of my first novel provided a brief escape from science. Prior to the book, my specialty had been cancer research. For nearly a decade, I loved the challenge of trying to find a cure. Hope kept me going, but that all changed when my father fought the battle with cancer and lost. This new project at Amulet, although much different than any of my previous work, brings me a new kind of hope.

CHAPTER 5

The Present
Age Forty-One
Monday

When I return home from Amulet, I find Aaron at the foot of the driveway, just inside the front gate. He stands there, hands wrapped around the handle of a rake as I pull up next to him, a pile of leaves at his feet. He's filthy. His white T-shirt and baggy green work pants are covered in smears of dirt. His face, thanks to a layer of sweat, is caked with grime so thick in places that it makes the wide band of scars, normally so obvious, almost invisible. His wispy white hair is tangled with bits of leaves.

I stop the car and lean my head out the window. "What happened to you?" I tease. "Looks like you've been rolling in those piles."

Aaron grins. "Only maybe once or twice," he says as he tips his head toward the yard. "So, what do you think?"

Behind him, the lawn is freshly raked, the flower beds near the carriage house are tidied and mulched, and not far from the front of the car, a small pile of sticks sends a billowing trail of smoke high into the air.

"I think you're amazing," I say and toss him the new pair of garden gloves I bought for him at the hardware store on the way home.

He tries them on, and as I watch, a flicker of movement near the edge of the yard catches my eye. In an explosion of leaves, the dogs materialize out of the woods and thunder toward us. They reach the base of the drive in no time. Attis and Nyx stop to prod at Aaron's pockets, hoping for one of the biscuits he always keeps there, but Quake runs straight for the car. He's more interested in getting his ears scratched and a kiss on the nose.

When Quake eventually steps away, Aaron comes over and leans an elbow on the side mirror. "So, how did it go today?" he asks. "The way you flew outta here this morning makes me think you read that article, even though I told you not to. That right?"

I flash him a playful grin. "What did you expect? When someone tells me not to do something, it's the first thing I do. You should know that by now."

He nods and looks back at the dogs. They're roughhousing behind him.

"I talked to Sterling," I say. "He claims this whole mess is Tom's doing."

Aaron turns back to me and squints as if considering this. "Tom, eh?" He nods again. "Only talked to that boy a few times, but I suppose I can see that. He's an interesting bird, that one."

"He sure is," I say, watching the dogs as they wrestle in the grass, "and he's certainly not stupid. I'll have to talk to him tomorrow. He needs to keep quiet."

"You're gonna relax tonight, though, right?" he asks. "Take the night off? Stop thinking about that place for a minute?" He looks at me down the bridge of his nose. "I'll be honest. You seem a little frazzled lately. I'm worried about you. You need to take a little break."

He's right, of course. I do need a break, but the likelihood of that happening tonight is slim.

Aaron reaches up and pinches my nose, no doubt knowing what I'm thinking. "Anything else you need done around here, Lady Jane?"

I look past him, at the perfectly manicured yard, and shake my head. "I can't even imagine what that would be. Looks like you've done it all. How about take your own advice and go relax?"

Aaron studies the yard and smiles. Telling him to relax is like telling a fish not to swim.

"You actually enjoy this, don't you?" I ask.

He gives me a wink. "I'm as happy as a clam, thanks to you."

His smile is all I could ask for.

"Well, the feeling goes both ways," I say. "So, how about you go kick back with a beer or something, because if you don't, I'll feel like I have to come back down here and help you … and to be honest, I'm ready to call it a day."

Aaron steps away from the car. He leans down and picks up the rake. "Well, that's exactly what you should do, then. Stop worrying about everybody else for once, and do something for yourself. Go on up to the house and kick back with one of those books of yours maybe. I promise I'll quit working before I drop."

I glare at him.

"No need to give me the hairy eyeball, young lady," he says. "I'll do what I want, and you know that."

He drags the rake around to the back of the car, and then he leans in and gives the rear bumper a slap as if the car's an old horse that needs a little reminder to get moving. "You get on up to the house now. I'll come up and check on you in a bit."

It's pointless to insist. No amount of coaxing will change his mind, so I put the car into gear. When I pull away from the gate and start up the tree-lined drive, the dogs follow. For a stretch, they stay close, but as I near the house, they break off into a carefree sprint across the lawn. They only double back once they see me gathering my things from the back of the SUV. They line up at the head of the walkway that leads to the front door, tails wagging enthusiastically.

"You should wag your tails," I tell them. "You don't know how good you have it, not having to work with people. It can be exhausting."

Quake and Attis flank me as we start up the walkway. Nyx, on the other hand, slinks through the grass on my left, her attention on a squirrel that sits a few yards away. Her head is low to the ground, her big paws stealthy. The squirrel hasn't noticed her yet, and she's getting pretty close. I'm in the process of watching this unfold when Quake cuts in front of me. He does it so quickly, that if his back wasn't waist high, I'd topple right over him. Instead, I'm forced to stop dead in my tracks, thighs against his rib cage. He's angled toward the house. His hackles are raised, and a low growl rumbles in his throat.

Quake likes to grumble, sometimes for no reason at all. The creak of an old floorboard or rush of wind through the eaves can set him off.

There are plenty of times, though, when his grumbles are warranted. I look toward the house and hope this isn't one of those times. I just don't have the energy for it. When he continues, I shift my bags onto the grass and take Quake's enormous head in my hands. I turn it until his nose is within an inch of my own.

"How about we give it a rest tonight, big guy? Can we do that? Ignore whatever you think you see? For me? Hmmm?"

Quake studies my face. His eyes shift in their sockets, eyebrows doing their little dance.

"I used to ignore those pesky shadows all the time," I tell him. "Can you give it shot?"

He backs out of my grip and gives a deep bark. I see it coming, but I still jump. Nyx, of course, takes this as an invite to play. She darts in from my left and lunges at Quake, nipping at one of his front legs. Attis then nips at Nyx, and before I know it, the three of them are gone, racing through the yard until they disappear behind the house.

I wait to see if they'll return, and when they don't, I head inside. In the foyer, I drop my bags onto the bench near the door, hang my keys on the hook, and glance up at Ares. He's perched on the top step of the curved staircase, looking down. As always, he makes no move to come and greet me. He just sits there, still as a statue, as if he just wants to keep an eye on me.

"Hello, handsome," I tell him. "Have a good day?"

He continues to stare.

Ares is my first cat, and I wonder if they're all like this. I don't try to coax him down. Instead, I look toward the living room, wondering what might have put Quake on high alert. I can see one arm of the sofa from where I stand, the grandfather clock beyond it. The house is unnervingly quiet. Maeve is still at work and won't be home until much later. I briefly consider searching each room like I've done a million times before, but I decide I have better things to do. I turn and dig in my bag until I find the yellow notepad from this morning and then head through the kitchen and into the library.

The last of the daylight streams in through the library windows, but I throw the light switch anyway, knowing it will be dark by the time I'm done. Two floor lamps illuminate either side of the room. My desk sits in the far corner, a beautiful nineteenth-century mahogany Dickens. It was my father's, and it's the only place I'll write. As I make my way over to it, I pass the two leather armchairs that sit angled in front of a huge stone walk-in fireplace. They're where I usually find myself at the end of each night.

At the desk, I turn to study the room, again thinking of Quake's grumbling, wondering if I'm alone. The placement of the lamps creates plenty of places for the shadows to gather. My eyes search the corners, but for now, it appears that I'm the only one here.

Except for the studio, the library is where I spend most of my time. Maeve and I have always been avid readers, which is why Aaron calls it our sanctuary. The walls are lined floor to ceiling with shelves, and thanks to Jillian's similar penchant for books, most of them are already full. Aaron carried nearly twenty boxes down from the attic once the library renovations were complete.

My collection of journals fills most of the shelves behind my desk. The habit was kick-started by my Gram Marie when I was a kid, and keeping them continues to be a passion of mine. My father kept them too, most likely at her urging, as well. I can remember him sitting at his desk for hours each night while I stretched out on the floor beside him with my own. Sometimes, if I got lucky, he'd hoist me up onto his lap and read an entry from one of the older ones out loud. He'd tell me about the times he and his friends got into trouble or how the woman next door taught him how to dance so that he could impress my mother. There were times when I'd drift off to sleep in his lap. When this happened, he'd shift me onto the couch while he finished. That same couch now spans the trio of windows that look out into the back garden here at the Baird. It's where I usually go to catch up on any sleep I've lost thanks to my recurring nightmares.

In addition to my own journals, I have a growing collection of ones written by others. These aren't easy to come by, but they're well worth the wait. A good friend of mine, Mr. Noah, has a knack for finding them. He owns a used bookstore here in town. He gave me my first a few years ago, a journal that belonged to a woman who spent her entire life as a gardener at an orphanage. I remember what Mr. Noah said when he handed it to me.

"I think you might appreciate a good journal," he said. "Those autobiographies you read are good in a pinch, but like my mother used to say, they're just canned versions of the real thing. Journals, on the other hand, those are what give you a true taste of the person who wrote it."

He was right. I've been hooked ever since, and I do get that true taste as I decipher the author's penmanship and take note of any grammatical errors they're prone to make. I learn what was important to them by their underlines on the pages and their notes in the margins. Things like this tell me so much more about the person than their words alone. Journals give a secret glimpse into someone else's life through their own eyes—often a glimpse that no one else was ever meant to see.

We haven't been able to locate my father's journals anywhere, and I can't help but wonder what was in them. I'd be curious to see if Gram Marie told him more than she told me. I should have asked them both more questions while I had the chance. We never seem to take enough time to ask our parents or grandparents about their lives while they're here, do we? We never think to ask them the simple things. What were you like as a kid? What was your favorite subject in school? How did you spend lazy summer afternoons? We never think to ask these questions until we're older, and by then, it's often too late. This is why I keep my journals for Maeve. I want her to know everything.

Before heading over to my desk, I reach out and touch the spine of my first novel. It sits eye level on a shelf near the library door, the title stamped in gold block letters. I think of the morning newspaper and of our lab results from this past week.

"Did I write you because I knew what was going to happen?" I ask. "Or is all of this happening because of what I wrote?"

This isn't the first time I've pondered these same questions, but it's the first time I've said them out loud. I can't seem to figure out how or why certain events from my novel keep weaving their way into reality. I'm not sure I can blame coincidence any longer. Foresight seems more fitting. It's why the painting of the urn surrounded by amaryllis and paperwhites worries me.

To the left of my novel is a red book that used to belong to Jillian Stiles. It was half full when Aaron and I found it inside the trunk of art supplies in the attic, the pages filled with sketches rather than words. I slide it out and run a thumb over the symbol that's pressed into the top right-hand corner. A small circle about the size of a quarter surrounds a perfect equilateral triangle. Branches, or maybe roots, extend outward from it on all sides. It's a symbol I've seen somewhere before although I can't remember where, but that's the least of my concerns at the moment.

Back at the desk, I grab a pencil from the crock Maeve made for me years ago in her second-grade art class and write today's date on the next blank page. This is how most evenings begin. Before long, Ares will be curled up at my feet, purring so loudly that I'll want to chase him away, although I never do. For now, I'm happy that it's just me in the library.

I flip through the yellow notepad from that morning and review my notes, thankful that I have them because my memory has already begun to fade. I use the notes to sketch the scene, a rough draft of the image I'll paint later. I pencil in Ares on his back paws in the window, a few scribbles to suggest the leaves and flowers behind him. I draw the edge of the cobblestone path at the bottom of the page, the basket of apples under the window, and a few other minor details. Then, unlike my first attempt at this same scene, I add the outlines of the three figures in the background, one of them with a hand raised. I stare at the trio, the one in the middle in particular.

Was it just my imagination? Wishful thinking?

I shake my head, and then I add a few arrows to the page, short notes at the ends of them, details on color for when I finally sit down with a paintbrush. Last but not least, I write the title for the piece across the bottom of the page: *Ares Revisited.*

I exchange my pencil for a pen, and then I open the desk drawer and pull out yet another journal, this one a recent gift from Jakob. The cover is a dark green, beautifully decorated, embossed with a gnarled tree. Now that Jakob and I have begun sorting through my dreams in his sleep lab, he likes me to record as much as I can about them. I take down the details from the night before, sure to document the smells and how they changed, the play on light, the graffiti on the walls, and the misplaced furniture in

Gram Marie's house. I write about the operating table and the man on it, and of course, I write about the cats, adding a guess at how many there were. Their numbers keep growing, and Jakob thinks this is significant. Most importantly, I note how I avoided changing anything this time, how I allowed the dream to follow its course without redirection. To close the entry, I add a few general notes about my day, including an overview of the article in the newspaper and Sterling's reaction to it.

By the time I finish, an hour has passed, and the sun has gone down. The room is darker now. The light from the desk lamp falls on Ares as he stirs at my feet. He must have crept in without my even noticing. I stretch my arms overhead, once more searching the corners of the room for shadows, thinking that they, too, might have crept in unnoticed.

When had I seen the shadows last?

I'm trying to remember just how long it's been when the spine of a bright yellow journal catches my eye. It's on the top shelf near the corner.

That's where it all started, I think.

This yellow journal was a gift from Gram Marie on my seventh birthday. It was my first and came with a little brass key. It's where I kept my ghost stories, the ones that only Gram Marie and I knew were true.

There comes a time when you can look back at your life and finally see it for all that it was. Gram Marie had said this in the hospital that day with a squeeze of my hand and a glint in her eye. I think I know now what she meant. Anyone reading my journals could easily spot the common thread that weaves its way through most, a thread that has been leading me to Amulet all along. My ex-husband read my journals once, and when he noticed that thread, he tried to make sure that no one else got the chance.

I remember coming home from work that night to find him at the kitchen table with three of my journals spread out in front of him. None had keys, but he still had no business reading them. This wasn't something I could ever say to Sam, though. I can still see him ripping out the pages, throwing them at me, telling me that I needed to grow up and quit believing in ghosts. I could only stand there and watch. When he was done, he told me to pick up the mess and throw it in the fireplace, and as I stood there watching years of memories turn to ash, I knew what I had to do.

"What doesn't kill us makes us stronger," my mother likes to say, and she's right.

After that night, I started keeping my diaries hidden, stashed in the bottom of what Sam thought was an old rag box in the basement. When I left him a few years later, I took the box with me. Sometimes, I wonder if my father might have hidden his journals too. Maybe we just hadn't looked hard enough to find them. *But why would he hide them? Were there things inside that not everyone should know?* I have a feeling this might be the case.

I sometimes wonder if he had a few like my *Notebooks of the Unexplained*, a small subset of my journals that I keep in a special place behind my desk. These are where I record all of the strange things I've experienced in my lifetime along with possible explanations for them, things I think Gram Marie might have shared to "get me on my way a little quicker."

Rowan claims that my lifelong curiosity of the supernatural is what draws this kind of energy to me. As a kid, when friends stayed over, we'd always sneak out to the TV long after Mom and Dad had gone to bed so we could watch scary movies. In my teens, my friends and I passed around horror novels and books on Victorian spiritualism. We were fascinated by mediums and séances. As an adult, I've simply continued along this path.

On the shelf below the yellow journal is another one I remember well. I stand and take it down just for fun. The worn brown cover is made from an old paper bag, one that's been decorated in true high-school fashion, mottled with notes, red hearts, and the name of my high school sweetheart in big bubble letters across the front. I thumb through it as I carry it over to one of the chairs near the fireplace, noting the dog-eared pages, the doodles, and the obsessively neat teenage scrawl inside. It doesn't take long to find the page I'm looking for. A skull and crossbones has been drawn at the top. I don't bother making a fire. I just fall into the chair, tuck my legs up underneath me, and start to read. The journal entry is lengthy, written more like a chapter from a novel.

"Maybe you're right, Gram Marie," I say out loud. "Maybe I was practicing to be a writer all along."

From the Journal of Nadia King
Age Fourteen

Last night was the full moon. We thought that was the perfect time to sit in the graveyard of the Old Mud Church and try our hands at the Ouija board. Donna, Jess, Emily, and I have been planning this for weeks. Everyone but us was at the middle school dance.

Emily did the research, and after reading some books from the library, including a few about séances gone horribly wrong, she decided that the Ouija board seemed a safer bet. We all agreed, adding that they probably wouldn't sell the boards in toy stores for ten bucks if they were dangerous. We didn't even have to buy one. I just grabbed the board from our game room at home, and off we went.

We squeezed into the graveyard through the big iron gate out front just after dark. The church steeple loomed above us, keeping watch as we weaved through the maze of toppling gravestones and the army of creepy shadows that crouched behind them. The grave we planned to visit was at the farthest corner of lot. Unlike the others, the moss-covered grave of Thomas Birch stood perfectly upright, his name still legible, probably thanks to the huge oak tree that stood nearby protecting it from the rain and wind. His perfect stone isn't why we chose Thomas Birch though.

Thomas Birch was a coal miner when he was alive, like many of the other folks living here back then, but as the stories go, he also had a certain reputation around town. He was apparently friends with a lady who lived on the other side of the railroad tracks, a lady who claimed to be a medium, not the kind of person you usually see in a small town like ours. Jess and I went downtown and talked to a few people in the nursing home who said they knew him. A few even told us they had been invited to séances at his house, said they were there when old Mr. Birch spoke to his wife after she died. Some of them believed it, and so do I. Nobody could remember the medium's name or where she was buried, but everyone knew where to find Thomas Birch. They said he was buried in the old graveyard because most of his family was there. We figured if we had any chance of contacting a spirit, he was our guy.

We dropped our backpacks onto the ground next to Birch's gravestone, and Jess arranged the circle of white candles around us. They had to be white because, according to the book Emily read, white would only attract good spirits. Since this was our first run with the Ouija, avoiding any bad ones sounded like a great idea. Once the candles were lit, Jess took the board out of her bag and placed it on the ground. There was just enough moonlight to see the alphabet arranged in two neat arcs across its surface, the YES and NO in the upper corners, and the row of numbers and a GOOD-BYE along the bottom.

I sat on the ground first, and Jess handed me the pointer, apparently called a planchette. I placed it on the board and looked up at the others who just stood there looking down at me, as if they were afraid to get too close.

Donna looked positively terrified.

"What are you waiting for?" I asked. "You can't play from up there."

I told them they had to sit cross-legged on the ground, so that our knees were touching, the board across our laps. I was the only one who had ever played before. I didn't tell them I had only ever played with Mom—and that she and I had only ever used the board like a Magic Eight Ball, asking silly questions like whether I was going to pass my science test or if I might lose a tooth. Mom and Gram Marie asked different types of questions when they played. I used to sit in the other room and listen.

"OK, everybody, put your fingers on," I said, "and, remember, don't push too hard. The pointer has to be able to move."

I watched as they reluctantly placed their fingertips on the planchette, and then I told them to close their eyes while I performed the invocation. This was something Mom and I had never done, so I had to memorize the one from Emily's book. Supposedly, the board can't work without one, which makes me wonder how the pointer moved when Mom and I played. I guess either the book is wrong, or the pointer only moved because Mom was pushing it. Either way, I decided we weren't taking any chances this time.

"Greetings, spirits," I said. "We are Nadia, Donna, Jess, and Emily, and we welcome you. Only spirits with good intentions are invited to use the board. Others are not welcome here. Move the pointer when you're ready, and give us your name."

I could hear Donna's quick breaths beside me, so I opened one eye and peeked over at her. Her face was scrunched into a grimace, and it looked like she might be crying. She had asked us to find someone else to take her place, but we insisted she come. I suddenly felt guilty for dragging her into this, and I reached out to put a hand on her arm. The second my fingers made contact, though, she practically leaped out of her skin and screamed. The pointer went flying.

"Sorry," Donna said quickly. "Nadia touched me, and I jumped."

"Nadia, that's not funny!" Emily said, glaring at me. "If you do it again, I'm leaving. I mean it!"

"It's not like I did it to scare her," I said.

"Come on," Jess said. "Just forget it. Everybody, move back in and put your fingers on. We're not gonna get anywhere like this, and we're running out of time."

Emily and Donna moved back in, and we readjusted the board on our laps. For the next fifteen minutes, we all sat there in perfect silence, fingers balanced on the planchette, arms and feet filling with pins and needles. Leaves rustled around us, but the planchette didn't move.

"I don't think we have any takers," Jess said finally, looking at me. "What do you think we should do? Call it a day? Close the session? Try again some other time?"

I hated to stop, but I nodded my head.

Jess cleared her throat, but before she could say the words that would close the session, I felt the planchette shift under my fingers.

"Wait," I said, glancing down. "Did anyone else feel that?"

We all watched as the pointer began a slow drift toward Birch's gravestone. When it reached the edge of the board, it did a quick U-turn and picked up speed. It began moving more easily, across the lines of letters and numbers as if someone was testing the process. It stopped and started, took short, staggered bursts, paused over random letters and circled others. It glided across the board, pulling us along with it.

I looked at Donna. Tears were streaming down her face. My own heart was pounding. The pointer had never done anything like this when I'd played with Mom. It always stopped carefully on each letter, spelling out words and sentences. I was about to tell everyone this when the pointer stopped. It paused over the H, then moved to another letter, then another. When it stopped over the fourth, Emily jumped up and backed away from the circle.

"I'm not staying if it spells things like that," Emily yelled, pointing at the board. "I told you this wasn't a good idea."

Donna pulled her hands away too. She wiped them down the front of her sweatshirt as if something nasty clung to them. She joined Emily outside the circle of candles.

Jess and I stared down at the board between us. The pointer sat perfectly still.

"Come on," I said, looking up at Donna and Emily. "We have one! You can't bail now."

"No way," Donna said, shaking her head. "I'm done."

Emily stepped behind Donna, also refusing to sit back down.

I looked at Jess. She nodded and shimmied closer until our knees were touching and the board was balanced between us. The second our fingers touched the planchette, it repeated the same four letters and added a fifth.

H-E-L-L-O.

Jess looked at up me, her eyes wide.

We answered in unison. "Hello."

The pointer then began to volley between X-O-X-O-X-O.

It kept going as Donna stepped in and leaned over us.

"What's it doing?" she asked. "Do you think that means hugs and kisses?"

The pointer immediately swung to the upper corner of the board and stopped over the word YES. We all looked at each other.

I started to ask another question when, out of nowhere, we heard leaves rustling. A group of boys came lumbering toward us across the graveyard, moaning like a pack of zombies. Donna quickly blew out the candles. The rest of us grabbed our things and scattered.

Back at Jess's house, Emily and Donna stood giggling at the front door, peeking through the curtain, watching to see if the boys had followed us home.

I pulled Jess into the dining room. "Tell me the truth," I said. "Were you pushing it?"

She looked hurt that I would even ask. "Of course, I wasn't pushing it," she said. "Were you?"

I shook my head.

After that, Jess and I were hooked. We played every time we got together. The more we played, the easier the planchette moved. It told us where to find things that we'd lost. When we asked to have a friend call us, the phone would ring within the hour. The more the board worked, the more we tested it, but we kept our secret to ourselves—at least for a while. We figured no one else would believe us anyway. We continued playing until the board gave us a reason to stop.

I flip though the same journal until I come to the next skull and crossbones in the top margin. The entry below is short, the handwriting shaky.

From the Journal of Nadia King
Age Fifteen

I just got off the phone with Jess. She was crying. Her words were all jumbled.

She says she heard something tapping at her window last night around three in the morning. Her bedroom is on the second floor, so I don't know how that's possible, but she swears it's true. She didn't get up to look, just pulled the covers over her head and tried to fall back asleep.

She was crying so hard on the phone.

She says she heard a voice while she was hiding under the covers. She said it was like someone was sitting right next to her bed, like they were leaning right up against her ear. She says they whispered her name. When she tried to ignore it, she said she felt the mattress sink down beside her, like when someone sits down on the bed. She jumped up and turned on the lights then, but her room was empty.

She thinks it happened because we forgot to close our last Ouija session. She said she looked it up. Apparently, spirits can hang around if you don't make them say goodbye. We definitely didn't close the board the last time we played. She and I were on it when Donna showed up at her house unexpectedly. When we heard Donna coming upstairs, we tossed the board under Jess's bed so Donna wouldn't know what we were doing. I don't think that's the only reason it happened though. I think it happened because I broke my promise to Jess.

Last night, I was over at Gretchen's house when all of this happened. We were in her basement looking for Monopoly, and I found a Ouija board on the shelf. Gretchen didn't know what it was, and when I told her what it could do, she didn't believe me. So, of course, I had to show her. We started playing at around three o'clock in the morning, which is when this happened to Jess. I only remember the time because Gretchen and I went into the kitchen to grab some cookies before we played. I was surprised to see how late it was.

I think our spirit went looking for Jess when he saw me at the board. I think he wondered where she was. I think he's somehow linked to the two of us.

Jess doesn't think we should play anymore, and I think she's right. What Jess doesn't know is that what happened to her used to happen to me all the time as a kid. She's afraid, and I don't blame her. I remember what it feels like to lie in bed and know that you aren't alone in the room. I told her we'd stop playing, told her I hated that she was so scared. What I didn't tell her is that I'm afraid too. I don't want to reopen those doors.

I lost touch with Jess after high school, but I never stopped wondering about that night, about how it was even possible. In my second year of college, I attended a series of seminars hosted by the university's Psychology Department. They were led by a guest lecturer, Dr. Phyllis Young. The title of the series was "Parapsychology: Fact or Fiction." Dr. Young lectured on psychic abilities mostly, but her last lecture was all about the history of the Ouija. I couldn't resist. I made it a point to catch her afterward.

When I told Dr. Young what had happened with Jess, she said I was probably right, that the spirit had likely seen us as a pair. Together, we were its conduit. She agreed that not closing a session could cause problems if you weren't careful. We talked about my other experiences too. Before she left, she gave me her card and said I should reach out if I ever wanted to learn more. I emailed her not long after that, and in response, she sent me a list of universities well known for their parapsychology departments. She said I should look into them, that I would be a natural. The closest was about four hours away, just outside of Philadelphia. I was actually considering a transfer until I met Sam. Once he was in my life, I stayed where I was. We got married not long after graduation.

Sam and I stayed where we were for a few years after that. He took a job with a local engineering firm, and I took one in a tiny academic lab doing basic research. He got transferred shortly after Maeve was born, to a site just a few minutes outside of Philadelphia.

It's funny how unexpected turns in events can sometimes lead us back in the right direction, to where our true fate lies. Without even trying, I eventually found my way to one of the institutes that Dr. Young had originally suggested in her email—the one that everyone now calls "the University."

CHAPTER 6

The Present
Age Forty-One
Monday

A far-off tapping catches my attention as I finish reading the last page of the journal. I turn and look toward the library door. Rowan is there looking back at me, the toe of one bright orange shoe clicking against the hardwood floor in front of her. Her long skirt is spattered with flecks of orange and pink, her blouse and scarf an exact match. Her short, dark hair is styled in perfect curls. No one would ever guess she's in her seventies. Her arms are wrapped around a paper bag.

Aaron stands beside her, still filthy from yard work.

"Welcome back, space cadet," Rowan says, her voice cheery. "Did you have a nice trip?"

I look at my watch and am surprised to see it's nearly nine o'clock.

"How long have you guys been standing there?"

"Not long," Rowan says, shaking her head. "I just dropped Mom off at Les Choux. She's helping Ella at the restaurant tonight with a huge retirement party. Ella gave me all of this for you." Rowan places the bag on the floor and pulls out a large bottle of wine and an equally large box of chocolates. "She thought you might need it."

"She might be right," I say. "How are my two favorite blue hairs, anyway?"

Rowan strides toward me and sets the box of chocolates on the small round table between the leather chairs. She rolls her eyes. "Those two will be running that place until they die, I swear."

"I certainly hope so," Aaron chimes in from the doorway. "They need to keep the treats coming." He holds up a to-go container. "Rowan brought me one of those hazelnut tortes I love. I think I hear it calling my name."

Rowan spins on a heel and looks at him. "Are you not joining us for wine? Plenty to go around."

He waves a dismissive hand. "You girls drink up and enjoy. Can't have the torte and wine both. Gotta keep my girlish figure," he says, patting his flat stomach as he walks over to the fireplace. "I did set this up earlier though. Figured someone we know would end up in here before the night was over." He shoots me a playful look, sets his to-go box on the mantel, and pulls a box of matches from the ceramic bowl next to it. Kneeling down, he strikes a match and touches it to a piece of balled-up newspaper on the grate. He blows on the kindling until the flames catch, and then he pushes himself back up to standing.

He makes it look so easy.

"That should do it," he says, tossing the box of matches back into the bowl. "You should be good for the night. There's more wood there in the bucket to keep it going." He points to a large copper pail at the side of the fireplace. "Now, if you girls don't mind, I think I'm gonna go hit the shower and see if I'm still underneath this dirt somewhere before digging into this dessert. Try to behave, all right?"

Rowan places a hand on her hip. "Us, behave?"

Aaron laughs on his way out the door. "You're right. Forget I even suggested it. I know better. You ladies enjoy."

Rowan waits until Aaron is out of sight, and then she turns to look at me. "He's an absolute sweetheart."

"I honestly don't know what I'd do without him," I say, placing the journals on the floor so I can get up to grab some glasses.

Rowan points a finger at me. "You sit and relax. I've got this. You just open that box of chocolates and eat a few, how's that? You're getting way too thin. You're worrying yourself to death over all this."

She wanders over to the liquor cabinet and pulls open one of the doors. From the top shelf, she grabs two wineglasses and, from the drawer, the corkscrew. By the time she returns, I've eaten two of the chocolates, and the fire has caught nicely, the lowest flames a hot blue. She studies them for a minute and then turns to me and shakes her head. "I don't know how that poor man can start a fire for us," she says, placing the glasses on the table. "It must remind him of the accident every time."

"The counselors say he's blocked a lot of it out, and I hope they're right. He never talks about it."

"The mind is a funny thing," Rowan says. "You and I know all too well how much it can block out. In his case though, it's a good thing. I don't know how else you'd cope with losing your whole family like that."

Rowan fills our glasses to the top, hands one to me, and sinks into the other chair. "You've got a good heart, Nadia. Not many people would have done what you did for him."

"Everyone in that shelter deserves some sort of break," I say. "I'm just glad I could help Aaron, at least. He'd give you the shirt off his back if you needed it, and if he didn't have a shirt, he'd help you find one. Did you see the kitchen when you came in?" I tip my glass toward the door. "He did the whole thing by himself. Design to completion. Incredible."

Rowan leans back in her chair, glass balanced in a perfectly manicured hand. "All I can say is if a book of mine sold like yours, and I had the chance to splurge a little, I would have picked less of a fixer-upper, but that's just me."

I laugh. "This house is definitely a lot more work than I anticipated, but it's coming along. Most of it thanks to Aaron."

"And what about Amulet?" she asks. "How's that coming along?"

By the time I'm done answering that question, we've finished two glasses of wine each. I share my concerns about Sterling and explain we might have to tell him something soon. I also tell her about my dream. When I'm done, we just sit there and stare into the fire, listening to the logs pop and crack.

When Rowan goes quiet, I know she's thinking, so I wait.

After a few minutes, she refills my glass and gives me a serious look. "What if I told you Sterling already knows what you're up to? Would that make you feel any better?"

I wait for her to smile, wait for her to tell me she's pulling my leg. There's no way Sterling would be so quiet if he knew what we were up to.

"I'm not kidding," Rowan says, leaning forward in her chair. "Listen, we both know Sterling is a hardheaded bastard, no doubt, and yes, we know how much he despises me and the work that Jakob does, but you've got him thinking, Nadia. He'll never admit this to you, but he's read your novel."

I want to ask how she knows, but before I can get the question out, she winks.

"A little bird told me," she says. "Sterling knows what comes next ... at least what happens in your novel. I'm not sure he truly believes all of it will translate to the lab, but he can't deny that your predictions have boasted a pretty good track record so far. You should talk to him, Nadia, and talk to him soon." She puts her empty glass on the table, draws her shawl up over her shoulders, and pushes herself out of her chair. "I'll let you stew on that one for a bit," she says, readjusting the waistband of her skirt. "I know it's a big pill to swallow. You've got some hard thinking to do, my dear, and we have some very interesting times ahead. It's nearly the big day. As for tonight, I think it's time for this old lady to get on the road. Don't worry, Aaron said he'd drive me home when I was ready."

I figured as much. He knows the drill by now. I stand to walk her to the door, but she just shakes her head.

"You might as well stay where you are, my dear," she says. "You'll just end up right back here after I leave anyway. Save the energy—you're gonna need it." She hobbles over and gives me a hug. "If I weren't so damn tired, I'd stay a little longer and have you read one of those journals to me. Maybe the one about the day we met. I'll bet that one's a doozy."

Rowan tweezes a white truffle out of the box for the road, and as she passes through the archway into the kitchen, she looks back with a wave. Not long after that, I hear the front door close behind her.

CHAPTER 7

The Present
Age Forty-One
Monday

After Rowan leaves, I put another log on the fire, slide back into my chair, and watch the flames catch. The weight of my body sinks into the cushions around me. I relish in the quiet, that thick heavy quiet that only comes at night. The logs in the fireplace crackle. Outside, the wind swirls, a soft whisper at the eaves. Every once in a while, a quick gust scrapes a gangly tree branch across one of the windowpanes, producing an eerie sort of warbling sound. I consider what Rowan said. *If Sterling has indeed read my novel, that's encouraging news, but is he really ready to know everything?* Unlike Rowan, I'm not so sure.

The wine has taken its toll, so I don't worry about this as much as I would have otherwise. The tip of my nose feels numb, and my eyes have a sleepy kind of quality to them. I teeter on the verge of sleep. Far off, back in the corner of my consciousness, a dream starts, some thought about a woman and her two young children, each of them wearing old-fashioned dresses with hems that brush the ground. They're standing next to a horse-drawn carriage. It's parked in the middle of a gloomy alley, a dim streetlamp overhead. The horses are fidgety, shifting on their feet as if they're anxious to get going. I'm about to walk over to them when a sharp crack breaks the silence. The horses rear and give a look of sheer terror, the whites of their eyes visible, ears pressed back against their heads.

I sit bolt upright in my chair, half in and half out of sleep.

Was the noise a part of my dream, or did it come from somewhere inside the house?

The dogs give me the answer. They were asleep on the floor when Rowan left, but the three of them are now staring toward the archway that leads into the kitchen, their ears perked, their heads held high. Quake's hackles are up, and once again, a low growl rumbles in his throat. He seems to be watching something in the darkness beyond. The idea of an intruder never even crosses my mind. Given what I just heard, I'm thinking along different lines. I wait for the noise to come again. Suddenly, the crackling of the logs seems too loud. The wind seems more of a roar than a whisper. The tree branches scrape at the windows far too often. I get out of my chair.

"You stay," I say, pointing at Quake in particular. "Stay. You hear? I'll be right back."

I know that if Quake stays, they all will.

Standing in the archway, I reach one hand into the darkness, feeling for the light switch, and when I find it, I flip it on. Light floods the kitchen, and I let my eyes sweep the room. The sound could have been a flowerpot falling from the bay window, but Ares is nowhere in sight, and the orchids are all still intact. The salt and pepper shakers are still on the island counter. The broom is still standing in the far corner of the room, propped against the wall just as I left it. I walk over to the patio doors and jiggle the handles. They're locked.

Turning back to face the kitchen, I give the room one final scan from that direction. The only thing that seems remotely out of place is a spattering of fingerprints on the door of the stainless-steel fridge. I start toward the sink to grab a rag, figuring I might as well take care of them while I'm out there. Before I even get to the island, though, I feel the left side of my face prickle. I know then that the noise wasn't Ares.

On that side of the room, a tall fern stands near the pantry. I can see it in my peripheral vision as I continue toward the fridge. The prickling sensation persists, but I try to appear disinterested. I pass the island on the right, and while making my way around the edge of it, I glance toward the pantry. A shadow stands near the pantry door, tall and narrow, no different than the ones that tag along behind us on a sunny afternoon.

Anyone else would have assumed it belonged to the fern, but I know better, and it knows that I know. I watch as the shadow hesitates, letting me get a decent look before it shifts its position and moves behind the plant. It's testing me.

Normally, they're quick to hide. I'll think I see them, and then they're gone, but this one wants to make sure I see it. They've been harmless so far, but they're getting braver, and the sight of them still makes me a little uneasy. This is how I know I'm not quite ready for the next step. The fact that I heard the sharp crack this time makes me think they don't care whether I'm ready or not. I think of Sir Anthony Bard, of the noise his wife heard as she passed his study. She heard the crack, and then he was gone. Who made the decision for him to cross the veil and enter the next level? Was it his choice or theirs? I decide not to stay in the kitchen long enough to find out.

Back in the library, I join the dogs on the floor. Nyx and Attis wander over and curl up next to me, but Quake continues his watch. His hackles are still up, and his eyes are still trained on the doorway to the kitchen, but that's just Quake's way, and I'm thankful for it. The shadows don't come near him, which is why I told him to stay in the library while I investigated. I needed to see for myself what was out there.

Jakob and I aren't sure what to make of the shadows yet. We can only guess based on what I've read in Bard's notebook. The sound is yet another mystery, although I have my own hypothesis. I think it's similar to the thunder we hear during a storm. When a lightning bolt cuts through the sky, the streak of energy temporarily displaces the air, leaving a channel in its wake. The channel remains open as the light passes through, but once the light has moved on, the displaced air collapses in on itself. This is what causes a thunderclap. If a shade is just another form of energy, and it has to break through the veil to be seen, maybe its movement has the same effect.

I look at the dogs and ruffle their fur.

"Guess what, guys?" I say. "After that little adventure, I'm not that tired anymore. My nice wine buzz seems to be gone, too. So, now what?"

Quake is still watching the kitchen. I grab his back leg and give it a shake.

"What do you say, big guy?" I ask when he finally turns to look at me. "Think another journal sounds like a good idea?"

Bard's journal is in the lab. If it were here, that would be my first choice. I'm only halfway through and extremely curious about what might be in the rest of it. I'm not sure how Mr. Noah got his hands on that one, but he did—and he's heard there could be more. The one he gave me is on loan, not mine to keep, but that's OK. I just need it for a little while.

I study the shelves behind the desk for a minute and decide on two journals this time, one with a badly warped spine, as well as the prettier one just below it. I carry them both back to the chair. The fire is getting low. It will be out shortly, but it should last long enough for what I have in mind.

I open the tattered one first. The smell of mildew escapes, a testament to its hiding place in the rag box under the basement stairs. Flipping through it, I see that most of the entries are messy and rushed. I could only spend so much time writing in the basement back then without raising Sam's suspicions. Somewhere in the middle of the journal, I find the entry I'm looking for. Two giant question marks flank the date at the top of the page. These were added months later, scribbled there when I went back to read the entry a second and third time in an effort to make some sense out of everything that happened that day. It was the day that Rowan and I met.

We have a bizarre history, Rowan and I, one prompted by a very strange beginning and held together by even stranger glue. Before meeting her, I wasted a lot of time wondering how I might have done things differently, how I'd go back and change things if I could. It was Rowan who convinced me that each step we take in life is, at once, a piece of our history as well as a part of where we're going, that the steps along the way aren't something we should ever want to change. Rowan insists that every life event has its purpose, that each person we meet teaches us something new about ourselves, and that every experience is necessary.

"Look forward for change," she says, "never back."

Above the two question marks is a faded coffee stain. I'd nearly spilled the entire cup that night when one of the neighbors slammed a car door outside on the street. I was on edge because I was writing in my journal at the dining room table rather than on the basement stairs. That night, I had the house to myself, but it still felt strange to be writing out in the open. Sam and Maeve had gone away for the weekend, home to visit his family. He told me they wouldn't be back until Sunday, but you never knew if that was actually true or not.

There were plenty of times when he said he was leaving, but he would show up at the house a few hours later—as if he thought he might catch me doing something that wasn't allowed. This could be a whole range of things based on Sam's definition. Something as simple as having a glass of wine was one of them. Normally, when Sam was away, I did treat myself to wine, but that night, I'd chosen coffee instead because I was chilled to the bone. I'd just gotten home from a day volunteering at the homeless shelter. The walk home from the bus station had been bitterly cold. Sam didn't like me going anywhere or talking to anyone. He didn't know about my work at the shelter, nor did he know about Aaron, who I'd recently met there. Aaron was my only true friend at the time.

From the Journal of Nadia King
Age Twenty-Seven

It was cold today, almost ten degrees below zero with the wind chill. By the time I stepped off the bus in the city, a layer of snow had covered the sidewalks. I got to the shelter around six o'clock this morning, but by eight thirty, there was no sign of Aaron, which seemed strange. When eleven o'clock rolled around and he still hadn't arrived, I decided to take a walk to see if I could find him. I searched for nearly two hours with no success. I was on my way back to the shelter when a sign at the far end of an alley caught my eye. I wandered closer to get a better look.

The sign turned out to be an elaborate piece of ironwork in the shape of Boreas, the north wind, the old man's features hammered into the dark metal. Elegant furls of air flowed from his mouth, each wisp formed by a thin strap of blackened iron. They twisted together in a mass of intricate detail, tapering off as they stretched out in front of him. The sign was absolutely gorgeous. Below it, suspended by two thin chains, hung a green serpentine nameplate, disproportionately tiny in relation to the sculpture itself. It bore only one word: Welcome. The sign hung beside a spotless shop window.

The glare of the sun on the snow and the light's reflection in the glass made it impossible to see inside. I cupped my hands against it to get a better look, like a child at the window of a candy shop. To my surprise, a woman sat only a few feet away, in one of two large wingback chairs. She didn't move, not even when our eyes connected. I felt my face flush and dropped my hands. I had no choice but to go in.

The bell above the door jingled as I stepped into the small room. The woman remained seated in her chair, but she offered a smile. She wore a long, flowery skirt and a blue blouse. A scarf was tied in a neat knot at the side of her neck. She had a round face and dark brown hair, and she looked to be in her early sixties. Her hands were folded in her lap. For some reason, she reminded me of a kindergarten teacher, one waiting patiently for the kids to settle around her for a story.

The room behind her distracted me immediately, so much that I even forgot to say hello. It was tiny and cramped, no better lit than it had appeared from the street. Three amber sconces hung on deep orange walls, giving the space a dim but fiery glow. Burning candles, arranged in groups of three, graced the length of a long white marble mantel behind the chairs. Above the candles, a colorful swirl of mosaic tile decorated the wall. Tiny shards of mirror were interspersed. They reflected the candlelight and projected dancing spots across the ceiling. *The Starry Night* by Van Gogh came to mind. The curtains at the window were made of heavy velvet, deep plum in color. They kept the room toasty despite the cold outside. No draft had a fighting chance against them.

The woman watched me take this all in without saying a word.

I felt the heat creep back into my feet. The room smelled of coffee and cinnamon rolls, making me wish I'd stopped at the café a few blocks back.

"Cozy, isn't it?" the woman said finally, making me jump.

Realizing I still hadn't said a word, I opened my mouth, ready to apologize.

She waved a hand in the air but never got up from her seat. "No need for apologies, my dear. It's your first time here. It happens to everyone. My name is Rowan, and you are?"

"Nadia," I said, walking toward her and pulling off one fuzzy white glove.

She smiled and hoisted herself out of her chair.

"I didn't mean to be rude," I said, extending my hand.

She took my hand in both of hers, and a sudden look of horror came over her face. "For goodness' sake! Your fingers are like ice cubes! How long have you been out there in this awful weather?" She grabbed my other hand and gave them both a rub. "I just put on some coffee. How about a nice big cup to warm up?" She patted the closest chair. "Have a seat. Stay a while."

"You must have read my mind," I said. "I was literally just thinking I should have stopped for a cup of coffee on my way. It smells amazing in here."

"Well," Rowan said with a chuckle, "you don't have to be a mind reader to see that you're chilled to the bone. Blue lips are usually a dead giveaway." She winked at me before walking toward the counter at the other end of the room. "Coffee is the perfect remedy."

As Rowan shuffled past me, I removed my scarf and coat, draping everything over the arm of the chair since there didn't seem to be anywhere else to put it.

At the counter, Rowan dug in the cupboard above the coffee pot.

"It actually smells like you might have my favorite flavor brewing."

"Well," Rowan said, "people do sometimes say I have a knack for the mind-reading bit, so, yes, the coffee is hazelnut, your favorite." She then proceeded to arrange a few mugs and spoons on a tray.

I wasn't sure if I'd heard her right. Hazelnut was indeed my favorite, but there was no way she could have known that. I was even more surprised by what she did next. Before pouring the coffee, without even asking how I took mine, she added two scoops of sugar and a small touch of oat milk, exactly as I would have done, as if we'd known each other for years.

I stayed for about an hour. We sat in front of the window, talking while people wrapped in hats and scarves passed by outside. Within ten minutes, I felt like I'd been reacquainted with an old friend. As the next half hour passed, however, I grew more agitated. I eventually stormed out.

I have no desire to ever speak to that woman again. I'm not sure why anyone would tell a perfect stranger the things she told me. I can't even remember what I said to her when I left. I was in such a rush to go that I left my coat and scarf hanging over the arm of the chair. Despite the cold, I refused to go back in to get them. I'm not sure how I'll explain this to Sam.

The good news is, I did see Aaron from the bus window on the way home. He was on the corner of Ninth and Walnut, huddled over a steam grate, an old woman squeezed up next to him. They were wrapped in blankets, and it looked like he was reading her a book. At least I don't have to worry about where he is tonight.

Opinions often change over the years. You either learn to appreciate someone more by hearing what they've done, or you realize that you have to get away from them because of how they treat you. Rowan is now one of my closest friends.

I didn't return to Rowan's shop until much later, but in the years that followed that first encounter, she was never far from my mind. Every once in a while, reminders of our conversation haunted me, and I eventually realized why she had told me all that she had. She wasn't trying to be cruel. She was just trying to prepare me for what was coming.

I lay the tattered journal on the floor and open the other, this one in much better shape. Sam was a thing of the past by the time I started working on this one. No more storage in the rag box, no more writing in a rush on the basement stairs.

The dogs shift on the area rug in front of me. The fire is nearly out. I don't have much time. I flip through the pages of the journal until I see a few more question marks at the top. I pass by those and continue flipping, searching for an exclamation point. I find it and settle in.

From the Journal of Nadia King
Age Thirty-Three

I returned to Rowan's shop today. With everything that's been happening, I just needed answers. I wasn't even sure if her shop would still be there, but it was.

She greeted me at the door, opening it before I could even touch the handle. Once again, she seemed to be expecting me. She was dressed in another colorful outfit, nails painted to match, hair in perfect curls. Her smile was as welcoming as it had been the first time. She hasn't changed, but my opinion of her certainly has. I can't be angry at her anymore.

I started to apologize, but like last time, she didn't give me the chance.

"I understand why you got so upset," she said, placing her hands on my shoulders. "I said too much too soon. There were just so many things you needed to know." She pulled me inside. "Let's get you in out of this heat. You'll melt if you stay out there, and we can't have that. We're going to need you."

We're going to need you. Those are the words she used. I have no idea what she might have meant by it, but that's exactly what she said.

At the counter, two coffee mugs waited next to the pot. I pointed at them and shot her a questioning look. "Coffee? It's a hundred degrees outside."

She proceeded to add sugar and milk to the cups just like last time, and then she raised one eyebrow at me. "And your point is?"

"Don't most people go for iced tea instead of coffee when it's this hot?"

"I suppose," she said matter-of-factly as she filled the cups, "but today, my company doesn't like iced tea, so why would I serve it?"

I narrowed my eyes at her. She was right again. "How do you do that?"

She laughed. "You'll find out in due time, my dear. For now, do you eat chocolate?" She pulled a box from the shelf, opened it, and held it out to me. "You don't look like you do, but you should. It's good for you. My mother's special recipe."

I chose the piece in the closest corner, a perfect square, a neat swirl on top. She took the one next to it and held it up in front of her as if inspecting a rare gem. "This, my dear, is the secret to staying young. Eat at least five a day, and you'll keep the wrinkles at bay. See here?" She jutted out her chin and rubbed her fingertips across her cheek. "A nice little layer of fat helps to fill in all the rough spots. Wrinkles don't have a fighting chance." She gave a wink and then reached up and pinched my chin.

I followed her as she carried the tray of coffee and sweets over to the chairs. My coat and scarf were slung over the arm of the one closest to me. Somehow, she knew I'd be back. How she knew was just one of the many questions I had for her. For the next two hours, she listened to my questions and tried to explain as best she could.

As I sit here writing this entry, I'm still not sure I understand any more than when we started. I'm not even going to try to write it all down right now.

"We should talk more," she told me as I was getting ready to leave. "I think we need to get you on your way a little quicker."

I spun and looked at her. It's not a phrase many people use now, is it? My thoughts returned to that day in the hospital with Gram Marie.

Rowan gave a little smile, one that I could swear was all too knowing.

I'm going back again next week, but before I do, I need to think.

CHAPTER 8

The Present
Age Forty-One
Monday

Rowan and I still pass entire afternoons in those chairs, but only when business is slow, which is rare. Rowan's psychic readings are known for being the best in the area. When I ventured inside her shop that first winter, she offered me a reading at no charge. I couldn't have afforded it otherwise. Rowan said that when she grabbed my hands, it wasn't only the coldness of them that made her ask me to stay. She said she knew immediately that we needed more time.

Like everyone who steps into Rowan's shop, I hoped to hear good news, some small glimmer of hope that life might get better than it was at the time. When she told me that I was going to lose my job, suffer through a messy divorce, and struggle for years to make ends meet, I was more than disappointed. When she told me that I should go back home to visit my father, that he wouldn't be with us much longer, that's when I stormed out. He was young, in his early fifties, a good chunk of his life still ahead of him—or at least that's what I thought.

When I returned to Rowan's shop that summer, I had indeed lost my job, gotten divorced, fallen into debt, and spent hours pacing the ground near my father's grave. Everything she told me had come true.

I look at the dogs. They're asleep on the floor. Every muscle in my body feels stiff. The clock on the mantel claims it's nearly midnight. I drop the journal onto the floor, stretch, and decide that the dogs have the right idea. It's been a long day. Crashing here in the library for the night seems as good an idea as any.

I swing my legs up over one arm of the chair and lean my head back against the other. The room has cooled substantially now that the fire has gone out. I reach into the wicker basket at the base of the chair, shake out my favorite fleece throw, and then pull it over me, tucking its edges underneath my chin and the sides of my legs.

Ares watches me from under the desk. As soon I'm situated, he comes over and leaps up onto my chest. He kneads the blanket with his front paws for a minute, and then he nestles himself into a tight ball under my chin. When he starts to purr, I let my eyes drift closed, and in no time, I fall into a very deep sleep.

Dear reader:

For a moment, forget everything you already know about Rowan, Jakob, Amulet, and my novel. I want to take you back a near decade, to right after I wandered into Rowan's shop for the second time. I want to give you more background, more about what happened between then and this very long Monday. You'll need to know what happened in between so you can be prepared for what comes next.

After my divorce and before we moved into the Baird, Maeve and I lived for a short time in a twin Victorian on Braeburn Avenue. The house was more than a hundred years old and sat in a neighborhood straight out of a Norman Rockwell painting. Flower beds were neatly tended, children played on front lawns, neighbors chatted on porches, and the ice-cream truck came at noon every Saturday. The years we spent there were a turning point for me. It was there that I started my first novel and finished it.

In my earliest conversations with Rowan, I told her about the things I thought I saw, heard, and felt in my Gram Marie's house as a child. I told her how they frightened me, how I tried not to think of them as I got older, and how the fears never truly seemed to go away. We talked about the willies and the drafts in the upstairs bedroom. We talked about the shadows and my nightmares. She asked me to tell her everything so that she could try to understand.

While we lived in the house on Braeburn, I worked closely with Rowan to further develop my psychic awareness, but to develop it fully, she said I'd have to conquer my fears.

You, dear reader, have probably grown out of your childhood fears. You're probably no longer afraid to let your feet dangle over the side of the bed or leave your closet doors open when you go to sleep at night. At forty-one, I still can't do either. I've seen enough to know that we should be afraid, at least a little. But we'll get to that.

First, I want to tell you more about Rowan.

Sincerely,
Nadia

CHAPTER 9

Rowan

Rowan Channing was born into a long line of sensitives. She's done some digging, and from what she can tell, the first record of any psychic ability was in her great-great-grandmother's generation. Adrianna was the first. Since then, fourteen women in Rowan's family have shown evidence of heightened awareness, and given these numbers, I think it's safe to assume that there were probably more before Adrianna. Keep in mind that psychic ability hasn't always been something about which to brag. It wasn't that long ago that bragging about these kinds of things could get you burned at the stake.

Whether a person is gifted or not, the same five basic senses that we learned about in elementary school apply: sight, sound, taste, touch, and smell. Everyone uses these same five senses to perceive our surroundings, but for most of us, perception is limited. Sensitives, on the other hand, are able to detect very minor shifts in each, triggers that most of us don't even notice.

The most gifted sensitives, like Rowan, possess a sixth sense in addition to the basic five. This extrasensory perception, or ESP, opens up a whole new world to its owner. Based on Rowan's family history, I'm convinced that ESP must have some genetic component. The fact that no men in her family ever carried the trait also seems to suggest that transmission is somehow linked to gender.

The most common gifts in Rowan's family are precognition and psychometry, both of which fall under the category of ESP. Precognition lets one see into the future, while psychometry provides a glimpse into the past. In the movies, the psychometrist is the one who is handed an object from a crime scene, and by touching it, is able to gather information about the person who touched it last. Rowan's grandmother, Triana, was well known for this. Over the course of Triana's lifetime, she worked with local police and helped locate more than twenty missing children.

When Triana passed away, Rowan and her mother, Rosa, left Rome for the States. Rowan was four, and Rosa was twenty-seven and recently widowed. They'd been here for only a month when Rosa found a bracelet in the street. Doing as her mother would have done, she picked it up and immediately realized that the woman who'd been wearing it last was in trouble. Rosa went to the police, but they never followed up on the lead. When they found the woman's body two weeks later in an empty warehouse, I'm sure they wished they had.

When the story broke, Rosa considered reaching back out to the police to offer her help in the future, but her friend Ella talked her out of it, telling her that a more normal life seemed a better choice given that she had Rowan to raise. "Things are different here in the States," she said. "People are less willing to accept certain gifts as truth."

A few months later, Rosa and Ella purchased a vacant storefront in the city and turned it into the busy restaurant it is today, Les Choux Charmants. The direct translation from French is the Charming Cabbages, but the name doesn't quite fit. Neither owner speaks a word of French and Les Choux doesn't offer any French fare, especially not cabbage, but four-year old Rowan suggested the name, and the two women never batted an eye.

Of all the women in the Channing family, Rowan is the only medium. Most people know that mediums are able to communicate with the dead, but what I didn't know before meeting Rowan is that mediums can also communicate with energies that have never been alive and never will be. The best examples of these are spirit guides, known to some as guardian angels.

I also never realized that being a medium could cause problems in school. Rosa was called in on more than one occasion by Rowan's teachers, many of them more concerned than angry. They were worried about Rowan's conversations with her "imaginary friends." They explained that Rowan went so far as to include these friends when she was asked to count the children in line at recess. Some teachers suggested a counselor, and the school nurse went so far as to suggest possible schizophrenia. Of course, Rosa knew better. Rosa never tried to explain her daughter's clairvoyance to the teachers. She didn't tell them, that to Rowan, shades were just as real as any other child in the room. Instead, Rosa talked to her daughter, taught her the difference between the living and the shades, and urged Rowan to keep this little secret to herself going forward.

The shades continued to visit, of course, but Rowan followed her mother's advice and didn't acknowledge them in public. She focused on school and took an interest in foreign languages, which came easily to her, thanks to the help of her imaginary friends who spoke a variety of them. Rowan worked as a translator for the United Nations after graduation, but that only lasted a few short years. As with me, fate found a way to put Rowan back on her true path.

She eventually left to open her shop in the city where she offered psychic readings three days a week. She spent the other four working for her mother and Ella at Les Choux. It was there that she met her first husband, Louis. He became a restaurant regular shortly after Rowan started working there and swore that Rowan was the reason for that. Rowan liked to tease him, saying he was only interested in Ella's famous éclairs. He ordered this same dessert every time without fail, and after a while, Rowan would bring it to him without even asking if he wanted one.

One night, when she brought him his coffee and dessert, Louis surprised her by getting down on one knee and asking for her hand. Suddenly the name of the restaurant chosen by four-year-old Rowan made more sense. Les Choux Charmants, previously assumed to be the Charming Cabbages, had nothing to do with cabbages at all. An éclair is made with choux pastry. Louis had been born and raised in France before coming to the States. And if a proposal over dessert isn't charming, then I don't know what is. Their marriage lasted only five short years before he died unexpectedly.

Rowan was widowed again by her second husband, Sal, at age sixty-five. He rarely came to Les Choux, but he regularly visited her shop for psychic readings. He was fascinated by her talent and spent most of their time together asking questions, trying to understand it, much like I do. This is how he, Rowan, and Jakob became close friends, and how Sal came to fund a good deal of Jakob's research.

Sal also designed and created the Boreas that now hangs outside Rowan's shop. He gave it to her as a birthday gift and hung it there the day before he passed away. As he left the shop that afternoon, he told Rowan she should offer her readings free of charge so that everyone could see what she can do regardless of whether they could afford a reading or not. When Sal died, he left her plenty of money to do just that. In fact, Rowan could have easily stopped working altogether if she wanted to, but she knew this would only break his heart. When I wandered into her shop a week later, she knew exactly what she had to do.

CHAPTER 10

The Past
Age Thirty-Three

A few months after I returned to visit Rowan, she and I sat parked in our respective wingbacks, both angled to face the big front window of her shop. The street outside was buzzing with people. It was a beautiful summer day. We had cups of coffee in hand, as always, and a plate of cookies on the table between us, big chocolate chip ones from the deli next door. They were our new favorite, a break from Rosa's homemade chocolates.

We'd just had another unsuccessful attempt at channeling my father, and Rowan was being uncharacteristically quiet. She sat there, looking out the window, elbows propped on the arms of her chair, the coffee mug cupped in both hands and pressed against her lips. She seemed deep in thought, and by then, I knew to give her the time she needed.

Outside, a golden retriever sat at the heels of tall blonde. It was staring up into a small tree, watching a bird in the branches. The woman tethered to the other end of its leash tapped a message into her cell phone. Farther down the block, a tiny Yorkie jumped up onto the bench near the bus stop and snuffled along its length, clearly enjoying all of the available smells. The Yorkie's balding owner held his own phone up at eye level, apparently speaking with someone on the other end of the line. Other dogs walked by and tried to sniff at lampposts or trash cans, but their humans just tugged them along.

Have we always been so disconnected with our surroundings? Or are we just getting worse?

When I looked back over at Rowan, she was studying me with a calculating grin.

"What?" I asked, self-consciously wiping at my chin. "Am I covered in cookie crumbs?"

"You have a few," she said, "but that's not why I'm smiling."

I looked down and saw that my shirt was indeed sprinkled with them and brushed them away. "So, why are you smiling?"

"I was smiling because you were so wrapped up in what was going on out there that you didn't even hear my question," Rowan said. "I was saying how I'm tired of talking about me every time you're here. I think it's time we talk about you for a change. I want to hear about *your* family. Beyond your father, I haven't been given much."

Rowan knew a lot about my father by then. With every failed attempt at contacting him, she'd ask for more information, hoping this might increase his energy enough to help him through. Nothing seemed to work.

"What exactly do you want to know?" I asked. "It's not like my family is as interesting as yours."

"Oh, I don't know about that," Rowan said, shaking a finger at me. "I have a feeling it might be more interesting than you think." She grabbed a cookie from the plate. "Your father's mother is one you call Gram Marie, right?"

I nodded as she took a bite.

"What about your mum's mum?" she asked. "She's still around, yes?"

I nodded again.

She asked about my mother, my sister, and Maeve. When she was done, she crossed her arms and looked at me. "Sounds like an awful lot of independent women, none of them with a man in their life for very long, including you. The similarities are interesting, don't you think?"

I squinted at her. "Similarities to …?"

"Oh, come on, Nadia," Rowan said, rolling her eyes. "You're a smart girl. You know what I'm comparing. The women in my family can't keep a husband around no matter how hard we try. I couldn't. Neither could my mother—or hers."

"But what does that have to do with anything?"

"There's got to be something to it, don't you think?" she asked, taking a sip of her coffee. "I'm not sure what that something is yet, but I've been trying to figure it out. But how about this? How do these women in your family feel about the paranormal? You haven't mentioned any gifts, but I feel like there might be a few who believe in it besides you."

I squinted at her again. "Why all of the questions about me all of a sudden?"

"Just humor me," she said. "I know you hate talking about yourself, but I'm curious, and you owe me." She smiled. "So, are they all believers? Any gifts?"

I looked out the window, thinking of the ghost stories with Gram Marie, how Mom and I used to play the Ouija, and how Mom and Gram Marie had played it as well. I thought of the tarot cards I found in Gramma Dessa's cupboard one day, and of the kinds of books she and my sister always read. When Rowan asked what I was thinking, I shared all of this.

"No gifts, at least I don't think, but obviously we all believe in it," I said. "Gram Marie was probably the most open about it. She's the one who bought the Ouija and talked Mom into playing. I actually think that's why Gramma Dessa and Gram Marie never got along."

"What do you mean?" Rowan asked.

"Mom told me a story once," I said. "Apparently, when Mom got pregnant with me, she and Gram Marie still continued to play with the Ouija board. Years later, at some family dinner, Gramma Dessa and Gram Marie got in a bit of a tiff. I guess Gramma D told Gram Marie that she should have known better, that this is why I always had nightmares as a kid, why I was so concerned about ghosts. She told Gram Marie that their playing with the board while Mom was pregnant is what opened certain channels to me. Silly, right?"

Rowan surprised me by shaking her head. "Not silly at all, actually. I never do a reading for anyone who's pregnant. It's one of the first things I ask when someone comes in. Don't you remember? It's too risky."

"Too risky? How? What do you think could happen?"

Rowan set her coffee cup on the table. "Let's just say that spirits are sometimes looking for a home, and unborn children can be an easy target. I don't have any personal experience with possessions, but I also don't want to take any chances. I think possessions are rare, mostly something for the movies, but I do wonder if being too close to spirits at an early age might have other consequences."

"Like what?"

"Well, look at my family," Rowan said. "Maybe we're living proof that being exposed to this kind of thing makes a difference. We've only seen the good effects, but what if early exposure makes it that much easier for a shade to lock onto a child once it's born?"

It was an interesting thought. *Expectant mothers are told to avoid plenty of other things while they're pregnant. Maybe this is no different.*

"Anyway," Rowan said, grabbing another cookie and turning toward me. "I think I want to know more about Gram Marie. Why do you think she had such a fascination with the board? She must have bought it for a reason. It's not the best method for spirit communication, but it does work. The catch is, it only works if you have the right partner. Sounds like your mother and Gram Marie might have been a good pair. Our types do tend to attract one another. Maybe that's what brought your mom and dad together."

"What do you mean when by *our types*?" I asked.

Rowan rolled her eyes again, ignoring my question, as if I should already know the answer. "Nadia, if you can work the Ouija successfully, which I know you have, it's time to move on to bigger and better things. I'd bet money that your Gram Marie didn't stop with the Ouija, given what you saw in her house."

"But what do you mean when you say *our types*?"

Rowan studied me. "I'll answer that question with a question of my own, if that's OK." She moved to the edge of her chair. "I'm extremely curious about something, Nadia. Have you ever heard of being born with a caul?"

"Of course," I said.

"Tell me," she said. "What does it mean?"

"It's when a child is born with a piece of the mother's amniotic sac covering its face."

"True, but that's the scientist talking," Rowan said. "What else is it?"

"Being born with a caul has a paranormal connection."

"Which is …" Rowan prodded.

"Being born with a caul is a sign that you're more prone to psychic ability."

Rowan pointed a finger at me. "That's my girl," she said, leaning back in her chair. "Cauls are rare, but they can run in certain bloodlines. Have you ever seen one?"

I shook my head. "Not a real one, but Gram Marie and I made one once."

Rowan cocked her head. "Made one? Out of what?"

"My Gram Marie was one of those ladies who owned every type of face cream imaginable. Every time I stayed over, right before bed, she'd sit in front of her mirror in the bathroom and go through her nightly routine. I always liked to sit and watch. She had this one fancy little glass bottle with a brush attached to the inside of the lid. The bottle was filled with this gooey pink liquid. She used to paint it all over her face, and once it dried, she'd peel it off. She said it was supposed to make you look younger. One night, after watching her, I asked if she'd put some on me, and I regretted it as soon as she started. The stuff in the bottle was cold and sticky. It smelled like medicine and took forever to dry. Plus, as it dried, it got tighter and itchier. All I wanted to do was wiggle my face to loosen it, but she told me I had to wait. When she finally peeled it off, it came away in one big sheet. There were holes where my eyes and nose had been. She told me that's how the doctors did it when I was born."

Rowan gave a nod. "Do you think that's true?"

"I don't know. I was too young then to ask her what she meant. She just smoothed the mask out onto a tissue, pressed down all the edges, then rolled the whole thing up into a tube. We tied one of my white hair ribbons around the middle of it."

"Did she say why she did this?" Rowan asked.

I shook my head. "I forgot all about until years later. I went over to her house for dinner the night before I left for college. After dessert, she handed me this gorgeously carved wooden box. Inside was the little scroll and a necklace. It took me a minute to realize what it was, and when I asked her why she'd kept it, she said it was for good luck."

Rowan pointed toward the fireplace mantel. On it sat a beautifully carved wooden box, very similar to the one Gram Marie had given me. "Mine is in there."

"Your what is in there?" I asked, afraid I already knew the answer.

"My caul, but not a fake one."

"Why?"

Rowan laughed. "For good luck, just like your grandmother said. It sounds like she knew what she was doing, and yes, it does sound like you might actually be a caulbearer, like me. That would explain a lot. In case you're curious, back in the day, the midwife who delivered the baby was the one who preserved the caul. She did something similar to what your grandmother did for you. After it was removed, she'd spread it out on a square of linen that had been soaked in salt water. The square was then rolled up, tied with a white ribbon, and left to dry in the sun. When the caulbearer turned eighteen, the veil was given back to them in a wooden box. It was meant to act as a talisman, strengthening their psychic gifts as they got older."

"Seems a strange thing to do," I said.

"Even stranger is what happened to some of the cauls once they were preserved," Rowan said. "Sailors often bought them. They believed that having one on board ship would protect them at sea—even keep them from drowning if they went in."

Rowan leaned forward and pointed a finger toward my neck. "Is that the necklace your Gram Marie gave you?"

I grabbed hold of the chain and pulled out the pendant, then held it out for Rowan to see. "I've worn it every day since."

Rowan rested the pendant on her palm and ran a thumb over the symbol. "Well, would you look at that! You know what the ankh stands for, I suppose?"

I told her what Gram Marie had told me while she helped fasten it around my neck. She said it was an Egyptian hieroglyph, combining the symbols for the god Osiris, lord of the afterlife, and the goddess Isis, queen of motherhood and magic.

Rowan handed the pendant back to me. "It symbolizes the connection between heaven and earth, supposedly providing its wearer a key to the afterlife."

I tucked the ankh back into my collar.

"I want to show you something." Rowan stuck out her leg, grabbed the hem of her skirt, and lifted the corner of it. At the top of her calf, neatly tattooed in black ink, was an ankh, nearly identical in size and proportion to the one on my necklace. She peered up at me. "So, tell me, Miss Scientist, do you still think it's a coincidence that you've found your way here to me? Do you think it's a coincidence that you, like me, and my mother before me, were all born with a caul even though it's so rare?"

She let the hem of her skirt fall back around her feet.

"You come to me, asking me to channel your father while you, my dear Nadia, clearly have a gift of your own, or at least the potential for one. You may not know how to use it yet, but it's there. The problem," she said, reaching over to pat my knee with her hand, "is that you're too afraid to try, and I don't blame you. You've seen a lot and without any instruction. On top of that, much of what you've seen is actually new to me. I need to hear more, but I think that you and Gram Marie were sensing something very real in that house of hers, something that you might have had every right to be afraid of. I want to work with you. We might actually have a lot to learn from each other."

Rowan stood up and wandered over to the counter. There, she ruffled through a drawer and pulled out a notepad and pen.

"I can't erase your fears, Nadia," she said, as she leaned over and scribbled something on the pad, "but I can certainly teach you how to use your gift if you ever want to give it a spin."

Rowan walked over to my chair and held out the small white sheet of paper.

"I think you should meet a friend of mine."

On the paper was a name.

"Jakob Fairheart?" I asked.

"He teaches at the University," Rowan said. "Look him up. He offers some pretty interesting classes. You should consider taking a few of them. Before then, though, I'll set up a time for the three of us to meet."

From the Journal of Nadia King
Age Thirty-Three

I met with Rowan today. She wants me to meet a friend of hers. Dr. Jakob Fairheart teaches at the University, which is apparently just a nickname for the Wayne Center for Psychological Studies, one of the most highly regarded paranormal research hubs in the United States, the same place Dr. Young mentioned when I attended that series of parapsychology seminars back in college. I just got done reading a few of his papers online.

According to one article, Dr. Fairheart believes that there's an anatomical reason for increased sensitivity, possibly a receptor that we haven't discovered yet. He compared it to the olfactory receptors in dogs, explaining how their sheer numbers give canines an advantage when it comes to smelling things imperceptible to humans. I remember having that same thought years ago. I may have even put it in one of my journals.

Another one of his papers spoke of three levels of existence: the realm of the living, the interim realm, and the realm of the shades. He spoke of the veils that separate each, quoting Sir Anthony Bard. Based on Jakob's case studies, it appears that shades have begun to communicate certain details about the second and third levels to certain sensitives who are alive today. He thinks the shades' eagerness to share this information— and the limited number of sensitives on this side of the veil—is causing a jamming of the signals, so to speak. He has a hypothesis. He's begun to correlate this imbalance of senders and receivers with the recent uptick in diagnosed schizophrenia. He thinks the "voices and hallucinations" they often hear might be more than what psychiatrists realize.

Jakob Fairheart also wrote a paper on a certain subset of shades he calls the Dark Ones, a sort of border patrol for the veils, whose job is to prevent too much communication across the levels. His younger mediums see them the most. Apparently, spirits are "permitted" to communicate a little, but they aren't supposed to say too much. The Dark Ones break the connection if boundaries are crossed. I can't help but wonder if these Dark Ones have anything to do with why Rowan can't reach my father or Gram Marie. I'm sure the two of them would try to tell me everything if we could just get through.

I think all of this could make a great premise for a novel. Gram Marie always said I should write, so maybe this is my chance. I could write about scientists who discover the receptors. They could work with psychics like Rowan to prove that abilities like hers actually have a scientific basis. They could maybe even meet the Dark Ones on the other side of the veil. I could include the stories of the shadows I used to see at Gram Marie's to give it a ghost story feel. Maybe some of the shadows won't be as forgiving as the Dark Ones. Maybe this new kind of shade can have an even darker purpose. Rowan did say that Gram Marie and I may have sensed something in her house that we had every right to be afraid of.

CHAPTER 11

The Past
Age Ten

When I was a kid, I always looked forward to visits with Gram Marie, despite what I sometimes saw when I was there. Her house was old and filled with plenty of good places for hide-and-seek. There were cupboards under the stairs, deep closets stuffed with coats and clothes, and plenty of beds to shimmy myself under. Hiding was one of my favorite things to do, and Gram Marie was always a good sport. We'd play for hours every time I stayed over. There were a few times, though, when Gram Marie didn't know I was hiding—and didn't know I was watching her. I wasn't doing it to be sneaky. I only did it to figure out who she was talking to under her breath whenever she went into the cellar.

The first time I heard it, I was coloring in the breakfast nook. I don't think she knew I was there. At first, I thought she was on the phone, but when she started down the cellar stairs, I knew that couldn't be right. This was back when phones were tethered to the wall with a cord, and the cord would never reach that far.

I heard her talking to herself again a few weeks later, and just like last time, right before she went into the cellar to do the laundry. This seemed suspicious to me, especially knowing that Phillipe, her old black tabby cat, and I never liked going down there. You just never really felt like you were alone, and based on the way Gram Marie was mumbling under her breath, she apparently felt the same way. I was determined to figure out what was going on.

One day, when I saw Gram Marie gathering laundry from the hamper, I told her I was going outside to meet a friend. While she was still upstairs, I hurried into the kitchen to put my plan into action. The base cupboard that was directly opposite the french door was to be my hiding place. I'd even packed my spy bag the night before, an old blue purse of Gram Marie's, filling it with all kinds of gadgets I thought I might need. I knew I had to move fast. I attached a short length of fishing line to the base cupboard's outside knob, making sure the knot was secure. I then opened the cupboard and quietly rearranged the pots and pans inside, creating enough space to climb in among them. Then I slid in. I used the fishing line to pull the door closed in front of me. I made it just in time.

A few seconds later, I heard Gram Marie unlatch the chain on the cellar door. I heard the door swing open with its familiar creak, and then I listened as her shoes tapped their way into the cellar. When I was sure she wasn't coming back up to gather another basket, I climbed out of the cupboard and crawled toward the open door. She was saying something as she moved around down there, but the words were muffled, nothing I could make out. I reached into my spy bag and pulled out my listening cones, red plastic party cups with the bottoms cut out. I slipped them over my ears, and once in place, they amplified Gram Marie's voice perfectly. I heard every word.

"I know you're here," she said, "and you can stay, as long as you do no harm, but I don't want to see you." She repeated it over and over again until she was back upstairs.

I hid in the same cupboard a few more times after that listening closely to make sure I'd heard her right. When she repeated the same words, I wondered if she was maybe talking to the mice that I sometimes saw down there. I actually believed this reasoning until the day I saw the shadows.

That day, when I crawled out of the cupboard, I looked up to find three of them huddled on the top step of the cellar stairs, just beyond the french door. It took me a minute to figure out what I was seeing. As much as I could tell, they looked like ordinary shadows. They were humanlike in shape and were about as tall as me, but they had no real facial features, which is probably why I didn't find them scary. I was more curious than anything. I didn't get too close—just close enough to know they weren't my imagination. They didn't really move at all that first time, but I could see their outlines wavering a little. I was studying them when Gram Marie called to me from the living room. I turned away for no more than a few seconds, and by the time I looked back, they were gone.

I stopped by the door often after that. Sometimes they'd be there, and other times, they wouldn't. Each time I saw them, there was usually a group, sometimes three, sometimes four. I got braver with each visit. I learned that if I stood there long enough, they'd move closer, allowing me to get a better look at them. After a while, it became a game. They eventually started to mimic any movements that I made, acting as if they were my reflection. If I waved, they'd wave. If I blew them a kiss, they'd do the same. I'd try to trick them by doing something quickly, but they always seemed to know what I was about to do and matched my moves exactly.

One day, I got a little too close to the french door and learned quickly that this wasn't a good idea. When you got too close to them, it was hard to move away. I started to feel dizzy. My vision darkened, and my ears began to ring. I worried that if I became too dizzy, I might faint, and if I did that, they might be able to slip under the door and touch me. They were shadows, after all. I had a feeling that their fingers would be cold, and I decided that I never really wanted to know for sure. I stopped going near the door after that, and even refused to go into the basement with Gram Marie. That's when I started to see them in other places, even upstairs, as if they'd come looking for me. It was then that I, too, started muttering Gram Marie's mantra under my breath.

"I know you're here, and you can stay, as long as you do no harm, but I don't want to see you." Saying it made them disappear, but somehow, I knew they were still there. I think that's when the willies started. Without actually seeing the shadows, though, I felt safer somehow.

CHAPTER 12

The Past
Age Thirty-Four

Rowan showed up at the house on Braeburn not long after dusk. When I heard the knock and opened the front door, I found her standing on the porch in yet another new outfit. A bright purple handbag rested on her wrist. A flashy scarf of the same color was twisted around her neck. She and Gram Marie would have gotten along well. Neither believed in leaving the house without jewelry and makeup, without being completely pulled together.

She immediately looked me up and down. "You're not ready to go?" she asked.

Unlike her, I was barely presentable. I was in my favorite sweats, my hair pulled back in a messy ponytail, dressed for an evening of unpacking groceries, a task I'd been in the middle of when the knock came. I frowned at her. "Ready to go where?"

"To meet Jakob, of course," she said, marching past me into the living room. She turned and put her hands on her hips. "At Les Choux. You don't remember?"

I tried to recall when she might have suggested this, but I came up with nothing. My confused look must have answered her question. She was obviously disappointed.

"Honestly, Nadia, what am I supposed to do with you?" She shook her head. "After all the work we've done, and you still can't read my mind?" She tried to look serious, but her face melted into a smile.

I rolled my eyes. "So, you're playing with me? Is that what this is?"

She pulled a tube of lipstick from her handbag and removed the cap. "Well," she said, running the color across her lips, "not playing exactly. I never actually asked you to go before now, but we are going."

I gestured toward my sweats. "Do you see me, Rowan? I'm not exactly ready to go anywhere."

"That can be fixed." She tucked the tube of lipstick back into her bag and pointed to the stairs. "Go on, up you go, snap to it."

"I haven't even showered yet today."

"Well, then, I suppose you'd better get a move on," she said. "Shower and throw on something decent. I'll finish the groceries while you pull yourself together. It's not that hard."

I opened my mouth to reply, but Rowan just waved her hands in front of her, as if sweeping me up the stairs.

"Go on. Up you go."

Fifteen minutes later, I stood in the kitchen, better suited for company in black jeans and a matching top. Maeve, who'd apparently known of Rowan's plan, sat at the table with her friend from next door. They were telling Rowan about the kinds of cookies they were going to bake while we were gone. Maeve looked at me and gave a sly little smile.

When Rowan and I arrived at Les Choux, the place was buzzing. Its wide front window showed a waiting area crammed with people. A valet took our keys as soon as we pulled up to the curb, and another gentleman in a red coat opened the front door of the restaurant for us. Smells of garlic and freshly baked bread wafted out.

Inside, the hostess, a young girl with long blondish hair, must have been watching for us because she immediately grabbed two menus and waved a hand for us to follow her. She led us through a maze of tables, all of them full. A violin, barely audible over the rumble of voices, played somewhere in the background, and as we passed the bar, I saw that my two favorite bartenders were working. They were busy, but they raised a hand when they saw us.

Jakob was seated in the main dining room at a table closest to the brick fireplace. He beamed as soon as he spied Rowan, and then he stood and gave his lapels a tug. My first impression was of a slightly underweight Santa Claus, right down to the full white beard, rosy cheeks, and tiny rectangular glasses. He pulled out the chair next to him and offered it to Rowan while I slid into the one across from her.

He stood there, palms resting on the table, and gave us one of the biggest smiles I think I've ever seen. "Well, now, aren't I just the lucky man tonight? Joined by two beautiful young ladies for an evening out."

His Scottish accent was heavy, something I should have expected, I suppose, given that most of his papers came out of the Koestler in Edinburgh.

"I do apologize for being so busy lately," he said, taking his seat. "I would have loved to have gotten together sooner, but I guess we should just be glad the stars have finally aligned. I believe a toast is in order, no?" With this, he reached for the bottle of wine propped in an ice bucket off to his right and began to pour. "Rowan tells me you'll be joining my classes this semester. Is that right, Ms. King?"

My eyes shifted to Rowan; she was nodding enthusiastically. I hadn't yet told her my concerns about how much these classes might cost or whether I could afford them.

"She said I should definitely consider it."

Jakob placed the bottle back on ice. "I think you should do more than just consider it, my dear. If you ask me, I think you should just agree to come. What can I do to convince you?"

"No convincing needed," I said. "I'd love to come. I just need to set aside the money, that's all."

He smiled. "Well, that's already been discussed. For you, there's no cost. According to Rowan here, we're going to need you—and if there's anything I've learned over the years, it's to trust this dear lady's judgement."

We're going to need you. Rowan had used those same words on my return visit to her shop that summer.

Before I had a chance to ask what was meant by it, Rosa came by the table, a white apron tied around her waist. Like Rowan, she was done up in lipstick and jewelry, and despite her age still moved as if she was twenty years younger. She slid a basket of rolls onto the table. Next to it, she placed a plate of freshly chopped herbs and hot pepper flakes, and then she drizzled the pile with olive oil from a decorative glass cruet.

Jakob thanked her and grabbed one of the rolls immediately. "Any other concerns or questions, Ms. King? Or does that settle it? Can I count on you joining us for class?" He tucked his napkin into the collar of his shirt and broke his roll in half.

"That was my only concern, so I think that settles it. Thank you," I said. "As for questions, I have plenty." I grabbed a roll for myself. "I think I'm most curious about how you got into this line of work in the first place. I'm not sure if Rowan told you or not, but I considered it once. I just never followed through."

Jakob dabbed a piece of his roll into the oil. "You can blame my sister for that. She was interested in this kind of thing long before me, as far back as I can remember. She was constantly pestering my parents with questions about reincarnation and past lives—although I'm not sure why. I was just there to overhear them all, and her curiosity got me thinking." Jakob grabbed a corner of his napkin and wiped at his chin. "I swear, you never knew what was going to come out of Evelyn's mouth next. When she was in primary school, she wrote a paper on 'survival after bodily death,' if you can believe that. Not for class or anything. She just wrote it and gave it to our parents for fun. I remember talking about it over dinner one night." He chuckled. "I suppose that gives you a little glimpse into our family dynamics, eh?"

I smiled. "Definitely sounds like interesting dinner conversation. Did you both work at the Koestler?"

Jakob shook his head. "I was the only one there. Stayed for quite some time though, and enjoyed every minute."

"Why did you leave?"

"I suppose you can blame that on my sister, as well," he said. "Evelyn came to the States long before me. She got sick a few years later. I decided to move here to be closer to her. I wasn't sure what I was going to do for work once I got here, but I knew I had to come. Thankfully, Professor Keeler, one of my colleagues at the Koestler, was kind enough to pull together a last-minute grant. Back then, there was nothing like the

Koestler in the States. Keeler just decided that you needed a Center for Paranormal Research here too, and she made it happen." He held up his hands. "Thanks to her, I got to spend a few good months of quality time with my sister before she passed, bless her soul. And thanks to our friend Rowan, here," he patted Rowan's hand and smiled, "I can still spend quality time with my Evelyn. One of the benefits of our type of work, eh, my dear?"

Rowan smiled and nodded. "A definite perk."

Two servers appeared at our table shortly after that and proceeded to lay out a dizzying assortment of appetizers. Plates were covered in everything from calamari to thin slices of tomato pie. All of it looked and smelled amazing.

As they were arranging the plates, Rowan turned toward the bar. Her mother and Ella were talking to a man in a gray suit. Both gave a wave.

"They work fast, those two," Rowan said, blowing them a kiss. "I should have known they'd put in an order." She turned back and gestured at the spread in front of us. *"Buon appetito."*

I scooped a healthy serving of gnocchi onto my plate. "You say your sister didn't work at the Koestler, but she must have done similar work, no? In reading your papers, it sounds like she was pretty involved."

Jakob shook his head. "This kind of work was more of a hobby for her. She was good at finding interesting people who needed to talk to me, and it was thanks to her that I got my first case studies." He tapped Rowan's hand. "She also introduced me to Rowan. Once word got around, though, people started finding me at the University on their own." He took a sip of wine. "The new sleep lab has been quite the resource too, actually much more than I ever imagined. I never realized how much of a role altered states of consciousness, like sleep, can play in this kind of thing. Evelyn was right when she said that dreams are often windows to the soul."

"And what about nightmares?" I asked, reaching for a slice of tomato pie.

He studied me with interest. "What about them?"

"You said your sister drove your parents mad with questions. I drove my parents mad with nightmares. I think they spent most nights talking me back to sleep when I was a kid."

"Really?" He squinted at me, brows furrowed. "When did the nightmares stop?"

I took a sip of wine. "I'm still having them, and most tend to have a common theme. Things chasing me, me trying to get away. Always filled with shadows and cats."

He seemed to consider this. "We'll definitely have to talk about those sometime. I have a child now who's dealing with similar things. We can compare notes." He took another bite of his roll. "I enjoy working with children. They're much less inclined than adults to lie about any experiences they have. They don't hide things, but they don't embellish either. They see what they see, and they're more than happy to tell you all about it." He smiled. "Children are more open to spirit communication overall, but I'm sure you were already aware of that."

"I read your paper that explains the reason why. It's pretty convincing," I said, nodding. "There's some solid scientific backing in there."

"That same science supports something we call *spontaneous recall* as well, the ability to remember past lives. This happens most right around age four, and it's why my sister became convinced that souls are recycled when we die. This is the thing she was most interested in. She spent a lot of time collecting recall memories from a handful of my young sensitives before she passed."

Two young children were sitting at the table next to us. They were walking their fingers through mounds of spaghetti and giggling hysterically as their parents talked. Their faces were plastered in red sauce. Discussing something as serious as past lives with children of this age seemed an impossible task.

"Recycling of souls always made more sense to Evelyn than ghosts," Jakob said. "To her, the idea of souls floating around looking for houses to haunt seemed silly, and I have to agree, although it does happen." He smiled at me. "As I said, she was fascinated with reincarnation, but she never really liked the idea of the same soul simply moving to a different body. After all, what fun is that?" He popped a piece of calamari into his mouth. "She preferred to think that the energy from past lives gets mixed up and redistributed, sometimes in larger chunks than intended. Mozart was always her example. She believed he was born with most of that musical knowledge already in his head. She claimed he got the lion's share of memories from someone who'd lived and breathed music before they died.

"Mozart died young, around age thirty-five, I think," Jakob said. "Evelyn was convinced the spirits took him early because he knew too much too soon, said they'd realized their mistake. She always gave the Dark Ones a little more power than I do. I think it was one of the only things that Evelyn and I ever disagreed on. You're familiar with the Dark Ones, Nadia?"

I nodded and looked at Rowan, wondering if she might bring up the shadows from Gram Marie's or ask whether Jakob thought the Dark Ones might have anything to do with her inability to reach my father.

Rowan's eyes caught mine, as if she knew what I was thinking, but before either of us could ask, Jakob said, "I do believe the Dark Ones work to keep the spirits in check. I think they prevent them from telling us too much. I don't think they have much power over the living though. I certainly don't think they can cut lives short. As for spontaneous recall, we rarely see it after age five. I blame the parents for that, not the Dark Ones. Parents tend not to believe that these memories are real, so they never ask their kids any questions about them. As a result, the transferred memories get discarded. Use it or lose it, so they say." He smiled. "As you probably already know, there's significant brain remodeling going on at that age, so it only makes sense. We lose millions of brain cells by age five, anything we're not actively using. It's why those first years are so critical to development. That's why Evelyn liked to engage children in conversations about their memories, so they'd stick, so the details wouldn't be lost. She believed we could learn important information from these memories, especially since these souls might have witnessed something during their transfer, details currently unknown to the living."

Jakob leaned toward me, his face serious, like a child who wants to share a secret.

"Trust me when I say there's so much more to this world, Nadia, than what most of us can see with our eyes. The three of us here are what they call *old souls*. There aren't many of us left. Most everyone else these days focuses on their cell phones and televisions. People like us do our best to avoid the noisy trappings of society. Old souls like the way things used to be. We like walks in the forest where we can hear the birds. We despise streetlights because they overshadow the wonders of the night sky. We avoid crowds and find quiet places to sit. It's not easy to hear the old signals anymore, Nadia, but some of us still take the time to try. My point to you is this. You should never ignore these important signals out of fear. Rowan and I can teach you how to sift through the good and the bad. These things aren't as scary as you might think, especially once you know how to play the game properly."

By the time I left that night, I had plans to start classes at the University in the fall. One evening course, one night a week. Rowan would come stay at the house with Maeve while I went. Even though Maeve was old enough to be fine on her own by that time, I knew she'd appreciate the company. Even at her age, I never wanted to be alone.

CHAPTER 13

The Past
Age Thirty-Four

Intro to Parapsychology was held in the largest lecture hall on the first floor of the University. Although it wasn't scheduled to start for another ten minutes, most of the chairs were already full when I arrived. I chose an empty seat in the lower level, just a few rows back from the front.

Jakob arrived a few minutes later, his entry marked by a hush that fell over the room. He climbed the stairs onto the stage, walked past the podium at its center, and stopped at the front edge, hands clasped behind his back. He was dressed in a neat, gray three-piece suit, the chain of a pocket watch trailing across the bottom of his vest in a neat swoop. When he caught my eye, he gave a smile and nodded.

"Welcome, everyone," he said finally, his voice resonating through the hall. "This is Psi 101, and I'm hoping it will be the first of many classes you'll be taking with me."

An old chalkboard spanned the full width of the stage behind him. He walked over to it and scratched his name across the top with a piece of white chalk. I thought about what he'd said at dinner about old souls. I hadn't seen a chalkboard in years. Even some of my own college classes had used video screens. I wondered if he'd had it installed on purpose.

He introduced himself as he made his way back to the center of the stage, telling the class most of the things I'd already heard over dinner at Les Choux. Once there, he grasped both sides of the podium and looked out at the group.

"So, who can tell me, what is parapsychology?"

Papers ruffled, but no one offered a response. I knew the answer, of course, but I had never liked speaking up in class. Apparently, I wasn't the only one.

A full minute passed, and Jakob shrugged. "Parapsychology is the scientific study of paranormal phenomena," he said. "We're going to talk about extrasensory perception today, but I think before we get into the 'extra' side of it, I want to talk about the basic garden-variety perception first. Think back to grade school for a minute. That was probably the first time you ever learned about the five basic senses: sight, sound, taste, touch and smell. Remember those?"

He glanced around the room. There were a few nodding heads.

"In high school, you probably learned how these senses work. You learned about the sensory receptors in your eyes, ears, mouth, skin, and nose and how they keep you in the know about your surroundings."

Jakob lifted a small silver bell from the corner of the podium and shook it. The sound carried throughout the auditorium. When the sound dissipated, he returned the bell to the podium. "You heard that because of the sound waves that issued from the bell's vibrating surface. Those sound waves traveled through the air until they came in contact with the auditory receptors in your ears. Those receptors converted the sound into an electrical impulse, and this impulse traveled to your brain where it was interpreted. You recognized the sound because you've heard a bell before. You had a frame of reference. If you'd never heard a bell before and hadn't seen me ring it with your own eyes, you would have been left wondering what had made the sound."

He paced the front of the stage as he spoke.

"The process is the same no matter what sense we use. The stimulus excites the receptor, the receptor converts the signal into an electrical impulse, and the impulse travels to the brain to be interpreted. The stimulus could be the scent of a rose, the sight of rainbow, the taste of a tuna fish sandwich, or the pain you feel when you drop a bowling ball on your toe."

A few stray giggles came from the back of the room. Jakob pointed a finger in that direction as if to thank them for their participation.

"So, what do you think happens when we start looking beyond those basic five senses? What about the sixth sense? How does that work?"

Once again, he stared out at a silent room.

"Still nothing, eh?" He rolled the piece of chalk between his palms. "Well, it's probably best you kept quiet that time because, to be honest, no one knows how that works just yet. In fact, not everyone even agrees that the sixth sense is real. The media has most people convinced that the sixth sense is just a fictional concept. If it's in the movies, it must be make-believe, right?"

He shoved his hands into his trouser pockets.

"Trust me when I say that nothing could be further from the truth," he said. "The sixth sense is very real. It's just very tricky to prove. And why is that?"

He cupped a hand to his ear, hoping for a response, but got none.

"It's tricky because we humans are nothing but arrogant bastards," he said.

This brought more giggles from the back of the room, and Jakob pointed again.

"You laugh because you know it's true," he said. "Right?"

He paced the edge of the stage again, hands behind his back.

"Let's look at a purely hypothetical situation, shall we?" he asked. "It just so happens that there's a form of color blindness known as deuteranopia. Deuteranopes, if you don't already know, see no difference between red, orange, yellow, and green. They can't differentiate between these colors because they lack medium wavelength receptors in the eye. Now that part's true ... but let me bend the truth a little here." He shook a finger in the air. "In truth, deuteranopia is very rare, but what if the *majority* of the human population suffered from it? What if only a few lucky people actually possessed these medium wavelength receptors? If that was the case, then only those lucky few would be able to see those four different colors, correct? Do you follow me so far?"

Jakob paced some more, head down.

"Now, let's say that these lucky few get together and agree between themselves that red is red, orange is orange, yellow is yellow, and green is green, and they present this to the rest of the population. What do you think would happen?"

This time, a man in the front row answered, "We'd say they were crazy."

"Correct," Jakob said, pointing at him. "People find it very hard to believe anything that they can't experience for themselves, don't they?" He put his hands on his hips. "So, how could the deuteranopes prove that these other colors exist?"

The same man answered again. "They'd have to isolate the receptors. Prove that they can detect medium wavelengths of light."

"Right again," Jakob said, stopping where he was in the middle of the stage. "Does everyone see how this little scenario is similar to the case for the sixth sense? The people who have it know what they see. The people who don't have it think the others are crazy. That's pretty much how it goes, right?"

Back at the chalkboard, Jakob wrote a list of four terms and underlined each of them.

"Paranormal phenomena," he said, "falls into these four broad categories. Life after death, including apparitions and reincarnation. Mind over matter, like psychokinesis and poltergeist activity. Informational talents like telepathy and clairvoyance. And finally, time anomaly, including precognition and retrocognition.

"Keep in mind, now, these categories have overlap. For example, let's say a spirit wants to contact someone who has an informational talent. The spirit has several options. It could appear as an apparition and be detected by clairvoyance, literally translated as clear seeing, or maybe, if the spirit was your great-aunt Bertha, she might choose to manifest as her favorite perfume. This would be detected via clairgustance, clear smelling."

Jakob began pacing again.

"Or, if the spirit wanted to get fancy, it could simply opt for detection by clairsentience. In this case, the spirit doesn't have to do anything at all. It just has to show up in the room. People with clairsentience don't see, hear, or smell anything. We simply detect a spirit when it's nearby. It's more of a gut feeling."

I thought of the willies. The chills, the ringing in my ears, and the butterflies in my stomach.

A man sitting near the window raised his pen into the air.

Jakob held out an upturned hand in his direction.

"So, what's that supposed to mean, exactly?" the man asked. "If they don't see or hear anything, how do they detect it?"

"Good question," Jakob said. Jakob went back to the chalkboard and added another term: *vibrational hypothesis*. "Anyone ever heard of this?" He tapped the words with his piece of chalk.

A few people raised their hands.

"Anyone want to tell me what it is?"

The hands fell immediately, and he laughed.

"Vibrational hypothesis," Jakob said, "is derived from some very basic principles of chemistry, and it plays a huge role in the sixth sense. You'll have to bear with me here while I get a bit technical."

I flipped to a new page in my notebook and wrote the term at the top of the page.

"As all of you know," Jakob said, "everything around us is made up of atoms. If we force ourselves to remember basic chemistry, we know that these atoms are in constant vibrational motion. The desk in front of you may seem solid enough from your perspective, but if you were to look at the same desk at its atomic level, you would see its atoms whirring about. These atoms come in different sizes and weights, and so they vibrate at different frequencies."

One girl sitting directly in front of me leaned toward her friend. "I didn't come here for a boring science lesson."

"I know," said the friend. "What's this got to do with anything?"

Jakob looked directly at the girls as if he'd actually heard them, which was impossible, and said, "I'm boring you with the science so you can understand one thing. Vibrational hypothesis is based on the belief that spirits have their own vibrational energy. In fact, scientists in the field of parapsychology believe that a spirit's vibrational energy is almost ten times higher than that of a human's."

Jakob walked back to the podium and rang the bell again.

"Sound waves, like the ones coming from this bell, also have different frequencies. Humans can detect between twenty and twenty thousand hertz." Jakob wrote the numbers on the board to the right of his previous list, the largest on top.

Jakob drew a line well above the second mark. "Up here is ultrasound. This is beyond human perception. Dogs, however, can hear frequencies up to fifty thousand hertz—and porpoises up to 150,000 hertz."

Jakob wrote these numbers, as well, each closer and closer to the top of the board.

"Sensitivity differs greatly between species. And how about this?" Jakob asked. "Let's do a little experiment here in class." He pulled a small object out of his jacket pocket. It looked like a deck of cards, but when he held it up to show the class, I could see a red dial on the front.

"This little box transmits sound. I'm going to set it to ten thousand hertz, well within the range of human perception, and hit the button on the back." He turned the knob on the front, lifted the box into the air again, and tapped the back. A pulse of sound filled the room. "Raise your hands if you heard that."

Everyone in the auditorium raised their hands.

"All right, now keep those hands up," he said. He lowered the box and fiddled with the knob again. "Let's try this frequency."

This time an even higher-pitched noise came from the device.

"Keep your hands up if you heard something," Jakob said. "If you heard nothing, put your hands down."

A few people lowered their hands. Heads turned to look at neighbors.

"OK, here we go again," Jakob said. "Once I press the button, keep your hands up if you hear anything—and drop them if you don't."

Jakob fiddled with the knob, held the box up in the air, and tapped the back.

I heard nothing, but goose bumps spread across my arms. The hairs on the back of my neck stood on end. I lowered my hand and looked to my left.

The arm of the man next to me was covered in goose bumps as well.

The girl on my right still had her hand in the air.

Jakob repeated this a few more times, and with each repeat, fewer and fewer hands were left in the air.

In the end, there was only one. It belonged to a little girl in the front row. She appeared to be about five years old. Jakob looked at her and smiled.

She waved at him with a hand no bigger than a doll's.

"Interesting, right?" Jakob asked the class, looking around the room as he tucked the device back into his jacket pocket. "So, what just happened? Why were some of you more sensitive to higher frequencies than others?"

The woman sitting next to the little girl, probably her mother, raised her hand.

Jakob pointed.

"We lose the ability to hear higher frequencies as we get older," she said, running a hand over the little girl's hair. "My daughter, Tina, is five. She hears everything."

She hears everything. Something about the way the woman said it gave me chills. It made me wonder if she was talking about something more than just the sounds given off by the box.

Jakob gave the little girl a thumbs-up and thanked the mother for answering. "Tina's mother is absolutely right," Jakob said to the room. "I increased the frequency each time, and I lost hands as I went, decade by decade. The last frequency was twenty-five thousand hertz, just beyond the human's upper limit, and our little Tina here was the only one who heard it. If I had to venture a guess, I'd say that no one else here is under ten except for Tina." He paused and looked out at the room. "Anyone else under ten?"

No one raised a hand.

"So, let's think about this for a minute," Jakob said. "If spirits have a higher vibrational energy, is this why children are more prone to seeing them? To me, this makes perfect sense. We need a functional receptor to detect a signal, but we also need the signal to be within that receptor's perceptible range. This, I believe, is how clairsentience works."

Jakob put his chalk in the tray below the board. He then spent the rest of the class going through each of the four categories one by one. He posed a similar scientific rationale for each, and by the time class was over, I'd filled a good portion of my notebook.

"All right, people." Jakob looked at the clock on the side wall and clapped his hands together. "I've filled your brains with enough for one day. You're free to go, but I'll see you all back here next week."

Students chattered as they filed out of the room.

From my seat, I watched them go, and when the room was empty, I approached the stage.

"Ah, young lady," he said, erasing the board and gathering his things from the podium. The bell gave a muffled tinkle as he placed it in his pocket. "Happy to see you here. Did you enjoy it?"

"Of course, only now I have more questions."

"Well, that's the whole point, isn't it?" he asked, grinning. "Questions keep you coming back for more."

He was right. They did keep me coming back for more. The fall semester passed quickly. The winter holidays came and went. In the new year, I started meeting with Jakob and Rowan outside of class to pick their brains about other things. I set up appointments for Jakob's sleep lab once every month. Each time, we monitored my sleep patterns and discussed my nightmares. He seemed intrigued.

Just before summer break, I started working on my novel, getting an outline down on paper, at least. The classes had given me plenty of ideas. That's not to say that writing came easily though. I quickly learned that writing a novel was much more difficult than jotting daily events down in a journal. Writing was an art, and I definitely needed practice.

I spent hours locked away in my upstairs office every night after work, but rarely walked away with more than a few pages done. Frustration became a constant companion, but I never gave up.

Feeling guilty about being so busy, I gave in and got Maeve the dog she'd always wanted. We actually brought two of them home from the rescue, thinking they could keep each other company. As puppies, they were about the same size, although you could tell that Quake was going to be a big boy given the size of his paws. We had no idea he was a Dane at the time. Our best guess was a big dalmatian given his spots. Attis was in for a rude awakening, though. His early habit of flopping down on top of Quake didn't last long. By the end of that year, Quake was twice his size.

CHAPTER 14

The Past
Age Thirty-Five

I'd just carried in the last of the Christmas wreaths from the front porch when Maeve galloped down the stairs. She leaped off the second step from the bottom and landed on the floor about a foot in front of me.

The dogs barreled down behind her.

"I'm going out tonight," Maeve said as she spun in circle, "to the movies with the gang. You remembered, right?"

"I remembered," I told her, tossing the wreath on top of the pile in the corner. There were ten in all, one for each window, and taking them down after the holidays was always a thankless chore. My fingers were frozen.

Maeve held out a hand for my soggy gloves. "What about you?" she asked, laying the gloves across the radiator to dry. "What are you up to tonight? Anything fun?"

"I think I may try to make some progress on this novel of mine. It's been slow going lately. I'm kind of stuck. I might head over to the college library and do a little more research."

Saying I was *kind of* stuck was an understatement. I had drawers full of notes, piles of ideas, lists of characters, and my outline, but after working on it for more than half a year, I had only about forty-five pages of anything that resembled a story.

Maeve stood on tiptoes and planted a kiss on my cheek. "Don't be too hard on yourself. It's not every day you write a novel. You can't expect it to be easy." She started toward the kitchen. "You'll figure it out."

While Maeve was getting ready to go, the dogs followed me up to the office and sat there while I gathered my things. Next to my laptop on the desk was a purple folder with "Important Notes" written in a diagonal across the front. I flipped it open. Stapled to the inside was a C-fold paper towel, often the closest thing to write on while working in a lab. A few messy thoughts were scribbled across the front in black Sharpie.

> Jakob's receptors. Found only in mediums/psychics? How do they work? Vibrational hypothesis? See class notes from fall semester. Spirits vibrate at higher frequencies than most can detect. Use this information for later chapters.

The rest of the folder was filled with articles copied from a neuroscience journal, articles I had yet to read. I stuffed the folder into my bag. Before adding my laptop, I tapped the mouse and watched as an image of a house filled the screen, an old white stucco and stone Colonial with a broad, sweeping porch. A few of the shutters were hanging cockeyed, desperately in need of hinges. Trees and a low stone wall filled the background. The gravel drive in front was overgrown with weeds. The house cried for restoration.

Maeve and her best friend had come across the house while exploring an abandoned lot a few blocks from our twin. According to the National Register of Historic Places, it was one of the oldest houses in town, built by the Baird family in the early 1800s. It had been a working farm until developers came in and took over the surrounding areas. Maeve and I fell in love with it immediately and walked the dogs there nearly every day.

I ran a finger over the roofline. "One day, if I can get this book written, and if it actually sells, I'll make you ours. Just wait and see."

Beside the laptop were two novels that I was reading at the time. I knew I shouldn't take them with me, knowing that if I did, it would be all too easy to push the laptop aside when I got frustrated. Then again, there were plenty of other books at the library to distract me, so I figured I might as well take my own. I threw them into my bag. This was probably why I never got much done.

It was a little past eight o'clock when I arrived at the library. The night custodian sat at the front desk, a crossword puzzle in front of him, pencil busy. Peter was a squat man with graying hair, his round glasses far too big for his face. He looked up long enough to give a quick nod in my direction but was back to work before I even tapped my ID card on the keypad and pushed through the turnstile.

I made my way through the lobby and into the main floor. On my way to the stairs, I saw two other people, an older man with a cane near the water fountain in the back and a young woman in baggy sweats coming out of the restroom, a backpack slung over her shoulder. At the top of the stairwell, I made a left and headed toward one of the long tables near the windows. A light snow was falling. In the courtyard below, a series of streetlamps lined the intertwining walkways. Each path was already coated with a thin dusting. One lonely trail of footprints led toward the dorms.

I put my bag on the table and pulled out the laptop. The stack of novels and pile of folders went next to it. In the bottom of the bag, there was a handful of spare change. I dug it out and made my way toward the elevators, remembering that there was a vending machine there. The quiet hum of the fluorescents buzzed overhead as I stood at the machine and considered my options. The noise made by my coins as they clattered through the inner workings of the machine and by the can as it clunked into the tray below disturbed no one. As far as I could tell, the entire second floor appeared to be as empty as the first.

I decided to take the long way back to my table, a detour through the last aisle of fiction, just to see if anything caught my eye. Halfway through, on my left at eye level, a book was propped up in a stand. On the cover, a man stood near a tall gravestone, one of his hands resting on top. His other hand dangled at his side, holding what appeared to be a book. The scene was backlit, the man's figure mostly just a silhouette. He wore a hat, a fedora if I wasn't mistaken, the outline crisp against the moonlit background. His chin hung toward his chest, and his face was turned slightly to the left, showing off a bit of his profile. It was the kind of cover that always caught my eye, dark and hinting at the paranormal, the kind I'd choose for my own novel if I ever got that far. The title, *Apparitions,* was written in a misty font across the front. The author wasn't anyone I recognized.

I pulled it off the shelf, and after reading a few lines from the inside cover, I tucked it under my arm and continued on my way, knowing full well that the last thing I needed was another distraction. As I approached the end of the aisle, a gap in the books on my right allowed a clear view of my table. I stopped. A man was standing there, his back toward me. He, too, wore a long coat, not unusual given the weather, but his hat appeared to be a fedora as well. He lifted each of my novels one by one and inspected them, turning them over to read the back covers. When he was done, he tidied the pile, glanced once around the library, and then continued on his way. He rounded the corner near the stairs and disappeared from view. I waited to make sure he wasn't coming back, and when he didn't, I made my way over to the table to see if anything was missing.

My bag and laptop were right where I'd left them. My stack of books, if I didn't know better, seemed to be untouched. I added *Apparitions* to the top of the pile and glanced in the direction of the stairs. The floor was empty. I placed my ginger ale on the table, deciding I'd drink it later, worried that if I cracked it open just then, the man might hear the noise and return.

The next two hours passed without interruption. I spent most of the time taking notes from several anatomy books that I'd found on the first floor, but I did make some progress on the story. When I began to yawn, I glanced at the books on the table and toward the bright orange couch near the windows.

A few seconds later, I was rearranging the cushions. I leaned one of them against the wooden armrest, creating a sort of makeshift lounge, stretched out on it lengthwise, and brought *Apparitions* to eye level. I opened to the first page and began to read.

Not long into chapter 6, my eyelids grew heavy, and about an hour later, I woke to the sound of footsteps approaching the couch, a soft swooshing on the industrial-grade carpet. Thinking it was probably the night custodian coming to tell me that the library was getting ready to close, I sat up and began readjusting the couch cushions. When I turned to explain that I was just packing up, it wasn't the stocky custodian who stood before me. It was a much younger, much taller man. He wore a hat and a long winter coat.

I leaped to my feet, but even then, he towered above me. He was at least six foot tall, maybe more. I probably should have been more alarmed, but there was something strangely familiar about him. He was handsome, with hazel eyes, the slightest trace of wrinkles at their corners. Wavy brown hair, almost shoulder length, peeked out from beneath the brim of his hat. His dark gray overcoat hung loosely from broad shoulders, making him look wider than he really was. The coat was unbuttoned in the front and showed off a dark suit and maroon tie underneath.

I was busy taking this all in when he thrust out a hand and offered an introduction. This caught me by surprise. *Apparitions* slipped from my fingers and landed on the floor with a thud, causing me to miss his name.

I shook my head and laughed. "Sorry. I guess I'm a little jumpy tonight." I took his hand. "My name's Nadia."

"I know," he said, holding my hand a bit longer than necessary.

I tried not to look alarmed, although I did wonder *how* he knew my name.

He gestured toward the table. "I hope you don't mind, but I was being nosy earlier. Your books caught my eye as I walked by. Interesting choices. Seems we have similar tastes."

He tilted his head to look at the book on the floor. I watched him bend to pick it up and couldn't help but notice his shoes. They were polished to a high sheen, so much so that the overhead fluorescents reflected in them.

"I saw you when you were here at the table," I said, as he stood up and handed *Apparitions* to me. "I was over there." I pointed toward the shelves. "I was getting ready to jump you if you touched my laptop."

He laughed, and then he nodded toward the book in my hand. "I didn't see that one before."

"I found it just before I saw you." I studied him. "You said you knew my name. Do I know you from somewhere?"

He took off his hat and placed it on the table. "I sat behind you in class."

"At the University?" I squinted at him. "I don't remember seeing you there."

He smiled. "That's probably because I sat behind you." He pointed to a chair. "Do you mind if I sit a minute?"

I shook my head.

"Look, I know I probably startled you," he said, taking a seat, "and I apologize, but I've been wanting to talk to you for a while. I just thought now might be a good time."

The hairs at the nape of my neck prickled. My eyes scanned the room.

"We can talk somewhere else if that makes you more comfortable."

I shook my head again. "No, this is fine. What did you want to talk about?"

He glanced down at his hands. "Nadia, what I'm about to say is going to sound strange, so just bear with me for a minute." He looked up. "I can't explain how I know what I'm about to tell you, at least not yet, but you can ask as many questions as you like once I'm done, OK?"

A faint ringing filled my ears.

He leaned forward and put his elbows on his knees. "I know you came here to write, and I know that you've found writing a novel is a lot harder than keeping a journal. You're getting frustrated, but you shouldn't. You can do this. You've always been good at what you do. That said, you've grown bored with your current career, and you think it's time for a change. I want to help you. That's why I've been wanting to talk to you."

None of what he said was common knowledge. *Had he spoken with Rowan?* "Go on," I said, my voice wavering slightly.

"You aren't going to ask how I know any of this?"

"Not yet," I said. "You have more to say, so go on."

He reached into his jacket pocket and brought out a dark green wallet. From inside, he pulled out a white business card and held it out to me. "Let me help you. Continue writing your book. I'll be here if you need me. I can work with you if you'd like. When you're done, you call this number. It's a publishing company. A woman named Lydia Winters will answer. She'll be expecting your call. Send her your story."

I didn't reach for the card. "You don't even know what my book is about." *If he knows this, I have to leave.*

He stood up from his chair, dropped the business card into my bag, and grabbed his hat from the table. "I just want to see you finish it, Nadia.

It'll be a best seller, I can tell you that, but I suggest you get to work. Quit reading those other books of yours and put your heart into it. That's all I ask." He started to walk away, but he turned back before he rounded the corner. "I'll be in touch."

When I was sure he was gone, I pulled the business card out of my bag. "Broadman Publishing" was printed across the front in neat blue lettering. There was a local phone number just underneath it. I turned the card over, hoping to find a name, but the other side was blank. I flipped back to the front and quickly memorized the number. It was unlikely that he could help, but if I lost the card, which I was often prone to do, I'd lose even that chance. As I tucked it back into my bag, the timer on my phone went off. It was midnight, and it was time to go.

When I got home that night, Maeve was curled up on the couch, reading, a red fleece blanket draped over her shoulders. The dogs were snuggled up next to her. "Hey, Mums," she said.

I hung my keys on the hook and dumped my bag and stack of books onto the floor just inside the door.

"You got more books? I thought you were going to the library to write?"

I squeezed in next to Quake on the couch and gave Maeve a full recap of my night. "So, what do you think?" I asked.

"I think you need to get some sleep," she said. "And when you wake up in the morning, I think you need to get serious and start writing."

"What about the number?"

She shrugged and shook her head. "Maybe it's nothing—or maybe it's not. At least you have it, right? Just in case? When the time comes, try it. Till then, I wouldn't read too much into it."

I leaned over and kissed her forehead. "The teenage voice of reason. What would I do without you?"

I tucked the corner of the fleece under her feet and gave each dog a good night scratch. "Don't stay up too late, kiddo, OK?"

Upstairs, in the office, I wrote the phone number on a bright yellow sticky note from memory and pinned it to the corkboard. "It's probably nothing, but she's right—why not give it a try when the time comes."

CHAPTER 15

The Past
Age Thirty-Five

That night, and for months after, I dreamed about being in a lab. Most of the equipment was similar to what I used at work, but there were cages, huge ones. They lined the walls, and they were usually empty. The man from the library was always there, the two of us rifling through notebooks and designing experiments. These dreams, interspersed with my normal playlist of nightmares, were a huge help with the novel.

In the sleep lab, Jakob and I made progress. My overnight stays, scalp dotted with electrodes, produced some interesting data. My brain waves, compared to other women my age, showed that my time spent in REM sleep, the time spent dreaming, was off the charts.

I added all of this to my novel, which was finally coming together. It was going so well, in fact, that I chose not to enroll in any upcoming classes at the University. When Jakob called to ask what had happened to me, I told him I was fine, just busy, that he would see me soon. In all honesty, I was afraid to do anything but write, afraid to break the rhythm for fear I couldn't get started again. During work, I kept a pile of C-fold paper towels nearby, ready to jot down any ideas that came to me. Sometimes, I'd scribble down whole chapters. I found myself hoping for red lights on the drive home, time to note a few quick thoughts on a pad of paper kept on the passenger's seat. It was as if that night in the library had opened the floodgates.

When the headaches started, I assumed they were just the result of working too many hours in front of a computer. After all, that's when they happened most. I only decided to call the doctor once the blurred vision and dizziness started—and when the pain became concentrated at the base of my skull. My father had suffered similar symptoms right before he was diagnosed with a brain tumor. A few months after that, he was dead.

Research told me that the location of a brain tumor typically determined the patient's symptoms. Patients with a frontal lobe tumor often experience changes in their behavior and emotions. Those with a tumor in the brain stem might suffer from hearing loss. Tumors in the parietal region generally cause impaired speech or an inability to write. At least I knew mine wasn't there.

While Dr. Maize waited for my test results, she asked me to cut back on my time spent in front of the computer to see if this helped. I told her that was out of the question. I was too close to being done with my novel. Plus, if it was indeed cancer, and if it was anything like my father's, I didn't have much time. I needed to finish.

Of course, I wove this morbid twist of fate into the story line. My lead scientist died about halfway through the book and crossed through the veil, thus gaining firsthand access to the information she needed to complete her research. I used her death to resolve the plot.

When my test results came back, I was told that there was no physical reason for my complaints. My vision was twenty-twenty, and my scans were clean. Dr. Maize assured me that the headaches and dizziness were due to nothing more than eye strain caused by excessive screen time. Again, she suggested that I cut back. Again, I told her I had no intention of doing any such thing. I instead relied on aspirin and walks with the dogs when the headaches got too bad.

During one of those walks, my neighbor, Diane, saw us and called me over. She was sitting out on her front porch in the dark, the red glow of her cigarette marking her location. Diane had moved into the neighborhood only a few months prior. The front of her house faced the side of mine. We realized early on that we shared similar interests. About a week after she moved in, she told me that her house might be haunted, and when I mentioned that I was working on a novel filled with ghosts, she and I knew we'd found our ongoing topic of conversation.

Diane walked across her narrow yard to meet us at the fence. As soon as she got there, she pointed up at my office window. "You're in there a lot these days, aren't you?"

I looked over my shoulder toward the house. The office light was still on. "Just trying to finish the book," I said. "Almost done."

Diane scratched at her chin and took a drag of her cigarette, studying me the whole time. "Ever feel like you have company when you're up there?"

I should have known this was coming. "Why do you ask?"

She shrugged. "I think you might have a friend, that's all. I was out here on the porch last night having a glass of wine, and when I looked up, I saw a woman standing there. Could have been the booze, I suppose, you know me, but I don't think so. It wasn't you or Maeve, though, I can tell you that. This woman had white hair, down past her shoulders." Diane pointed again, this time to the left of the window. "I only noticed her because of the streetlamp, there. Your office light wasn't on at first."

"At first?" I asked.

"Yeah. When the office light came on, it was like she was never there." Diane dropped what was left of her cigarette onto the grass and used her slipper to stamp it out. "All I could see then was you. You walked over, closed the blinds like you always do, and that was the end of the show." She held up her hands and shrugged.

Quake tugged on his leash.

"Looks like the big guy's ready to go," she said and started back toward the porch. "Just figured I'd let you know. Good luck with the book. Keep me posted. Who knows, maybe your new friend is lending a hand."

From the Journal of Nadia King
Age Thirty-Five

Today, Diane told me she saw a woman with white hair in the office window. I know Diane loves her wine, and what she said may not be true, but it got me thinking.

What if my recent dizziness and chills aren't tied to the headaches at all? What if the willies are coming back, given my work with Rowan and Jakob? Is that possible? Could something like this come back with practice, even after being suppressed for so long? If that's true, then maybe Diane is right—and I do have a visitor.

What did Gram Marie used to say? "I know you're here, and you can stay as long as you do no harm, but I don't want to see you."

Diane said maybe she's here to help with the book. If that's the case, she can certainly stay ... but I still don't want to see her. I'm not quite ready for that yet.

CHAPTER 16

The Past
Age Thirty-Seven

I sat in the office and stared at the last two words on the screen: The End. My cursor hovered next to them. Attis lay on the floor at my feet, an empty box near his front paws. Quake was on his bed in the corner. I considered pinching myself to make sure it wasn't a dream.

I looked down at Attis. "Do you think it's bad luck to kill off my main character? Should I fix that before I call?"

Attis only groaned and fell onto his side.

I looked back at the screen and moved the cursor to the printer icon. Nearly two hundred pages churned out into the tray. I gathered them and put them in the box. For some reason, I just needed to see it on paper. Although it was after midnight, I knew that Maeve would still be awake in her room, likely with her nose in a book. I leaned back in my chair, eyes on the ceiling.

"It's done!" I called.

Her bedroom door flew open a second later, and I listened as her feet pattered down the hallway toward the office.

I swiveled my chair toward the door in time to see her peek around the doorframe.

"It's done?" she asked. "The whole thing? Totally done?"

I pointed to the box. "Totally done."

Maeve threw her arms around me. "I knew you could do it! Never doubted it one bit."

"So, what do you think?" I asked. "How about a trip to the diner?

Chocolate chip pancakes to celebrate? I'm starving, and my head is pounding."

She stood up and held out her arms. "Can I wear this?"

She was dressed in fuzzy leopard-print pajama pants, a tie-dyed T-shirt, and two unmatched socks.

"Why not?" I said. "Anyone out at this hour needs a little excitement in their lives."

She shook her head. "I'm kidding," she said. "I'm not going out in this. Give me a minute to change."

She trotted off, and while I sat there waiting for her to come back, I looked at the yellow sticky note on the corkboard. The phone number for Broadman Publishing stared back at me. Then, I lifted my bag from the floor and dumped the contents out onto the desk. There was a journal, a handful of gum wrappers, a few pieces of change, and several paper clips. There was an extra flash drive—but no white business card.

Maeve appeared a few seconds later, freshly dressed in black yoga pants and a sweatshirt, her hair pulled up in a ponytail. She glanced at the mess on the desk and shot me a puzzled look.

"I wanted to see if that business card was in my bag," I explained.

She raised her eyebrows. "And was it?"

"Of course not."

She shook her head, grabbed my hands, and dragged me out of my chair. "Mums, sometimes I worry about you. Let's go get you some food."

CHAPTER 17

The Past
Age Thirty-Seven

The next morning, I sat in the office with my coffee. My phone was on the desk in front of me, the yellow sticky note next to it. Quake was at my feet this time, his big head resting across his front paws.

"So, what exactly am I supposed to say if someone answers?" I asked him.

Quake closed his eyes.

I looked back at the sticky note. I doubted the number would work, but I had to at least give it a try. I picked up the phone and dialed.

After about five rings, a woman's voice answered, "Hello. This is Lydia Winters. How can I help you?"

It was one of those moments that take longer in your head to process than it should. While the phone was ringing, I'd convinced myself that this was silly. Now the woman whose name I'd been given was on the other end of the line.

Lydia's voice came again. "Hello? Is anyone there?"

Quake lifted his head, as if to remind me to speak up.

"Yes," I said. "Sorry. This is Nadia King. I was given your number a while ago. I've been working on a novel. The man who gave it to me said to reach out to you directly once I was done. He said you might be expecting the call?"

There was a long silence before she answered. "What did you say your name was again?"

I repeated it, and there was another long pause. I wondered if she might be trying to figure out a way to politely end the call, but when she spoke again, it was with a hint of curiosity in her voice. "And who did you say gave you my name?"

There was no good way to explain why I didn't have the man's name, so I went with the simplest option. "We only met briefly," I said. "I'm afraid I can't remember. I'm terrible with names."

I heard papers rustling in the background. "Not a problem," she said, "I was just curious. Can you hold for one second? I need to grab something."

"Of course, take your time."

I listened as an old Beatles tune played on the other end of the line. My mind was reeling. A few seconds later, there was a click, and the music stopped.

"Sorry about the wait, Ms. King. First of all, why don't you give me your phone number and email? I want to make sure I have them in case we get disconnected, or if I have any questions."

I gave them to her, and she repeated both back to me.

"Do you have a pen and paper handy?" she asked. "I'm going to give you some information. I'll put everything in an email when we hang up, of course, but I just like to share it in person, as well. Call me old school, but I don't trust computers sometimes."

I took down the information, and when I asked how much it would cost to start the process, she insisted that there was no charge—it had already been taken care of.

"That's all we really need to do for now, Ms. King. I'll start to review your manuscript as soon as I receive it, and you should probably expect a call back within the month. Do you have any questions for me?"

I told her I didn't, but that was a lie. I had a million questions. She explained a few last steps, but I barely heard any of it. The ringing in my ears had become a constant hum. Something was coming.

"Before we go," Lydia said, "I do have a question for you, if you don't mind."

Gooseflesh covered my arms.

"Could the man's name have been Remmington? Does that name ring a bell at all?"

I felt my heart catch. It wasn't a common name by any stretch, and yes, it certainly did ring a bell, even though I had no reason to link it to the man I'd met in the library.

"Ms. King, are you there?"

The hum in my ears grew louder. I looked at Quake. He was looking back.

"I suppose that could have been it," I told her, trying to remember that night in the library. "What does this Remmington look like?" I asked, unable to help myself.

She explained that he was tall. Longer hair, hazel eyes. Maybe early fifties. It was a description that could have fit a lot of people. Then she added two final details.

"He always wears one of those old-time hats. I forget what it's called. And every time I see him, his shoes are absolutely spotless." She laughed. "Not that you'd ever notice something as silly as that."

I recalled the man's shoes, how they'd reflected the light from the library's fluorescents and my head began to pound. *Remmington. Is it possible?* I actually felt like I was going to be sick. I needed to get off the phone.

"Not silly at all," I said. "I actually did notice his shoes, and you're right. They were absolutely spotless. I think we're talking about the same man."

When I finally put the phone down, I rubbed at the soft spots behind my ears. They were throbbing. I looked at Quake. He seemed concerned. I considered calling Jakob, but I remembered that my next sleep session was booked for the following day. I could just talk to him then.

Plus, I needed a minute to think.

CHAPTER 18

The Past
Age Thirty-Eight

After my call with Lydia Winters, things happened quickly. My book hit the shelves, word spread, and sales escalated. Shortly after the launch, *Psience* topped the best sellers list, just as my visitor from the library had promised.

Lydia stopped by the house one afternoon to drop off some paperwork. We'd begun discussing plans for a second novel. As I was reading through the documents at the dining room table, she got up to refill our coffee cups in the kitchen. When I went in to join her, I found her standing in front of my laptop. It was propped open on the kitchen counter, and my screen saver, the photo of the Baird, was on full display.

She pointed at the screen and looked at me. "Where did you get this?"

"My daughter took that photo. It's a house just up the road, near the dog park. Abandoned, I think. She and I have fallen in love with the place. It's sort of been my motivation while writing. I always said that if the book sold we'd find the owner and make an offer."

Lydia raised an eyebrow.

"I know, it doesn't look like much," I said. "It's in pretty bad shape, but there's just something about it. I don't know what it is."

"You're surely not serious, are you?" Lydia had a puzzled look on her face. "At the rate your book is selling, you'll be able to do much better than that."

"I'm completely serious," I said. "For some reason, I can see Maeve and me living there."

She looked at the screen and then back at me. "What would ever make you want that house?"

I shrugged. The photo certainly didn't do it justice with the shutters askew and the front porch practically caving in. "I'm not sure. Maybe just because it looks spooky?"

Lydia laughed. "Well, I'll agree with you on that one." She picked up the carafe and poured our coffee. "And you're 100 percent right. The house is in terrible shape. It's been empty since my grandmother died. I pay someone to keep up with the lawn, but that's about it."

I was in the process of grabbing the milk from the fridge, but I stopped and stared at her. "Wait … what did you say?"

"That's why I was so surprised you had a picture of it on your laptop," she said as she pointed at the image. "I used to sit out on that porch all the time. Anything to keep from going inside. Granny loved the place … lived there her whole life. Who knows, she's probably still in there somewhere." Lydia looked at me, laughed, and then shook her head. "The place always gave me the creeps. Too many rooms, too many shadows. Something always creaking or banging." Lydia stirred her coffee. "You ever heard of Jillian Stiles?"

I shook my head.

"Well, that was Granny," she said. "The eccentric artiste, at least that's what the papers called her." She smiled. "People would drive for miles for one of her paintings. Had a real knack for figuring out just what people wanted to see."

"So, you own the house now?"

She nodded, taking a sip of her coffee. "Yep, and I have no idea what to do with it. Nobody wants it, and I don't blame them. I'll certainly never live there. If you really want the place, you can have it. The house—plus all of Granny's creepy things that are still up in the attic."

All I could do was look at her. I wasn't sure what to say.

Lydia took another sip of her coffee. "I'm serious. If you really want it, we can make that happen. You'd be doing me a favor. Package deal, house and everything in it. Bargain-basement price. Give me your best number."

CHAPTER 19

The Past
Age Thirty-Nine

Aaron was eating his lunch at one of the long tables in the dining hall of the shelter when I arrived. I could see the back of his head, and his white hair was longer than it had been in a while. We'd have to take the scissors to it soon. He was wearing a black T-shirt, the name of some long-forgotten rock band across the back. As I got closer, I could see that he was hunched over a plate piled high with barbeque chips, both hands wrapped around the sides of a sandwich. He didn't see me as I came up behind him, but when I squeezed in next to him at the table and he realized it was me, his eyes lit up. He put down the sandwich, snatched the napkin from his knee, and dabbed at his mouth.

"Well, now," he said, one of those huge smiles on his face, "aren't you just a sight for sore eyes? Must be my lucky day. You get off work early?"

I gave him a wink. "It *is* your lucky day. I have a surprise for you."

"That so?" He took a sip of his water. "Do tell."

I told him about the property while he finished his lunch, about how much work it needed, about the little carriage house at the end of the drive, and about the role I thought he might play in it all. He looked at me as if waiting for the punch line.

"That little carriage house would be perfect for you," I said.

He wiped his hands on his pants and tugged at the white tuft of a beard that covered his chin. Then, he scrunched up his face. "You want to give me a house?"

"Like I said, it would be perfect for you."

He shook his head and laughed. "Deary, I always knew you were plum crazy, especially for hanging out with an old fart like me, but this little idea of yours is over the top." He popped the last chip into his mouth. "You're a sweet girl for thinking of me, and I do appreciate the thought, I really do, but I could never let you do that."

"Sure, you could. It's easy." I stood up. "Come on. Let's go for a drive."

Aaron glanced around the lunchroom. Twenty or so people filled the tables.

"Well?" I said. "Are you coming or not?"

He eventually shrugged and got up from the table. I hooked an arm through his and led him to the car. In less than an hour, we arrived at the Baird. The driveway was nothing more than a poorly mowed path covered with a sprinkling of gravel, easy to miss if you weren't paying attention. Two stone pillars flanked either side of it, both nearly covered in ivy. The pillars were the base remnants of an old gate, made of hand-cut blocks of stone. They stood about five feet tall, the one on the left canted at a bad angle. They reminded me of two decrepit sentinels standing guard.

The car tires crunched on the gravel as we turned into the opening and wound our way between a row of old trees. The stone carriage house came into view first. Set back in the high grass on the left, its roof and sides were covered with grapevines and brambles. The small front porch was cluttered with garden tools.

"That's the one," I said, stopping to let Aaron take a look.

He studied it, and the corners of his mouth turned up in a smile.

Farther ahead on the right was a rapidly deteriorating barn, and behind that, the cornfield, the stalks already knee-high.

Aaron rolled down his window and leaned his head out. It made me think of Attis who liked nothing better than a nose full of air as we drove.

"God, do you smell that?" Aaron said, turning to me, his smile wide. "Fresh air. Nothing like the city, is it?"

The breeze carried the smells from the nearby fields and the sharp bite of freshly mowed grass. According to Lydia, the land surrounding the house had been rented to a few farmers. They grew their crops and tended to the grass in the summer and plowed in the winter so the place didn't fall completely into ruin.

Aaron pulled his head back into the car. "How far to the house? Can we walk the rest of the way?"

I angled the front end of the Escape into the grass and shut off the engine. By the time I made it around to Aaron's side of the car, he was already at the edge of the cornfield, his hands deep in his pockets. He turned to me, no longer trying to hide his smile. It was good to see him happy. We started up the drive.

As we got closer to the main house, a stone wall came into view. About four feet high and capped in slabs of slate, it stretched from the edge of woods on the left to the cornfield on the right. The driveway cut through it, and beyond the opening, a gravel circle met with a lush green lawn that was freshly mowed. Aaron stopped to admire the stonework, but I continued through the opening. Thick brush crept up to the house from the left, and among the brambles, I could see the small family graveyard that Lydia had mentioned. It was just beyond the slate patio. Aaron saw it too, but he kept walking.

He stopped in front of the steps that led up to the porch, hands on his hips. He shook his head, and then he looked back at me and pointed toward the house. "Damn troublemaker kids," he yelled, pointing to where a band of graffiti covered the stucco. "Why do they go and do stuff like this? Too much time on their hands these days, that's what I say."

Near the area that had been painted, one of the windows was broken. I could only hope the kids hadn't gotten inside.

Aaron climbed the front steps and worked his way down the length of the porch. He stopped at the window and leaned in close, hands cupped over his eyes. "This can all be fixed, you know," he said, turning back to me. "Not sure if I ever told you, but I used to do this sort of thing, fixing up old places, before the …" He looked down at his hands for a minute and then back up at me. The smile was gone. "You know," he said, turning back to the house. "Before."

Even from the distance, I could see tears welling up in his eyes, and for the first time in ages, I actually noticed the scars on his face and arms. Things like that tend to disappear once you get to know someone like

Aaron. I didn't know the full story behind the scars, and until then, I knew nothing about his previous work. I climbed the stairs, thinking I should offer a hug, but as I got closer, Aaron quickly pulled out a handkerchief and wiped at his eyes.

"Yeah," he said, leaning back, a hand over his brow like a visor as he inspected the roof. "Historic renovation. That was my specialty." He shot me a smile. "And now you show me this? What are the chances?"

I wedged in next to him at the window and peered inside. The room was filthy, but it wasn't in terrible shape. There didn't appear to be any graffiti on the interior walls. I stepped back and put an arm through Aaron's again. "So, what you're telling me is that you'd know exactly how to revive this place? Is that right?"

"I know how to do pretty much everything," he said. "Plumbing, electric, plaster. Loved them all." He rubbed at his chin. "Nadia, this place could be fixed up nice."

"Sounds like you're the man for the job, so, what do you say?"

He leaned back again and eyed the overhanging roof. "Do you care if I take a few more minutes to look around? Maybe peek in a few of the other windows around back?"

"Be my guest, boss. I want your professional opinion."

"Boss?" He laughed, waving a hand at me as if that was the silliest thing he'd ever heard. "That's a good one."

Aaron disappeared around the corner of the porch. Once he was gone, I wandered over to get a closer look at the gravestones. Lydia said she'd never gotten close enough to see whose names were on them. There were five in all, clearly old but still readable, patches of moss clinging to the sides of most. Baird was the last name on each. Hidden in the overgrowth behind them was a cluster of rosebushes, their bright red flowers poking out among the vines. I wondered if they had been planted there on purpose.

It was almost dinnertime when we pulled up at the shelter. A line was forming at the door. I told Aaron I had an appointment with Jakob and couldn't stay.

Aaron climbed out of the SUV but paused on the curb, hand resting on the door. There was a gleam in his eye, like a child who'd just been promised a pony for Christmas. "Nadia, I don't know why you'd ever offer something like this to me, but if you really do mean it, I'd love nothing more than to move into that little house at the end of the drive and help you fix that place up." His eyes were glassy again.

"I do really mean it, Aaron," I said. "I can't imagine going if you didn't come along."

He gave a nod. "Then, I accept. I don't know what I ever did to deserve this, but I accept."

From the Journal of Nadia King
Age Forty

Aaron and I had coffee on the front porch this morning. We stood there looking out over the property through a mist that hung in the air just above the surface of the lawn. Neither of us said a word. Most of the time, like today, the house is peaceful.

My second novel is coming along, even without Remmington's help. Neither Lydia nor I have seen him in ages, although we talk about him often.

The nightmares haven't stopped, but sometimes the chases are shorter—if you can call that an improvement. This is only because my pursuers often catch me before I make it to the room at the end of the hall, a room that's no longer dark, but instead, blindingly bright. Every once in a while, I'm the one on the stretcher, the green drape thrown across my own body. When this happens, the shadows take turns wheeling me through Gram Marie's house, which is still in shambles, furniture scattered, and graffiti on the walls.

The cats are still there too, dozens of them, with fur in every color. They follow the stretcher through the house. Their eyes, still the same luminescent green, are always locked on mine. Once we cross into the bright room, the cats still stop at the threshold and refuse to follow us in.

Rowan thinks these nightmares mean that my captors are trying to show me what they want me to see. Rowan thinks the brightness of the room means I'm getting closer to the answers. She thinks the cats represent spirits that are waiting to speak with me. They stand at the doorway, instead of coming in, because they haven't been invited yet. They're waiting for me to make that decision.

As for the shadows I see in the house when I'm awake, I've stopped using Gram Marie's mantra. I've told them they can stay, and I've told them that I want to see them. They've been happy to oblige. They only present themselves as shadows, though, never anything that looks remotely human. Maybe that's better. I'm still not sure how I'd react to anything more.

With the nightmares, and all of the lost sleep, I've come to rely heavily on naps. The couch in the library has definitely been getting some use.

CHAPTER 20

The Past
Age Forty

I was asleep on the couch when I heard Remmington's voice. "Nadia, are you there? Can you hear me?"

I sat up, confused for a second. It was as if I'd somehow summoned him by writing in my journal that I hadn't seen him in ages. He hadn't yet visited me at the Baird.

When he called again, I practically ran to the foyer. I yanked open the door and found him standing there in his dark suit and tie, as usual. When I glanced down at his shoes out of habit, I saw that they were spotless, as always, although I couldn't imagine how, given the current state of the lawn. Aaron had just finished the landscaping, and mud was everywhere.

Remmington was never one for hugs, but I gave him one anyway. "You're a sight for sore eyes," I said. "It's been a while."

He took off his hat.

I noticed that his hair was shorter, his face thinner.

"I suppose I am a little overdue in my congratulations on the book," he said, offering an apologetic smile. He looked around. "And on the house."

"You knew, didn't you? That I wanted this house and that it belonged to Lydia?"

"It's possible," he said, smiling over his shoulder as he ducked through the stone archway that led into the kitchen.

I'd forgotten how tall he was. My father probably would have had to do the same thing. In the kitchen, he made his way over to the bay window where he stuffed his hands in his pockets and stared out at the yard. The gravestones were visible from there, something I'd realized I should probably fix. The sight of gravestones with your morning coffee wasn't the most cheerful way to start the day. He seemed to be looking right at them.

"Can I get you something to drink?" I asked. "Lemonade maybe? It's fresh made."

He spun on a heel to face me. "I'd love that. I actually can't remember the last time I had a lemonade. My mother used to make it all the time."

"One glass of lemonade, coming up, then," I said, grabbing the pitcher from the fridge.

He pulled out a stool at the island and placed his hat on the counter near the sugar bowl. "So, things are going well for you," he said, more a statement than a question.

"Thanks to you," I said, as I filled two glasses and pushed one toward him. "I'm not sure how you made it all happen, but here I am."

Remmington shook his head and took a seat. "I didn't make anything happen. You did all the work, not me."

"You made this house happen," I said.

He smiled. "OK, I admit it. I suppose connections do come in handy sometimes."

I looked at him more closely. From where I stood, I could see that his hair was not only shorter, but that he'd gone a little thin on top. *Had it really been so long since I'd seen him?*

He took a sip of his lemonade and winced.

I pushed the sugar bowl toward him. "You might want some of this. I'll get you a spoon."

I turned, but instead of opening the silverware drawer, I opened the cupboard above the stove and began to rummage. I could hear Remmington talking in the background, but I wasn't really listening. The cupboard was packed with everything from bug spray to cotton balls, and I couldn't find what I needed. "They must be in here somewhere," I muttered.

"What are you looking for?" This, I heard.

"Something for this blasted headache," I said, still rummaging. "They stopped for a while, but now they're back."

I suddenly realized what I'd done and turned toward Remmington. "Well, that was rude of me. I went to get you a spoon and then totally forgot about you."

He smiled. "It takes a lot more than that to hurt my feelings, Nadia." He pointed at the open cupboard behind me. "Second shelf. Small clear bottle. I can see them from here."

I turned and looked. The bottle of aspirin was literally right in front of me. I grabbed the spoon for Remmington first, and then I popped two of the white pills into my mouth. I washed them down with a sip of lemonade. He was right. It definitely needed more sugar.

"Maybe you should take a little break from writing," he said, picking up the bowl and pouring a stream of sugar into my glass first and then his own. "Do something else for a while. I think I have a project you might be interested in."

Just then, the cat strolled into the kitchen. I was surprised to see him since Ares usually hides from visitors. He stopped near Remmington's shoes and looked up.

Remmington studied the cat. "Why's he looking at me like that?"

I laughed. "Probably because you're on his stool."

Ares turned to me and blinked, as if confirming that I'd gotten it right. I picked up my glass of lemonade and tipped my head toward the foyer.

"Let's go into the living room," I said. "There are plenty of seats in there for all of us."

Remmington reached down and ruffled the cat's fur.

Ares accepted the attention but then quickly plodded away. He stopped just under the stone archway and waited as Remmington gathered his things. When he saw that we were finally coming, he darted across the foyer.

I followed close behind, passing through two wide sheets of late afternoon sunlight which streamed in through the glass panels on either side of the front door. The glare sent another wave of pain through my head, and Remmington grabbed my elbow to steady me.

"Are you sure you're OK?" he asked.

I pressed the heel of one hand to my forehead. "It's just the headache. I'll be fine." But then a thought struck me. *The brightness of the room means you're getting closer to the answer. The cats are spirits waiting to talk to you. They stand at the door because they haven't been invited in yet.*

Ares stood at the door to the living room and watched as Remmington steered me past him, to one of the two couches that faced each other, a coffee table between them. This small grouping of furniture and the rug underneath seemed to create an island in the center of the overly large room.

"My furniture used to fit so perfectly in the twin," I said. "Here, it looks a little sparse, doesn't it?"

Remmington took a seat on the opposite couch and glanced around the room as he placed his glass on a coaster. "Let's just call it cozy," he said, as Ares leaped up next to him and curled into a ball. The cat wrapped his fluffy tail around his face. It covered everything except his green eyes, which were trained on me.

I gazed at the cat in disbelief and eventually had to look away as he continued to stare. I took a sip of my lemonade. Remmington had gotten the sweetness just right. "So, what were you starting to say in the kitchen before our little friend there got bossy and chased us out?"

Remmington scratched the top of the cat's head, and Ares closed his eyes. "I was saying that I may have found some research that might be of interest to you. Work by a Professor Jorg Sterling." He held up a finger. "That's Jorg with a J, not with a Y, even though I know that's how it sounds. You should look him up. You might run into him soon, and when you do, I want you to be ready. You'll want to get on his good side right from the start, if you're smart. In fact, I suggest you do a little research beforehand. Read a few of his papers. Let him see that you know his work."

"What type of research does he do?"

"Let's just say you'll notice some similarities between his work and your first novel."

I leaned closer. "What kind of similarities?"

"He's just recently discovered a new type of cell very much like the ones you described in your novel. The work leading up to this discovery should sound very familiar to you. When you talk to him, I wouldn't mention that you know about the cells though since that hasn't been published yet. Maybe skip any mention of the supernatural as well. If you can avoid those two topics for now, you just might get a chance to prove your theory."

I shot him a puzzled look. "I don't understand. If Dr. Sterling's research has something to do with my book, then why wouldn't I talk to him about the cells he's found or anything related to the supernatural? That was the whole point of *Psience*. And if this connection might allow me to prove my theory, why wouldn't he and I discuss it?"

Remmington shook his head. "Just trust me on this one, Nadia. Stick to discussing his published work for now. You can see if he chooses to mention anything more."

"So, how do you know this Professor Sterling?"

"Let's just say he's a friend of a friend … and leave it at that." Remmington smoothed the hair on Ares's back, and the cat began to purr.

"Why do you watch out for me like you do?"

"Why shouldn't I?" he said. "You spend a lot of your time helping others, so maybe I think you deserve to have someone do the same for you. You and my daughter are very much alike, but I haven't been able to help her as much as I've wanted to, so here I am."

"You never mentioned a daughter."

He shook his head. "We've sort of lost touch. I've tried reaching out to both her and her mother plenty of times, but they refuse to see me." Remmington glanced at his watch, and I knew this meant he was about to leave. He lifted Ares off the couch, set him on the floor, and brushed the fur off his pants.

I followed him into the foyer where he stopped at the base of the stairs and turned in my direction. The sky was fading to a light pink beyond the front door.

I studied his face, his hazel eyes, and tried to see the familiarity I'd noticed in the library. In a strange way, he reminded me of my father. They had the same complexion, but my father's eyes were a deep brown. Both had dark hair, only my father had much less of it. And of course, my father never wore a suit—not even to my wedding. "So, if I hadn't gone to the University, do you think we ever would have met?"

Remmington placed his hat on his head and tucked his hands into his pockets. "Without the University, would we have met? I don't know if I can answer that. You never know where life will take you. Sometimes, if you're lucky, or if you work hard enough, paths double back and give you a second chance at something that's important to you. I don't know what would have happened if you hadn't gone to Jakob. The fact is that you did, and here we are. That's all that matters right now."

I heard the phone ring and looked over my shoulder toward the sound.

"Go on and get it," he said, reaching for the door. "It could be important. I have to get going anyway. We'll talk soon."

And with that, he was gone.

By the time I picked up the phone, it had already stopped ringing. There was a missed call from Jakob. Seeing his name reminded me of an order I'd placed for him earlier that month. I'd have to call Mr. Noah and see if it was ready. If it was, I'd make a surprise visit to see Jakob in person rather than calling back.

I set the phone down next to my laptop and looked at the screen. I'd written fifty pages that morning before my nap, so it was no wonder I had a headache. Being hungry probably didn't help either, so I made my way back into the kitchen.

I grabbed an apple from the bowl on the counter and then stood at the window just as Remmington had. The dogs sprinted along the edge of the property outside. I was thinking about what Remmington had said when Ares rubbed up against my leg. I looked at him. "Jorg Sterling. Jorg with a J—not a Y. So, what do you think about that, Mr. Fuzzball? Should we look him up? See if his research has anything to do with my novel?"

The cat stared at me with interest, so I bent down and picked him up.

"Remember, though. Even if it does, I can't talk about it," I said, scratching his ears. "What do you suppose that's all about? I guess we'll just have to wait and see, won't we?"

CHAPTER 21

The Past
Age Forty

That night, before dinner, I made a quick call to Mr. Noah to ask if he had been able to find the almanac for Jakob. It was the only one Jakob needed to complete his collection, and he had apparently searched everywhere—at least everywhere except the Attic.

Mr. Noah answered after two rings and confirmed that, yes, he had it stashed away and that he'd see us in the morning. When I asked Maeve if she wanted to run errands with me the next day, and I mentioned that two bookstores were on my route, she was immediately interested.

The Attic, Mr. Noah's bookstore, was a favorite of ours. It was only open on weekends, and he sold nothing new. Every book on display was handpicked by Mr. Noah himself, gathered from antique shops and auctions throughout the week. Back at the Attic, he organized them in a way that made perfect sense to him—even if it made no sense to anyone else. The Attic wasn't a place you shopped when you were in a rush. It was more of a browser's paradise.

The old renovated barn sat in the middle of nowhere. Maeve and I followed the long, winding back road for miles, seeing nothing on the way but trees, grass, and an occasional cow. We turned into the small parking lot shortly after ten o'clock, pulling up to one of the old iron hitching posts. Only one other car was there, a tiny red Fiat, which belonged to Mr. Noah.

A dented cowbell clattered as we stepped into the small room at the front of the barn, a space previously used as a wash bay for horses. Mr.

Noah was right where I expected him to be, settled in his rocking chair next to a potbellied wood stove. The fire was going, and the room was more than toasty. Still, he wore a red flannel shirt with a blue sweater vest pulled over it. He had a book in his hands, of course. Sandy, his wirehaired Jack Russell was fast asleep at his feet. She was deaf, so the sound of the bell made no difference to her. Mr. Noah heard it, though. He held up a finger as he finished his page, and then he carefully set his book in his lap and squinted in our direction. His smile was quick and warm. "Well, I'll be," he said, his face lighting up, the words tinged with a southern drawl. "Zat you, Maeve? And my Nadia too?"

"None other," I said, stripping off my jacket.

He shoved his stockinged feet into a pair of wool-lined moccasins and shuffled over to us. He grabbed our hands and gave them a squeeze. He was tiny man, barely five feet tall and probably no more that ninety pounds soaking wet. Something about him reminded me of Geppetto from *Pinocchio*. If my memory served me correctly, I was pretty sure his ninetieth birthday was just around the corner.

He shook a finger at me. "Let me go get that book for ya." Before I could say anything, he shuffled across the room and disappeared behind a heavy brocade curtain that hung just beyond the counter.

Maeve headed in the opposite direction and disappeared through the door that led out into the stacks.

I knelt down next to Sandy. Her nose twitched as I pulled a dog treat out of my pocket. She was going on fifteen, but she could still smell a treat from a mile away.

Her tail gave a wag as Mr. Noah popped his head back into the room. He pointed a crooked finger at the door Maeve had gone through.

"Why don't you go take a gander out there in the stacks with your girl," he said. "I want to clean up this almanac for ya. Meant to do it last night, but got a lil' sidetracked with my book. I shouldn't be long."

"Take your time," I said, waving him on. "I'll go have a peek. Where are you keeping my journals these days?"

"Second floor, back in that corner by those rocking chairs. Oh, there's some good ones up there right now. Found 'em this week."

Beyond the door was a short hallway with a low ceiling. The walls were lined with rows of handcrafted shelves. Books that couldn't fit on the shelves were jammed into wooden milk crates. These were stacked anywhere they'd fit, some of them five high. I passed through without stopping and climbed the rickety stairs at the end, hoping as I always did, that they'd hold. On the second floor, I found the journals right where Mr. Noah said I would, beyond a circle of old wooden rocking chairs. A pile of them was stacked neatly on a stool in the corner. I took the full stack over to one of the chairs and thumbed through each of them, eventually picking one written in 1910 because I saw the word *ghost* sprinkled throughout. I would have gladly taken the entire pile, but I knew that Maeve would find something for sure. With the almanac, that would be three books in total, and at the Attic, if you bought three books in one visit, another would magically appear in your bag when you checked out. Mr. Noah kept a pile of his personal favorites at the ready.

Mr. Noah was leaning on the counter when I stepped back into the front room. He was leafing through a hardback. When he heard me coming, he closed it and held it out to me for inspection. It was the almanac. "Have a look."

The book's burgundy cover was gently worn, but it was in much better shape than expected given its 1758 publication date. I flipped through its pages and glanced over the poems, weather charts, and astrological information.

"Jakob will be thrilled," I said.

Maeve returned just as I closed it. She added two more books to the pile, and Mr. Noah gave her a nod.

He ran the numbers in his head. "Fifty sound like a fair price?"

"Sounds like a steal to me," I said, placing that and twenty more on the counter.

Mr. Noah tucked the bills into the old-fashioned cash register and bagged the books. "Always a pleasure seeing you two young ladies," he said, passing me the bag.

We headed south into town from there. Town traffic was heavy, as usual. We were forced to crawl through a line of stoplights before turning into the busy outdoor mall that Maeve and I had nicknamed the Twilight Zone. I found a parking spot right in front of the bookstore.

When we stepped inside, the smell of coffee greeted us. Shelves full of movies, music, and electronic readers filled the front room. Tables piled high with puzzles and bookends were beyond that.

Continuing through a section of games, I turned to Maeve and asked if she thought they might have any books.

She chuckled and pointed toward the escalator. "I'll be over there if you need me. Rowan's going to teach me Russian. I want to see if they have a workbook."

I watched her go, noticing the number of people milling about. The checkout line extended well into the row of display tables at the front of the store, each strategically placed to catch the shoppers' eyes as they waited. This is where I was headed. It was October, after all, which meant that anything remotely spooky was likely on display.

I found the book I'd come for just beyond a cauldron overflowing with Halloween scarves. There were two left, one stacked neatly on top of the other, my name across the bottom in big block letters: Nadia King. The fact that it was sitting there seemed too surreal. This was my first time seeing it in a store, something I'd avoided, convinced that if I saw my book before seeing Remmington again, it would be bad luck. I couldn't use that as my excuse any longer.

Two older women ambled over to the table as I stood there, one dressed in various shades of blue, the other in red, both topped with a matching hat. They looked to be in their late seventies.

The one wearing red snatched up a copy of my novel and handed it to her friend. "This is the one," she said, as if they'd just been talking about it.

The other woman studied the front cover and frowned. "You're sure?"

"Of course, I'm sure," Red said, sounding indignant that her friend would even ask the question.

Blue squinted at the image on the cover. Centered above my name was a french door, like the one in Gram Marie's cellarway. Eclipsing the frame on the right was a shadow, nearly human in shape. A little girl stood in front of the glass, a plastic party cup held to her ear.

Red looked at me and patted the last remaining book with her hand. "You should grab this one before it disappears, deary. It's a good one."

I smiled, and when the two women walked away, I did pick it up. Of course, I didn't need to buy a copy. I already had one at home, but I wanted to buy one just because I could. I flipped through the pages as if I'd never seen it before. *Did I really write this? Is it really here?*

Someone leaned in close to my ear just then and barked, "Boo!"

I spun to find a witch's hat, purple feathers decorating the brim, blue eyes and beard underneath.

"Jesus, Jakob!" I said, realizing who it was. "Why would you do that?"

Jakob gave a hearty witch's cackle, which made everyone in line gawk in our direction.

"Why wouldn't I do it?" he said, pulling me into a hug. "A boo is the perfect greeting for this time of year, my dear. You should know that better than anyone." He pointed to the book in my hands. "Finally giving in, are you? Does it feel strange seeing it here?"

"Very," I said. "I only wish Gram Marie could be here to see it too."

Jakob raised an eyebrow. "You know what I say to that, don't you?"

I nodded. He and Rowan would both say that Gram Marie *is* still here to see it.

Jakob tilted his head toward the coffee counter. "Have time for an espresso—or are you in a hurry? I've been wanting to talk with you."

"Never in too big of a hurry for you." I started in that direction. "I did see that you called yesterday. Sorry I never called back. Maeve and I were actually planning to swing by the University on our way home. We have something in the car for you."

"See there," Jakob said. "Providence and destiny, my dear. Fate knew we needed to meet, and here we are." He bumped his shoulder against mine. "So, what's in the car?"

"It's a surprise. Let's get coffee first. You can tell me what's on your mind. After that, we'll gather Maeve and head outside."

We found a table near the window, but Jakob started talking before we even sat down, clearly excited to share his news. "I called because I was recently speaking with a friend of mine about his work, and in the course of the conversation, he said something that struck me as odd." Jakob took the lid off his tea and set the cup aside to cool. "When he realized what he'd said, he tried to backpedal, but of course, me being me, I questioned him further, and what I learned was quite fascinating actually." Jakob narrowed his eyes. "Nadia, are you by any chance familiar with the work of Patterson and Goodall? Their work with primates?"

I felt the hairs on the back of my neck prickle. *Jakob's going to tell me about Jorg Sterling. Jorg, with a J, not a Y,* I thought.

I told him that I was. I'd actually idolized Goodall as a child. My Gram Marie often told me stories about her work in Tanzania, how Goodall spent her whole life immersed in the world of wild chimpanzees, something I said I was going to do when I grew up. Like her, I, too, had a stuffed chimp instead of a teddy bear. Goodall's stuffed friend was named Jubilee, mine was Feather, although I'm not sure why I ever picked the name. I only became familiar with Patterson's work with sign language much later in life.

Jakob nodded. "My friend, Dr. Jorg Sterling, does similar work, at least similar in the fact that his focus is on primates and how they communicate. He's published a few papers in recent years. I'm not sure if you've seen those."

I told Jakob that I had, but I didn't say that I'd only read them the night before as directed by Remmington.

Jakob leaned across the table as if he wanted no one else to hear what he was about to say. "Nadia, I wanted to talk to you about the work he's doing right now, work that's not yet published … work that you and I need to get involved in. He's identified some new cells in the brain." Jakob folded his hands. "The similarities between Sterling's cells and the ones in your novel are remarkable, and I don't quite know what to make of it. I know I shouldn't have said anything to Sterling about what you wrote, but I just couldn't help it."

I thought of Remmington's warnings.

"Of course, Sterling demanded to know where I'd read about these cells," Jakob said, "and as much as I tried to avoid telling him that it was in a novel, your name came up in the end. Here's the thing, Nadia. I actually feel like Sterling might be able to use what you've written. You've done an excellent job of thinking things through. Your experiments might work for him, given what he's found already, and if his cells are anything like what you describe in your novel, we can't miss this opportunity." Jakob's face took on a worried expression. "Nadia, I have to ask you a question, and please don't get angry with me for asking it. How did you come up with the experiments in your book?"

This was a question I wasn't yet prepared to answer in full—not even to Jakob, someone I trusted completely—so I offered a partial answer instead. "The work I do in the lab now really isn't that different than what I wrote about in the book. The psychic receptors that my scientists discovered are just cells, and I work with cells every day. Cancer cells or glial cells, they're pretty much handled in the same way. I don't work with fMRI, but I got all of that information from books."

I failed to mention Remmington's involvement.

Jakob looked nervous. "Nadia, Sterling wants to meet you."

And there it was. Another promise of Remmington's come true.

"He gets back from Vienna tomorrow," Jakob explained, pulling a white sheet of paper from his inside jacket pocket. It was folded neatly into thirds. "He gave me this before he left."

I unfolded it. It was a typed letter. The first line suggested a meeting time, the second an address. In the middle of the page was a campus map, a red X in the center. At the bottom was a list of bullet points. Sterling's signature followed, including the PhD.

"He couldn't have just called?" I asked.

"That's Sterling for you," Jakob said, shaking his head.

I pointed to the bullets. "Is this a list of Sterling's publications? Does this mean I'm supposed to read these before I go?"

"I would, if I were you," Jakob said. "Get on his good side, Nadia, right from the start. That's my suggestion."

"So, is this an interview?"

"Let's hope so," Jakob said. "If you want the job though, don't mention any of the things that you and I and Rowan usually talk about. Stick to straight science, my dear. Trust me on this."

I tucked the letter into my purse just as Maeve appeared wearing the same witch's hat that Jakob had on earlier.

"I thought I saw you," she said to Jakob, smiling down at him from the side of the table. "Did Mom tell you? We have something for you in the car."

"Your mother said as much." Jakob peered into my empty cup. "What do you say we blow this popsicle stand and go see that surprise?"

Maeve and Jakob bought their matching hats, and I bought my novel, which I tucked into my purse on the way to the car. Maeve took the keys and ran ahead. She dug the almanac out of the back seat and had it ready by the time Jakob and I got there. As she handed it to Jakob, the look on his face was priceless.

"No, it's not," he said, complete surprise in his voice as he turned it over in his hands. "This is *Poor Richard's Almanack,* the twenty-sixth. The very last one prepared by Franklin himself. How on Earth did you find this?"

"Mr. Noah worked his magic like I said he would."

Jakob pulled us both into a hug. "Thank you both so much. I dare say that tonight, I see myself with this book in my lap and a bourbon on the table. I may not move until tomorrow."

"My idea of a perfect evening," I said. "You're very welcome."

CHAPTER 22

The Past
Age Forty

A sharp wind was blowing when I arrived at the spot Sterling had marked with an X on his map. Only a handful of people were in the courtyard, most of them bundled up in scarves and hats, making it difficult to find someone who fit Jakob's description of Sterling.

Two women and a man stood in line at a shiny metal food cart. The women had their arms wrapped tightly around themselves, outwardly shivering. The man behind them seemed unfazed by the cold. He wore a dark blue ski jacket and seemed to be about the right build. The hair peeking out from under his yellow hat appeared to be the right color as well. As he stepped up to order, I thought I saw him glance in my direction, so I started toward him. I watched as he took his cup from the vendor, expecting him to head toward me once he had it. Instead, the man turned and walked off in the opposite direction. I stopped where I was and scanned the courtyard, but no one else seemed to be standing on their own. Most were in pairs or groups.

Not sure what to do, I glanced once more back toward the food cart. The man in the blue ski jacket stood just beyond it. He was leaning against a waist-high brick wall, and he seemed to be watching me impatiently, arms crossed in front of him, paper coffee cup in one hand. Deciding this must be him, I started over.

"Dr. Sterling?" I asked as I approached him.

"Miss King," he responded flatly with no hint of a smile. Above his scarf, blue eyes regarded me with what appeared to be pure annoyance—although I wasn't sure why.

I extended a hand. "It's a pleasure to meet you," I said. "Jakob speaks very highly of you and your work."

He shook my hand, squeezing a little harder than necessary. "Jakob speaks highly of everyone. He even speaks highly of you, although given what I've heard, I'm not sure why."

This comment would have bothered most people, but my years with Sam had hardened me. I let it go.

"Jakob said you wanted to talk," I said, watching as a paper cup skittered across the courtyard. The wind was picking up. I tightened my scarf.

"You read the papers I put in the letter?" he asked.

"I did. You've done some impressive work." I hoped this might put him in a better mood. "I'd love to hear more."

"I'm sure you would," he said, sipping his coffee. "So, what else of mine have you read, Ms. King? Clearly much more than what I provided in that list, given what Jakob told me. Maybe you can explain how you got your hands on my *unpublished* work."

I frowned at him. "I'm not sure what you mean. How would I have read anything that you haven't published yet?"

He laughed. "I think that's the question of the day, isn't it? Obviously, you got access to it somehow. How else would a perfect description of my work be sitting in your novel for everyone to read?"

I watched him sip his coffee, surely cold by then, and I didn't know what to say. *Did Jakob know this was why Sterling wanted to speak with me? Surely not.*

He glared at me. "Not so easy to answer once you're confronted about it, is it, Ms. King? No worries, you can take your time, but before we leave here today, I need to know the answer to that question. If someone from my lab gave you this information, then that someone needs to be fired. Clearly, that must be the case because, as far as I know, no other lab is doing anything remotely similar."

I frowned at him again, trying to understand what he was saying. "Are you suggesting that I got the idea for my book from your research?

That I've stolen your work? Because if that's what you think, then you're wrong, Professor. If there are similarities, then I'm sorry, but if that's the case, they're purely coincidence."

"Oh, come on, Ms. King, let's be serious here. It's not like this is a little coincidence. You mention my *exact* discovery in your book. Jakob told me about your cells, your so-called *vibrioglia*. I need to get to the bottom of this. If there's someone in my lab who's leaking information, I need to know who. If some other lab is doing similar work, and that's how you got the information, I need to know that, as well, because if that's the case, I need to do all I can to stay ahead of the game. It's pretty simple. So, who's your source?"

"Look," I said, holding my palms up to the professor, "there seems to be a huge misunderstanding here. Even if we are talking about the same kind of cells, it doesn't matter, right? Yours are the real thing. Mine are fiction. There's no reason to be upset. It's not like we're competing to get an article in a journal or to get funding for a project—"

"And that's another problem! My discovery is out there in some ridiculous novel about the occult. How's that going to look when I finally publish?"

I nearly laughed, but I quickly realized he was serious. His face had gone a deep shade of red, not likely from the cold.

"Look," I said, digging in my purse, remembering that I still had the copy of my book in there from the other day. I held it out to him. "You can take this and read it, and then you'll see that I haven't stolen anything. Jakob and I have been talking about psychic receptors for a while now. I simply ran with the idea and made up a story around them. I gave a fictional cell a fictional name and a fictional function. That's it. From what Jakob said, it sounds like he didn't even know about this new work of yours until recently. The only other person who helped me write the book ..."

I stopped mid-sentence, realizing my mistake, but it was too late.

Sterling took a step closer. "Who else helped you write the book?"

Again, I didn't know what to say. I needed time to think.

I held the novel out to him again. "Just take this and read it. There's absolutely no way you've found exactly the same type of cells that I wrote about in here. Mine are rogue glial cells that can differentiate at will, cells that increase proliferation in response to nonverbal communication, for goodness' sake. There's no way that can be real. On top of that, my cells are found in the primate brain stem of all places, which makes absolutely no sense given their function, but that's why I put them there. That's the beauty of fiction. You can say anything you want, the more unbelievable, the better. That's quite a few specific details that would have to match, don't you think?"

Sterling pushed the book away. "Yes, quite a few."

Finally, I thought.

But then Sterling took another step closer. "That's what I've been trying to say, Ms. King. That's the reason why I wonder how that exact type of cell appears in your novel and in my lab at the same time. When Jakob first told me, I chalked it up to coincidence too. But when he started telling me more details, the things you just mentioned, it all started to make sense. It wasn't a coincidence … at all. It couldn't be."

"So, what are you saying? Are you saying that's what you've found?"

"I don't know why you look so surprised, Ms. King." He lowered his voice. "Yes, my lab has found a cell of unknown origin in the brains of primates, quite possibly a glial cell, at least that's what it looks like on first inspection. We've identified its primary location in the brain stem, which happens to be exactly where your cells are found. We have pictures to prove it. We use fMRI, functional magnetic resonance imaging, to observe them. The only question we have yet to answer is the cells' function. That one is throwing us off a little. Jakob never mentioned the function of your cells, but that really doesn't matter to me. We don't have that answer yet, which means you can't have it either."

My head swam. The air suddenly seemed colder. If what he was saying was true, how was that possible?

"If you don't tell me who gave you this information, Ms. King, I'll find out myself. It can't be that hard."

"Look, there's no one to find, but if you feel like wasting your time, that's up to you." I turned to walk away.

"Don't walk away from me," Sterling called, again reminding me of Sam.

I turned and held out the book to him one last time. "Take it," I said, my patience worn thin. "Maybe you should try the experiment in chapter 17 if you think your cells and mine are the same thing. Let me know how that works out."

Of course, I didn't really think the experiment would work. This was just anger talking. Surprisingly, Sterling snatched the book from my hand.

And what if it does work, Nadia? This is what crossed my mind as I stood there waiting for him to throw my book on the ground. When he didn't, I said, "I have a request. If you try the experiment from chapter 17, and it works, will you call me?"

He laughed. "I doubt you'll be hearing from me anytime soon, Ms. King."

"This may surprise you," I said, standing there, "but I honestly hope you're wrong. Good luck, Dr. Sterling."

A group of students was huddled downwind in the shelter of a nearby doorway. I could feel their eyes on me as I walked away in the direction of Les Choux. I pulled out my phone and called Jakob. When he asked how it had gone with Sterling, and I told him, he apologized.

"I'm headed over to Les Choux," I said. "I need something to warm me up after that. We've been outside in the cold the entire time."

Jakob must have called ahead because, the minute I got there, Rosa immediately led me to a booth and delivered a hot cocoa. A minute later, she returned with a huge slice of chocolate cake, complete with a dollop of whipped cream and pile of fresh raspberries.

"I'll wrap what you don't eat," she said, patting me on the shoulder. "No need to make yourself sick. I'll put together another piece in the back for Maeve."

I watched her head toward the dining room after leaving my table, and as she passed the bar, I noticed a man sitting there, a tall glass of what appeared to be milk in front of him. He obviously spent more time in the gym than I did. His broad shoulders and chest seemed to test the fabric of his T-shirt. His long, dark hair was a mass of tiny braids, all pulled back from his face in a loose ponytail. I thought I managed to turn away before he caught me looking, but apparently, I hadn't.

A few minutes later, he stood next to my table. "Care if I sit?" he asked, pointing to the seat across from me. Up close, he was unnervingly handsome. His eyes were an extraordinary shade of blue-green, his skin the same color as my cocoa. He pointed back toward the bar. "That little lady over there said it might be OK if I came over." His words flowed in an easy Jamaican rhythm.

I glanced over at Rosa who smiled and stopped clearing the bar long enough to give me a thumbs-up. I gestured toward the other seat, and he managed to slide in, but it was a tight fit.

"I don't think booths are made for linebackers," he said, laughing, as he shifted the table a few inches in my direction. "Name's Xavier, by the way. And yours is Nadia, according to the little lady over there. I just wanted to come over and make sure you were OK after your little run-in out there with Sterling."

I realized then that he must have been one of the students I'd seen congregated near the doorway as I was leaving the courtyard.

"So, you know Professor Sterling, do you?"

He nodded. "All too well, I'm afraid. I actually work for him in the lab."

I made a face and took a bite of cake. "Sorry to hear that."

Xavier laughed. "I knew there was gonna be trouble when I saw you walk over. The courtyard is where Sterling holds all of his screaming matches. I considered saving you, but I wanted to see if you were as tough as you looked. What was the book you gave him?"

"Just something I thought he should read. We'll see if he takes me up on it." I took a sip of cocoa. "So, can I ask you a question since you work with him?"

Xavier said I could.

"This work you're doing in the lab right now, and the cells you've found, do you have any reason to believe they're tied to psychic abilities?"

This time, Xavier's laugh could be heard a few tables away.

"Sorry," he said. "I wasn't laughing at you. It's just that Sterling has some pretty strong opinions about that type of thing. Might fire me on the spot if I even used those words in his lab. He does have a friend who works on that kind of thing though. He comes to the lab sometimes ... was there a few weeks ago. Name's Jakob Fairheart, I think."

I told Xavier that I already knew Jakob, which seemed to interest him.

In fact, for the rest of the evening—until Les Choux closed—psychic ability was our main topic of conversation. We exchanged numbers before we left, and he promised to keep me updated on any progress they made in the lab.

When I got back home, I had an email from Jakob.

My dearest Nadia,

I spoke with Sterling this evening and told him I was very disappointed with the way he handled your discussion. He may be reaching out again soon. He said you gave him your book. I'm not sure that was a good idea, but I seriously doubt he'll read it. Wish I could be there, but my plane departs in ten minutes. Please just be careful about what you say if you speak with him again before I'm back.

All my best,
Jakob

CHAPTER 23

The Past
Age Forty-One

Sterling called a week later. He asked if I'd meet him on campus again, this time at Stan's, a local pizza shop. He said he'd talked with Jakob and promised to be on better behavior this time. He even said he'd buy me a slice of pizza if I'd be willing to come and speak with him again.

When I got there, he was standing outside, wearing the same blue ski jacket as before. This time, though, he actually offered a smile as he held the door open for me. Inside, there was no line, just a long counter covered with every type of pizza imaginable. A massive man stood behind the counter. He was tall with heavily muscled arms, both covered in a mural of tattoos, his white apron spotless.

"Slices are buy one, get one today, folks," he said in a voice that suited him perfectly. "What can I getcha?"

Sterling asked what he would recommend, and the man pointed to one covered in artichokes and Kalamata olives.

"Momma's favorite," he said, "but only if you like a good dose of garlic."

Sterling looked at me, and I nodded. We told him we'd take two each, and after a quick toss in the oven, they were on our plates and being carried to a table at the back of the shop.

"I know I wasn't exactly on my best behavior last time we talked," Sterling said, taking a seat. "I suppose Jakob told you he gave me hell for being so confrontational?"

I smiled and placed my plate on the table. "He might have mentioned it."

Sterling shook an overwhelming amount of hot pepper flakes over his pizza. "Well, if you hang out with me long enough, you'll know that's just how I am. I'm still not all too pleased about any of this, but Jakob is a good friend of mine, so I agreed to listen when he insisted that I hear you out. He apparently thinks we should talk about your experiments. At least, this time, he told me you're a scientist—and not just a writer. What kind of work do you do?"

I explained that I worked at a regional biotechnology company and that my focus was cancer research.

"So, why in the world would a scientist ever want to waste their time and energy writing a novel?"

"I don't think you'd like the answer to that question." I reached for my water. "We should probably just stick to the science."

"Fair enough." He nodded. "You're probably right. I get the impression that you and Jakob see eye to eye on quite a few things, which is actually part of why I wanted to talk to you. I've known Jakob for a long time, Ms. King. I know you haven't, but it doesn't take that long to realize what he's like. He believes in the work he does. Eats, lives, and breathes it, I think. He also knows how I feel about it, although this never stops him from nagging at me. Over the years, I've learned to tune him out when he starts, but when he started talking about your cells this time, *that* caught my attention. When he stopped by that day, he didn't know anything about what I'd just discovered. Do you know why?"

I shook my head.

"I didn't tell him what I'd found because I knew what he'd think, and I knew I'd get one of his little speeches. I knew he'd try to twist what we were seeing in the lab to match his receptor theory. I've been hearing about that one for years—ever since Evelyn died—but the main reason I didn't tell him about my most recent work is because I didn't want to get his hopes up." Sterling looked at me with true concern in his eyes. "Ms. King, I don't know if you realize this or not, but your book hit Jakob very hard. I don't know what's in there, but I can tell you this, I think it's exactly what he's always wanted to hear, and now that he knows about what I've found, I think he's mixing your book with reality. I'm actually worried about him.

"When Evelyn died, he became more determined than ever to prove his theories. Of course, we all hate to lose someone like that, but what Jakob doesn't understand is that there's no talking to someone after they die—no matter how much you might want to. Dead is dead, right? Am I pissed that your book talks about my discovery? Yes, I am. But what upsets me more is the fact that Jakob now has some kind of hope that these cells of mine are identical to the ones in your novel, that they could be what he's been looking for all this time. He needs to stop talking about your cells as if they're real. He needs to stop thinking that my work is somehow going to help him talk with Evelyn again."

"So, why am I here?" I asked. "My book is already out there. It's not like I can take it back."

"Obviously." Sterling folded his hands on the table. "But if I do the experiment from chapter 17, and it doesn't work, well, then, Jakob will have to realize we're not on the same page, won't he?"

"And what if you do the experiment in chapter 17—and it does work?" I knew this was risky to ask, but couldn't help it.

"If I do the experiment in chapter 17 and it works, I don't think that necessarily proves Jakob's theory either, right? I only gave it a quick review, but that experiment, as far as I can tell with my limited expertise in your field of research, could prove a lot of things. Who knows, it might even support my own theory, but I'd need your opinion on that. As you can probably tell from my papers, Ms. King, cells aren't exactly my specialty. They seem to be yours though. I did look you up. More than twenty scientific papers to your name. Not bad." He took a drink of his soda. "My entire career up to this point has involved living, breathing animals, not cells. Now that my work has come down to the cellular level, I'm at a loss, and I could use your help."

"So, what are you saying?"

"I'm saying that I hope the two of us, together, can talk some sense into Jakob by figuring out what these cells really are."

"Are you asking me to join your lab?"

"That's what it sounds like to me. So, what do you say?"

I wasn't sure if I should take him up on the offer or not. He wanted me to help him disprove my own theory. But what if the opposite happened?

"Well?" he asked again.

I finished my last bite of pizza.

"I think I need to see the lab first and hear about the project before I make a decision," I said. "So, how about a tour?"

CHAPTER 24

The Past
Age Forty-One

We arrived at the Science Center just as class dismissed. A wave of students emerged from two sets of double doors, both set into the front of a beautiful gray stone building. Huge stained glass windows studded the facade, making the center look more like a church than a research hub.

The interior was just as impressive. An intricate mural spanned the high ceiling. Pink marble floors were buffed to a high shine. On each side of the room, a staircase followed a wide arc to the pillared second-floor balcony. Colored light filtered in through the stained glass, warming every surface it touched.

"Welcome to our home," Sterling said. He pointed to the upstairs balcony. "Our lab is on the second floor."

He led the way. At the top of the stairs, we made a quick right and passed by a circle of chairs, each filled with a student actively typing on his or her laptop. We continued through a door marked "Staff Only."

"I've been working with chimps for almost fifteen years now," Sterling explained. "We have about five on site at the moment, but none are up to Einstein's caliber." He turned and looked at me. "I'm sure you remember him from my papers?"

"How could I forget a chimp named Einstein?"

"True." Sterling nodded. "Anyway, he's been our driver here for a while … learned a ton in such a short amount of time. That's why these past few weeks have been so hard for me."

"What's happened these past few weeks?" I asked, following him into a narrow corridor.

Sterling stopped in the middle of the hallway. "Jakob didn't tell you?" I shook my head.

"Einstein's on life support ... has been for a few weeks now. He had a significant stroke, which is why I'm so set on figuring out what these cells are." He turned and pushed through another set of doors on our right and into a hallway more like the ones I was used to. Square fiberglass tiles covered the floor, a drab mix of cream and pale green, and the walls were painted an equally dull beige.

"But there was another chimp that showed promise, wasn't there?" I asked.

Sterling nodded. "That was Zena. Unlike Einstein, she was born and raised in captivity, pretty sickly from day one and a pretty slow learner ... that is, until Einstein arrived."

"Einstein wasn't born in captivity?"

Sterling shook his head. "We found him lying in the road in Tanzania as we were on our way back to the facility one day. We were over there doing a field study. We weren't sure what was wrong with him. We threw him in the Jeep, took him back to camp, and after a quick exam, realized he'd just suffered a heart attack. He was about four years old. Luckily, a guy on the team knew of someone back here in the States doing transplant research, and we brought him back. They performed the surgery, and we all reaped the benefits."

There was a clang of metal on metal from one of the open doors on our left. I stepped up beside Sterling and peered in. A chimp was sliding a metal cup along the bars of a giant floor-to-ceiling cage. The cage was outfitted with a hammock and plenty of toys.

A woman in a white lab coat stood next to it. She was peeling a banana.

"That chimp there is Gracie," Sterling said. "Our newest addition. She can get a bit rowdy at mealtime."

"What about Einstein? What was he like?" I asked. "I know chimps can be a bit unpredictable, can't they? Plus, it's not like he was used to being around humans. Was he aggressive ... at all?"

"Aggressive? No. Einstein was just the opposite," Sterling said, continuing down the hall. "When we approached him in the road, he actually reached his arms out to us. Nobody knew what to think. He was weak but a big boy at the time. And as you said, chimps can be unpredictable, so we were very wary. Once we got him on the truck though, he never gave us any reason to worry. Not that day or any other. He actually seemed to enjoy human contact. The only times he ever got upset was when he was left alone. That's why we eventually moved him into our constant observation room with Zena."

At the end of the hall, I followed Sterling into what I assumed was the observation room he'd just mentioned. On the far side, near the big windows, stood two very large cages. They were outfitted with ropes and tire swings, but no chimps. Off to the left, two desks had been arranged so that their front edges were touching. The shelves that lined the walls held neat rows of binders and books. Two doors branched off the main room on either side, and the one on the right hung open, revealing more cages. The one on the left, behind the desks, was closed.

In the back of the lab, a man and woman were huddled over a computer, both of them facing away from us, pointing at something on the screen. The woman tapped the man on the shoulder, and when he turned to face her, she spoke to him using her hands. Once she'd finished, they both turned to face us.

"Nadia, I'd like you to meet two of our crew, Mary and Paul. Mary, here, taught the rest of us sign language, so she's the expert. She can also read lips, so be careful. Can't get anything past this one."

Mary slapped Sterling's arm playfully. Her shoulder-length, frizzy blonde hair stood out at every angle, framing a pretty face. She was a tiny woman with delicate features. If I had to guess, I'd say she was in her early thirties.

Sterling pointed at the man on her right. "Paul, here, only pretends to know what he's doing."

"Thanks, Sterling," Paul said, offering a hand complete with black nails and skull rings. His pale arm, poking out of a black T-shirt, seemed almost too long for his body. He had a beautiful smile, his perfectly white teeth accentuated by a thick layer of black lipstick.

"Paul and Mary, this is Nadia King," Sterling said. "She's here to see what we've been working on. I was just telling her about Einstein." He looked at Paul. "She asked if he was aggressive."

Paul actually laughed. "Definitely not a word I'd use to describe Einstein. He was a sweetheart." Paul elbowed Mary. She watched him while he spoke. "Remember that time I was in here super late—and Einstein got out of his cage?"

Mary put a hand over her mouth and giggled.

"Scary at the time," Paul said to me, "but looking back, it's funny. It was like one o'clock in the morning, and I was at my desk. Einstein was over there in his cage." He pointed toward the other room. "I had my headphones on, jammin' out to Iron Maiden, when all of a sudden, I felt this tap on my shoulder. I whipped around, and Einstein was squatting on the floor beside my chair. Talk about a scare. This wasn't long after he arrived, so we didn't have a lot of experience with him yet. I don't know if you know it or not, but chimps can be pretty nasty when they want to be—and Einstein was a big boy. I literally froze. Had no idea what to do. Next thing I know, Einstein holds out his hand, and there's the padlock from his cage, draped over one of those big, long hairy fingers of his. Bugger figured out a way to undo it." Paul laughed. "He just kind of sat there looking at me until I took it from him. Once I took it, he turned around, waddled over to Zena's cage, and put his arms through the bars. It took her a minute—she was probably as scared as I was—but she finally went over to him. I wasn't sure what was gonna happen. I think we were both about shitting a brick."

Sterling cleared his throat.

"Sorry," Paul said. "Anyway, after that, the two of them became best buds. Once the two of them started hanging out, we started seeing improvements in Zena's mood ... and in her health."

"Like I was saying," Sterling explained, "Zena was a pretty slow learner before Einstein arrived. Once we saw the effect he had on her, though, we started keeping them together for everything, even during sign lessons. At first, we worried it might be a distraction, but then we saw that Zena actually learned more when the two of them were together."

Paul nodded. "At first, we thought it was just because Einstein calmed her down. Zena used to get pretty agitated when she couldn't understand something, but Einstein never let that happen. Even before Zena got visibly flustered, Einstein would put his arm around her and stroke the top of her head until she figured out the word. He'd even clap after she got it, just like we did."

"Within three months of Einstein's arrival," Sterling added, "he and Zena were at the same comprehension level. Zena took two years to learn her first thirty signs. In a total of three months, Einstein learned those same thirty—plus twenty more that we taught them both. It was pretty incredible."

Paul spun his chair to face us. "Of course, this brought a whole new set of questions to the table. First off, what would happen to Zena's rate of learning if we went back to separate lessons? In other words, could she learn new information more quickly now on her own—or did she still need Einstein there while she learned it? Second, would Zena try to teach Einstein any new words that we taught her while she was alone?"

"We had a hard time separating them at first," Sterling said. "They'd gotten so used to being together."

"Yeah," Paul said. "The first week was rough. Zena took a lot longer to focus once Einstein was in the other room, but once she realized she got to see him after she learned a new word, she started learning pretty quickly. The first word she learned on her own was *truck*. To test my second idea, we left the toy truck in her cage after the lesson, and then we brought Einstein in and left the room." Paul pointed to several cameras mounted near the ceiling. "These cameras monitor the cages when no one is here in case of an emergency. We used the videos from that night to see what happened after we left." He raised his eyebrows and smiled. "It was pretty cool. First, Zena showed Einstein the truck, and then she signed the word. When he repeated it, she clapped her hands. She taught him just like we did. We did it again a week later with a doll and got the same result. Then, one day, we made a mistake. When we were done with Zena's lesson, we accidentally put the new prop back in the toy box over there instead of leaving it in Zena's cage."

Paul pointed to the box in the corner. The lid was up. It was filled with everything imaginable. Plastic fruit. Balls in every color. Toy trucks. Dolls. Blankets.

"The videos from that night are kind of freaky," Paul said. "We watched them a couple times the next day to try to make some sense out of what we were seeing."

"Why?" I asked. "What did they do?"

Sterling grabbed a stool and rolled it over so I could sit down.

"For a few minutes after we brought Einstein back into the room, he just sat there in his cage, looking at Zena like he was waiting for his lesson. That's when we noticed that there was nothing in her cage, no prop for her to use to teach him the new word. We almost turned off the video, thinking it was gonna be a bust, but then Mary, here, held up a finger. She was watching the screen. Something had her attention. Einstein and Zena sat there staring at each other for a really long time, both of them perfectly still. For a minute, I actually thought the cameras had frozen, but then I noticed the cheerleader's pom-pom in the toy box. The heater vent was right above it, and the strands were moving.

"All of a sudden, Zena leaned forward, tapped her forehead, and then signed the new word that we'd just taught her. Einstein watched her, but he didn't move. She did this a few times, and they'd just stare at each other in between. Then Einstein clapped his hands. He stood up and made the sign, which is no biggie, right? He was just imitating her. Then Zena pointed at the toy box. That's when Einstein did the most amazing thing.

"He reached through the bars of his cage, did his little magic trick to remove the lock, and made his way over to the toy box. We could only see his back while he was rooting through it, but when he turned around, he was holding up a pair of green gloves. Zena looked at him and clapped her hands.

"The gloves were the prop we'd used, the prop we forgot to leave in Zena's cage. Mary and I just looked at each other. I mean, think about it, how did Einstein know what she wanted him to find? Sure, he could mimic the sign, but he'd never seen the gloves to make the connection. You can't teach a chimp a sign for something without showing them the prop. It's not like Zena could be like, 'Hey, go look for this thing called a glove, it fits over your fingers, you wear them in the winter to stay warm, they're green, and this is how you make the sign.' It was almost like she must have sent him some kind of mental picture of the gloves or something. That's the only possible explanation."

Some sort of telepathy, I thought. *Communication without words.*

"Which is why we moved toward fMRI, functional magnetic resonance imaging," Sterling said. "Neuroimaging tracks blood flow and can show us what's going on in the brain. With fMRI, we can pinpoint the area of brain activity to within millimeters."

I looked at him and nodded. "My scientists used fMRI, as well, so I'm familiar with how it works."

Paul looked down at his hands.

Sterling apparently didn't know this, judging by the look on his face. "Well, your fake scientists might have used traditional fMRI, but I'll bet they didn't use the same device we do to get the scans." He looked at Paul. "Where's Curt?"

Paul cocked his head toward the door on the left. "He's in the back."

Sterling left the room, and Paul leaned in closer. "I heard about your book on the radio a while ago. All of us here have read it. Cool stuff. Just so you know, though, when Xavier told us you were coming, he said we shouldn't talk about it. Said Sterling would probably kill us if we did."

Sterling returned a few minutes later with a very tall man who looked to be in his late twenties. He had sandy blond hair and narrow, slightly hunched shoulders.

Xavier followed them in with a large cardboard box in his hands. He nodded in my direction before going through the door on the other side of the room.

Sterling stopped in front of us and clapped Curt on the shoulder. "Nadia, this is Curt Brannigan, our engineer. I told him you were interested in seeing his helmet."

Curt gave a shy smile, and then without saying a word, he handed me what appeared to be a miniature yellow bike helmet. My arms broke out in gooseflesh. The one in my novel had been blue.

The helmet was light and padded inside with what appeared to be lambswool. A chin strap dangled below. A device that resembled a kitchen timer was attached to the back, its five buttons concealed under a locked shield of plexiglass. In the front, a set of goggles had been permanently attached, the rims shaped like hearts and decorated with a pink sparkly material, like the pink aluminum foil they wrap Easter candy in.

I ran my finger over the glasses. "What's this?" I asked, pretending not to know.

Curt's face flushed. "It's a remote device for measuring neural activity, sort of a mix between your traditional fMRI and the electrodes used for MEG." His voice was surprisingly deep. He talked slowly, probably so that I could follow. "The interior is lined with electrodes that monitor brain waves. That way, there's close contact with the scalp at all times. Less chance of error in signals, especially for chimps. The box on the back records their brain activity and relays the information to a wireless system.

"As you probably know," Curt explained, "in a traditional MRI unit, any type of movement can distort the images and prevent accurate readings. You can't really tell a chimp to sit still. That's why I designed this." Curt pointed at the helmet in my hands. "I tried to make it a little fun too. The chimps love the glasses. Sometimes they don't even want to take off the helmet. Over there is a picture of Einstein wearing it."

He pointed at the framed eight-by-ten photo hanging on the wall near the workstation. I walked over to get a better look. In it, Einstein was sitting in a child's yellow lawn chair. He was wearing the helmet and holding a banana. His right foot rested in the grass, his left was propped up on the seat, and his long toes were curled underneath the chair's front edge. His eyes were hidden behind the glittery hearts, and his face was plastered with an enormous grin, his top lip flipped back to show off a row of intimidating teeth.

"That one you're holding is adjustable," Curt said, "but I'm working on making custom helmets for each animal. They're most sensitive when they have a snug fit."

"So, these helmets transmit the signals to a computer?" I asked.

Curt flicked a hand over his shoulder and pointed toward a computer workstation in the opposite corner of the room. A huge flat-screen hung on the wall behind it.

"Yeah, the station is set up with an image processor," Curt said. "The processor reconstructs and aligns all of the data by comparing each image to common coordinates. The final MR image comes up on this screen over here." He tapped the monitor behind him.

I glanced at Sterling. If he knew that all of this—from the helmet, to the data processing, hell, even down to the details of the room—was sitting in my novel, I wasn't sure what he would do. I didn't have the heart to tell Curt that my helmets had one advantage over his. Mine offered much better spatial resolution. This was one thing I'd researched. Sterling's device could show differences of millimeters, but the ones my scientists used could detect individual brain cells. Like I'd said to Sterling in the courtyard that day, when you write fiction, science knows no boundaries. Everything is possible. If you can think it, you can have it.

"Kid's a genius," Sterling said.

Curt lowered his head and put his hands in his pockets.

"Yes, he is," I said, handing the helmet back to Curt. "You do nice work."

Curt smiled and walked toward the screen. "I'll show you the output ... if you want."

Paul and Mary stayed where they were, but Sterling and I joined Curt near the workstation. Here, there was a full-sized scientific poster on the wall. In the bottom right-hand corner was a smaller picture of Einstein in his lawn chair. Four larger images filled the rest of the space, each one showing a light gray sagittal slice of the brain positioned over a black background. The orientation of the brain was as if you were looking at someone's profile. This "someone" was clearly a chimp given the shape of the skull, most likely Einstein given that his photo was included in the arrangement.

I leaned in to look at the images more closely. Overlaying the gray brain tissue were bright yellow, orange, and red blobs in various sizes, the colors overlapping and bleeding into each other as if they were put there by a child who didn't have full control over his or her crayons. From my research, I knew that the different shades of color indicated various levels of brain activity. Their placement indicated which part of the brain was active when the scan was taken.

Sterling stepped in closer to explain, tapping each image with the cap of a pen as he did. "In this first one, Einstein was looking at picture books, so there's activation in the brain's occipital lobe. Here, when he listened to music, we saw activity in the auditory cortex of the temporal lobe. This one here shows the areas of activation when he's making noises. And finally, this one here shows partial activity in the parietal lobe when Einstein and Zena were signing."

"Of course," Curt added, "these images are just a portion of the full panel collected during each session. The helmet acquires hundreds of images from all three planes. The processor integrates them all and generates a full-activation map."

I pointed to the yellow smear on the last frame. "When you say there was partial activity in the parietal lobe when they were signing, does that mean there was more than just this one activation cluster?"

Curt said, "The other signal isn't captured on those images. This poster was only used to demonstrate proof of concept, to show that my helmet worked. I have the other images saved though … if you want to see them."

I nodded. *I certainly did.*

Curt started bringing up files. As he punched at the keyboard, a series of images appeared along the top of the screen, four sagittal sections of Einstein's brain, the ones from the poster. When he hit another key, a second row of images appeared directly underneath. These were coronal sections, views of the brain from a different angle, not a profile, but as if you were looking at the subject face-to-face. A faint outline of the neck and ears surrounded the wrinkled brain in the center.

Curt highlighted the row of coronal sections.

The series showed a progression. The brain image on the left side of the screen had very little color, but as you moved to the right, more yellow appeared.

Curt pointed to a small yellow blob on the first image, on the very left edge of the brain, and said, "Here's that signal in the parietal lobe, like you saw in the poster over there. But, as you can see in this view, we also have this big vertical streak of signal right up the middle here."

He ran his finger up and down the screen, tracing a thin line of bright orange, the color indicating that this signal was stronger than the activation in the parietal areas.

"You can't see this cluster on the other view because you're looking at the brain from the wrong angle. You need to be looking at it straight on to see it. What's interesting is that this signal down the middle got stronger the more we worked with Zena and Einstein." Curt turned and looked at me. "I have the entire activation maps on file if you're interested in seeing them."

"Maybe later," I said, my eyes still fixed on the screen. *Definitely later.*

Curt nodded and went back to explaining. He shook his head. "At first, I thought it was a glitch in the system, you know, maybe something gone wrong with one of the probes on the back of the helmet, but after a couple of repeats, we saw that the signal was reproducible. Even different helmets gave us the same result. Also, Einstein's signal was always a lot stronger than Zena's."

I stepped closer to the screen. The first two images only showed activation in the language centers of the parietal lobe, seen as two diffuse blobs of color, like yellow balloons floating on either side of the head, a little above the level of the ears. The two images on the right, however, clearly showed three distinct activation clusters. The parietal clusters still resembled a child's artwork, diffuse yellow blobs with wavy edges, but the bright orange signal down the middle was much more defined. This crisp line started at the level of the cerebellum, near the top of the neck, and divided the brain into two distinct halves, left and right.

Paul joined us at the screen. "Two months after we first started seeing that weird dividing line, Zena and Einstein started crafting whole sentences in sign. They used words we hadn't taught them, but words that Mary and I probably used every day. Einstein's signal was always stronger than Zena's, but Zena's signal definitely increased over time."

"Once we saw the trend," Sterling added, crossing his arms in front of him, "we had to admit that the signal was real. There's some literature to suggest that activation in the cerebellum can be associated with language tasks, but it's not common."

Curt cleared the screen and brought up a video. It showed two chimps, each of them wearing a helmet. They were in a room by themselves, one inside a cage, one outside. They were facing each other. I don't know sign language, but it looked like they were having a full-fledged conversation. On each side of the screen, a few inches beyond the edge of the video feed, a 3D brain rotated in cyberspace.

"These floating brains," Curt said, pointing to them, "are in real time. They show the integrated signals recorded by the helmets while Einstein and Zena are signing in the video."

He froze the screen, and the brains stopped mid-spin.

"When we first started noticing the signal, it was just this one linear tract of cells, one thin orange line right up the back of the head." Curt ran a finger over the traces of orange on each of the floating brains. "Paul called it the *Curious Tract* in the beginning, or CT for short. The name stuck, so that's what we still call it now."

Curt brought up another image.

"After a couple of weeks, though, the activation clusters changed. That single line started to branch. Pretty soon, it started looking more like a tree. You can see it here." Curt pointed. "The center line still runs up from the cerebellum near the neck, to the pons, to the ventricle, even all the way up to the auditory centers. The diagonal branches, here, stretch out to the visual cortex. The activation hits nearly every sensory area."

Curt cleared the screen and brought up a single coronal slice, one from somewhere deep within the center of the brain. The gray tissue was overlaid with a glowing orangish-red tree, one that extended upward and branched out over the regions he'd just described.

Seeing it literally took my breath away. I swallowed hard. Somewhere in chapter 10 of my novel was a very detailed description of what I was seeing in front of me. "And you think this activation is in response to sign language?"

Sterling opened his mouth to answer, but before he could say anything, Xavier's voice called out from behind us, "Hey Sterling, could you give me a hand?"

I turned toward Xavier and found him looking at Paul. Xavier nodded and then shot me a smile.

Sterling got up. "I'll be right back. Hold that thought."

As soon as Sterling left the room, Paul scooted his chair close to mine.

"Nadia, there's no way that signal is in response to sign," Paul said as he looked at Curt. "Watch the video again. You're about to see something way freaky."

Curt ran the video again, but this time, in slow motion.

Paul narrated as I watched. "Look ... when Einstein and Zena are signing, there's only activity in the parietal lobe, the language centers, which is exactly what we'd expect. This branching signal in the back only comes up when they're pausing, when they're just sitting there staring at each other. Now, keep in mind, there's always a delay between the task and the onset of a signal with fMRI, but it's only three to five seconds. Plus, Curt's helmet is way better than that. Their pauses, like this one that's coming up, are all about a minute long. Watch ... the CT goes orange the entire time. When they start signing again, the signal fades. Something's going on while they're just sitting there."

Mary tapped Paul's arm to get his attention.

Paul translated as her hands danced.

"Paul and I did another run with just Einstein," she signed. "When Paul and I were signing with him, the parietal areas lit up. When we stopped signing, and he was just sitting there, the scans were blank. No orange at all. The CT activity isn't associated with sign language, but Paul and I think it may be associated with another type of nonverbal communication, one we don't currently know much about."

"Xavier said you know Jakob, right?" Paul asked.

I nodded.

"He was here one day talking to Sterling. When Sterling left to get on a call, we pulled Jakob aside and showed him this video. Our theory," Paul said, looking at me, "matches yours, Nadia. We think what's lighting up is some kind of psychic receptor. We think we're detecting areas of the brain used for some sort of telepathy. Chimps may lack the anatomy they need for spoken language, but they're definitely communicating."

"And what does Sterling make of all this?" I asked.

"I'm not sure Sterling knows what to think. He claims the tract is made of stem cells, which could be true, even with our assumptions. The difference is that Sterling thinks they can differentiate and heal the brain after stroke. I don't know if Sterling told you, but Einstein had a stroke a few weeks ago. Honestly, I think Sterling's just grasping at straws.

It's what he wants to believe, and it's what he wants us to prove. Like I said, these cells may very well be stem cells, but I doubt they're the kind Sterling's thinking of."

Curt said, "Paul thinks better resolution in the images would let us get a closer look at what's going on, so I started working on a way to increase the sensitivity of our helmet. I coupled the MRI with an oscillator to enhance the signal."

So, Curt is already creating a more powerful version of the helmet—just like I had for my novel.

"When it's done," Curt said, "we should be able to see individual cells. There's just one problem."

"What's that?" I asked.

Paul said, "Not long after Curt started working on this new helmet, Zena suffered a large-scale seizure. She died a few days later. Einstein was absolutely devastated. He refused to leave his cage. He wanted everything of Zena's in there with him, and he refused to take off the helmet. That's when things got even stranger."

Curt swiveled around on his chair and punched a few keys on the keyboard, bringing up a video from the surveillance cameras. It showed Einstein alone in his cage. Zena's cage was empty. Einstein was wearing the helmet and was holding a pillow across his chest, presumably Zena's because he was sitting on his. Scattered around him were all of the props. A 3D brain floated next to the video on the screen. A bright orange-red tree was glowing within it.

"Now remember," Paul said, "we typically saw the CT signal when Zena and Einstein were in the room together and when they weren't signing. This video is from the night she died. Like I said, he wouldn't let us take the helmet from him, and he got pretty aggressive when we tried, which was completely unlike him. We figured maybe it just reminded him of Zena, so we let him keep it, but honestly ..." Paul looked toward the door on the other side of the room, maybe wanting to be sure Sterling hadn't come back, "I think he wanted to keep it on to show us something. Watch him."

The video continued to play. In it, Einstein tapped his forehead, and the tree glowed. His hands danced.

"What's he saying?" I asked.

Curt paused the video.

Paul looked at me and gave an answer I hadn't expected. "He's saying, 'I hear you. Don't be afraid.' He keeps saying it over and over."

Chills coursed up my arms. *Is it possible? Do we actually have proof that Einstein and Zena had been using telepathy to communicate while she was alive, and now, here, in this video, proof that they were continuing to communicate after she was dead?*

Curt said, "We have a video from the night before Einstein took a turn for the worse, too, the night before Sterling put him on life support. The brain activation looks very similar to what you just saw here. He just says something else at the end."

Paul answered before I even had the chance to ask what Einstein said. "He says, 'Don't be afraid. I'm coming. I'll be there soon.'"

Paul leaned back in his chair, hands clasped behind his neck. "The power of the mind, baby." He shook his head. "I heard once that the human brain weighs about three pounds, but contributes to one-fifth of our total energy expenditure every day. What do you suppose it's doing with all those extra calories?"

I started to say something, but Sterling walked in and said, "Don't you start with that power of the mind thing, Paul." He walked over to one of the desks and shuffled through some papers. "You work *here*, remember, not with Jakob. If you want, I can fire your ass, and you can go over there and work with him. You just let me know."

As Sterling continued his search, Xavier leaned into the room, one hand against each side of the doorframe. I saw him exchange a glance with Paul.

Paul shook his head, using only the slightest movement.

Sterling grabbed the paper he needed and joined Xavier back at the door. "I'm going to leave you in their hands for a little while longer, Ms. King, if that's OK," Sterling said. "I've got some business to take care of upstairs. I'll find you when I'm done?"

I told him that would be fine.

When Sterling left, Xavier rolled a chair over to where we were sitting.

"So, what does everyone think?" I asked. "I'm not sure I understand how Sterling has come to his conclusions given what I've seen today."

"We all think your ideas make a lot more sense."

Even Curt nodded at this.

"We've been talking about your book quite a bit since I saw you at the restaurant," Xavier said. "Obviously, only when Sterling isn't around. Ever since we started seeing the CT in the scans, we've had questions. The four of us tried to investigate a little on our own without causing too much of a stir. We've been collaborating with a few other primate groups. We let them use our helmets and have collected quite of bit of data. It looks like all of the apes who were rescued from the wild show mild CT activity. Those born in captivity have lower levels, or none at all. Exactly what you would expect, right? It would make perfect sense for animals born in the wild to use something like telepathy to communicate. They'd need it for survival, to coordinate hunting or food gathering. Those born in captivity wouldn't need it as much, but I would expect them to still have the anatomy to support it, like Zena did, just in case they ever got the chance to use it."

"Did Sterling have anyone collect brain tissue when Zena died?" I asked.

Xavier pointed at a freezer. "We've got fixed tissue blocks and slides from the CT area, cerebrospinal fluid too."

"But no live cells?" I asked.

"We tried to grow some," Paul said, "but it didn't work very well. We learned pretty fast that cell culture wasn't our specialty. We brought up some equipment from the basement, borrowed some materials from another lab upstairs, but things got contaminated pretty quickly."

Xavier pulled me into the next room and showed me the equipment they'd used. A rusty incubator sat in the corner. A heavily pitted biosafety cabinet stood next to it, looking far from sterile. It was no wonder their cells hadn't survived.

Xavier ruffled my hair. "This is why we need you."

"What did you do with the slides?" I asked. "There must be something that makes Sterling think they're stem cells. He's not stupid."

"We stained them for surface markers," Xavier said. "That's what initially made Sterling think they're radial glia. He knows that kind of cell isn't typically found in the adult brain, but that's what the slides showed."

"Well," I said, "sometimes research finds things in the most unexpected places. That's why we collect the data first and analyze later—and set no expectations. Maybe they are radial glia. Maybe it's just that no one has ever looked for them there."

"Now, that's the kind of conversation I like to walk in on." It was Sterling. He cruised into the back room with Paul and Mary following close behind. "Real science, none of that hocus-pocus bullshit. And Nadia's right. These cells are something new, so we can't simply expect them to fit current descriptions. We're on the verge of something big here. I can feel it." He tipped his head toward the door. "Let's go up to my office, Ms. King."

Sterling's office was on the third floor. He took a seat behind his desk, turned on a lamp in the corner, and gestured toward the chairs in front. I took the one closest to me. The first thing I noticed was the framed picture on his desk, angled so that anyone sitting where I was could see it. *Wife and daughter, maybe?* The two of them were leaning in, cheeks touching, huge smiles on their faces, a bright blue sky behind them.

"So, what do you think?" Sterling asked.

His question seemed to come from a distance. My mind was elsewhere, wondering how all of this had happened, how his work was so in line with my novel. It seemed impossible that I was actually sitting there.

"Will you be joining us?" he asked.

Of course, I wanted to accept immediately, but I didn't want to sound too eager—plus it didn't make sense for me to join just yet. "Unfortunately, I think we'll have to wait and see what happens with Einstein first, and go from there," I said. "Without live cells, I can't try any of the experiments from my book, so I won't be much help."

Sterling looked down at his desk.

"Sorry," I said, realizing that even someone like Sterling had feelings. "That came out harsh. I'm just saying that maybe you should give this some time. If Einstein recovers, you can continue with fMRI and figure everything out that way. If it doesn't look like he's going to recover, then you can call me. If it comes to that, I can certainly help with the in vitro work. Obviously, in the meantime, we can prepare for both scenarios, maybe even try to locate another lab where I can grow the cells if we get them. That old equipment you have downstairs isn't going to work. Plus, you can still play around with the slides you've collected from Zena's CT."

Sterling shook his head. "Look, I know I probably come off as a hard-ass, but Einstein means the world to me. Trust me when I say it's not just the research I'm interested in here. I'd love to get my hands on these cells, but I want Einstein back to health even more."

"You'll know when it's time to make the next move, and people will just need to understand that you're doing it for the right reasons. Let's just be ready in case the worst happens."

Sterling pressed the heels of his palms to his eyes.

"Listen, I know you don't want to hear this right now," I said, "but if you start to see a decline in Einstein's condition, you're going to have to move quickly. Once his heart stops, you'll only have a couple of hours to collect the cells from the CT. We need to get them in culture right away."

Sterling's eyes went to the photo on his desk. "I had to do this before, you know?" He looked at me. "It doesn't get any easier the more you do it."

His eyes were glassy, and I figured Sterling wasn't the type of person who wanted you to see them cry, so I stood to go.

"Take your time," I said. "Do what you need to do. You know where to find me when you need me."

I pulled Sterling's door closed behind me and was surprised to find Xavier waiting in the hall. He was seated on the floor, back propped against the wall, a set of headphones over his ears. His eyes were closed. I tapped his knee with the tip of my boot. He looked up and slid the headphones down around his neck.

The green eyes get me every time, I thought, and I did my best not to look away.

"How did it go in there?" he asked.

"Not too bad," I said. "Are you waiting to talk to him?"

Xavier shook his head. "I've talked to that man enough today. I was actually waiting for you." He stood up, grabbed his backpack from the floor, and slung it over one broad shoulder. "Figured I'd escort our beautiful novelist back to the train station."

This time, I had to look away; otherwise, he'd see me blush.

"It's good that you're here," he said, giving me a gentle hip check before he started down the hall. "This isn't going to be easy for Sterling. He doesn't like not knowing what to do. And if these cells turn out to be anything like the ones in your book ..." Xavier turned and gave me a look. "If that happens, Sterling's gonna lose his shit." He pushed open the stairwell door.

"We can't assume that's what these are," I said. "Seriously, what are the chances?"

Xavier stopped on the stairs, turned back, and shook a finger at me. "You need to stop that. Deep down, you know that's exactly what they are. You just don't want to admit it yet. And you know why you don't want to admit it? Because there's no easy way to explain how you knew to write about them." He spun and continued down the stairs.

We stepped out into the second-floor hallway, and I followed him to the door of the primate lab.

"You know what my great-grandmother always tells me?" he asked.

I shook my head.

"You need to trust your gut, and if you do that, the whys and hows will work themselves out."

As he said this, a scrawny man in a white lab coat popped out of the lab. He stopped just a few inches in front of me and stood there, pale blue eyes darting back and forth across my face. Bony fingers worked at his top button. His sharp cheekbones and pointy nose matched his jaggy blond hair. His front teeth were far too big. It's awful to say, but he reminded me of a rat.

Xavier put an arm around my waist, and the man took a step back. "Nadia, this is Tom. He works in our lab."

Tom's eyes darted up to meet Xavier's, but then they quickly flicked back to mine. "I heard you talking about the book earlier." His words were spoken so quickly that I nearly missed them. "I read it too, you know?" His head gave a quick jerk. It could have been a nod or a nervous twitch. "You're the author, right?"

I nodded, too caught up in his mannerisms to answer.

"I thought so," he said. "I really liked it." He rubbed at his dry lips with one of those bony hands. "I can talk to ghosts too."

Xavier said, "Tom, where's Bea?"

"In the basement," Tom said. "Pulling a sample for Dr. Fostenau. Want me to show you where?"

"No, thanks, Tom. We'll find her." Xavier steered me around Tom toward yet another set of stairs.

I waved goodbye, but Tom just stood there and watched us go. "He works in your lab?" I asked, once we were out of hearing range.

"He and Bea help take care of the animals," Xavier said. "Bea's wild, but she's harmless. Tom, though, something about him just doesn't give me a good vibe. He lost his wife a few years back, which is sad, but he hasn't been quite right since."

"And why are we looking for Bea?"

"If Einstein passes, she's the one who can help us get the cells. I want you to meet her. Her specialty is autopsies, so we call her Brainy Bea. She's the one who made Zena's slides for us."

At the bottom of the stairs, we stepped into a long basement hallway. A single line of bare bulbs dotted the ceiling along the corridor. Rows of large gray metal drawers lined one wall, floor to ceiling.

I pointed at them. "Are there bodies in those?"

Xavier nodded. "Yup. This basement connects to the hospital," he explained, pointing to the adjoining corridor. "Those drawers are used for temporary storage until they can get around to the autopsies. It's surprising how many Bea does in a day."

"Who's talking about me?" The voice came from around the corner.

The next thing I knew, a squat woman with dark, wiry hair whipped around the corner on our right, wheeling a stainless-steel cart. She was wearing a blue surgical gown and matching Crocs. On the cart was an oblong metal pan. A long autopsy knife lay across the top of it, and as she got closer, I could see a mass of gray tissue inside. Convoluted and slick, it was a brain without a doubt, and human by the size of it.

"Well, speak of the devil," Xavier said.

Bea stopped dead in her tracks. "And, what, may I ask, is a sexy guy like you doing in a dungeon like this?" She turned to me. "And who do we have here? None other than Nadia King, perhaps?"

Word seemed to travel fast. I reached out a hand, but she raised hers in the air, both covered in latex gloves. "Don't want to shake these babies." She wiggled her fingers. "They've been busy."

My eyes went to the pan on her cart.

"Oh, don't mind that," she said, waving her hand over it. "Just something I found along the way." She laughed. "Tom was just down here … in case you were wondering how I knew it was you. Told me you were up in the lab today. Didn't think I'd get a chance to meet you, but here we are. Love the book, by the way." She turned to Xavier. "So, what can I do for ya? You don't ever come down here to see me unless you need something. So, what's the mission this time?"

Bea listened as Xavier told her exactly what we needed when the time came. She said she'd get everything ready. She also offered to keep her eyes peeled for equipment we might be able to use. Her daily rounds took her all over campus. She said if she saw anything up for grabs, she'd let us know.

From the Journal of Nadia King
Age Forty-One

I had a visit from Remmington last night. He pulled up in an old Cadillac, not banana yellow like Gram Marie's, but a glossy black one. He had a visitor with him, which was unusual. He's never brought a visitor before. When he helped her out of the car, I immediately thought of the woman

Diane said she saw in my office window at the house on Braeburn. Her hair was straight and long, stark white. The color added years to her youthful face.

Remmington led her to the start of the cobblestone walkway without an introduction, which I thought was odd as well. She smiled as she passed, and I noticed one small, but not unattractive mole high on her left cheek, something Gram Marie would have called a beauty mark. Apart from the resemblance to my supposed ghost from Braeburn, she also reminded me of someone else, although I can't place who.

Remmington released her hand, and she walked the length of the path on wobbly feet past the edge of the patio, then out into the grass, across the back garden to the low stone wall that surrounds the Baird family's gravestones. Ares followed her.

When I asked Remmington who she was, he said I should call her Ms. Sterling, but he refused to elaborate further. I have no idea if she's related to the professor or not. He asked about our meeting at the Science Center and whether I'd decided to join the lab. I told him the same thing I told Sterling, that it didn't make sense to join just yet.

"The lab needs you," he said. "But Ms. Sterling needs you even more."

Why does everyone keep saying that they need me?

CHAPTER 25

The Past
Age Forty-One

Sterling stood before us. It was a little past five in the evening. His eyes were red, their lids puffy. He stood behind a chair, which he'd placed in the front of the lab, his hands resting on the back of it.

Jakob sat in a chair to Sterling's right. His head was down, and he was staring at his hands, which were clasped between his knees. Curt Brannigan, the mastermind behind the helmet, was leaning against the doorjamb, his shoulders even more slumped than usual, his hands at their customary stations in his pockets. One of his feet traced a wide arc on the floor in front of him.

To Sterling's left sat Mary and Paul, her head leaning on his shoulder. Her eyelids were raw. Her frizzy mass of blonde hair quivered every time she tried to stifle a sob. Paul's arm was around her but seemed to offer little comfort. A few others I'd never met stood in the background, most of them young and likely standing together out of shyness.

Xavier stood beside me, and Tom was nowhere to be seen.

Sterling had called me around noon and asked if I could come in after work for a lab meeting. His voice had been steady and businesslike on the phone, but I knew why he was calling.

I'd phoned Xavier right after we hung up and asked him to find Bea as soon as he could.

Jakob got out of his chair and stood next to Sterling. "We have sad news," Jakob said. "At eleven o'clock this morning, a huge player in Professor Sterling's research … all of your research … passed on.

As most of you know, Einstein has been on life support. After careful consideration, a difficult decision was made. It was time to let go."

Sterling said, "I think all of you here know how much Einstein meant to me. His life has been in my hands since we met. He would have surely died on that road if we hadn't brought him back, so when I made this decision, I could at least take a little comfort in that. I hope he enjoyed his extra time with us as much as we enjoyed our time with him." Sterling's voice cracked, and he took a second to compose himself. "In some ways, Einstein will still be helping us as we shift focus a bit—in ways he couldn't even imagine.

"I wanted to get everyone together here today to say goodbye, but also to share our plans for the lab moving forward. We intend to continue our research on what we've been calling the Curious Tract, a grouping of cells we discovered in Einstein's brain. Our goal is to figure out what this CT really is and what it does. As you all know, Einstein was very fond of his helmet, especially after Zena passed. He's actually been wearing it ever since. I kept it on him, even in the ICU, thinking it might give him a reason to fight his way back. Unfortunately, that just wasn't the case, but we have been collecting images over these past few weeks. The CT cells have been highly active the entire time. The signal remained red until five minutes before the time of death, and then the glow simply faded. It was as if Einstein knew it was time to shut down.

"Once life support was removed, an autopsy was performed. Tissue from the CT was excised and sent off to the histology lab. They prepared tissue blocks and microscope slides."

Sterling looked at me. "I sent a few of the frozen sections to a lab on the third floor for laser microdissection. I flew in one of Brannigan's old associates, Dr. McCulvey, to do the work. He was one of the authors on the paper you gave me, Ms. King, apparently an expert in the procedure. He should have cells for you by tomorrow morning."

Laser microdissection is extremely tricky. With it, a highly skilled technician can extract individual cells from a frozen section of tissue. Scientists in my novel used the procedure. The article I'd given Sterling was from a prestigious scientific journal, and McCulvey was indeed an expert. I'd seen laser microdissection performed by him once in a hospital pathology lab long before writing about it in my book. He'd hosted a demo session where the group sat around a large rectangular table fitted with microscopes. These microscopes were all connected in series with fiber-optic cables. McCulvey, lead pathologist at the time, sat at the head of the table and performed the dissection on the main scope while the rest of us simply observed what he was doing through our own eyepieces. The high-powered laser he used worked like a jigsaw, carving out individual cells from a frozen liver specimen. The tissue was frozen so that the heat generated by the laser didn't destroy the cells. Once excised, the cells were immediately placed into a petri dish that contained a nutrient-rich broth.

When done correctly, freezing doesn't kill cells. They can remain frozen for years and still be viable upon thaw. Once placed in the broth, though, cell growth resumes, and the cells divide just as they do in the body. Kept under the right conditions, the dish can fill with exact replicas, clones, of the original cell in just a few days.

Sterling had moved quickly. I could only hope that Brannigan had secured the device we needed for the first experiment.

When Sterling dismissed the group, I found Brannigan at his desk.

"I have the machine in the back," he said, before I even had a chance to ask. "You want to see?"

"Have you adjusted it yet?"

"All done."

Brannigan was indeed a genius. In the back room of the lab, a new biosafety cabinet had been installed to replace the rusted one. The glass sash in the front was lowered. Inside, a fluorescent light shone down on the smooth stainless-steel surfaces. The interior workspace was nearly six feet wide and about two feet deep. The motor hummed with an efficient purr as its interior air circulated through a system of HEPA filters designed to maintain the sterile environment inside.

In the center of the workspace was the machine I'd asked Brannigan to find. It looked exactly as I'd imagined it would when I wrote about it. Its square gray base was no bigger than a toaster. On it were two black dials, a number pad, and a digital display screen like the one on an alarm clock. Two electrical cords extended from its right side, one yellow, the other black. The black cord was plugged into the electrical socket inside the cabinet. Attached to the end of the yellow cord was a frosted spiral bulb about the size of a closed fist. The collar of the bulb had been mounted on a chemistry stand, basically a vertical metal rod set into a sturdy base.

The device was a multi-wave oscillator, an updated version of the Rife machine, a contraption most often used in alternative medicine. Newer models are used in ultra-frequency therapy, which is supposed to strengthen the immune system by producing high-energy waves. The waves are delivered to the patient by placing the spiral bulb in close contact with the skin over the area of interest. Treatment is painless. These energy waves cause cells to vibrate, but only the cells with the same baseline vibration as the one generated by the oscillator. The Rife is typically used to help with healing, but this isn't how we planned to use it.

For our application, we wouldn't be dealing with a body. Our target would be inside a petri dish. Thus, a microscope had been placed beside the apparatus, its viewing stage set to the same height as the frosted spiral bulb. This is where the dish of cells, the ones extracted from Einstein's brain would be placed.

Our setup required one further modification. Straight off the market, the machine offers frequencies in the range of ten thousand to twenty thousand hertz. Our machine, modified by Brannigan, would offer a much wider range.

From the Journal of Nadia King
Age Forty-One

I reviewed the experiment from chapter 17 earlier today. I want to make sure I get it right when we perform it in the lab. Brannigan is still playing with his device, making sure it's ready.

Jakob and I met tonight over dinner to go over a few other things as well. He told me that if this first experiment works, he and Rowan are planning to fund any research that follows. There's no way we can let Sterling know that Rowan's involved—or he'll start questioning our motives. I think Jakob honestly believes that my cells and Sterling's are one and the same. I wish I shared the same confidence.

Jakob has also decided that we can't continue this project in Sterling's current lab. He's going to see if we can take over some of the space on the first floor at the University. We should know in a few days if this is possible.

I told Jakob I'll join Sterling's lab full-time if this first experiment is a success.

CHAPTER 26

The Past
Age Forty-One

Xavier and I sat at one of the desks in the front room of Sterling's primate lab, flipping through lab notebooks and reviewing the results of the previous two weeks of experiments. Sterling was chatting with Paul in the adjacent room, but their voices were barely audible. Einstein's helmet sat on a shelf just inside the lab door, a constant reminder of where this work all started.

Professor McCulvey had been successful with his dissection. Hundreds of cells had been isolated from Einstein's brain, and each one had been placed in its own dish to grow. These dishes, each assigned a specific ID number, filled the two new incubators behind us.

Given the results of our preliminary experiments, we had indeed isolated our target, cells from the so-called Curious Tract, or if you wanted to use the term I'd chosen for my novel, *vibrioglia*.

"So, what do you think?" Xavier asked, closing the notebook we'd just reviewed. "Remind you of anything?"

Two things were certain: these cells weren't what Sterling thought they were, and Sterling wasn't happy. He stormed into the room.

"Paul just gave me the update," Sterling said, a definite note of irritation in his voice. "So, if they aren't neural stem cells, then what the hell are they?"

I pulled on a pair of sterile gloves and opened the incubator door. "That's what we're here to find out." I removed dish number 037. The dish was made of clear plastic and was about the same size and shape as a hockey puck. It was filled with pink liquid, growth medium, which supported the cells growing inside. I slid the dish onto the stage of a nearby microscope, leaned into the eyepiece, and took a peek. The cells growing in the dish were some of the prettiest I'd ever seen, attached to the plastic with long, threadlike extensions. They were also some of deadliest, able to produce a lineage that could morph into a glioblastoma, the rare and malignant tumor that killed my father.

"I looked at them earlier," Sterling said. "They're definitely some sort of stem cell."

"Sort of," I said, still staring at them under the scope as I adjusted the focus. I picked up the dish and carried it over to the biosafety cabinet.

Sterling followed, right on my heels.

Brannigan had already turned on the interior light. The glass sash was raised just high enough for me to reach through and place the dish on the stage of the microscope that had been set up inside. I slid the dish as close to the spiral bulb as possible and removed its lid. I then adjusted the frequency device, setting the number pad on its base to the desired value.

On the bench next to the biosafety cabinet, Brannigan had set up a computer. He was clicking away at the keys while a digital camera, connected to both the microscope and the computer, allowed us to view the contents of the dish in real time. On the monitor, a live image appeared. The cells looked healthy and sat in clusters of eight to ten, resembling miniature islands.

I'd invited Jakob to come for the demo, and he stood on the other side of Sterling. Both men had their eyes on the screen.

"All set to record, Ms. King," Brannigan said.

I nodded and gave the dish a gentle swirl. On the monitor, the cells remained in place, proving that the clusters were firmly attached to the bottom of the dish and not just floating in the growth medium. The display timer on the base of the device showed 00:00:00 hours.

"So, what are we doing?" Sterling asked.

"Just watch," I said, stepping back from the biosafety cabinet to join the rest of the team who had now congregated around the monitor.

Brannigan hit a button on the keyboard to apply the frequency. For thirty seconds, the image on the monitor remained unchanged.

I'm really here, I thought, *looking at a machine I dreamed up, watching cells so much like the ones in my novel that it's almost scary. What happens if this works?*

According to my novel, the cells needed just a few more seconds to respond.

Brannigan shifted his weight from foot to foot.

When the timer hit 00:00:45 hours, Sterling thrust a hand in the direction of the cabinet. "So, what the hell are we waiting for here? What's supposed to happen?"

I looked at Jakob. He was still watching the monitor. I began to worry that I had indeed gotten his hopes up, but then I saw him smile.

Brannigan pointed at the screen. The cells began to change shape, first the cluster right in the middle of the field, and then a few more on the periphery. The cells' long extensions retracted, making them look more like ovals than delicate stars. The timer was at 00:00:50 hours, exactly as it had been in my novel.

"Dear God," I said, not believing what I was seeing.

By 00:01:00 hours, only one minute after the frequency was applied, most of the cells were in motion, gliding across the dish as if we were watching time-lapse photography. Each rounded cell body sent out a leading edge, like the tentacle of an octopus, reaching away from each cluster. This pseudopod then pulled the cell in that direction. The cells moved away from each cluster like synchronized swimmers. Once repositioned, the cell divided into two.

Cell division is a normal process. It's how we grow and how we replace injured tissue. The only difference is that, generally, the process happens much more slowly. When the timer reached 00:02:00 hours, the entire dish was filled, but the cells were no longer clustered in small islands. They were instead arranged in an organized network of lines, much like the veins on a leaf—or the tree-like image Brannigan had captured with fMRI when Einstein and Zena were communicating. The experiment had worked.

Tom appeared just then, stepping through the door on the other side of the lab. He didn't know about this experiment. Xavier had advised me not to include him. I watched as he flipped over a page on his clipboard and began walking toward us.

I casually reached over and switched off the computer monitor.

Xavier gave me a confused look, and I shifted my eyes in Tom's direction.

Xavier opened the incubator door, and I returned the dish to its shelf, being sure to remember the number written on the outside.

When I closed the door and turned around, Sterling was there. "I'll see you in my office in five minutes," he said as he left the lab.

Tom took a few steps in my direction, but Paul and Mary pulled him into a conversation.

Xavier put his hand on the small of my back and led me into the other room.

Jakob came with us, but only stayed for a minute. Before leaving the lab, he leaned in and whispered something into my ear.

Brannigan showed up a few minutes later. "Guess Sterling's gonna want some answers, huh?"

"I'm sure," I said. "Want to come along?"

"Not really," Brannigan said, stuffing his hands in his pockets, "but I guess I don't have a choice, do I? You did say he hasn't read your book, right?"

I shook my head. "At least we can be thankful for that."

On our way to Sterling's office, I shared what Jakob had whispered to me, and when we arrived, we found Sterling perched on the edge of his desk.

"So, who's going to explain to me what just happened?" Sterling asked—without even waiting for all of us to step inside.

"Actually," I said, "Jakob thinks we should do that at Les Choux. He said to tell you he's on his way over there now."

Sterling pushed off his desk and came straight at us. "We're not going anywhere until someone explains what just happened down there. I need to know, and I need to know now."

A quiet knock came at the door. Sterling rolled his eyes and turned to find Tom's face peering around its edge. "Tom, we're busy right now," he barked.

"But, it's important ..."

"I said, I'm busy. Find me tomorrow morning. I want that report you and I talked about by nine o'clock. We can talk then."

Tom tried again to work his way into the room, and I could see Sterling getting more frustrated. I felt bad for Tom. It wasn't his fault that Sterling was upset.

I said, "Sterling, we should get going. Jakob will wonder where we are."

Sterling shot an angry look in my direction and then pushed past Tom out into the hall.

As we walked to Les Choux, Sterling pulled out his cell phone and called someone, presumably Jakob. He walked far enough ahead that we couldn't hear any of the conversation, although we could tell he wasn't happy. He only dropped his phone back into his jacket pocket once the restaurant came into view.

Inside, Rosa led us to the table where Jakob was waiting with a bottle of champagne in front of him. Jakob didn't even wait for us to reach the table before he grabbed the bottle and popped the cork.

The couple at the next table looked over as he began to pour.

Jakob picked up his glass. "To brilliant discoveries," he said, smiling as he lifted it into the air.

Xavier, Brannigan, and I each picked up another and did the same.

Sterling pulled out a chair and took a seat.

Jakob frowned at him. "Sterling, this is your good news more than anyone's, so I'm not sure why you're refusing a toast, but I suppose that's up to you." He tapped his glass against ours and then tipped it toward Sterling. "Cheers."

Sterling waited until we took our seats. "So, now that you've gotten that out of the way, would someone mind finally telling me what the hell just happened back in my lab?"

Everyone looked at me. The experiment had been my idea, after all, so it was only right that I should explain.

"To put it bluntly," I said, "I think it's safe to say you've identified a new type of cell. I'm certainly not an expert in the field, but in all the reading I did in preparation for my novel, I didn't come across any other cell type that would have behaved like that, and believe me, I did my research."

Sterling frowned. He looked first at me and then at Jakob. "So, are you saying you didn't expect that experiment to work? Is that what I'm hearing?"

"I saw nothing in the literature to suggest that it would," I explained.

Sterling looked honestly perplexed. "So, then why did we do it?"

I shrugged. "I suppose just in case it did."

"And now that it has?" Sterling asked. "What does that mean?"

I said, "Honestly, Sterling, I'm pretty sure it means that my other experiments will work too." I wanted so badly for it to be just Jakob and me at the table. There was so much I wanted to discuss with him—things I could never discuss with Sterling there.

Sterling sat back and sipped his water. He seemed to be thinking. "So, how much more work do you think we have to do? Because if it's a lot, I'll have to start a new grant proposal. We'll need to get more funding. Right now, I only have enough to support my current project. There's no extra."

The last thing I wanted was for Sterling to write anything about this in a grant. I wanted no one else to know about the work we were doing. I looked at Jakob, and he nodded. It was time to tell Sterling our plan.

I said, "I actually think we should do the work as a satellite company—one that focuses specifically on this discovery. I think we should keep the funding separate from your other project."

Sterling turned to Jakob. "She keeps looking at you. Have you two been discussing this behind my back?"

Jakob said, "Sterling, listen, Nadia's right. It's important that we keep things quiet right now—for everyone's good. You may not have read Nadia's book, but a lot of people have, and if any of them catch wind of this work and notice the similarities, your research might be called into question. Isolating this project from your already published work might be your best option. Keep the two projects separate—that's all we're saying."

Sterling frowned. "This has nothing to do with her book. We're talking about real science here. Real cells. We just observed them in the lab. Remember? This isn't fiction."

"So, let's not give anyone the chance to make that conclusion, then," Jakob said. "There's no getting around it, Sterling. Your work and Nadia's have quite a few things in common, and that's not a bad thing. It's actually a reason to celebrate, which is why you're here." Jakob pushed the remaining glass of champagne toward Sterling.

"Sterling, we're not saying that your cells are the same as the ones in my book, but if anyone gets wind of this work and notices the similarities, they'll try to link the two for sure. If we create this satellite company, and keep this project isolated, your original work is protected no matter what. The discovery of the cells stays with your current lab. We just think we should perform any further work with them under a different name."

"Plus, I think we need to keep Tom away from this project, Sterling," Xavier said.

"Why? Tom's a hard worker."

"And that's exactly why he should stay on the other project," Xavier said. "You'll need reliable people over there too. Plus, you know what he's like. I guarantee he's read Nadia's book, and if he gets wind of this, he's definitely going to make those connections and start talking about them with whoever wants to listen. It's not gonna be good. Word will get out fast. The less he knows, the better."

Sterling looked at Jakob. "And if we form this company, where would we do the work? And where will we get the funding if I don't submit for a grant?"

"I'll provide funding," Jakob said quickly, "but I'm only offering it if you agree to form the satellite and hold off on submitting any preliminary papers."

Sterling frowned at him. "You don't have the money for this. And why would you offer funding for my project even if you did? You have your own research to worry about."

"I do have the money for this," Jakob said, "and I'm offering because that's what my niece and my sister, Evelyn, would want me to do."

I saw Sterling flinch, but I wasn't sure why.

Jakob kept going. He told the team about what he and I had already discussed, obviously without mentioning Rowan's involvement. "There are a few vacant labs in my building," he said. "The one in the back half of the first floor is already fit for purpose. We might need a few more pieces of equipment, but not much. There are more than enough offices available on the upper floors, as well." He cast his eyes around the table. "Plenty for all of you."

"So, will we call it Amulet?" Xavier asked.

I nearly choked on my water. I couldn't believe Xavier would even ask this. If Sterling hadn't read my novel, he wouldn't know that Amulet was the name of the fictional biotech that discovered my vibrioglia, but even so, it was bold for Xavier to suggest the name.

Sterling picked up his glass of champagne and downed it. "I don't care what the hell we call it. If you're all crazy enough to go to these extremes to get more data, you can call it whatever you want. I'm in." Sterling looked at me. "So, what about this consultant of yours, Nadia? This scientist who helped you write the book? Will he be joining us as well?"

I felt Jakob look at me, but I couldn't turn to face him. Of course, Sterling hadn't forgotten about what I'd said that day. This was one part of the courtyard conversation that I hadn't yet shared with Jakob.

"Consultant?" Jakob asked.

Sterling laughed. "What? You didn't tell anyone else, Nadia? Not even Jakob? That's surprising." Sterling glanced around the table. "Didn't anybody else wonder how she got these ideas for her book? You all keep talking about the similarities between her book and my work, but how do you think that all happened? I'll tell you how. Someone else is doing the same work, and somehow, Nadia got her hands on it. Too bad for them. Looks like we'll be the ones reaping the rewards."

Jakob got up from his chair. "Well, it seems to me we have a lot more to celebrate and not enough drinks to go around. Nadia, what do you say? Want to help me gather a few from the bar?"

I got up and followed him.

As the bartender pulled together another round, Jakob leaned in close. "Don't let Sterling get you flustered. We all know how he is. I'm just relieved he didn't put up much of a fight about this new company. As for this consultant of yours, I'm sure you haven't told me for a reason, so let's talk soon, all right? For now, let's just enjoy the moment." He bumped his shoulder against mine.

I nodded and bumped him back. We would talk later. We needed to.

For the next hour, the group talked mostly about Einstein. Sterling seemed relaxed, and after a few drinks, even Curt Brannigan got chatty.

I listened, but all I could think about was the fact that Amulet was a go. We were about to see if the rest of my book played true. Jakob would call the University VP in the morning and seal the deal for the extra lab in the back. Based on our calculations, and if we really pushed, we could be up and running in about a month.

Things were going well until Rowan arrived. From the second she stepped up to the table, I watched Sterling's mood change. Jakob greeted her with a hug, of course, and grabbed a chair for her from another table.

"Well, if it isn't our local fortune-teller," Sterling said as Rowan slid in next to him. "To what do we owe this pleasure?"

"Oh, for heaven's sake, Sterling, calm your horses," she said, adjusting her skirt. "I'm not here to cause trouble. I only came over to see why everyone looks so happy. Let's keep it that way, shall we?" She patted his knee. "No need to be a party pooper."

Xavier scratched the back of his neck and looked at me as if to say, "Here we go."

Rosa passed by the table and dropped off a glass of red wine for Rowan. She planted a quick kiss on her daughter's cheek before leaving.

"Nadia and Sterling's experiment worked today," Jakob said. "We're celebrating."

Before Rowan could respond, Sterling was standing. "She doesn't need to know anything about this project, Jakob, so let's just stop this conversation right now."

"Oh, come on, Sterling," Jakob said. "Sit down with us. There's no need—"

"No, it's time for me to go," he said. "I'm sure your friend here will find less scientific things to talk about, and I don't really feel like listening to any of that." He looked down at me. "I'll see you in the lab tomorrow?"

I nodded and watched him walk away. Rowan called after him, but Sterling kept going, either because he didn't hear her or had decided to ignore her. I guessed it was the latter.

"Well, then," Rowan said, "that worked like a charm." She rubbed her hands together. "So, tell me now, how did it go?"

Everyone took turns explaining all that had happened, and then Rowan looked at me and smiled. "So, are you convinced yet?"

"Convinced?"

"About your gift, of course," she said. "You dream of the future, you paint the future, and now we know you can write about it as well. You're obviously a *pre-cog*. What other proof do you need?"

"A what?" Brannigan asked.

Rowan sipped her wine. "It's just another way of saying that our Nadia seems to have a knack for predicting the future."

Xavier suddenly seemed concerned. "I think we all agree that Nadia's nailed this experiment," he said, "but she can still be wrong about other things, right? I mean, not everything has to play out like in the book. Precognition can't be 100 percent accurate, can it?"

I'm sure he was thinking about the chapter where Juliet Savini, my lead scientist, dies. I know that's where my mind was. *At least he doesn't know about my painting of the amaryllis and paperwhites, my favorite flowers, surrounding an urn with an indecipherable nameplate.*

"Yeah," I said, "I wouldn't mind being wrong on a few points."

Rowan had to know what we were talking about, but she didn't answer.

"Do you think Sterling will read the book now?" Brannigan asked.

Rowan smiled. "He will eventually if we keep talking about it, and he should. We actually need him to."

"I wouldn't mind getting a few more experiments under our belt before he does though," Jakob said.

Brannigan cleared his throat. "So, I don't mean to sound stupid here, but I have to ask something." He glanced around the table. "Is there a scientific explanation for what happened today? Cells moving around like that seemed a little far-fetched when I first read the book, but it was fiction, so I just sort of took it at face value since pretty much anything can happen in a novel, you know? But now that I've actually seen it happen, I'm wondering why it would."

Brannigan was justifiably confused. We hadn't shared any of this background with him.

Jakob was happy to explain. "You saw the cells start moving when your machine applied a high frequency."

Brannigan nodded.

"You saw them arrange themselves into a branching pattern," Jakob continued, "one very similar to the pattern you saw on Einstein's brain scans when he and Zena were communicating, correct?"

Brannigan nodded again.

"So if you put two and two together, this means that the cells isolated from Einstein's brain are likely some kind of psychic receptors that can receive telepathic messages."

Brannigan said, "I get that, but why did they move?"

"I think they move to help amplify whatever signal is coming in. That tree-like structure on the scans connected many different sensory areas of the brain. No matter what sensory area is hit first, these cells seem to reach out to all of the others." Jakob took a sip of his drink. "Vibrational energy typically goes undetected by most people—except for sensitives like Rowan here. I'm not sure if you two have officially met, but Rowan is a medium. That's why she's so interested in this project. If these cells are what we think they are, that might explain how she sees what she sees." Jakob went on to explain the vibrational hypothesis. "In my field of research, we believe that spirits possess a higher vibrational energy than the living. That's why ghost hunters carry around EMF detectors, right? They use them to pick up this energy. Your modified Rife machine actually generates electromagnetic frequencies, EMFs, and the cells respond. If your cells can respond to mechanically generated EMFs, don't you think they'd respond to other things that emit that same kind of energy?"

Brannigan seemed to consider this. "So, you're saying these cells can detect ghosts?"

Jakob gave a catty smile. "I think that might be one side effect." He leaned forward on his elbows. "Let me ask you this, Brannigan, think about their location on the scans. At the back of the head, right? When you're in a dark room all by yourself, and you get that feeling that you might not be alone, where do you feel the chills first?"

Brannigan rubbed the back of his neck.

Jakob tipped his head. "Bingo."

When I got home that night, Maeve was at the kitchen island with a book in her hands. Ares was on the stool next to her, watching with intense interest as she turned a page.

I slid a slice of Rosa's famous blackberry pie across the counter. "Rosa sends her love," I said.

Maeve took the fork I was holding out to her and dug in. "So how did it go in the lab today?"

I rested my elbows on the counter, chin on my hands, and gave her a minute to swallow. "What would you say if I told you it went just like it did in the book?"

She gave a disbelieving look. "You're kidding, right?"

I shook my head. "Literally. No joke. Just like in the book."

She made me tell her everything.

"But, how do you even explain that?" she asked when I was done. "I mean, the shark painting was freaky enough, Mums, but this is even weirder, don't you think?"

I stole a blackberry from the edge of her plate. "I don't know what to make of it, to be honest. Of course, Rowan doesn't seem surprised, but that's Rowan. She's been dealing with this kind of thing her whole life."

"And what about Sterling?" Maeve asked. "I'm sure he handled this well."

I laughed and filled her in on that too. "I'm just glad he hasn't read the book."

I watched as she scraped the last remaining pieces of crust and stray berries into a pile and scooped them into her mouth.

Once she swallowed this, I told her the best part. "Sterling asked if Remmington was going to join us."

Maeve let her jaw fall open. "What? How in the world did he know about Remmington?"

"I sort of let that slip when I met him that day in the courtyard. Sterling told everyone at Les Choux tonight."

"Who else was there?" Maeve asked.

I rattled off the names.

"But I didn't think you told Jakob about Remmington yet."

"I haven't, but I'll have to now."

"Have you told Rowan?"

I shook my head. "I haven't told anyone except you and Lydia. He keeps reminding me not to say anything about him. I worry that, if I do, things will go down the drain."

Maeve just shook her head. "Sounds like a pickle. I guess you'll have to tell them soon, huh?" She got up from the stool, tossed the paper plate in the trash, and tucked her book under her arm. "It's just gonna get weirder if you don't. I already told you what I think is gonna happen. I bet you a hundred bucks I'm right." She gave me a peck on the cheek. "That pie was frabjous, Mums. Just what I needed. A good old sugar crash to put me right to sleep."

"Frabjous?"

Maeve held up her book. On the cover was a girl in a blue dress, a cat, a rabbit, and a deck of cards. *Alice in Wonderland.*

"Ah," I said. "Now I get it."

Maeve disappeared behind me into the foyer. I heard her feet bounding up the stairs, and not long after that, the sound of the dogs as they followed her.

I stood there in the kitchen, the same worrisome thought coursing through my head from earlier that evening. *Why had I decided to kill Juliet Savini?*

Instead of heading upstairs, I rounded the corner into the library. My painting of the amaryllis and paperwhites hung over the fireplace. I'd modified the original to make it more suitable for display since a painting of an urn didn't seem the cheeriest of wall hangings. I'd added more flowers. They now filled the container, making it look more like a vase than an urn. I'd added some in front too to cover the blank nameplate.

Despite the modification, I knew this wasn't how the painting had started. I knew this—and so did Rowan. Exactly *why* it had started as it did was my biggest concern.

I grabbed my novel from the bookshelf and made my way over to one of the chairs in front of the fireplace. I pulled the blanket out of the basket, threw it over my shoulders, found the pages I was looking for, and prepared for the worst.

CHAPTER 27

Psience

J uliet Savini was my lead scientist, her character closely modeled
after myself. She led the work at Amulet and was the one who
had discovered the vibrioglia. She was determined to prove their
function. Like Sterling, her original work was with primates, and her
team had proven that telepathic communication was the reason for the
activation seen by fMRI. Juliet also believed that these cells could do
more. Like Jakob, she thought they could give us access to spirits tethered
to all other levels of existence. In other words, they could allow us to
speak with the shades.

Juliet Savini, like me, was also a huge fan of Sir Anthony Bard, and of
course, Amulet had access to all of his journals. My novel provided some
details of Bard's work. I needed my readers to understand what Juliet was
trying to do. She had studied his notebooks and was determined to follow
his lead. She knew traveling through the veil was the only way to get the
information she needed. She tried everything that Bard described in his
notebooks, but she couldn't replicate his results.

Late one night, frustrated with her lack of progress, Juliet scribbled
a few final thoughts into her notebook and shut down the lab for the
night. She packed the notebooks and Bard's journals in her bag and left
for home.

It had been snowing for most of the day. The roads were icy. She was
tired, and as she rounded the curve no more than a mile from her home,
her car veered off the road, sending her into a stand of pines.

My book leaves the reader wondering whether Juliet might have done this on purpose. After all, she was desperate to get the answers she needed.

A colleague of hers, Professor Fairleigh, woke up from a dream just as she went into that stand of pines. In his dream, Juliet pulled up next to him at a rest stop in a car he recognized, a red sedan that used to belong to his sister. Margaret had lost control on a patch of black ice years before, and the red sedan had fallen into a ravine. Seeing this same car in his dream made him worry that something might be wrong.

Professor Fairleigh immediately tried calling Juliet, but he got no answer in the lab or on her cell. He threw on some clothes and drove to the rest stop he'd seen in his dream, easily recognizable from the landmarks: a curve marked with a yellow warning sign, an old stone barn and silo, a billboard advertising a local radio station, and, of course, a tall stand of pines. When he arrived, Juliet was unresponsive.

He called 911, and as he stood there waiting for the ambulance, he noticed the notebooks on the passenger's side floor. A C-fold paper towel was tucked into the front of the one on top:

> What about dreams? It's how Sir Anthony Bard used to visit his wife. How did he do it? How does one prepare for something like that? Maybe we should have a code word that only we know. That way, if something ever happens to one of us, and if the others see the code somewhere, they'll know we made it through. They'll know to keep working to prove our theory, to prove that the realm of the shades does exist. SPIRIT1?

One month after Juliet Savini's car went off the road—one month after she died—a power failure shut down the entire Amulet facility. The outage lasted for thirty minutes, and when power was finally restored, every computer monitor displayed the same strange message. SPIRIT1 was repeated end on end, filling each screen.

CHAPTER 28

The Past
Age Forty-One

When I arrived at the Science Center the next day, Sterling wasn't in his office, which seemed strange since he'd asked me to meet him there before he left Les Choux.

Paul was in the lab though, so I asked if he'd seen him. He pointed to a large yellow envelope on Xavier's desk.

My name was scrawled across the front.

Xavier came in from the back room as I was standing there looking down at it. He placed a stack of notebooks on the desk. "That was there when I got in at six this morning. Looks like Sterling's writing."

I picked it up. "You don't think he's changed his mind, do you?"

Xavier shrugged. "There's only one way to find out."

I unhooked the clasp and pulled out a white sheet of paper that had been folded in half. Sterling's first sentence didn't leave me hopeful. I held the paper out to Xavier, and he took it. "You read it. I can't."

"I won't be returning to the lab for a while," Xavier read. "While I'm gone, go ahead and move whatever you need for the company to the new space if that's what everyone agrees is best. I've already told Jakob the same and have given him permission to make any other decisions he thinks will be beneficial to the research. I'll leave the new lab renovations in your hands as well. It sounds like you already have a plan. I'm not going to be much help right now. I just need some time."

I felt guilty. We were essentially chasing Sterling out of his own lab, taking over his discovery, and using it for our own purposes. Worst of all, we were keeping secrets from him and pushing him to continue when he really just needed time to adjust to the loss of Einstein.

In the letter, Sterling provided instructions on who should work where and on what project. Sterling would divide his time equally between both facilities when he returned. Brannigan and Xavier would work solely for Amulet, just as I would, and Paul and Mary would stay in the old lab with Tom. It would have been nice to have the two of them with us, but Sterling explained that their expertise fit much better with his behavioral and cognitive work, at least for now. Plus, a new chimp, Einstein's replacement, had arrived and needed their attention.

Leaving Paul and Mary in the primate facility will also help keep Sterling's focus elsewhere, I thought selfishly.

At the bottom of the page, Sterling gave very specific instructions regarding Rowan.

"One final thing, and I'll only say this once," Xavier read. "Tell your friend Rowan to keep her nose out of my business if you want to continue to work on this project. If I see her in the lab, you won't have that luxury."

Xavier handed the paper back to me. "He doesn't seem to like her much, does he? What's their story? Do you know?"

"No idea," I said. "He probably just doesn't like her because of what she can do."

From the Journal of Nadia King
Age Forty-One

With Sterling gone these past few weeks, it's been quiet. He's called once or twice, but he's never asked to speak with me. He's only spoken with Jakob, who says he's doing fine. Apparently, Sterling has stepped away once before. Jakob says he'll be back when he's ready.

Jakob and I have been using the freedom to plan the new lab space exactly as we need it, and we've been meeting regularly with the design team to keep things moving. We'll continue working out of Sterling's old lab while Amulet is under construction.

Xavier has repeated most of the preliminary work just to be certain of what we saw the first time. The data from the first and second runs are identical, which is good. Given that, the plan is to continue with the second experiment from chapter 19 once the new lab is ready.

CHAPTER 29

The Past
Age Forty-One

I t wasn't long until Amulet—once just a figment of my imagination—became a reality. The labs in the back of the first floor of the University had been successfully converted into space that suited our needs perfectly.

Jakob and I stood in the doorway taking it all in.

The walls were painted a crisp white, and the floor was tiled in a calming blue. New equipment lined the walls, including a set of biosafety cabinets and two incubators. I didn't think we'd be needing these much longer since our work with the cells was nearly done, but Sterling would have questioned it if we hadn't installed them. After all, he was still under the assumption that we were here to prove that his cells were the next medical miracle.

In the center of the room were two long counter height lab benches with plenty of drawers underneath for storage. The benchtops were an industrial black epoxy. Stainless steel stools were pushed into the leg wells, and a series of computer workstations and large monitors sat on top. This was all we really needed for our work moving forward. No cages were required in this lab. We could use the ones in Sterling's other lab, if necessary, in the future.

"Come on," Jakob said. "I want to show you something else." He led me up to the second floor, taking the stairs but cursing his knees as we went. "I swear all I do is pop and crack anymore. This getting old is for the birds."

At the top of the stairs, we rounded the corner and continued down the hall. He pointed into a room on the left as he passed. "That's Brannigan's office. You'll be up here, across from Sterling and right next to Xavier."

We stopped in front of an open door on the right.

"So what do you think?" Jakob asked, hands on his hips.

A broad expanse of windows filled the opposite wall. I wandered over to them and looked down at the courtyard below. Hundreds of students milled about. "I think I still feel like this is all a dream. Please tell me it's not."

"Not a dream," Jakob said, shaking his head. He pointed toward the corner. "There's a gift for you there."

A large cardboard box took up most of the small table in the corner of the room.

"Go gather your things from the car, settle in, and then open the gift. Let me know what you think." He looked at his watch. "I've got to head back upstairs for an appointment. I'll see you tomorrow morning."

I watched as he hobbled out of sight, and once he was gone, I went over to the box. "Lift Carefully" had been written across the front.

I placed my hands on either side and lifted. Underneath was a microscope.

A tag dangled from one eyepiece:

For quiet contemplation. Enjoy.

It might seem strange to have a microscope outside of the lab, but Jakob had placed it in the office for a reason. Juliet had a microscope in her office. She spent hours there, looking for things the others might have missed. A small box of slides sat near the base of the scope. I lifted the lid and pulled one out.

All in all, there were maybe fifty in total.

When Jakob wandered in the next morning, he found me seated at the scope, slide 025 on the stage. He pulled out the chair on the other side of the table and groaned as he settled into it, his knees offering the familiar pop and crack that he'd pointed out the day before.

"Thank you for this," I said.

He nodded.

"Have you heard from Sterling?"

"He actually called last night." Jakob picked through the box of slides and held one up to the light. "He said he might be back later this week, which reminds me …" Jakob stood up. "Come on … while the cat's away, I want to show you his office. It's where Evelyn used to sit when she came to visit. Claimed the room had good energy." Jakob tapped his elbow against mine as we crossed the hall. "Maybe some of that will rub off on Sterling, eh?"

Jakob hit the light switch, and two small Tiffany lamps illuminated opposite ends of a huge antique desk. Behind it, wooden bookshelves stained in a deep walnut lined the wall. Jakob went around the desk and stopped in front of a small window on the other side. "Come here. You'll like this."

We stood shoulder to shoulder in front of a thin rectangular window made of leaded, beveled glass and looked out onto the street below. In the upper-left corner, the head of a gargoyle leaned out into the open air. A few others dotted the neighboring roofline.

Jakob locked his hands behind his back. "My Evelyn loved her gargoyles. Had them all through her garden." He turned and looked around the room. "She spent a great deal of time in here when she'd come to visit. She chose the lamps, the desk, and most of the books that you see."

A soft knock came at the door and Xavier peeked in.

"Oh, it's you," Xavier said, stepping inside. "I saw the lights on and thought maybe the boss decided to grace us with his presence. Any word yet? Tom called me this morning and asked for him. Apparently, he hasn't been over there either."

"I was just telling Nadia that he called last night. Might be back later this week. I actually wonder if he might be taking the time to read Nadia's book."

I looked at Jakob. "Do we want that?"

"I'm beginning to think we might."

CHAPTER 30

The Past
Age Forty-One

Brannigan and I were setting up the final computer in Amulet's labs when we heard Sterling's voice in the lobby. He was talking with Erma. We stopped what we were doing and looked at each other, not sure what to expect if he came in.

Erma was rambling on like she does, and then Sterling cut her off, saying that he had to go. We assumed he'd come into the lab, but he didn't. He'd either left the building or gone upstairs.

We didn't see much of him during his first week back. He would just come into the lab, grab a few notebooks, and carry them up to his office. The second week, he did come in and sit while Curt and I were observing some cells under the microscope. He asked what we were looking at, and he had us explain the progress we'd made while he was out. By the third week, Sterling hardly left the lab. He was usually the first to arrive in the morning and the last to leave at night. He watched the videos over and over again, but hardly spoke to anyone.

As more experiments from my novel proved true at Amulet, the shadows continued to make their appearances at the Baird. Remmington, on the other hand, rarely showed his face. I talked with Xavier in the lab, and I saw Jakob everywhere: in class, at Amulet, and in the sleep lab. Of course, Rowan and I continued to meet as we always had.

She had her theories about the shadows, my novel, and how I should be paying more attention to Xavier. She repeatedly brought Xavier up in conversation, and I repeatedly put her off, even though I knew, deep down, that he was definitely one of the reasons I didn't mind spending so much time on this project. But there was work to do, things to understand, and still so much to explain to Sterling. I had to stay focused.

CHAPTER 31

The Past
Age Forty-One

On Friday morning, I sat in my office at Amulet, behind the desk, one ankle crossed over my knee, watching as four tiny birds danced around on a branch outside the expanse of windows. My chair was angled in such a way that I could see Sterling's office across the hall. His light was on. The door ajar.

I'd decided that this was probably the best time to sit down with him and try to explain everything. It would give him the weekend to digest what I needed to tell him, and it would be two days before I had to see him again, which was good, especially if he reacted in the way I expected. Paul and Mary had also mentioned that his work in the behavioral lab was going well, that the new chimp's word count was already approaching that of Einstein's, so I knew he'd be in a good mood. I sat there for nearly fifteen minutes going over what I wanted to say to him in my head. If my mother had been there, she would have pulled me to my feet and told me to get moving. "No better time than the present," she'd say, and she'd be right.

I pushed myself out of the chair and made my way across the hall. Sterling didn't notice me standing in the doorway at first, so I tapped gently on his door. He'd been running a white handkerchief over the tops of the Tiffany lamps, but when he looked up and saw me, he immediately rolled the cloth into a ball and tucked it inside a desk drawer. His face was somber.

"How are things?" I asked from the doorway. "Sounds like work at the other lab is going well."

Sterling folded his hands in front of him and gave a forced smile. "The new chimp is up to forty signs ... so I guess that's good. Learning quickly." He glanced down at his hands. "Not as sharp as Einstein, of course, but she'll do."

I nodded. "Do you have a minute to talk real quick?"

"Of course. Come in. Have a seat." He gestured toward one of the two Windsor chairs that faced his desk and then pointed at his monitor. "I spent most of last night here, reviewing the data again, trying to get a grip on what's been happening. Looks like things are going well here too."

"They are, which is why I wanted to come talk to you. I thought maybe we could discuss what we're seeing."

Sterling leaned back in his chair.

We spoke for over an hour, but the only thing I could bring myself to talk about was the data we'd gathered while he was away. I listened to his interpretation of it and nodded, but never touched on anything that I meant to discuss. When I left his office, I told myself I'd return in the afternoon to get everything out in the open. I just wanted to talk to Jakob first, to see if he had any suggestions about how to approach the topic. I needed to bring Sterling up to speed before the weekend. I needed for him to understand what all of this data really meant.

CHAPTER 32

The Past
Age Forty-One

Sterling left the building at noon, not long after we talked, and he didn't come back. I stayed at Amulet until five o'clock, using the last few hours to review data in my office. My mind kept wandering. I wanted to get a head start on plans for Monday, but I just wasn't up to it.

I cocked an ear toward the door. Reggae bounced in the background, telling me that Xavier was still in his office. I gave the notebook in front of me one last cursory glance, and then I closed it and headed down the hall.

Xavier was at his desk, hunched over a notebook of his own, his pen busy. A lock of braids brushed the page.

I leaned on the doorjamb and waited for him to finish, not wanting to break his train of thought. On his desk, next to the notebook, there was a gallon water jug and the blender bottle he used for his protein shakes. Both were empty. His gym bag sat on one of the two steel-framed chairs in front of his desk.

He dropped the pen and rubbed at his face with both hands.

"Knock knock," I said.

He turned toward the door.

"Didn't want to interrupt," I said. "You seemed busy."

He looked at me out of the corner of his eye. "And you look like you're up to no good."

I shrugged. "Maybe. How do you feel about a happy hour?"

"Over this?" He gestured at his notebook and then flipped the front cover closed. "Does that answer your question? Should we call Jakob?"

Part of me wanted to say no, but I nodded.

I stood in the doorway as he called, noticing the stark contrast between his and Sterling's offices. Xavier's had minimal clutter. Modern furniture. Everything gray, white, and sleek. He had the same expanse of windows as I did, the same view of the courtyard below. No gargoyles for either of us.

Xavier put down his phone. "Jakob said to go ahead without him, said he needs about half an hour to wrap things up. Said he'll meet us at the pub when he's finished." He slid his pen back into a silver cup at the top corner of his desk, tucked his blender bottle in the side pocket of his gym bag, and slung the bag over his shoulder. "Go grab your stuff. I'll meet you in the lobby. I wanna go make sure the lab is all buttoned up before we head out."

I called Rowan as I closed up my office.

She answered on the first ring. "How about I pick up Jakob on my way then meet you and Xavier at your house in an hour?" she asked. "That way you have time to take care of the dogs, and we can all ride together."

I knew this was just her way of forcing Xavier and me to spend some time with each other. More than once she'd made it very clear that I shouldn't let this one get away.

Downstairs in the lobby, I waited for Xavier near Erma's desk. Without her there, it was unusually quiet. Erma usually leaves by four o'clock on Fridays. A pile of papers was neatly tucked away under the counter for the weekend, and her chair was pushed in just right. Xavier rounded the corner as I was studying the pictures of her grandkids that circled her monitor. He was bundled in a peacoat, a red scarf around his neck. I told him about the change in plans, that Rowan would be picking us up at my house, and he made no argument.

A blast of wind hit us as we stepped through the revolving door. The evening was chillier than I'd expected, although that didn't seem to stop people from coming out. A team of university workers was in the process of decorating the campus trees with thousands of tiny white lights, and on the main streets of town, we had to navigate through a crowd of holiday shoppers, each weighed down with bags. Xavier told me about his upcoming holiday plans as we went, his breath escaping in large white plumes, reminding me of the sign of Boreas outside Rowan's shop.

I'd gone over to help Rowan decorate the night before. We both thought it was a bit early, not even Thanksgiving yet, but if she expected to get the holiday shoppers, she decided that she probably needed to look festive too. Boreas was now draped in lights and swags of pine. Once again, as we decorated, Xavier had been the topic of conversation. I looked over at him and couldn't help but smile. *Maybe she's right. Maybe I would be crazy to let this one go.*

A passing siren wailed as we crossed at the corner of Seventeenth and Broad, cutting Xavier off mid-sentence. He pointed toward a life-sized golden Buddha that sat cross-legged just beyond the next curb. Behind it, in the yoga's studio's front window hung a red sign:

Beat the Holiday Stress. Join Us for Guided Meditation.
Gift Certificates Available.

Once the siren faded, he said, "Ever try it?"

"Try what?" I asked, my thoughts stuck on last night's conversation with Rowan.

He pointed again at the sign. "Meditation."

That accent could sell them a thousand gift certificates, I thought. I looked at him and smiled. "I'd do anything if they said it like that."

He threw back his head and laughed, and then he leaned in and tucked an arm through mine. "A sucker for the accent, eh? I had no idea."

The corner of his scarf brushed my face. It smelled of an earthy cologne. I made no attempt to pull away as we continued along the row of brightly lit shops.

"My great-grandmother meditates every day," he said. "Good for the soul, she says, but then again, she says the same thing about her brandy." He shrugged. "She must be doing something right, though. Turns one hundred soon and still gets around like she's in her eighties."

The parking garage came into view as we rounded the next corner. To the right of the entrance, a man sat on the ground, his back against the front wall, an empty cup in front of him. His legs were extended out over a grate. A ratty blanket covered them, and threadbare socks protruded from its edge. Steam billowed up around him. Xavier slipped his arm out of mine and dug in his pockets. When he leaned over and dropped a few dollars in the man's cup, the man held up a finger and asked us to wait.

He rummaged through the worn backpack at his side, removed something shiny, and held it out to me.

I reached out and took it. It was angel. He'd molded it out of what appeared to be an old foil sandwich wrapper, most likely fished from the trash can on the corner. A loop of plastic had been threaded through its back, just below the halo, turning his miniature sculpture into an ornament that could be hung on a Christmas tree. It was well done. I could only imagine what he could do with the proper materials.

"Thank you," I said. "This will look beautiful on my tree."

Xavier extended a hand toward the man. The man just stared at it, as if no one had ever done this, but Xavier only leaned in closer, waiting until the man eventually took it and returned the handshake.

Back at the car, I hung the angel on my rearview mirror, a reminder for Aaron and me to swing by the garage the next day. The temperature was only going to drop. Aaron and I would pick the man up and take him to the shelter, maybe even give him some proper art supplies so he could show the others how to make ornaments. They'd be putting the tree up there soon if they hadn't already.

As we pulled into the drive at the Baird, I warned Xavier of the canine welcoming committee. I told him they'd likely swarm the car when we pulled up to the house, which was exactly what they did.

Xavier didn't even hesitate. He climbed out and let the three dogs surround him, tails wagging as they sniffed at his outstretched hands.

When I came around the side of the car, Xavier was rubbing Quake's ears. "This is the kind of dog I'd need if I ever got one," Xavier said, looking at me.

"I agree. Next to you, he almost looks normal sized," I said.

The dogs took off again as we stepped into the foyer. It smelled of paint, but the drop cloths that had been spread across the floor when I'd left that morning were now neatly folded in the corner of room, which meant that Aaron was already done. He must have finished early. The walls were dry, and Gram Marie's mask collection stared at us from every angle. The masks were hung as tastefully as if on display in an art museum. The empty boxes were stacked neatly next to the drop cloths.

Xavier's eyes swept the foyer walls as he took off his coat. "Impressive," he said, turning a full 360 degrees as if looking for the best place to start.

Aaron had done a wonderful job. The last time I'd seen all of the masks in one place was when they'd hung in Gram Marie's office. There were nearly forty in all, each of them brought home by Gram Marie from different places around the world.

"Kinda creepy," Xavier said, circling the room. "Not gonna lie." He stopped in front of the only empty spot on the wall and put his hands on his hips. It was next to my first painting of Ares.

Xavier pointed at the void. "Let me guess ... you're saving this spot for a few shrunken heads maybe? Is that why I'm here?"

"Funny." I pointed at the painting leaning against the stairs. "Looks like Aaron is leaving space for that."

Aaron apparently hadn't given up the fight just yet. He kept insisting that I hang Jillian's painting next to mine. This time, he'd even brought it down from the attic.

Xavier walked over and squatted in front of it.

"It came with the house," I explained. "Painted by the lady who used to live here."

He pointed at the woman standing in the garden wearing the robe. "That sort of looks like you."

I shrugged. "It gets weirder." I pointed to my painting of Ares on the wall. "That one over there is mine. I didn't know hers existed until after I was done."

Xavier got up and walked over to mine. He studied them both, head shifting back and forth like he was watching a tennis match. "You only painted one of these?"

I nodded.

He looked as confused as I was when I first saw Jillian's. "But how is that possible? They're both so similar in the way they're painted ... not to mention that they look like two halves of the same painting."

I only shrugged again. "Still trying to figure that one out myself."

He shook his head as if trying to make himself stop thinking about it, and then he ran a hand over a mask that hung on the other wall. The carved wooden face was eerily realistic, the wood a flesh tone shadowed with gray contours around the eyes and in the hollows of the cheeks. Frayed twine had been embedded along the top edge, like a shock of hair. "Don't these things give you nightmares?"

"That one did," I said, looking again at the chikunga with the same fear I had as a kid. It looked like a corpse, one that could come alive at any second. "These were all my Gram Marie's. She used to tell me stories that went with each of them. That one there, the one you just touched, is called a chikunga. It was given to my Gram Marie by some tribal leader after she spent a few months with his clan. She was some sort of sociologist before she got married, I guess. That particular one was supposedly used during sacrifices, and if that's not enough to give you nightmares, I don't know what is."

He nodded. "I don't know, but if you ask me, old houses are creepy enough without all of these." He put his hands in his pockets and turned to face me with a serious look on his face. "So, tell me, Nadia King, if these masks don't scare you, what does?"

I told him about the shadows in Gram Marie's house, about the drafts in her upstairs bedroom, and about the shadows I'd been seeing at the Baird lately. "Not knowing what my Gram Marie knew also scares me. She knew something, but she never had the chance to tell me what it was. I want to know why the shadows are back. I want to know what they want, and I want to know why my grandmother didn't want them near me. But do you know what really scares me? Are you ready for a laugh?"

He waited.

"I think the only thing that might really bother me is if I saw an actual ghost. You know, like the ones in the movies? The ones that look like real people. Seeing one of those would freak me out."

"Really?" He screwed up his face. "You, of all people, would be afraid to see a ghost?"

"I know, right?" I led him into the living room. "Knowing me, you'd think I'd want to see one, but in reality, I'm just a big scaredy-cat. It's easy to write about ghosts in a book, but seeing one in person? I don't know. I go through phases, I guess. Sometimes I wish I could see them, and other times I don't. I think it's just one of those things that has to happen before you know how you'll really react."

Xavier went over to the framed photographs on the mantel and picked up the one in the center. It showed Aaron and the three dogs in the garden. Aaron was grinning, his arms draped over Quake and Nyx. Attis was sprawled out on the lawn in front.

"Who's this?" Xavier asked. "Grandfather?"

I shook my head. "No. That's Aaron. You'll meet him at some point. He lives in the carriage house we passed on our way up the drive. He's also the reason you smell paint right now. He's been helping me get this place back in order. This room was actually white when I left this morning."

Xavier spun to take in the deep red and gave a nod of approval.

"I didn't see his truck when we came up the drive or I would have stopped and asked him to join us for happy hour. He's probably out buying more supplies for tomorrow."

Xavier returned the photo to the mantel and strolled over to my largest painting yet. It took up most of the far wall and showed a bright orange moon suspended over the rose garden out back. The stone wall in front of the roses was tangled in dark green ivy, and beside it was a stand of trees. I liked how it had turned out. I'd gotten the light just right. It touched the roses just enough to make them visible.

Xavier studied it for a minute and then pointed. "Is this the same woman from the other one?"

"What woman?" I asked. *That painting is just a landscape. There are no people in it.*

I walked over to where he stood. His finger was pointing to an area of the painting near the stone wall, beside one of the trees. As I got closer and squinted a bit, sure enough, I could make out the profile of a woman. Her back was pressed against the tree, her face turned slightly toward the observer. She was barely visible. Her hair, falling over her shoulder, caught a bit of the moonlight. You had to look hard, but if you did, you could definitely see her. *Did I put that there?*

"What?" Xavier asked, looking at me. "You look confused."

I shook my head. "Nothing."

"It doesn't look like nothing." He turned to face me. "But if you say so." He wrapped his arms around me, clasping his hands at my lower back. "So, what do you think, Ms. King?" he said, eyeing me with interest. "Will all of the experiments from your book work as well as the first few?"

My heart pounded. Not knowing what to do with my hands, I placed them on his chest.

"I think Sterling's reading your novel," Xavier said, calmly, as if standing this close was perfectly normal. He looked down at me. "With all the data, he's got to be curious, don't you think?" He reached up and brushed a wisp of hair out of my eyes. "I don't know if I told you or not, but my great-grandmother senses things too—like you and Rowan." He placed his thumbs on my temples. "She says she feels a chill here when they're around—or sometimes back here." He scooped the hair off the back of my neck and brushed his fingers along my hairline.

Chills coursed up my back.

His hands returned to my waist. "How do *you* know when they're here?"

"The shadows?"

"Anything."

I explained the cascades, how Gram Marie used to call them the willies, and how the feelings were getting stronger the more time I spent at the Baird. "Rowan thinks my work with her and Jakob is increasing my sensitivity. She says it's like practicing the violin. The more you practice, the better you get. She thinks that's why the shadows are more obvious now. She thinks they've always been following me, but I just couldn't see them very well."

"So, what happens if she's right? What if you turn around one day and find someone standing there?" He pulled me closer. "What would you do?"

I laughed, thinking of how often I'd wondered the same thing. "I don't know."

"You know what I think you should do?" he asked.

I shook my head.

"I think you should stop thinking so much—and just go with your heart."

Just then, a car pulled into the driveway. The light from the headlamps swept across the living room, and a horn blared.

Not so perfect timing, I thought.

Xavier smiled at me, maybe thinking the same thing. He leaned in and kissed my cheek, pausing at my ear long enough to whisper, "Sorry for being pushy."

I tilted my head back and smiled up at him. "I kinda like it. You have permission to continue."

As we climbed into the back of Rowan's car, she turned around, smiled at me, and then flicked her eyes toward Xavier. I felt my cheeks flush and was glad it was dark. She asked if Aaron was coming, and I told her that he didn't seem to be home.

"We're going to Burke's," Jakob said. "A little hole-in-the-wall pub not far from here. You should text Aaron and tell him to stop by."

The pub was indeed a hole-in-the-wall, a shabby little building set off by itself, a menagerie of neon lights filling the two front windows. Inside, beyond an empty stage scattered with a few amps and speakers, we found a booth in the corner. Xavier and I sat on one side, Rowan and Jakob on the other.

As the server dropped off some water, Xavier looked toward the bar and waved.

Bea was standing next to a tall man in a baseball cap, her hair as wild as it had been when we'd met her in the campus basement. She gave Xavier a thumbs-up, flagged down the bartender, and pointed at us.

The bartender looked over, nodded, and in a few minutes, a round of beers arrived at our table.

Xavier raised a glass in Bea's direction and took a sip.

For a while after that, the three of them discussed plans for what might come next, but I didn't say much. I had other things on my mind.

About twenty minutes in, Rowan tipped her bottle in my direction. "What's going on in that head of yours over there, my dear? You're being awfully quiet."

Xavier and Jakob stopped talking and looked at me.

Maybe now's the time, I thought, *especially without Sterling here.* "I have something I want to ask everyone, and I need everyone's honest opinion," I said, looking at each in turn. "Doesn't anybody but me wonder why this is happening? I mean, I spent most of today reviewing the data we've collected so far. Every bit of it matches what I put in my novel, as if we've been following some sort of script or something. How's that even possible?" I shook my head. "You all seem OK with it, like this is all perfectly normal. Doesn't anyone else think this is a little strange?"

Rowan looked at Jakob and then back to me. "Are you still having the headaches?"

"They stopped for a while, along with the dreams, but now they're back."

"Which dreams?" Jakob asked.

The ones I've never told you about, I thought. "Remember when we were at Les Choux and Sterling mentioned a consultant? He said that someone had to have told me about his work."

Jakob nodded.

I wasn't sure where to start. I thought about Remmington and his appearance in the library: how he'd urged me to move forward with writing, how he'd given me the phone number for the publisher, and how he'd popped up here and there along the way to offer guidance regarding the book. He asked that I not tell anyone about him. He'd reminded me of that more than once. My fear was that if I did, he might not come back, leaving me stuck in the middle of a novel with no ending. I couldn't worry about this anymore though. I needed to tell them about Remmington.

Xavier reached over and took my hand.

"I don't know if the dreamwork I've been doing with you, Jakob, has anything to do with this or not, but I feel like I'm going crazy. My dreams—and nightmares—are more vivid than ever, but without them, I'm not sure I could have finished the first book. I must sleepwalk, too. Sometimes I drift off in one room and wake up in another." I looked at Jakob. "Remember that day I ran into you in the bookstore? When I apologized for not returning your call?"

Jakob said that he did.

"I fell asleep in the library but woke up standing in the foyer with the phone to my ear." I looked around the table. "You've all had recurring dreams, right? Where you're always in the same place or with the same people?"

The three of them nodded.

"In my nightmares, I'm usually in Gram Marie's house. In my dreams, there's this man. He's always wearing a dark suit, and his shoes are always spotless. He's dressed like that every time I see him. The first time I saw him was when I fell asleep in the college library. He gave me the phone number for the publisher. I told Maeve about it when I got home. I didn't expect the number to work, but it did. Everything he's told me in my dreams has come true. He even told me I'd meet Sterling before you mentioned him to me, Jakob." I hesitated to say the next part. "His name is Remmington."

Rowan didn't look surprised.

"What's even weirder," I continued, "is that Lydia, the woman at Broadman Publishing, sees the same man in her dreams. Same suit, same shiny shoes. He told her I'd be calling about my novel before I even did. Needless to say, she was a little surprised when I described him to her. We've talked about him between ourselves—but never with anyone else."

Jakob looked at Rowan and smiled.

I kept going. "He sometimes brings this woman with him. He calls her Ms. Sterling. She's got long white hair and a mole on her cheek." I touched my left cheekbone.

Jakob looked at Rowan again.

"I almost feel like I know her from somewhere," I said.

"Do you recognize the man?" Rowan asked.

I shook my head. "He seems familiar, but he doesn't look like anyone I know. When the book took off, I just told myself that maybe all authors have a Remmington, you know, like a really creative imaginary friend, just in your dreams, feeding you ideas. Now, I just feel like I'm losing my mind."

Rowan laughed. "Well, if you didn't have friends like us, they might tell you that you were."

Beyond Rowan's head, I saw Bea get up from her chair and walk toward the restrooms.

"We don't think you're crazy," Rowan said. "In fact, Jakob and I have been wondering about this for a while. Believe it or not, there's a simple explanation."

Xavier turned to Jakob. "Do you think she chose the name Remmington as a play on words? You know, rapid eye movement, REM sleep? Isn't that when you dream? During REM?"

"You do dream during REM," Jakob said, "but I don't think that's why Nadia's visitor is named Remmington." He looked at Rowan.

"Remmington is Nadia's father's name." Rowan looked first at Xavier and then to me. "You truly don't know what's happening, do you, Nadia?"

I truly didn't.

"Someone is trying to help you," Rowan said, "maybe more than one someone, maybe a few people. They know you're afraid to see them in person, so they've found another way to talk to you that you'll accept. They have information for you, so with no other option, they've found you in your dreams."

"It's fairly common, actually," Jakob explained. "Your father likely understands your fears better than anyone, so why wouldn't he take this route to get in touch with you?"

I shook my head. "But that doesn't make any sense. My dad wasn't a scientist. He couldn't have come up with the experiments in my dreams. Plus, Remmington doesn't even look like my father. Dad certainly never wore a suit. If my dad decided to show up in my dreams, don't you think he'd want me to know it was him?"

But in a way, I'd had a feeling, hadn't I? Like I knew him from somewhere, even when I first saw him in the library. There were hints that it was him all along, weren't there? I'd even picked up on a scent. Like cinnamon, but not really. Old Spice, the cologne I'd given him every year for Christmas as a kid. The eyes that were slowly changing color as time passed, changing to match the color of my father's. He was the man on the stretcher, too, wasn't he? Draped in green cloth, the top of his head exposed. That was where they had tried to remove the tumor. Where there was now patch of thinning hair.

Jakob said, "In cases of dream intervention, it's quite common for spirits to mask their identities, at least initially. They're hesitant, just like we are. When they break into our dreams, they know that the dreamer is already a little confused with what's real and what's not. Even you said sometimes you aren't sure if you're dreaming. If you thought you were awake, seeing him as he was when he was alive would make you afraid, and your fear would block reception. That's the last thing he wanted. He has information for you, Nadia, and he has no other way to express it. That information is why we keep saying we need you."

"You father's a smart man," Rowan said. "I think he knew that if he came to you as your father, you wouldn't do anything he suggested. Just as you said, he wasn't a scientist, but you are. He just needed to prompt your thoughts. His suit threw you off, but even so, he gave you the right name."

"I didn't even know his name until I talked to Lydia," I said. "She's the one who asked if it might have been Remmington who had given me the phone number."

"Again, he didn't want to be that obvious," Rowan said.

"But why would he go to Lydia?"

Jakob laughed. "Spirits can go wherever they want, Nadia. He got into her dream as easily as he got into yours. I'm sure he knew you wanted the house, and I'm sure he knew she worked at a publishing company. He may have even known that Jillian's energy was needed to bring you full circle. He hit the jackpot."

Before I could ask any more about this, a hand landed on my shoulder. I looked up to find Aaron smiling down at me. He smoothed a hand over my hair and gave me a surveying look. "You look a little peaky, my dear. You feelin' OK?"

"I think maybe she just needs another drink," Xavier replied. "Things are getting pretty heavy over here."

CHAPTER 33

The Past
Age Forty-One

"Hello?" The voice was muffled and seemed to come from far away.

Sunlight warmed my left eyelid. The right one was still pressed into my favorite pillow. I rolled over onto my back and turned my head toward the sound.

The bedroom door creaked open.

"You alive?" Maeve asked, peeking in. "You never sleep in this late."

I laid a hand across my forehead. The headache was enormous, and this time, it had nothing to do with writing—just too many drinks the night before.

Maeve held out a glass of orange juice and placed two white tablets on the nightstand. "In case you want them."

I sat up. "I think I might."

She handed them to me, and I washed them down with the juice.

"When did you get home last night?" I asked.

"Long before you," she said, smiling. "I only came upstairs because Jakob called a little bit ago and asked if you and I were coming to the seminar today."

"Oh my God," I said, looking for my phone on the nightstand. "What time is it?"

"Seven thirty," Maeve said, heading toward the door. "We're good. I told him we'd be there. Coffee's on, and breakfast is in the works. I'll see you downstairs. Gonna go make sure the pancakes aren't burning."

I jumped in the shower, and by the time I got to the kitchen, Maeve was setting plates out on the counter. She pushed a large cup of coffee in my direction. "I hear you finally told them about Remmington."

This was probably why Jakob had asked if we'd be coming to class that morning. Our conversation last night had most likely spurred an idea for his lecture topic.

We arrived at the University just before nine. People were still lingering in the halls, and even Jakob stood near the door, talking with Professor Weiss from down the hall.

Maeve gave Jakob a hug as we squeezed by and stepped into the auditorium.

For a Saturday morning, the room was surprisingly full. My headache had diminished, but the voices in the hall still sounded louder than normal.

Maeve and I found two empty spots near the front. Jakob wandered in not long after us. He stepped up onto the stage, but instead of taking his normal position behind the podium, he went straight to the chalkboard. He waited there until a hush fell over the room, and then he wrote two words on the board: *shifted perception*.

We scribbled the words into our notebooks as he made his way to the podium and rested his arms across the top.

"In previous seminars," Jakob said, "we've talked about increased sensitivity and psychic gifts. I've talked to quite a few of you about things you've seen, and I've been asked by others if it's possible for them to learn one of these talents. One thing we haven't really touched on, though, is how some of you in this room might not want to come in direct contact with a spirit—no matter how great it sounds on paper. So, let's see a show of hands. If given the chance to come face-to-face with a ghost, how many would pass?"

About half of the people raised their hands. I was one of them. Maeve wasn't.

Jakob paced the edge of the stage. "Most spirits know that there are people out there who have no desire to see them, so they try to follow the rules, and they try not to scare anyone. But, when they have something important to say, they sometimes must find other ways to get their message across." He pointed at the board as he walked over to it. "Shifted perception is a way that spirits can communicate with the living without being so obvious, in other words, without scaring the pants off the recipient."

A few giggles came from the back of the room as he wrote two more words on the board: *dream intervention.*

Jakob looked at me and smiled. "Dream intervention is a type of shifted perception. As most of you know, I run a sleep lab upstairs where we've monitored a few of my younger psychics while they move through the different stages of sleep." He turned again to the board and added four more words to the growing list: *Beta. Alpha. Theta. Delta.*

"These are the four states of consciousness. Beta is defined as complete consciousness, the state that most of you should be in right now unless, of course, you were maybe out a little later than planned last night."

A few people chuckled.

Maeve nudged me with her elbow.

"Alpha phase," he said, "is when we're technically conscious, but our subconscious is more easily accessed. During this state, we're relaxed, most susceptible to light hypnosis and daydreaming.

"After alpha, we progress to theta, a state in which we waver in a light sleep but are still aware of what's going on around us. Meditation occurs primarily in theta. And finally, the fourth stage is delta. This is where we fall into a deep sleep. In delta, you are no longer fully aware of your surroundings, but you can still remember what happens in a dream. This is when dream intervention occurs."

Jakob circled the word delta. He then extended an arrow out from the circle. Near the point of the arrow, he drew a horizontal line and divided it into thirds. He placed a few ZZZZs at the far left of the line and drew an alarm clock at the right.

"Spirits are patient," he said. "They have all the time in the world. They wait until we enter delta to cross the veil, over here by the ZZZZs. Then they wait some more before they intervene. They only step in when we're in late delta, right before we get dumped back into the real world, possibly by an alarm clock or some other noise that they anticipate."

Jakob scratched an X on the timeline, close to the end with the clock.

"If dream intervention occurs over here, near the X, at a time closer to the end of delta, there's a much better chance of recall when the recipient of dream intervention wakes up."

A woman near the stage raised her hand.

Jakob pointed at her.

"But how do they know when to intervene?" she asked.

"The answer to that is simple," he said. "Spirits know their target's cycle. They anticipate the target's actions and coordinate their own accordingly. They watch us as we set our alarm clocks. They know our habits, whether we normally wake up before the alarm goes off, or if we usually hit snooze a few times before we actually climb out of bed. They know how long we nap. They also know how we'll react to certain cues, and they use all of this information to make sure they intervene at the precise moment when recall is most likely. I'm sure everyone here has seen a movie at some point where a spirit is hovering near the bed while a person sleeps. This probably isn't far off from the truth, actually. Spirits know that sleep opens doors that aren't available at other times. When we're asleep, our inhibitions are lowered. They know this is when they need to act."

If what Jakob is saying is true, what exactly does this mean? Are we being watched all the time? Studied? I glanced around the room, at the empty seats, remembering how Remmington had said he'd sat behind me in class. *Is that possible?* A low hum of chatter coursed through the auditorium. Apparently, others were thinking similar things.

Jakob tapped on his microphone. "All right, everybody. Let's quiet down. We have a lot to get through today."

He waited until the chatter stopped, and then he spent the next half hour going over examples of dream intervention. Of course, people had questions. When no more hands were raised, Jakob went back to the board and wrote two more words: *automatic writing.*

He drew a line under them, rubbed his hands together, and stared out at the class. "So, who here can tell me about automatic writing?"

Jakob smiled in my direction. He pointed, and I froze.

Then I heard Maeve's voice next to me.

"Automatic writing is when someone writes under the direction of a spirit, sometimes willingly, sometimes not. They might not even know it's happening until it's over."

I looked at her. *How long had she known?*

"Nicely put, my dear," Jakob said, giving a quick bow of his head. "What about psychography? Care to have a go at that one?"

"That's when someone purposely channels a spirit in order to write," Maeve replied without hesitation.

The guy in front of us turned around in his chair to see who had answered.

"Nicely done, again." Jakob walked toward the podium. "As it turns out, both of these phenomena are quite common really. As Maeve just told us, with psychography, the writer usually knows what's going on, but with automatic writing, the recipient is often oblivious to their role in the process. Sometimes, the only telltale sign that they've been participating in this little exchange of information is a pounding headache." Jakob blatantly stared at me.

I shot a questioning glance at Maeve.

She shrugged and gave me a grin that had "I told you so" written all over it.

Jakob said, "The headache that accompanies automatic writing has been described as starting at the base of the skull, at the back of the neck. It generally radiates upward and downward equally. It typically commences with the start of writing, and it ceases shortly after writing stops. Dizziness is a common complaint, as well.

"What's odd," Jakob continued, "is that even though this type of headache can be crippling, the writer continues to write. Looking back on it, they sometimes say it's like a runner's high. Once the pain peaks, they barely notice it. The subject carries on, often at a frenzied pace, sometimes writing hundreds of pages in one sitting."

I closed my notebook. There was no point in taking notes. This was my life.

When class was over, Maeve and I met Jakob near the stage.

"Well, that puts a whole new spin on things," I said.

Jakob gathered his notes from the podium and looked up at me as he tucked them in his bag. "For me? No. But for you? Probably." He erased the board. "I'm headed over to see an old friend of mine after this. If you think my lecture put a spin on things, you should come and hear what she has to say."

I turned to Maeve.

She shook her head. "You go ahead. I'm gonna go meet Jenn outside and hit the food cart. She has a break between classes, and I'm starving. Take your time, though. Just text me when you're done."

On the other side of campus, Jakob and I stepped into another building, one I'd never been inside before. A huge skeleton of a *Tyrannosaurus rex* greeted us as we stepped into the lobby. A much smaller skeleton, a *Deinonychus,* according to the nameplate on the floor, had been placed in front of it, poised in a run. It glanced back up over its shoulder, as if it knew it should be moving faster. Glass display cases lined the perimeter of the room, and as we made our way to the elevator at the far end of the hall, I saw that they were filled with primitive tools and an assortment of human skulls. Above us, suspended from the ceiling, as if in flight, there was a trio of pterodactyls.

I wondered at the breadth of their wingspan as we stepped into the elevator, guessing it had to be at least thirty feet before the doors slid shut, removing them from view.

When the elevator reopened on the second floor, a huge medieval wooden door had taken their place. Arched and studded with black iron rivets, it would have been more at home on the front of a castle. It was attached to the frame with long, decorative hinges.

"Have a look at the knocker," Jakob said as we stepped closer. "Clever, eh?"

The knocker was made of heavy black iron, a human jaw, teeth and all. The bottom half, the mandible, if I remembered my anatomy correctly, was mounted on the door. Jakob grasped the top half, the maxilla, lifted it, and proceeded to rap the upper and lower teeth together. Two seconds later, a woman's voice called out, inviting us to enter. According to the metal nameplate hanging to the right of the door, the voice belonged to Dr. Evangeline Potvin, director, Paleoanthropology Department.

The high-ceilinged office inside was huge and had a very Gothic feel. Red curtains framed the narrow windows, and just inside the door, a long table, maybe fifteen feet or so, was draped in a red velvet runner. Carved legs, shaped like claws, poked out from underneath. More skulls, like those in the lobby, were arranged along its length. Beyond the table was a huge, polished desk that matched the size of the room. Behind that was a tiny woman.

She stood as we rounded the long table. She wore a frilly-collared white blouse and a tailored blue suit jacket. Her long, gray hair was pulled back in a chignon, her ears decorated with a pair of small diamond studs. Her face was heavily wrinkled as if she'd spent years in the sun, which she probably had, given her title and surroundings.

"Well, I'll be," she said. "Is that Jakob I see?"

"And Ms. King," he added, gesturing in my direction.

"Ah, yes, Ms. King." The woman came around the side of her desk. She would have been a perfect match for Mr. Noah, no more than five feet tall and no more than ninety pounds soaking wet. Her black pencil skirt revealed two thin legs. On her feet were a pair of heels that even I wouldn't attempt to wear, but she seemed to manage just fine. She reached out a hand in greeting.

"So, I finally get to meet you," she said, her voice raspy. "Our friend here kept promising I would, but I was beginning to lose hope." She pointed a finger at me. "I've been dying to show you something, so let's not waste any more time. Follow me." She went over to the long table. "Have a look at these with me, would you?"

I followed but stood opposite her, on the other side of the table, suddenly feeling like a shopper at a macabre sale booth. She placed her hands on top of two of the skulls.

"What in the world *am* I doing with all of these?" she asked. "That's what you're wondering, I'm sure. I saw you eyeing them up when you came in." Her raspy voice took on a cadence that reminded me of Katharine Hepburn, one of Gram Marie's favorite actresses. "I started collecting them forty-five years ago, when my great-uncle gave me one. He'd found it on a dig in Somalia, nothing special, but I didn't know that at the time. I thought it was the best gift anyone had ever given me. Little did he know the monster he created. They're my absolute obsession now, and I have some pretty good ones." She looked up and down the table. "Brain size and evolution, my dear, that's what I study. Are you familiar with the Neanderthals?"

"I am actually," I said. Oddly enough, this was another fascination shared with Gram Marie. She'd had shelves filled with anthropology books in her office. We used to read them for fun when I was a kid. I remember being amazed when she first explained evolution to me, all of the differences and similarities between us and apes. Because of her, I took a class in college, and I wrote a research paper on the Neanderthals specifically: how they lived alongside early modern humans, the theories of their extinction, and how a certain percentage of the current population still shares Neanderthal genes. I had my own ideas about why they had gone extinct, and they didn't agree with the ideas popular at the time.

Dr. Potvin nodded. "I had a feeling you might be. We'll get to the Neanderthals in a minute," she said, making her way to the very end of the table. "First, let's start here, shall we?"

She picked up a skull.

"This one here belongs to one of our earliest ancestors. As you can see, it's much smaller than ours." She held it up next to her face. "Of course, smaller skulls mean smaller brains. Cranial volume increased as our species advanced." She put down the skull and walked the length of the table, laying her hand on larger and larger skulls as she went. "The increase in size was primarily due to the addition of more and more cortex, the cognitive portion of the brain. Our earliest ancestors didn't have much of this. They didn't need it. Their brains contained the same sensory areas as those found in modern man, but given the much tighter cranial cavity, these areas were squashed in next to each other. This, of course, meant that our earliest ancestors didn't have to think much to survive. They acted primarily on instinct. The visual and auditory centers butted right up against the nerves that controlled motor action, so early man immediately ran when a saber-toothed cat got a little too close. The signals traveled quickly." She shot me a little grin and moved farther up the line of skulls.

"Now, as you know," she said, "later in man's evolution, we developed vocal cords. These gave us the ability to speak, but in order to do that, we also needed a speech center in the brain, more cortex to translate the words into a message that could be understood. Most paleoanthropologists will tell you that language development made us a more advanced species." She shook a finger at me. "I beg to differ."

She picked up the biggest skull on the table and handed it to me. It was heavier than expected, crude with a strong brow line.

"That's Neanderthal," she said. "Ms. King, did you know that Neanderthals had a slightly *greater* brain volume than modern humans, on average?"

I nodded. "Their cranial capacity topped ours by more than 15 percent."

Dr. Potvin nodded and looked at Jakob. "Smart girl. I like her." She shook her head. "The Neanderthal is still a mystery to me. I'm still not sure if they're a part of man's lineage or if they stand somewhere outside it. What we do know is that this extra 15 percent was enclosed in the occipital bun, that bulge you see on the back."

I rotated the skull in my hands.

Dr. Potvin reached across the table and tapped the bulge with a red fingernail. "What I think is that we lost this region of the brain after we learned to speak." She picked up a smaller skull and held it close to the one in my hands. "This skull here belongs to modern man."

I looked at the two, taking in all of the differences, the most noticeable being the overall shape. The skull she held was more rounded, with a flatter face and diminished brow. The Neanderthal skull in my hands was nearly one and a half times the depth, shaped more like a football. I turned mine over and peered inside, through the foramen magnum, the hole on the underside, where the nerves from the brain pass through to join the spinal cord. I wondered what Rosa would sense if she held this. *How far back would psychometry allow her to see?*

Dr. Potvin placed the modern skull back on the table.

"Neanderthals didn't speak," she explained. "We know this by looking at their anatomy. Several perfectly preserved specimens were discovered in the late seventies. They had a hyoid bone, the bone that supports our tongue, but it was crudely developed. We don't believe it was attached to the surrounding musculature at all, and hence, not functional. There was something else," she said, pointing at me. "A rudimentary voice box had started to form in Neanderthals as well. Based on the structure, it could have only produced very high-pitched sounds." She paused. "As you know, cavemen are typically depicted as grunting beasts, but based on what was seen in these specimens, that may not have been the case."

Dr. Potvin studied me intently from the other side of the table.

"So," she said, "knowing what I've just told you, Ms. King, think of the cells you've just found. Think of where you've found them. Near the back of the head, no? And to what frequency do they respond?"

Jakob took a seat near Dr. Potvin's desk. His elbows rested on the arms of the chair. His hands were steepled, the tips of his fingers resting on his lips. He'd clearly heard this speech before.

"Isn't it strange?" Dr. Potvin asked. "From an evolutionary standpoint, it's thought that these Neanderthals might have been a transitional species. They were so close to developing an audible language, but they fell short. So, how did they communicate? Is it possible they used telepathy, like Sterling's chimps?"

Jakob said, "I told her about Einstein and Zena, what the team saw on the scans. Don't worry; Evangeline won't tell anyone."

"Nadia, Neanderthals were the first to bury their dead nearly one hundred thousand years ago," she said. "They were the first to place objects in the graves. Makes me wonder why." She studied me, and her gray eyes flickered. "I mean, if they could communicate among themselves using telepathy, what else did that brain of theirs allow them to do? Why were they so worried about taking care of the dead?"

She walked over to her desk. "I don't know about you, Ms. King, but I see a connection. What if they cared for the bodies of the dead because they believed the spirit still needed that physical beacon in case they ever needed to return? Think of the Egyptian mummies and how they left food and wine, even servants, in the tombs."

I stared at the skull in my hands, at the occipital bun. *Had this been the origin of our CT cells?* I looked at Jakob and then at her. It was all coming together.

"Don't be angry with Jakob for telling me about your work," she said. "I haven't told another soul—nor would I ever. Jakob knows where my loyalties lie, but if you could prove this, Nadia, I'd be forever grateful. Your research suggests that primates may have retained the anatomical structures necessary for this type of communication. Rowan's abilities suggest that a few of us may have also retained at least some of these vestigial structures. Your CT cells, if proven to still exist in humans, would be a missing link. Better yet, if these cells still exist in the human brain, that means we may still have a chance to regain these lost arts. Just think of what you may have found."

When my cell phone rang, I placed the skull on the table and dug in my purse. It was Maeve. She was wondering when we might be ready to go. I told her we'd be down in a few minutes.

From the Journal of Nadia King
Age Forty-One

So much has happened these past few days. I was awake most of last night just thinking about the conversation at Burke's Pub, the seminar with Jakob, and our visit to see Dr. Potvin. I could probably measure my headache on the Richter scale right now, so I thought getting some thoughts out of my head and onto paper before bed might help to clear my mind for work this coming week.

Maeve went back to school early this morning. She's got some exams coming up. Aaron is at the soup kitchen. Cold weather always brings extra mouths to feed. So, here I sit, in the library, the house to myself, the dogs gathered around me, trying to figure out what all of this means. Even the shadows must be giving me room to think. I haven't seen any for days.

Jakob says he expected automatic writing all along. It never even crossed my mind. As for telepathy, I have no doubt that's exactly what was happening with Zena and Einstein. Potvin's theory seems to support this from both an anthropological and a sociological standpoint. Zena was born and raised in captivity. Prior to meeting Einstein, she'd never been around native apes. Her initial scans showed very little activity in the CT region. She was closer to humans who have shied away from nonverbal communication for one reason or another, either due to lack of receptors—or just parents who failed to encourage their use. Einstein, on the other hand, had been born in the wild. His use of telepathy was driven by instinct. His CT signal had always been strong.

Einstein taught Zena how to use her "lost art," to use Potvin's words. He helped Zena recognize the gift she'd always had. Teacher and student, much like Rowan and me. In both cases, the anatomy was always there. Zena and I just didn't quite know how to use it.

Then there's Mary, the one who's worked most closely with Sterling's chimps, teaching them a language that she'd been forced to use. Mary was born deaf. She was the first to work with Einstein. Was she possibly conveying mental images to the chimps while teaching them without even being aware of it? Is it possible that Mary's deafness put her more in tune with telepathy? Could this be why Einstein learned so much more quickly at the start?

Potvin's ideas even support what the team saw in Einstein's CT after Zena's death. What was that spooky comment Einstein had signed after she died? *Don't be afraid. I'll be there soon.*

The signals in Einstein's CT after Zena died could only mean one thing. Einstein was somehow still in touch with her. Potvin talked about how the Neanderthals had been the first to bury their dead, the first to leave gifts in their graves. Was it possible that the occipital bun, and the brain matter contained within it, conferred more than just the ability to communicate with the living through telepathy? Could they also communicate with the dead? Was their disappearance really due to extinction—or was it more in line with the work of Sir Anthony Bard? Did they escape this physical world on purpose? Is that why they cared for the bodies of the dead?

Our work at Amulet has already proven that CT cells respond to higher frequencies. Potvin claims that Neanderthals were only capable of producing higher-frequency sounds. Both situations fall in line with the vibrational hypothesis. It only makes sense that both telepathy and spirit communication should be detected by the same mechanism, the same receptors. It makes sense that our CT cells are the missing link.

So, where do we go next?

We need to prove to Sterling that we can control cellular activation, that we can turn the CT cells off and on at will. I have some ideas for how to do that. I think we can use Rowan, and me, to prove this. If we can demonstrate what I think we can, I don't know how Sterling will be able to deny the full function of these cells. He's a scientist. He can't dispute scientific facts. He's aware of developmental anatomy. He knows that we lose brain cells after we're born, especially ones that aren't being put to use. He can't dispute evolution either. In fact, he'd probably be more than happy to agree that any type of cell related to psychic ability should be the first to go. He can't dispute genetics. Rowan and I were both born into families with a history of psychic ability, so we'd be likely to have more CT cells than most. And finally, he can't dispute sociological impact. Rowan and I both grew up in families who believed in certain things, families that let us freely investigate them, so we probably retained more of these cells than most.

The only thing I can't figure out is how psychic ability explains precognition. It's one thing to pick up on a signal that others aren't aware of, but seeing the future seems to require more than just a receptor. My only guess is based on something Potvin said. If these cells connect us somehow with spirits, maybe the spirits are our link to seeing the past and the future. Maybe spirits, without a body to call home, without a need for a physical location, have access to all planes of existence, all planes of time, and maybe they are the missing link for precognition and psychometry. I'm going to meet with Jakob tomorrow and tell him my ideas. We should do these next experiments soon.

I closed the journal, and on my way upstairs for the night, I walked by the chikunga in the foyer. I ran my fingertips along its high cheekbones.

"Only those with good intentions shall enter here," I said out loud, repeating something Gram Marie had said years ago when I watched her hang it in her office. I brushed a strand of twine out of the mask's eyes and climbed the stairs.

Before turning off my bedroom light for the night, I set my alarm and looked around the room. The dogs were sprawled on the floor, and the cat was curled up at the bottom of the bed near my feet.

"The alarm is set for seven o'clock, Dad," I said out loud. "In case you were wondering."

CHAPTER 34

The Present
Age Forty-One
Sunday Night

Sleep comes quickly, and the dreams are vivid—more vivid than ever before.

The nightmare plays first. I climb the damp stairs in Gram Marie's house. When I look back through the railing, the figure with the broad shoulders is gone from the window. The cats are waiting for me on the landing and in the hall upstairs. When I bend to stroke the biggest, the smell comes, the scent like cinnamon, but not really. The cats don't follow me into the bedroom as I try to get away. A man, his face draped in green cloth, is on an operating table, the top of his skull removed, his brain exposed. He seems familiar to me. When the lights go out, a cold hand grasps my shoulder.

I wake up, but only for a minute. I fall asleep again almost immediately, right back into the dream. The scene has changed though, as it often does when we're asleep. I'm no longer in Gram Marie's house. I'm in the Baird, in the chair in the library. I'm drenched in a cold sweat, a newspaper at my feet. I change into my favorite pair of jeans and a black T-shirt in the laundry room and then carry the newspaper upstairs. The bedroom door is closed.

I know who's waiting for me inside given the conversation in Burke's Pub, but I'm still afraid to go in. This time, I know I'll have to see him for who he really is. I know he won't be wearing the suit or shiny shoes, and for some reason, the whole idea of seeing a ghost, even this particular ghost, still frightens me. I know his name is Remmington—but not just any Remmington.

I take a deep breath, summon the lucid dreaming skills taught to me by Jakob, and tell myself not to be afraid. *You'll see him as he really is, Nadia, but he's still just a dream. He's not really there, at least not yet.*

Ares is in the dream too. He looks at me as if to say, "Well, what the hell else are you going to do at this point if you don't go in?"

When I open the bedroom door, the man on the bed looks exactly as I remember him, at least how I remember him before he got sick. He sits there, propped up against the headboard, leaning against a huge pile of pillows, finally wearing something other than his "power suit," which I've grown so accustomed to seeing him in over the years.

I see him for who he really is, just my father in his sweatshirt and jeans, no longer any need for masquerade. The room smells of Old Spice.

He promises to help with the final experiment at Amulet, agrees that it's time.

I wake on Monday morning to the sound of my alarm, only to find the dogs sprawled out on the rug in front of me. Ares sits in the doorway.

Later, when I see the figures in the bay window from the cobblestone path, I know they're real. This is the next step. I'm awake, seeing something that I always thought I'd be afraid to see, but from a far enough distance so as not to be afraid, as if they know this might help ease me into my new awareness. The three of them, one of them my father, are testing the waters, seeing if this is OK.

Dear reader,

I won't bore you with the remaining details from that very long Monday. I'm sure you recall how I talked with Sterling at Amulet that morning about the article in the paper, how I shared a bottle of wine with Rowan when I got home from work, and how I fell asleep in the library with the cat on my chest after leafing through a few of my journals. It's where this whole story started, so let me pick it up from there. It's time we continue on to Tuesday, to the week leading up to my final experiment. It's time to see if I can prove my theory.

Sincerely,
Nadia

CHAPTER 35

The Present
Age Forty-One
Tuesday

When the phone rings bright and early, I find myself on the chair in the library, Ares stretched comfortably across my chest on top of the fleece throw. He starts to purr.

I look past him at the room beyond, a bit disoriented, like when you wake up in a hotel room that first morning of vacation and look around, only to find windows in all the wrong places. The smell of the fireplace helps jar my memory. The empty wineglasses on the table do the same. By the time my phone stops ringing, I've put the puzzle pieces together.

My legs dangle over one arm of the leather chair, and my toes are numb, full of pins and needles. I look at my watch. It's 6:30 a.m.

The phone starts ringing again, and I dig my hand in between the seat cushion and the back of the chair to pull it out. Rowan's name is on the screen.

"You do know it's six thirty in the morning, right?" I say, holding phone to my ear.

"Of course, and I'm not happy about being up at this hour either."

I rub my eyes. "So, why are you awake?"

"You should ask your father that question," she says with a yawn.

I sit up and swing my legs around to the front of the chair. "What do you mean?"

"I mean, he made a visit. Pulled me out of a lovely dream, was having lunch with Michelangelo in a garden, and he just walked right in, told me that he needed me."

I hold the phone to my ear and shuffle into the kitchen for a glass of water. At the sink, I notice the paint on my hands. I turn them over. It's on both sides, and all down the front of my shirt too.

"Why now?" I ask, carrying my glass through the back hallway and into my studio. "You've tried to reach him before, and it never worked."

"I might have fibbed a little," she says. "I have tried to reach him before, and I've *told* you that it didn't work, but let's just say he and I have been chatting. We both wanted you to see him on your own. We knew you could do it."

I can't be angry at her for this. When others do things for you, it becomes easy to take a back seat and let them continue without learning how to do it for yourself. I look into the library as I pass. Ares has taken my spot on the chair.

"He's happy you've finally realized that it's been him all along, but he's worried about what other things you'll try before you're ready. That's why he came and woke me."

At the studio door, I pause, taking in what I see, unsurprised.

"You said your Gram Marie's house was different in this last dream, didn't you?" Rowan asks. "That there was graffiti on the walls? Overturned furniture?"

I walk over and study the painting on the easel. The red painting journal is on the bench near my unused brushes, open to my notes from the day before.

"Sort of like the Baird was when you moved in," Rowan says. "I think this means we can find out more now. I think we can find your Gram Marie. I think she's in there."

I pick up a lid that belongs to one of the opened paint tubes and screw it back on, and then I move the paintbrush that's caked in red into a jar of turpentine.

"Why do you think that?" I ask, admiring the shading in the basket of apples underneath the window. *I've gotten better.*

"You'll see soon enough," Rowan says. "This is how it starts. From now on, things may not be so subtle for you. I want you to keep an eye on the shadows. Like Jakob said, sleep is close to the veil. Dreams are often the closest some people ever come to their loved ones, but you're a step further, Nadia. Just remember what I've told you. Loved ones aren't the only things that can get through. We should catch up later today ... after you get home from work."

I study the painting, the figures in the bay window, one of them clearly my father. Another one is the woman Remmington brought to visit the garden, Ms. Sterling. The last is an older woman I don't recognize. I'd apparently had a busy night. My thoughts had found their way out of my head and onto paper—or onto canvas in this case.

"I'll call you before I leave the lab," I tell Rowan before hanging up.

CHAPTER 36

The Present
Age Forty-One
Tuesday

When I arrive at Amulet, I go upstairs to my office. As I'm unlocking the door, Sterling calls to me from his office across the hall. I turn to find him at his desk, staring at his monitor. He waves me in. Before he has a chance to speak, I decide that now's the time for the discussion I should have had with him on Friday, especially if what Rowan said last night is true, and he's read my novel.

"Sterling, we need to talk about what your cells really are."

He nods, as if he might have known this was coming.

I sit in one of the chairs. "You must know by now why Jakob is so interested in this work, why he's been spending so much time here with us, especially while you were out."

Sterling presses his fingertips to his forehead and massages his hairline. He then runs both palms over his face.

"Like you said yesterday, your discovery is going to be big news," I say. "You're definitely onto something here, Sterling, but it has nothing to do with recovery from stroke. Your cells respond to high-frequency just like Jakob and I thought they might. You saw that happen in the lab. And that wasn't a fluke. We've repeated that same experiment three more times while you were out and got the same results. Brannigan has also been playing with different frequencies. He's found one that makes the cells migrate until they form that tree-like aggregation from your scans."

244

Sterling listens, but thankfully, he doesn't say a word.

"I read over the autopsy report the other day," I say. "Gross inspection of Einstein's brain showed that the meshwork of CT cells seemed to cover only certain regions of the cortex. The sensory regions most densely covered were the ones involved in language comprehension."

"Which is what we would expect, right?" Sterling asks. "I mean, that was the whole point of my research."

Of course, this is true, but there's more, and I can see that he knows it.

"Originally, we thought your cells were glial cells, just there for support. Further studies have shown that they can actually conduct impulses, like neurons. They secrete chemotactic factors too. These are what draw other cells toward them, which explains why the CT looked so expansive in the images over time."

Sterling narrows his eyes.

"Sterling, you must know by now that these signals are tied to more than just comprehension of sign language." I take a deep breath. "Has Jakob ever mentioned the vibrational hypothesis to you?"

He says nothing. I don't really expect him to, even if Jakob had mentioned it.

I continue. "This hypothesis claims that most psi abilities are due to an increased sensitivity to certain vibrations." I rest my forearms on his desk. "Look, I know this isn't something you want to hear, but there's a huge possibility that your lab, and Amulet, have just proven that psychic ability is real. That's something that no one has ever done, Sterling. Consider that experiment with Einstein. The signals you saw in the CT were most prominent while he and Zena were just sitting in their cages, when they weren't signing at all. That's when the cells lit up the most. Sterling, this would only make sense if those cells were picking up something that wasn't detectable to anyone else, some sort of telepathic signal between Einstein and Zena. That's the only explanation for it. Think about it, the only way Einstein could have known to grab the green gloves from the toy box was if Zena communicated some sort of image to him. She didn't have the gloves in her cage. She taught him the word without an object for reference. You realize this, right?" I sit back in my chair. "Sterling, you may have originally been looking for something else in those scans, but you caught the activation of the CT on video."

I give this a minute to sink in. Of course, none of this explains why the activation continued after Zena died or why it was still evident while Einstein was on life support, but that conversation can wait for another day.

Sterling stands and begins to pace around the room, eventually stopping in front of the bookshelves, his back toward me. "It makes sense," he says. "I mean, why wouldn't animals communicate like that? Before Einstein and Zena could sign, what other option did they have?" He turns and looks at me. "But telepathy, Nadia? Do we really have to call it that? I know that's what it looks like, but agreeing to use a term like that goes against everything I've ever believed in."

"But ... you do agree?"

He lets out a long breath. "Of course, I agree." He shakes his head. "I'm not stupid. I just needed some time away from this place to digest it. My whole project was put into place to prove that chimps were smart enough to communicate. Turns out I've just been focusing on the wrong language." He goes to the window and stuffs his hands in his pockets. "These past few months have been hard for me, Nadia. There's been a lot going on, and this whole thing with the newspaper just added more insult to injury." He turns and looks at me. "I've never been very good with apologies, and I know that I probably owe you one, but the best I can do is say that I trust you. I can tell you're a damn good scientist. I want you to know that I'm ready to hear what comes next when you're ready to share."

This is completely unexpected, and it takes a minute to sink in. "That means a lot, Sterling," I say. "As for what comes next, I have a few more details to work out, and then we'll give it try."

"*Can* I trust you, Nadia?" Sterling asks.

It's a loaded question, and he knows it.

"Pretty soon, I think we're all gonna have to put our cards on the table, Sterling, and no matter what, we'll have to face them as a team. So, yes, you can trust me."

I step out into the hallway and glance back over my shoulder.

Sterling remains at the window, staring out.

I want to ask what he's thinking, but I'm not even sure he knows.

I spend the afternoon working through the details of that final experiment, jotting down an outline in one of the laboratory notebooks on my desk.

Final Experiment

Purpose:

In vivo demonstration, willful activation of the CT.

Phase I:

Set a timer for five minutes. Nadia wears the helmet and begins writing something she's memorized. Brannigan obtains normal scans, activation observed in the parietal lobes.

Set a timer for five minutes. Remmington tells Nadia what to write. Activation observed in the CT.

Final five minutes. Nadia returns to writing from memory. Activation of the CT fades.

Phase II:

Set a timer for five minutes. Rowan wears the helmet while she meditates. Minimal activation in any sensory area.

Set a timer for five minutes. Rowan channels Remmington. Activation observed in the CT.

Final five minutes. Rowan breaks the connection with Remmington. Activation of the CT fades.

Data Acquisition:

Brannigan to capture fMRI images every ten seconds. Based on past observations with Einstein, the CT should glow red within one minute after onset of activity. A five-minute window for psychic interaction should be more than enough to observe the signal.

Points to Consider:

- How do we ensure Remmington's participation?
- Do we need to share this plan with him prior to the experiment—or will he simply know to be there?

Before leaving Amulet, I remember that I'm supposed to call Rowan. I know if I call her, she'll head over the house right away. I know if I call and say that I'm heading home in a few hours, she'll know that I'm lying. The truth is, I want some time alone at the Baird before she gets there. I'm sure she knows this, too.

I decide I'll call later—after I take a nap. My father and I need to talk.

CHAPTER 37

The Present
Age Forty-One
Tuesday

No one else is home, and I fall asleep on the couch in the library. Gram Marie's house is in the distance. I'm standing in the shadows of the trees. This time, I cross the yard without any hurry and easily mount the three concrete steps up to the patio. The steps are free of leaves, and the sliding glass door is intact. An easel waits a few feet in front of me, and beside it, there is a high wooden stool. There's a table with a cardboard box on top of it, one overflowing with crinkled tubes of oil paints. Beside that, an old applesauce jar is filled halfway to the top with cloudy turpentine.

The cats are there too, maybe ten of them. They pace, occasionally walking across the loaded painter's palette, which is next to the legs of the stool, its surface dotted with a rainbow of hues. As they weave in and out of the furniture's legs and mine, they leave intertwining trails of multicolored footprints on the patio's blue outdoor carpet. When I bend down to pick up the palette, they stop to look at me

"I'm not here for you," I tell them, and they immediately disappear.

A low meow comes from my left, and when I turn toward the sliding glass door, Ares is staring back at me through a freshly shattered pane. He stands in the breakfast nook, atop a pile of broken glass, his eyes trained on me. He meows again, and his eyes wander off to my right—to the half-finished painting on the easel. I know what he wants me to do. He wants me to finish it.

I look at the canvas, assess the work in progress, and take a seat on the stool. The image is beautifully rendered, the perfect likeness of Ares, the colors exact, right down to the watery green of his eyes. Behind him, the background is colorless, the outline of the door lightly sketched in pencil. The paint is still wet. A long-handled paintbrush in the easel's tray is tipped with a touch of green. I place it in the turpentine and set to work refilling the palette.

Ares sits quietly while I arrange my workspace. When I grab a new brush, a breeze blows past me. It carries the scent of jasmine, another common smell in my dreams. I try not to think about what it might mean. I have an idea, but that's not why I'm here. I dip the paintbrush into the dollop of black and use it to create a shadow on the floor behind Ares. I make it long and lean, unnaturally thin. It's clearly not the shape of a cat even though it's meant to belong to Ares. As I reload the brush, I sense movement in my peripheral vision. When I turn to see who's there, I find my father standing in the door. He's dressed in sneakers, jeans, and a gray sweatshirt.

"I was hoping you'd show up," I say.

He opens his mouth to speak, but there's no sound. It's as if someone has pressed mute. I close my eyes and rewind, reminding myself to stop blocking the things that scare me. A gust of wind tousles my hair, and when his mouth moves again, I can hear him.

"Jakob has taught you well," he says. "You learn quickly."

"I'm trying," I say, and then without wasting any time, I explain why I've asked him to come. I tell him that it's time for the final experiment, that we can't wait any longer.

He listens to my plan, and when I'm done, he agrees that it should work—if all goes well. "Is that the only reason you wanted to talk to me?"

"If you have time, I have plenty of questions."

"I have all the time in the world," he says, "and I'll try my best to answer your questions, but I have a feeling I know what they are, and if I'm right, we'll have to be careful. There are rules we have to follow when speaking with the living, certain things we're allowed to share—and other things that we aren't. If you promise not to look over here, I'll try to give you some of both. You sit and paint. Don't put me in the picture.

Don't let them know you can see me. They won't listen to us unless they have a reason to."

Somehow, I know who "they" are, and I already know that the questions I mean to ask are not allowed. I choose a dark shade of brown with my brush and trace over the lines sketched in the background, filling in the doorframe, shading it, as he talks.

"Before you ask your questions, I want to tell you something. I was there when you first moved into the Baird," he says. "I watched you walk down the cobblestone path, saw you turn around to face the bay window, as if you sensed *something*. I waved to you over the orchids, hoping that you'd see me, but you convinced yourself I was just a reflection in the glass. I was disappointed, but I understood. It's what most people do."

I pick up some blue paint to fill in the patio floor.

"They told me you might be more accepting over time, especially if I came to you in the dreams first. I'm happy they were right. I've missed you."

"Dreams are a psychic's training wheels," I say, repeating something Rowan said at Burke's as we were leaving.

We both laugh.

"Believe it or not," he says, "being on this side is just as hard as being on yours. Even shades have a learning curve. I haven't been here that long, so it's like being the youngest on the playground. Sometimes you just have to sit and watch to learn the game."

Out of the corner of my eye, I see Remmington bend down and pick up Ares. He flops the cat over one shoulder, and Ares begins to purr.

"I learned dream intervention to help you, but it also helped me because it requires less energy. We're both getting stronger, which is why I need to tell you a few things before you get too brave with this growing talent of yours. Then I'll let you ask your questions."

I paint another shadow in the background.

"There's a vortex in the Baird," Remmington explains. "It makes the door between your world and mine weaker. I believe you've already sensed that, given your decision to stop meditating. This vortex makes it easy for even weaker spirits to come and go as they please, which is why the shadows are so strong there, and that's why you have less control over them than you're used to. I'm not the only shade that's been trying to speak with you, Nadia. You just don't hear the others yet because a part of you is still leery of the process. Your mind is still filtering the input. But now that you and I are talking like this, arranged by your choice, now that you're willing to see me and accept who I am, this same type of contact may come from them as well. Before you open yourself any further, Nadia, you have to learn how to block out the signals you don't want to receive. This is what Rowan wants to talk to you about today, and it's very important that you listen to what she says. Some of the shades I've met in the Baird are desperate to make contact with anyone. Once they know you can see them and hear them, you have to be selective. You have to learn to control the volume. If you don't—and listen to me very carefully when I say this, Nadia—if you don't exert control, shades can quite literally make you lose your mind."

I look at him, but he shakes his head. I return my eyes to the canvas.

"You also need to tell Rowan and Jakob that Evelyn was right. The Dark Ones do have the ability to stop the living. It's harder for them, and it takes much more energy, but they can do it when it's absolutely necessary. The final thing you need to know is something that I definitely should not share. By giving you this information, I run the risk of not being able to speak with you ever again. The Dark Ones can and will silence me. Do you understand?"

"Then don't tell me," I say, turning his way. "I don't want to lose you again."

"Look at your painting, Nadia," he says calmly. "I *have* to tell you. I have to take the risk because you have to finish your work at Amulet. You're the only one who can put the final pieces together."

I study the canvas, but I don't want him to continue. *It's not worth the risk.*

"It *is* worth the risk," he answers, reading my mind. "You need to know that being a guide for the living is like playing a game of chess. Our job is to lay out clues, to give options to the living. We put other people in your path to see if you'll take the opportunities or pass them by. Every living thing is given a guide, but not many choose to use them. Some can't even sense us anymore, while some of the ones who can pretend they can't. You've been very good at using the clues we've left for you and taking the opportunities. You've trusted your instinct. You've believed that we were here. Fear was the only thing preventing you from using all of the information we tried to give you, and now you've conquered that.

"Nadia, this game of chess can't go on forever. The end is coming sooner than you think. Evolution is still at play, and right now is natural selection's final hour. Those who can sense their guides and utilize the information we provide will be able to bridge the transition before it's too late. Do you understand what I'm saying?"

"What do you mean by the end?" I ask, keeping my eyes on my brush.

"I mean that the world you live in is tired," he says. "It's overpopulated and filthy. Cruelty has become commonplace. No one cares anymore. Most put no thought or effort into preserving a balance. They're using up the resources like they'll be available forever, but that's just not the case. What I'm saying is that the physical world you're living in right now can't hold out much longer. In your current state, Nadia, you need a physical space to inhabit. You need clean air, water, and food. In my current level of existence, I don't need any of that. My energy can exist without a physical space. What you need to know is that there's a level between yours and mine. I don't know all of the details, but I do know that death is not required to enter. A physical body is not needed there either. Sir Anthony Bard went searching for a way to bridge the veil, a way to lose the connection with his physical body, because of what I just told you. He's made it across, but he's too selfish to share what he's found. He's also too afraid to go back to your side for fear he can't make it back to ours. If something were to happen to the world tomorrow, he knows he's safe where he is. You've nearly figured it out, Nadia. You're getting close to what he knows. You need to solve the puzzle. Good people are relying on you."

A shrill noise pierces the air, and I look toward the house. Remmington's image wavers, as if he's a projection going out of focus, and he turns to face the interior of the house.

A dark shadow, the largest I've ever seen, stands in the corner of the breakfast nook.

Ares sees it too. He lets out one of those eerie yowls, the kind you hear in the middle of the night when two cats accidentally come face-to-face outside.

My father turns back to me with an urgent look on his face. "Don't stop painting! And don't look at me. Focus on the canvas—on anything but me."

I feel my heartbeat race as I dip my brush into the gray. My ears begin to ring, and goose bumps spread across my forearms. I focus on the lines created by the brush.

"We have to be very careful now," Remmington says quietly. "The Dark Ones are here. Remember what I said and pretend you can't hear me. If they think you can't hear, they won't pay as much attention."

I give a barely perceptible nod.

"Before I say anything more, I want you to know that I love you and that I'm so happy that we've had our second chance. If anything happens to me, you have to promise to continue your work, no matter what. Promise me that."

Tears start to well in my eyes. I hold them back, knowing that any show of emotion will just confirm that I can hear him speaking.

"Is this what happened to Gram Marie?" I ask, suddenly afraid that I already know the answer. "She got in trouble for telling you too much, didn't she? That's why Rowan and I can't reach her."

A tingling starts in the pit of my stomach, and when I look toward the house, another shadow appears in the background, just beyond the doorway into the kitchen.

Remmington sees it too.

"Never mind, don't answer," I say quickly. "We should go now. Promise me you'll come to the lab tomorrow, that we'll talk then."

"I want to answer your question about Gram Marie first," he says. "The Dark Ones would want you to know this story. It shows they're in control. It's what prevents most people from asking questions."

I take another paintbrush and fill it with white, and then I use it to highlight a few of the hairs on Ares's face, around his eyes and on the bridge of his nose.

"Yes, your Gram Marie told me too much. She used to visit me in my dreams after I was diagnosed with cancer. Those last few weeks, when all

I really did was sleep, she was there every time I closed my eyes. She told me what it was like over here, that I didn't have to be afraid, that I didn't ever have to lose contact with anyone if I didn't want to. At first, I thought the dreams were just a side effect of the morphine. I thought my mind was just conjuring her up to help get me through. She was allowed to tell me all of this, but then she started telling me about the things you'd seen and heard in her house, how she'd tried to protect you from them. I never realized you saw them too, although I guess I should have suspected as much given the nightmares you used to have. I don't think she understood what those things were until it was too late.

"She learned a lot when she first crossed over, and she told me everything, but she didn't know there was a risk of losing contact with me by doing so. They started watching her more closely when she came to visit me—just like they're watching me right now. She was sharing the final puzzle piece when they dragged her away. I haven't seen her since.

"When the Dark Ones decide you've said too much, your energy gets divided. This is why we can't reach your Gram Marie anymore. Her soul is no longer whole. As long as a person's energy remains whole after death, it's possible to maintain contact with them, but when the energy is split, there's nothing to make contact with. The divided energy gets moved back into your level of existence, recycled back into the living, split into more than one individual. The division ensures that the knowledge that soul collected is dispersed. Each recipient gets just a little piece of what that original soul knew, so that the gathering of information has to start all over again. I think they do this because they aren't sure whether our level has a maximum capacity or not. I think they fear that bringing over too many souls may cause the same overpopulation here that you see there."

"Our types tend to attract one another," I say. "That's what Rowan told me once."

"And she's right. This splitting of energy has been going on for a long time. It's what creates soul mates. Think about it, if two people who received a piece of the divided energy from one soul would ever meet, they'd naturally feel an automatic connection to each other. Finding a soul mate is truly finding another piece of yourself. These are the friends and couples who pick up the phone at the same time and finish each other's sentences. Everything your Gram Marie knew is now spread out across multiple people. Not one of them knows the whole truth, but they know parts of it, and they're trying to find each other. If they can all find each other and share the information they've gathered separately, they'll be able to put the pieces together."

The left side of my face prickles. I know I shouldn't look, but I can't help it.

Behind Remmington, a group of shadows gathers. They move in closer, just as they moved toward the basement door when I was a child.

My head begins to throb.

"Turn away," he says. "Stop trying to see them. Don't give them any more energy than they have already. I can't lose touch with you like I've lost touch with my mother, Nadia. If they take me away, there's no coming back."

I wipe my eyes with the back of my hand and try to focus on cleaning my brushes.

"Nadia, you've been searching for the final pieces of the puzzle your whole life. You've been drawn to certain houses, and you can tell when another part of you is close. I can't say any more, but I can tell you that the ones who share Gram Marie's energy are all around you. You just have to pull them together. Find the truth so I don't have to tell you because I don't ever want to lose touch with you again."

There's a long pause. I can tell he has more to say. I can sense that he's considering whether he should continue or not. I don't end the dream. I wait.

"I've been gathering information, Nadia. Information that I need to tell you. I put it all in my journals, but—"

Pain suddenly radiates across the back of my head.

"I have to go now," he says as a shadow twists around his arm. "With or without me, you'll find a way to get here. Just remember, death isn't the only way."

"Tell me you'll be at Amulet for the final experiment," I say. "Promise me."

"If I'm not, Sterling's wife can help you. Now, break the connection, Nadia. Do it now. Wake up."

Quake begins to bark, and when I open my eyes, I see a trio of shadows scatter behind him, each moving to a separate corner of the library. Quake waits until they blend into the true shadows of the room, and then he trots over to the couch and nudges me with his nose. I can only hope that he's chased them away in time.

CHAPTER 38

The Present
Age Forty-One
Tuesday

Quake sits with me while I make the call to Rowan to tell her that I'm home. My eyes never leave the corners of the room, alert for any movement.

When Rowan asks if I just got there, I have no choice but to tell her what I've done.

"I swear, Nadia, you're worse than a kid with a new toy," she grumbles. "Determined to play with it, even when someone tells you not to without supervision. I'm coming over."

She arrives at the Baird twenty minutes after we hang up. She doesn't even knock; she just uses her key and comes in. When I meet her in the foyer, she's already tossing her coat over a hook. Her quilted overnight bag sits on the floor next to the coatrack.

"I want to hear every detail. Skip nothing," she says, turning to me. "God, I should have known you wouldn't listen when I said I wanted to talk to you first before you went digging." She shakes her head and ushers me into the kitchen. "You're just like me. It's a wonder our mothers are still alive."

Over coffee, I explain what happened in the dream and show her the notebook, my plan for the last experiment. "So, what do we do now?" I ask.

"The only thing we can do is move forward and see how it goes," she says. "I hope you didn't throw a wrench into this, Nadia. I truly do. If we follow your plan and realize your father is no longer available, well then, maybe he's right, maybe Ms. Sterling can take his place. You do realize, however, that by doing what you've done, you've attracted unwanted interest from their side." She walks over to the bay window and looks out.

It's the first I realize it's been snowing.

"I wish you'd called me sooner, Nadia, I really do." She turns and looks at me. "At least your father gave you some of the same warnings that I would have. There's more, but we can talk about those later—as long as you promise to quit dabbling until we have the chance."

"No more dabbling until we talk more," I say. "At least not on purpose."

She smiles and shakes her head. "In case you didn't notice, I brought my bag. If we're doing this experiment tomorrow, I figured it didn't make much sense for me to drive home tonight in this snow. Have a room at the inn for an old woman?"

"There's always a room for you."

She turns and looks out the window again. "Incredible," she says. "Unseasonably warm at the start of the week—and now this? Go figure."

CHAPTER 39

The Present
Age Forty-One
Wednesday

The weather grows progressively worse through the night and works its way into a near blizzard by the morning rush hour. Even though the main roads have been plowed, they're already covered in another three inches of snow by the time we reach the highway.

Aaron, concerned that Rowan and I have too much on our minds to drive safely, volunteers to shuttle us to the lab. He's read my novel several times by now, and given the unexpected snow, he's also likely thinking about Juliet Savini's accident. I'm sure he's hoping to prevent yet another prediction of mine from coming true.

We crawl along at a snail's pace, his Pathfinder staying just under the speed limit the entire way. From the passenger's seat, I barely notice. My mind is on other things. *Have I thrown a wrench into this? Will Remmington be there?* This one experiment could make or break our hope of convincing Sterling.

I stare out at the snow, watching it fall. Huge flakes pelt the windshield, making it look like we're driving into a tunnel, headed up into the clouds. This makes me dizzy, so I angle myself toward Aaron and Rowan instead.

Aaron's eyes never leave the road. His hands are locked on the steering wheel, poised at ten and two.

Rowan has her eyes closed.

"My dad loved the snow," I say. "We both did. If it stormed on a weekend, we'd spend most of the day outside, and we wouldn't come in

260

until I was frozen to the bone. Mom would always have hot chocolate waiting for us." I look down at my gloves. "He used to pack a snowball so tight that it stung like a rock when it hit you. Maybe this storm's a sign that he'll show up."

"Your dad wouldn't miss this for the world," Aaron says.

"Rowan, you haven't heard from him, have you?"

Rowan opens her eyes and shakes her head. "Not since he woke me up at that ungodly hour yesterday."

By the time we roll into the visitors' parking lot near Amulet, it's eight thirty in the morning. The lot is mostly empty and thankfully so.

When Aaron turns onto the newly plowed surface, the back end of his Pathfinder skids sideways. Rowan braces herself, but Aaron easily regains control and inches his way toward the edge of the lot, closer to the building.

"Damn it," I say, pointing at Sterling's red BMW. "Sterling's here already. I was hoping we could get Rowan inside before he arrived. A test run would have been nice."

Aaron puts the Pathfinder in park, reaches over, and lays a hand on mine. "You need to quit worrying. Like I said, your dad wouldn't miss this for the world."

"Do you want to come in?" I ask.

Aaron shakes his head. "I think I'll pass, if you don't mind. Too much suspense for this old heart. You can fill me in once it's over. I might just head over to the bookstore and relax for a bit."

Rowan leans up and kisses Aaron on the cheek. "Smart man. Sort of wish I could do the same." She shimmies out of the car, pulling a purple scarf up over her hair.

I climb out to join her, wishing I had a scarf of my own. Snowflakes pelt my face and show no sign of letting up. At this rate, the snow could be past our knees by the time we leave.

Aaron backs out of his parking space, cutting the wheel so that he stops right in front of us. He rolls down the passenger side window. "Good luck. Just call when you need me, OK?"

We both blow him a kiss and watch as a plume of exhaust follows him out of the lot.

Rowan tucks an arm under mine. "The moment of truth awaits, my dear. What do you say? Shall we go inside and get this party started?"

I guide Rowan to the side of the building rather than going in through the revolving door. There's an off chance, although unlikely given the holiday break, that Erma might be at the front desk, and I need Rowan's presence to remain a secret for as long as possible—at least until we're ready for her in the lab. Sterling will have enough questions already. Seeing Rowan would only bring more.

I swipe my key card across the access block near the first set of double doors. When it beeps, we push through and enter the small vestibule beyond them. Just ahead, another set of doors leads into the west wing hallway.

As I'm about to push them open, I see Sterling through the tiny rectangular window. He's standing near the elevator, a stack of papers balanced on one arm. He's shuffling through them, and he looks up just long enough to press the button for the second floor. When the doors slide open, he hops inside.

"That was close," Rowan says from behind me.

"Too close," I say. "At least now we know where he is. Come on. Let's go."

She and I scurry to the first-floor break room. From there, I call Jakob's office.

He picks up on the first ring. His hello sounds as anxious as I feel.

"It's Nadia," I say, watching Rowan as she touches up her lipstick in a small compact mirror. "We're in the break room. We just saw Sterling get in the elevator. Can you come down and get Rowan?"

He appears in the break room less than a minute later, and after a quick exchange of hugs and well-wishes, he whisks Rowan off to his office on the third floor. She'll wait there until she's needed. She thinks Remmington will tell her when it's time to come downstairs, that is, *if* he's able to join us.

I head in the other direction, toward the lab, knowing that Sterling will probably be there soon.

Brannigan is hard at work when I get there, hunched over a computer in the corner of the room, his fingers gliding over the keyboard at warp speed. An enormous flat-screen monitor hovers in front of him, displaying a series of empty white squares. These are direct-input feeds from the newly designed helmet on the bench beside him. With Brannigan's recent updates, our helmets collect fMRI data and have additional MEG-like capacity.

Magnetoencephalography, MEG, detects brain activity with much more precise temporal resolution than fMRI alone. MEG takes measurements directly from the activity of the neurons, while fMRI signals are based on increased blood flow in response to that activity. Due to its direct detection, MEG erases the lag time between brain activity and signal. It gives a reading comparable to that achieved by intracranial probes.

The statistical software program Brannigan designed takes the two feed loops and superimposes them, accounting for any time delays of fMRI and the low spatial resolution of MEG. The result is an exact representation of the ongoing activity in the brain—with spatial and temporal resolution being nearly 100 percent accurate. The 3D image produced on the screen is a compilation of all input. Brannigan is a genius.

I remove my coat and wait just inside the door, not wanting to interrupt him.

Without even looking up from his work, Brannigan uses his left hand to flag me over. "You've got to see this. It's amazing." He brings up a video and hits play.

I sit in the chair next to his. On the screen, I watch Paul as he dons one of the new helmets and latches the strap under his chin.

"This was taken late last night, using the new system," Brannigan says. "Paul went through that battery of sensory tests we designed, each exactly one minute long."

The battery of tests includes a variety of tasks—things like reading, talking, listening, and eating, really anything that involves the senses— all completed while wearing the helmet.

Brannigan points to the screen. "A description of each task shows up here in this text bar below the image as soon as it's initiated. My goal with the new helmet was to be able to see activity in the expected brain centers within one second of task initiation. Keep an eye on the stopwatch over here." He gestures toward a digital timer in the lower right-hand corner of the screen.

In the video feed, Paul is seated at a table. He picks up a book and reads until the timer goes off. Three boxes across the top on the monitor present three separate views of Paul's brain. From left to right are the coronal, sagittal, and transverse perspectives. Below them, dead center, is one larger collective three-dimensional reconstruction, made using the data gathered from the previous three. This final 3D image looks as if someone has literally removed a full-sized brain and suspended it in midair with invisible strings. Unlike a real brain, though, this one is completely transparent, allowing us to see every activity center from every layer, all the way to the brain's most central regions, as if the viewer is wearing x-ray goggles. By moving the mouse, Brannigan can grab the image and rotate it, letting us see the brain from any angle.

As I watch, the four images on the monitor shift and change. Red, orange, yellow, and green clouds appear in all of them, the different shades representing the intensity of the signal detected in Paul's brain in response to the task at hand. At one-minute intervals, new words scroll across the bottom of the screen.

Subject reading. Subject talking on the phone. Subject listening to music. Subject eating. Subject tapping fingers of left hand.

"The timing is almost exact," Brannigan says excitedly, "give or take a few milliseconds, and the activity map of the brain is textbook. Look here, the expected brain regions light up every time, exactly on cue."

As each new task dialogue appears in the scroll bar, the associated signal shifts to a different brain region in synchrony. The crispness of the lines is breathtaking, the edges of activation clearly delineated. My heart races. With this tool, and my father's help, there's no way our final experiment can fail.

He'll be here, I think. *He has to be. We haven't come this far for nothing.*

"Whose brain is that?" Sterling yells from the back of the room. He flops a pile of papers onto one of the benchtops and comes over to where Brannigan and I are sitting.

Brannigan pivots his chair to face the professor. "Paul's. He gave the new helmet a test run last night. It works just as well as we hoped."

Brannigan hits rewind and replays the video for Sterling.

Sterling stands behind us and sips his coffee. Bringing food into a lab is a big safety no-no, and Sterling knows how I hate it. I remind him every time. It's probably one of the reasons he continues to do it. I bite my tongue this time, not wanting to create any ripples before we even get started.

"Play it again," Sterling says as soon as the video times out. He sets his cup on the desk directly in front me, places his palms next to it, and leans in close to the screen.

When the final image freezes, Sterling stands up and claps Brannigan on the back. "This could be our big day." He looks at me. "Our boy Brannigan here makes it look easy, doesn't he?"

Sterling picks up his cup and walks away.

We both watch him go.

Sterling catches Xavier at the door and pulls him aside for some unheard dialogue.

After Sterling leaves, Xavier comes over and sits down next to me. "Paul and Mary are almost here. I just talked to them. They had to find something to keep Tom busy before they could escape."

Tom was always asking questions about Amulet. We hadn't given him a key card, and it was driving him crazy.

Paul stomps into the lab a few minutes later. He brushes a layer of snow off his coat and onto the floor. "Geez Louise, it's a freaking blizzard out there."

Mary shuffles in the door behind him, her frizzy poof of hair topped by a layer of white.

"Sorry to keep you guys waiting," Paul says, rubbing his hands together. He drags two chairs over to where we're sitting: one for him and one for Mary.

"Looks like the gang's all here," Sterling says, walking back into the lab with Jakob at his heels. "Time to see what Nadia has in store for us."

Xavier looks at me and points to a long table at the front of the room. On it are two of Brannigan's new helmets, my laptop, a video recorder, and a small video projector. In front of the desk, an old-fashioned projector screen hangs from a metal tripod. Xavier picks up the recorder and carries it over to Jakob.

Sterling stands next to Jakob in a red fleece, hands in his pockets.

"You can use this to film Nadia," Xavier tells Jakob. "The video feed will be directed to Brannigan's computer screen, so the recording includes both the scans and Nadia side by side."

I join Xavier at the front table where he pulls out the chair for me so I can sit down in front of my laptop. As I log on, my hands are shaking.

Xavier apparently notices. He stands behind me and rests his palms on my shoulders.

Brannigan comes over too. He checks the wiring on the helmets, and then he hands one to Xavier.

Xavier places it on my head, and I adjust the chin strap. The fit is tight, but it's not uncomfortable—although I do feel somewhat ridiculous sitting there in front of everyone with it on. I think of the picture of Einstein in the lawn chair, more than happy to be wearing one complete with glittery heart-shaped glasses. *At least this one doesn't have those,* I think.

Brannigan gives the helmet a wiggle and does one final check, making sure all contact points are secure. He looks at me and gives a thumbs-up.

Xavier leans in close to my ear. "You ready?"

I give a single nod. "Ready."

Xavier turns to the group and explains what we're about to do. He tells Brannigan to play the video of Paul, describes what we're seeing, and then points at me. "Nadia's first task will be typing. She'll do this for about five minutes. This will give us an input feed and establish a baseline image." He walks over and points at Brannigan's monitor. "You can watch her brain activity scan on here. We don't expect any CT activity at first." He holds up a timer. "I'm going to set this for five minutes."

A series of beeps follows as he programs the timer and puts it on the table in front of me.

I can't stop worrying. I have no idea if my father is going to show up or not. If he doesn't, the experiment will fail—and it will be my fault. Two times now, he's warned of possible failure, and God knows he has a good record with predictions. *Did he know that I was going to be impatient, to pressure him into telling me more? I can only hope not.*

Xavier says, "When the timer goes off, Nadia will switch to another task, one that she believes will prompt activity in the CT. I'll reset the timer when she starts. She'll continue with that second task for five more minutes. When the timer goes off, she'll return to typing, and that will conclude our first experiment."

"So, what's her second task?" Sterling asks. "What's expected to activate the CT?"

I turn and look at him. "You'll have to wait and see."

Suddenly, my head begins to ache. Either the helmet is too tight, the stress has gotten to me, or my father is nearby. I hope for the latter. I turn and nod at Brannigan.

Xavier slides into the seat next to me.

Brannigan's fingers rattle across the keyboard as he sets up the program.

I take a deep breath, close my eyes, and make a wish. *Dad, this is it. I need you here. Please tell me they didn't take you.*

Xavier's shoulder presses up against mine. "Everything OK?"

I haven't told him about my most recent dream. "I certainly hope so."

When Brannigan announces that we're ready to start, the room goes silent.

I position my fingers over the keyboard as Xavier grabs the timer.

"Here we go." Xavier presses the start button.

I begin to type. The words of my favorite nursery rhymes pan across the screen. Concentration is difficult with everyone watching, and I can't stop worrying about whether Remmington will show up or not. I even worry about whether my worrying might distort the scan. *I have to calm down.*

As we enter the fourth minute, I fall into an easy rhythm and begin to relax. When the timer goes off, I pause and let my fingers rest on the keys. I'm reminded of that night in the graveyard of the Old Mud Church, the first time Jess, Donna, Emily, and I tried our hands at the Ouija, our fingers poised on the planchette, not sure what to expect.

Xavier resets the timer, reprogramming it for another five minutes.

A hear a shuffling of feet to my right, where Sterling and Jakob are standing, and assume that both of them have moved closer. *Did Rowan tell Jakob about the dream? If so, is he as anxious as I am?*

"Next phase." Xavier turns toward Sterling as he presses start.

I stare at the screen of my laptop, waiting for the ringing in my ears, the chills, the butterflies in my stomach, the crickets or the grasshoppers, some sign that he's coming, but nothing happens. Thirty seconds pass. Again, I think of that day in the graveyard, how we'd almost given up. I think of the shadows behind my father in the dream.

As more seconds tick by, my hope begins to wane. I close my eyes and try to imagine my father sitting across from me. I imagine him dressed in his jeans and a sweatshirt, how surprised I was the first time I saw him, his back against the pillows on the bed. I feel tears welling up in my eyes and open them to look at the screen.

Paul and Mary shift in their chairs behind me.

A bead of sweat trickles down from the top of my head, tickling my scalp as it works its way behind my left ear. The room seems to grow warmer with every second that passes.

"Whatever you're doing isn't working," Sterling says. "There's no CT signal on the scan."

I block him out and focus harder, determined to prove this to him.

At minute three, a stabbing pain arcs across the back of my head, near the base of the helmet. Ringing pierces my eardrums, and as my fingers begin to move across the keyboard, relief washes over me not only because the experiment is working, but because this means my father is nearby. I hear Sterling talking to Jakob, but I try not to listen. I close my eyes again, letting my fingers do whatever they want.

"I'll be damned," Sterling's voice says. "It's the CT."

Chair legs screech against the floor, and I hear people moving toward Brannigan. I keep my eyes closed and keep typing. I feel someone close to me, behind me and on my right, and I think it might be Sterling—until I hear him on my left near Brannigan. I think of Jess and the way she felt the bed sink down next to her as she hid under her covers. I think of the game we used to play as kids. *Who is the Watcher now?*

"But she's not doing anything different," Sterling says. "What's going on? Is it a glitch?"

When the timer goes off, the pain at the back of my head subsides. I hear Xavier reset it, and for the last five minutes, I revert to the nursery rhymes. When the final timer goes off, I unbuckle the strap of the helmet and pull it off my head. My hair is drenched in sweat. I feel hands patting my back, and I assume this means the experiment was a success.

Xavier's arms wrap around me, and he whispers, "You had me worried for a minute there."

"I was worried, too," I say.

Before I have a chance to explain, Jakob ushers us over to the monitor to join the rest of the group.

Brannigan is seated at the computer loading the file. Images form on the screen. Jakob's video feed appears in a box to the right of the 3D brain. In it, I sit at the laptop, typing. During the first five minutes, the 3D brain shows normal activity in the language centers. A layer of red covers the motor centers as well, those responsible for making my fingers strike the keys. No activity is evident in the CT.

When the first timer goes off, I shift nervously in my seat. At 00:02:30 hours, I close my eyes. What I see next makes me lean forward to get a better look at the monitor. Just beyond my laptop, a shadow lurks in the background. It's a tall, humanlike form, and it's shaking uncontrollably. I look around the room, but no one seems to notice anything out of the ordinary. When I look back at the monitor, the shadow steadies itself and moves closer to me. I see it place a hand on the back of my head at 00:03:00 hours. My fingers begin to move.

In the center of the monitor, the 3D brain glows brightly. A faint shimmering of yellow appears first, presenting as a disorganized cloud of color in the middle of the brain's writing centers, just like in the previous segment, but this time, a yellow cloud also appears at the base of my skull. Each yellow cloud then breaks into small thin threads of activity. The threads eventually turn a deep orange and then red. They wind their way toward each other, meeting in the middle, and from there, they spread out across the cortex until they take the form we've seen a hundred times before: the shape of a heavily branched tree.

I look back to the video feed. The shadow is still there behind me, arm outstretched, fingers stroking my hair. I look at Xavier.

He raises his eyebrows and mouths a silent word: "Weird."

I want to ask him if he sees it too, but I decide to ask him later.

When the timer goes off in the video, the shadow recedes. The colors on the scan fade as I stop typing. My frontal lobe glows a faint green.

Brannigan turns off the video feed and expands the 3D image of the CT.

Sterling leans in, studies it for a minute, and then turns to me. He shakes his head and puts his hands on his hips. "All right. I give up. What did you do?"

I glance at Jakob—and then Paul and Mary. None of them say a word. I look back at Sterling. "One experiment doesn't prove anything, right? Isn't that what you say?"

Sterling turns to Jakob, but he only shrugs.

"Let's try one more before I tell you what I did." I point at the image on the screen. "See how these branches, here, reach out to cover the back of the cerebellum, where you originally detected activity in Einstein?"

Sterling nods.

"Then, up here," I say, pointing to the branches that stretch out across the top half of the brain. "This is the location of the writing centers. The signal suggests those two areas are communicating with each other."

Sterling nods again.

"I think the CT works to connect multiple brain centers, depending on the task at hand. The cells aren't isolated to only one region of the brain. They're mobile. Obviously, the writing centers weren't involved in Einstein's case, yet here they are lit up in mine. Bea got permission to gather some samples of human brain tissue during a few of her autopsies. We've found populations of CT cells in about 25 percent of them. Xavier and Brannigan also visited a few other locations that work with primates and ran some preliminary tests. We repeated the original studies you did with Einstein, and 100 percent of the animals born in the wild showed similar activity. This is true for only 50 percent of animals born in captivity. All activity observed in nonhuman primates showed up in similar brain locations. In humans, the localization varies, and I think I know why."

Jakob gives me a nod.

"I need a few minutes to set up for this next experiment." I grab Rowan's quilted bag, place it on the long table, and shift my laptop to the side. From the bag, I withdraw three white candles and arrange them in a triangle in front of the chair. In my periphery, I see the door in the back of the lab move as if pushed by a draft. A part of me wonders if this might be my father on his way to gather Rowan from Jakob's office.

Xavier sets up the projector, and when he turns it on, a series of still frame photos appear on the screen at five-second intervals. The first is three oranges in a green pottery bowl. The second is two lemons on a blue windowsill. The third is a green vase full of bright yellow flowers. They continue, all simple images. Rowan requested this slight modification to the original plan. She was worried that if her first task was meditation, another spirit might see her and decide to reach out before the timer went off. Mindful observation seemed a better choice.

I use a match to light the candles, and Xavier turns off a few of the lights.

"What the hell's going on?" Sterling asks. He turns to face Jakob. "What's this all about?"

"Sterling, just sit down and be quiet," Jakob says, using a tone I've never heard before. "Your cells are going to be the biggest discovery of the century. If you want to know what they do, just sit back and enjoy the show."

Sterling doesn't look happy, but he does as he's told.

Jakob adjusts his camera to account for the dimmer light, and when Rowan steps into the room, he pulls her into a hug.

Sterling glares at her. I half expect him to get up and leave, but he doesn't.

Jakob whispers something in Rowan's ear, and when she smiles at me, I assume he's told her that my first experiment worked.

Xavier carries a helmet over to the table and helps Rowan into it.

I watch Brannigan as he sets up the computer for another scan. When he nods in my direction, I move to the front of the room to announce what will happen next. "The same format applies in this next phase of the experiment," I say. "Rowan will begin with a simple task to establish the initial input feed and baseline. After five minutes, she'll switch to a task that should induce CT activity."

Rowan, now donning a helmet, nods at Sterling.

Surprisingly, he nods back.

Jakob steps in front of Rowan and begins the video, and Xavier starts the timer.

Rowan sits facing the projector screen, her hands folded in her lap, as the images play in a continuous loop. She watches them: three oranges in a green pottery bowl, two lemons on a blue windowsill, and a green vase full of bright yellow flowers. On and on they go, cycling for a full five minutes. On the monitor, her 3D brain is suspended by the invisible strings. Clouds of yellow cover the visual cortex, but the CT area remains devoid of color.

Instead of watching the video feed, I watch Rowan directly. My eyes scan the area around her, watching for anything out of the ordinary.

When the timer beeps, Xavier turns off the projector.

The candles flicker.

Rowan doesn't move. She continues staring at the blank projector screen, her hands still folded in her lap.

At 00:01:00 hours, her fingers twitch. I catch the movement because I'm watching for it. After a few more seconds, her palms come together. She brings her pointer fingers to her lips. A pale blue light appears in front of the blank projector screen, and I turn to see if anyone else in the group has noticed.

Xavier looks at me and winks. "He looks just like you described him."

I look back at the screen, but all I can see is a faint shimmering against the white backdrop. I try to see more, but I can't. On the video feed, the blue light is there. A full red tree-like structure dominates the 3D image of Rowan's brain, much larger and brighter than the one that formed in mine. Thick branches stretch out from a solid trunk. Tendrils cover the region near the base of her skull and travel outward, encompassing both the visual and auditory cortices.

When Rowan speaks, a yellow cloud fills Broca's area, the speech center. "I'm glad you could make it," she says. "We were hoping you could." She nods. "Of course, I'll repeat what you say."

Rowan sits quietly, apparently listening to someone only she and Xavier can see.

"Dr. Sterling?" Rowan says.

He sits forward in his seat.

"This discovery of yours has been a long time coming," Rowan says. "Pay attention. I want you to try to believe what you're about to witness."

On the monitor, the CT glows brightly, but then Rowan shakes her head and falls silent. In the video, I see a shadow appear beside her. I look at her directly and see the same.

"You know I can't do that, not yet," Rowan says. "You have to trust me, Evelyn. Now is not the time."

Jakob looks at Rowan, his eyes wide.

Sterling looks at Jakob.

This was not part of the plan.

"All right," Rowan says. "If you insist, I'll tell him." She turns her head slightly in Sterling's direction. "I have a message for you."

The timer sounds, but Rowan keeps talking.

Xavier shuts it off, but the CT glows brighter than ever.

I glance over at Sterling. *If looks could kill,* I think.

"Jorg, please. You need to accept what you're seeing right now for your daughter's sake—if not for your own," she says. "It's me, Evelyn. I want to be able to talk with you both."

Sterling is in Rowan's face in seconds, his body visibly shaking. "Is this some kind of sick joke?" he screams, his nose inches from hers. "Do you think this is funny?"

Rowan stares up at him, a hazy look in her eyes as if she's just woken from a deep sleep.

Color drains from the 3D image on the monitor, and Xavier turns on the lights.

Jakob puts down the camera and says, "Sterling, please sit down. Give us a minute to explain."

Sterling turns on me next. "Is this your idea, Nadia?"

Jakob starts to say something, but Sterling doesn't wait to hear what it is. He storms out of the lab. Jakob places a hand on Rowan's shoulder. She still looks dazed.

"Evelyn wasn't supposed to come," Rowan says. "I knew she wanted to, but I told her it wasn't a good idea. She's waited so long to talk to him, and she thinks he's close to believing. Jakob, you know I sometimes can't control who speaks, especially when they're so driven to be heard. She thought it was her only chance to make him see. She's worried about him ... about Sophia." Rowan turns to me. "Nadia, Evelyn wants you to go talk to him. She thinks you can convince him, but she says you have to hurry."

I look at Jakob and ask, "Why is Sterling so upset that your sister is here?"

Jakob takes my hands in his. "My sister, Evelyn, was Sterling's wife."

Suddenly, the unlikely friendship between Jakob and Sterling makes sense.

CHAPTER 40

The Present
Age Forty-One
Wednesday

S terling's office door is closed when I get there. I raise a hand to knock, but I lower it when I hear him murmuring inside. The light underneath the door flickers as if he's pacing back and forth in front of it. Like him, I need a little time to collect my thoughts. I have no idea what Evelyn expects me to say.

I walk to the window at the end of the hall and look outside. The snow is falling heavier than before, and the cars on the street are nothing but white mounds. The University's grounds crew is hard at work with plows and shovels, but they're hardly making a dent.

I glance up at my reflection in the glass, and the hall lights behind me flicker. A woman with long white hair is standing outside Sterling's door. When I turn, the lights go off completely. When they come back on, the woman is gone.

Sterling pulls open his door and steps into the hall. He looks left, then right, and he spies me at the window. "Nadia?" He turns in the other direction as if searching for someone closer. "Did you just knock?"

I'm not sure if I should tell him what I saw, so I just point at the window. "It's still snowing out there. I don't think we should keep everyone here much longer."

"They can go … if they want. They don't need to wait for me."

"I'll go tell them. How about I bring you a coffee back? Maybe we can sit and chat for few. Would that be all right?"

Sterling looks again in the other direction and then back at me and nods.

Downstairs, Jakob looks surprised to see me back in the lab so soon. "You want me to go talk to him?"

I shake my head. "I can handle it, but if I'm not back in twenty, come save me."

"Don't be much longer than that," Jakob says. "Aaron's here. He's in the lobby. He says the roads are getting worse. He wants to make sure you get home safely."

"Tell him I'll be there in a few—and tell him not to worry about the accident I wrote about in my book. It's not going to happen. The experiments worked, so we have all the answers we need. It's done."

Jakob nods.

I look at Xavier and Brannigan. They're near the monitor. Rowan stands off to their right, chatting with Paul and Mary. I want to stay, to hear what they're saying, but Sterling is waiting. I stop in the break room and grab two coffees from the machine.

When I get back to Sterling's office, his door is open. His elbows are propped on his desk. His hair is a mess. He looks exhausted.

I hand him a coffee and take a seat in the closest Windsor chair.

"Thank you." He takes a long sip from the cup. After a pause, he looks at me, his face like that of a lost child. "So, tell me what just happened."

This is the conversation I've been dreading all along. I know I need to be careful with my words while still telling the truth.

"When you got up there, how did you turn on the CT? We saw it light up on the screen, but why? You were just typing. That's all I saw. What was different between your first five minutes and the next five? And what the hell did Rowan do? She just sat there staring at the screen until she started with all of her gibberish."

"I'll tell you what happened … if you promise to listen and keep an open mind."

Sterling sips his coffee and nods.

"By now, I'm sure you know Jakob's hypothesis: that there is survival of a soul after bodily death. Those two experiments we just did, as well as your work with Einstein and Zena, prove this. They prove that at least two of the psi abilities Jakob studies are real. Telepathy and clairvoyance, for sure. Maybe others."

Sterling rubs his forehead.

"Your cells are receptors, Sterling, no different than any other sensory receptor in the body. They detect signals, just like the rods and cones in our eyes detect light. As for how they do it? That seems to be a little different than most other sensory cells. For the five basic senses, the signal goes from the receptor to a processing center in the brain, one designed specifically to interpret that one particular type of stimulus. Your cells act like sensory cells, but they're also the relay system. When they detect a signal, they line up to form a network, a network that can invade *any* of the sensory processing centers in the brain. This allows the signal to be interpreted in a lot of different ways, depending on which areas they touch."

Sterling shifts in his seat, but he remains quiet.

"You've seen how these cells respond in the petri dishes when we hit them with high frequencies. They congregate and form a tree-like structure. Today's experiment showed that they do the same in vivo. As you also just saw with me—and Rowan—the CT cells in different people respond in different ways. Once stimulated, these cells reach out to various brain regions, depending upon the individual and the task at hand. When I wore the helmet, the CT branched out to the writing centers. For Rowan, the tract wrapped around her visual and auditory processing centers. It's the same type of signal, the same cells responding to the vibration. The signal is just relayed and interpreted in different ways."

"And the source of this vibration is what?" Sterling asks.

I let out a deep breath. "You're no dummy, Sterling. You've been friends with Jakob for far too long to ask that question. You know the answer. You know what Rowan does for a living. When you saw the signal light up in her visual and auditory centers, what did that say to you?"

Sterling rolls his eyes and looks away.

"While you were away, we compared our results with data from Jakob's lab," I say. "We conducted a few studies with several of his confirmed psychics and found a direct correlation between psychic activity and

CT activity. I'm not sure if you're aware or not, but psychics can detect spirits in different ways: some through sight and others through hearing or smell. Each and every time we ran a study, the activated brain regions corresponded to the psychic's particular gift. We've also determined that not everyone has CT cells. This tells us that they're more of a vestigial structure in modern man, no longer needed in our species, but not yet removed from our anatomy. Once we learned to speak, we lost the need for them. Jakob's friend, Dr. Potvin, agrees that evolution has been pushing these cells to extinction in humans, but she also seems to think they're making a comeback."

I think of what Remmington said about the world not lasting forever. *Maybe the cells are making a comeback because we need them.* Natural selection's final hour, he'd said.

Sterling narrows his eyes.

"Think about it," I say. "Think of how many people today are questioning the connection of mind, body, and spirit. Look at the number of yoga and meditation studios out there now. Look at how many people come to Jakob's classes. People are feeling the pull again, maybe not all the time, but they can sense it gaining strength. Sterling, you can give them answers, a reason to believe in what they're sensing. Think about it. Your data might very well prove that we don't have to lose contact with our loved ones when they die. Imagine how that will make people feel."

He leaps up from his chair and walks over to the tiny window, shaking his head.

"Sterling, don't fight this. You know a part of you wants to believe."

He stuffs his hands into his pockets and stares down at the street.

"Sterling, do you remember when I told you that someone helped me write my book?"

Sterling turns to look at me. His eyes are red.

"That was my father. He died years ago, but he's the one who helped. That's what was happening when you saw my CT light up today. My father, Remmington, was there, telling me what to write. My father is my consultant."

Sterling reaches up and pinches the bridge of his nose. He shakes his head and then looks at me. "Nadia, listen to yourself. You're a scientist, and you're talking crazy. Death isn't a way station. It steals the ones we love right out from under our noses, and then they're gone for good. There's no more contact after that. Sure, you can always hope for one more conversation, one more touch, one more day, but it's never going to happen. Your time with that person is over, and you'll never get a second chance. You need to accept the fact that your father isn't around anymore. He's gone, Nadia. He's dead. He wasn't in the lab." A tear runs down his cheek. "It took me years to get over the loss of my wife, to accept that I was never going to talk to her ever again, and you need to do the same. I don't know what happened down there, but I can tell you right now, it has nothing to do with your father! It's that woman, Rowan, playing with your mind, just like she did with Jakob, just like she did with my daughter, just like she tried to do with me, even today." He starts toward the door.

I reach out and grab his arm.

He could easily pull away if he wanted, but he doesn't. Instead, he stops and looks at me.

"Sterling, I've read the notebooks from cover to cover, sometimes twice. I've compared them to my journals. I've compared all the dates. Your primate studies were underway at the same time I was researching primate work for my novel. Neither of us knew what the other was doing back then, but somehow, we were both doing the same work, just in different ways. You had a lab. I didn't. That's what Jakob would call synchronicity. My father knew about your work. I don't know how, but he did, and he led me to you. And here we are."

"So, you've kept me in the dark all this time?" Sterling asks. "Is that what you're saying? That you knew you were leading up to this all along? You used my cells and purposely misled me?" He puts his hands on his hips. "Amulet wasn't created to keep things quiet; it was created to keep me preoccupied, keep me in my other lab while you did whatever you wanted with my cells here. Was that it?"

"You kept yourself preoccupied! You're the one who kept disappearing. As for misleading someone, why didn't you tell me that you read my novel? You knew this was coming—so don't try to put all the blame on me."

The door creaks open, and Jakob peeks around it. He doesn't ask if he can come in; he just wanders over to the other side of the room and takes a seat in the chair near the window. "I could hear the two of you from the other end of the hall, you know." Jakob looks at Sterling. "I came up here to tell you it's time to stop fighting yourself, Sterling. Quit being so hardheaded—just this once. This has to do with more than just work. This is personal for you, and you know it. A part of you wants to believe that Evelyn is within reach. You never believed it before, but now you're curious. I can tell. It's OK to change your mind. No one will think any less of you. Actually, I can think of at least two ladies who'd be extremely pleased if you did. I know Evelyn would love to talk to you again, and I know Sophia would love that you finally got the chance."

Sterling remains near the door as he listens to Jakob.

I keep hoping he won't turn and go. *He's so close to letting himself accept this.*

"Sterling, do you remember when Sophia would write letters to you and say they were from Mommy? Do you remember your response? You told her to grow up and accept that her mother was gone. You can take that back if you just forget about protecting your pride for two seconds and just admit that you were wrong. You must see what's happening. You must know that Sophia wasn't making it up now."

"Let's not talk about that," Sterling barks, but I can hear his voice crack.

"Why not?" Jakob asks. "Because it's too hard to admit that you were wrong? Because you don't want to make things right? Think of what could be done with this information."

Sterling looks up at the ceiling, blinking his eyes to hold back the tears. He shakes his head. "Amulet, huh? The Academy for the Metaphysical Understanding of Life Energy Transmogrification. Isn't that right, Nadia? When I read your book and saw that, I knew I should probably get out. Now I wish I had."

It's my turn to shake my head. "I'm sure your wife is glad you didn't."

The look he gives me makes me realize I've gone too far.

"You know nothing about my wife!" Sterling jabs an index finger in my direction, "So, don't even pretend that you do. You know nothing about any of this. When my wife got sick, do you have any idea how hard it was for me to give the doctors permission to take her off life support? How hard it was for me to tell our daughter that her mother was gone? How hard it was to keep breaking Sophia's heart every time she insisted that she could talk to Evelyn? For years, I told my daughter to quit dreaming, to quit being silly. Of course, I missed Evelyn too. I would have given anything to talk to her, but I had to be the adult. I told Sophia that hope for contact was unrealistic. You want me to change my mind now? Go back and tell my daughter that I was wrong?"

"What's the harm in that, Sterling?" Jakob asks.

Sterling presses the heels of his hands to his eyes. "Jakob, when you took Sophia to visit Rowan, you went against everything I tried to teach her. After that, Sophia begged me to talk to Rowan, begged me to listen. Rowan overstepped her bounds. The more she meddled, the easier it was for me to take a harder stance. Now I see all of this, and I realize I was wrong all along. It kills me that there's been a way for me to talk to Evelyn all this time and to know that I haven't even tried. If contact is possible, then I've failed both my wife and my daughter for years. This is what I'm struggling with right now, Jakob. Do you see?" Sterling goes to the coatrack and pulls on his jacket. "I need time to think about this. I need time to process what just happened, to figure out where to go from here."

When he leaves, I look at Jakob, expecting him to go after Sterling, but he doesn't. Instead, he pulls off his glasses and wipes at the lenses with a handkerchief.

Jakob sighs. "Churchill had a saying: 'Man will occasionally stumble across the truth, but most of the time, he'll pick himself up and continue on.'" He holds his glasses out at arm's length, inspects them, and then slides them back onto his nose. His cheeks are flushed. "Sterling's pride is the problem here, Nadia, and he's the only one who can adjust that. I suspect he'll go and talk with Sophia, and if he does, I suspect she may be able to convince him to listen. It's out of our hands now. We've done what we can. Let's give him the time he's asked for. I'll reach out to him or Sophia tomorrow and see if they've made any progress. As for now, I think you'd better get back down to Aaron and get home. We should all get home before the roads get any worse."

CHAPTER 41

The Present
Age Forty-One
Wednesday

As Jakob and I step out of the stairwell into the west wing corridor, Aaron sprints toward us, his white hair flying. He's out of breath by the time he reaches us. "I don't think Sterling should be driving." He bends at the waist and rests his hands on his knees to catch his breath. "He pulled out of the lot going way too fast. Jakob, can you call him? Tell him to come back? Tell him that I can take him home? I tried to stop him, but he just waved me off."

I put a hand on Aaron's shoulder. "I'm sure he'll be fine. We talked with him. He just needs some time to think. I'm more worried about you. You OK?"

Aaron shakes his head and looks up. "I really don't think he's going to be fine. I have a really bad feeling, Nadia. He looked like he was crying."

"Maybe that's why he didn't stop," I say. "He probably didn't want you to see."

Jakob pulls out his cell phone and begins to dial.

Aaron and I both watch. From where I'm standing, I can hear Sterling's voicemail recording.

Jakob grimaces and drops the phone back into his front shirt pocket.

He looks worried, but he doesn't let Aaron hear it in his voice. "Like Nadia said, I'm sure Sterling will be fine. We'll give him thirty minutes, and then I'll try calling again. By then, he'll either be at home or at Sophia's; both are close."

282

Aaron keeps shaking his head. "You can't go that fast on these roads, especially in that little sports car of his."

At first, this thought does make me worry, but then I realize something. "Aaron, Sterling's definitely not going to let anything happen to that car of his. That car is his baby. He'll slow down once he sees how bad the roads are."

Aaron seems to consider this.

"Come on," I say, taking him by the elbow. "I want to show you something."

When we get to the lab, everyone is crowded around the monitor.

Xavier is pointing at one of the images. He stops as the three of us get closer, and everyone turns to see who has come in. "Where's Sterling?"

I give them all an update and tell them that Sterling has left for the night. No one seems surprised.

Jakob keeps checking his watch as Xavier continues with his explanation. When Xavier finishes, Jakob pulls his phone out of his pocket, looks at the display, and starts to punch in the numbers again, but as he does, the phone rings in his hand. I assume this must be Sterling calling back. Jakob looks up at me, smiles, and puts the phone to his ear. "Sophia, is your father with you?"

Before Jakob can say anything more, Rowan walks over and places a hand on Jakob's shoulder.

Jakob offers a series of responses to the person on the other end of the line. "Yes. Yes. Yes." The tone of his voice isn't right. "I'll be there as soon as I can."

When Jakob lowers the phone, his face is blank. Rowan runs a hand up and down his back. I look at Rowan, fearing the worst, and she nods.

Bad weather. A car crash. A red car. Juliet Savini. Jorg Sterling. "J. S.," I say out loud without meaning to. *Jesus, Nadia, you should have caught that sooner.*

Aaron, standing next to me, grabs my hand.

"That was Sophia," Jakob says finally. "Sterling's at Piermont General. He's in the ER. His car veered off the road. He's not doing well."

We immediately gather our coats and meet at the front doors of Amulet.

Rowan grabs Xavier's arm. "You ride with them," she says, "I'll go with the kids."

Aaron and I climb into the front seat of the Pathfinder. Jakob and Xavier climb into the back. I immediately text Maeve to tell her where we're going. I don't offer too much detail because I don't want to upset her. I just want her to know that I'm OK. She's been on edge all week, and I'm sure today's bad weather hasn't helped.

As we drive, the snow continues to fall. Visibility is low. Aaron drives fast enough to get us to the hospital quickly—but slowly enough to keep us safe. He keeps his flashers on the whole time. My Amulet key card is in my hand, and my index finger traces the symbol of the ankh on the front. *You didn't offer much protection today, did you?*

When we arrive at the hospital, Aaron pulls up to the emergency entrance to drop us off.

Jakob sprints to the door, and when he looks back, I wave for him to go ahead.

"You go ahead too," Aaron says. "I'll park in the garage and be right back."

Xavier and I find Jakob inside, his arms around a young woman in the waiting room, presumably Sophia. She's tall and lean. She has her head on his shoulder, but she steps back as we approach. Jakob introduces us, and I can see the resemblance immediately. She's striking, even under these circumstances. Under the tears, her eyes are as blue as Sterling's. She has the same sharp jawline. Her hair is dark, but her skin is paler, more like her mother's. She's young, maybe in her early twenties, but more composed than most of us. She thanks everyone for coming before looping an arm through her uncle's and accompanying him to the nurse's station. There, they speak quietly with a doctor before following her through a set of doors.

When Aaron arrives, we take off our coats and find a seat in the waiting room. I sit between him and Xavier. Rowan and the others wander in not long after. Rowan sits directly across from me.

As Paul, Mary, and Brannigan settle in around her, a little girl down their row looks our way. She's no more than four or five years old. Her bright pink polka-dot dress seems to be the only happy thing in the otherwise dreary waiting area. She studies us intently, her tiny hands playing with the ends of a white satin ribbon that acts as her belt. She seems to be singing to herself. The woman next to her, probably her mother, doesn't seem to notice. Her hands work furiously at a white handkerchief.

The little girl gives me an inquisitive look, and after a few minutes of studying my side of the row, she leans forward in her chair so that she can see farther down her own.

Rowan leans forward, looks in her direction, and lifts a hand in a wave.

The little girl returns a bashful smile and taps her mother's arm. When her mom leans in closer, she reaches up with cupped hands and whispers something in her ear. The woman nods, and the next thing I know, the little girl climbs off her seat and comes our way. She stands in front of Aaron, looking up at him, and bites her lip.

He smiles at her and gives a little wave.

She looks at the empty seat next to him, seems to consider something, and then climbs up onto the one next to it. She cranes her neck up at Aaron, and when he turns to look at her again, she raises her eyebrows at him. Aaron is used to the attention. Children are always fascinated with his scars. Some are afraid, but most are only curious. I'm not convinced this is why the little girl has come to sit next to him, however. She keeps looking at the empty seat between them, then up at Aaron, and smiling. She doesn't say a word.

After a few minutes, she hops down from her seat and skips back to her mother, her sandy blonde hair swinging behind her as she goes. A poodle barrette sits high up on her head. When she scoots back up into the chair next to her mother, her chubby kid legs jut straight out in front of her. The lower half of her calves and pink sneakers stick out over the edge of the chair. She taps her toes together while she whispers something more to her mom.

A few seconds later, she pulls her feet in close to her as if they might be in the way. She looks up as if watching someone tall pass by, and then she leans forward again to gawk at Rowan.

Rowan's hands are pressed together in front of her face, pointer fingers resting against her bottom lip. Her eyes are closed, and her eyelids flutter.

I look back at the little girl. She's watching. Her eyes go from Rowan to an invisible someone who might be standing directly in front of Rowan's seat, between the two of us. I see nothing.

As I'm trying to make sense of this, Jakob and Sophia return.

Jakob has his arm around Sophia's waist. "Sterling suffered numerous internal injuries," he says. "There was nothing more they could do."

Sophia appears calm, but my heart goes out to her. Losing both parents at such a young age can't be easy.

Aaron crumples forward in his seat and covers his head with his hands.

I put my hand on his back. *He'll be blaming himself for this. He and I will have to talk later.*

"My father came to visit me when he took that break from the lab," Sophia says. "He told me what you've been working on. He tried to give me the book you gave him, Nadia, but I'd already read it. Uncle Jakob bought it for me right after it came out. My dad had an idea you were doing more than what you were telling him, but he wasn't sure he wanted to know. I told him to read the book, and he finally did. He and I talked about it a lot these past few weeks. I could tell he wanted to believe, but the pragmatic side of Dad just couldn't allow it. Uncle Jakob just told me about the experiment you ran today. I knew it would only be a matter of time before you figured it out."

Sophia wipes at her nose with a tissue.

"I actually talked with Dad a few minutes before the accident. He said he was on his way over … said he had good news. I want you to know that he wasn't against you. Of course, I'm sad I didn't get to see him one more time before he had to go, but at least now I know for sure that I can talk to him if I want." Sophia smiles at me. "It's amazing what you've done, Nadia. I guess we just have to find some way to make the process a little simpler for everyone. I want you to know I'm here if you need any help."

A nurse appears and motions to Sophia.

Sophia walks over and accepts her hand. As they move down a long hallway to the right of the nurses' station, Jakob perches on the seat next to Rowan. He leans in and whispers something, but his words are too quiet to hear. When he stands, he takes Rowan's hands, holds them for a second, and then follows Sophia.

Once he's out of sight, I slide into his seat and lean in toward Rowan. "Who were you talking to a little bit ago? Was it Sterling?"

Rowan smiles and pats my knee. "Do you really think Sterling would reach out to me, of all people, even if he knew he could? He's still too proud to admit that he was wrong. I think it might be a while until we hear from him." Her eyes scan the waiting room. "Hospitals are filled with random spirits, Nadia. I see a lot while I'm here … and so does she." Rowan leans forward and points to the little girl in the polka-dot dress. She's spinning in happy circles in front of her mother.

Rowan tilts her head toward Aaron, who is still buckled forward, head in his hands. "He doesn't look so good. Let's get him out of here for a minute and go have a chat."

Rowan squats in front of Aaron and puts her hands on his knees.

Aaron looks up at her. "I should have stopped him! I should have tried harder to make him stay."

People turn to look in our direction.

Rowan pats his knees. "Let's go outside for a second, my dear. Come on."

She and I loop our arms through his and make our way toward the front doors.

"I could have driven him," Aaron says. "Why didn't he just let me drive him? I could have prevented this whole mess. I always get there too late. I'm always too late." He rubs a shirtsleeve over his face and bursts into a sob.

Rowan stops and pulls him into a hug.

The people who were watching look away.

"Now, you listen here," Rowan says. "This is not your fault; it's never been your fault." She tucks her fingers under his chin and tilts his head up so he's looking directly at her. "I need to tell you something, Aaron."

I know what she's about to say, but I wonder if this is the best time.

She rests her forehead against his. "Aaron, I know you probably don't remember a lot of what happened after the fire. Nadia tells me you've blocked a lot of that out, but you came to see me. You came to my shop in the city. Do you remember that?"

Aaron shakes his head.

"It couldn't have been long after the fire. You still had bandages on your face and arms. You were carrying a book, a photo album. You left it at my shop. You only stayed a few minutes, and you didn't say much while you were there, but I knew instantly what happened because you weren't alone when you came in—even though you thought you were. Your family stayed after you left, and they told me everything."

Aaron looks at her and wipes at his eyes.

"Your wife and children were all there with you that day," Rowan says. "For a minute, I thought for sure you could see them. Your eyes went right to where they were standing. Then you looked at me, started crying, and ran out the door. I called after you, but you didn't come back. You never came back."

The little girl in the polka-dot dress comes over, grabs the leg of Aaron's pants, and gives them a tug.

He looks down at her, and the girl's mother nods in my direction.

"They're here now too." The little girl points to the waiting area. "Lilly told me who you were. She said she hates when you're sad, and she asked if I could come over and give you a hug for her."

Aaron looks back toward the chairs, drops to the floor, and starts crying harder than ever.

The little girl wraps her chubby arms around his neck.

He seems to squeeze her almost too tightly, as if he desperately needed the hug.

She pats the back of his head with her tiny hand and sits down next to him.

I look at Rowan, and she also has tears in her eyes.

"Lilly told me all about the scary fire," the little girl says. "She says you did all you could to get them out of the house, just like you tried to help that man today. She saw you trying to get back inside. Even after that big, mean fireman told you no. She's just so, so glad that nothing bad happened to you. She doesn't want you thinking anything is your fault— not from the fire and not from today, 'cause it's not, and she knows it."

Aaron pulls a handkerchief out of his back pocket and blows his nose.

"I believe Lilly is your youngest," Rowan says. "Katelyn, two years older. Anne is your wife. I can give you the album if you want it."

"Annie always kept the albums so nice. It's the only one I could grab. God, I think of them every day."

"As well you should," Rowan says. "But try to focus on the good memories—and not the sad ones. Your girls want to see you happy. It hurts them to see you so sad."

Aaron looks at the little girl. "And what's your name, little one?"

She beams and sticks out her hand. "My name is Elizabeth, but you can call me Lizzy. I told Lilly to call me that too. Our names are almost the same."

Aaron takes her hand and kisses the back of it. "Well, then, sweet Lizzy, I want to thank you for coming over here. You are a dear, dear girl. You tell your mommy that you made an old man's day. How 'bout you go back over there and sit with Lilly while I go find myself a bathroom and clean up a bit. Can't have a grown man leaking all over the waiting room like this, can we?"

Lizzy shakes her head and chuckles into her hand.

When Aaron returns from the restroom, we give Lizzy a wave and head out to the car. We meet up with the rest of the team back at Amulet. In the parking lot, we all take turns pulling each other into hugs.

I'd like to go back inside—and consider sending Aaron home, telling him I'll just sleep in my office for the night—but I can't do that to him or Maeve. They'll both want to know I'm safe, especially after tonight. I look at the team. They stand there as if waiting for someone to tell them what to do. "Why don't you guys take a few days off? We can regroup next week."

Xavier shoots me a questioning glance.

"Seriously," I say. "I think we all need a minute. Be sure to text me when you're home."

CHAPTER 42

The Present
Age Forty-One
Thursday

I wake up to a world that's covered in a thick blanket of white. Standing in front of the bay window with my coffee, I feel the pull of Amulet, but considering what's happened, I don't want to drive unless it's safe. I call Aaron and ask if he's looked at the main roads lately to see if they've been cleared. He tells me that the plows and salt trucks have been out all night and that cars are moving along just fine.

An hour later, when I pull up to Amulet, I see that the grounds crew has already cleared the parking lot. A massive pile of snow is the only evidence that it was once completely covered. The pile takes up most of the parking spaces, so I swing my Escape into the spot right next to it, shut off the engine, and look at the building. *Yesterday, I came here worried only about how the experiment might go, how Sterling would take it, wishing I didn't have to contend with his opinions. Now, here I am, wondering what I'll do without him. Be careful what you wish for, as my mother would say.*

I wait for two students to pass in front of the car before climbing out, and then I follow them down the sidewalk to the front door. Coarse grains of rock salt crunch underfoot, making me think of Maeve when she was little. Every time she heard this, she used to yell, "Fritos!" claiming the noise reminded her of people eating potato chips. It's funny how moments like that get stuck in our minds, no matter how inconsequential they are at the time. I can only hope that Aaron has similar memories of his children.

Inside the front lobby is the Christmas tree Erma put up before leaving for break. I plug it in and place a card and a bag of gourmet chocolates on her desk. She'll be devastated when she hears the news. I turn the corner beyond her desk and head down the hall toward Amulet. The halls are quiet since most of the students have gone for break. The door to the lab is closed, which means that everyone listened to my suggestion and took the day off.

He should be here, I think as I unlock the door. *We should all be here celebrating.*

We'd left in such a hurry that most of the monitors are still on. Papers are strewn everywhere. Sterling's coffee cup sits on the benchtop. I touch it and think of how mad it made me when I saw it yesterday. The helmets on the table look as if they'd just been taken off. I run a hand over one of them. *Brannigan did an amazing job with the upgrades. He'll have to apply for a patent soon.*

I spend the morning tidying up, signing off on the notebooks, and backing up the computer files. While I'm watching the videos of the experiment, I hear a noise behind me. I turn to find Jakob. He's carrying a carafe of coffee.

"I thought you might need this," he says, putting it down on the bench next to a few scattered notebooks. "If you're anything like me, I'm sure you didn't get much sleep last night."

"Don't you know there's no coffee allowed in the lab," I say, and I feel my eyes sting.

Jakob, who's heard me say this a million times to Sterling, smiles and shakes his head.

I tap the side of the pot with my pen. "I wish he was here so I could yell at him again about it."

Jakob drags a stool over from the next bench. I'm not used to seeing him without his suit jacket. He's in khakis and a sweater. His beard is less tamed than usual. "I'll leave you be in a minute," he says. "I know you want to be alone, but before I go, I want to give you something to consider." He studies me, his eyes looking more tired than I've ever seen them before. "You realize that this accident is probably the only way Sterling could be convinced that there's something more, don't you?" He looks at me over his glasses. "Also, I want you to know that Sophia will be fine. I stayed with her last night. She plans to go see Rowan later today ... expects to hear from her dad soon. I don't think Sterling will let Rowan channel him just yet, but I'm absolutely positive he'll find a way to reach Sophia. Sophia just needs to brush up on a few tricks. She'll be talking to both of her parents in no time, thanks to you."

"Do you think Sterling did it on purpose?" I ask.

Jakob seems to mull this over. "Sterling was pretty brazen, but I don't think he would do that to Sophia."

We sit and talk for few minutes, and eventually, Jakob pushes himself off the stool. "I'm sure we'll have more answers in due time, my dear, but for now, I'm going to head up to my office. I need to look into a few things. Yell if you need me, OK? And don't leave without saying goodbye."

"I'll stop by when I'm done here," I say. "Don't let me stay past eight. I don't want Maeve to worry."

I watch him go and then pull a messy stack of papers toward me. After shuffling them into a neat pile, I carry them over to the computer workstation closest to the incubators. I finish typing the last report around six thirty. *This would have been Sterling's job if he was here.* I slide back from the bench and look around the empty lab. "Damn it, Sterling, why were you so fucking stubborn?"

As soon as it's out of my mouth, the lights dim, flicker a few times, and then stabilize. I glance at Sterling's coffee cup next to me and then up at the lights. My pulse quickens. "If that was you, do it again," I say. "I dare you."

I wait, but the lights don't waver. *It could still be him,* I think. *Probably just refusing to give me the satisfaction.*

I pull a pencil out of a beaker and begin pecking at the keyboard in front of me. I think of Sterling, how he must have been trying to piece everything together over the past several months. I want to know what he thought of my book, what he'd been thinking while he watched us yesterday. I think of Juliet, how she helped Dr. Farleigh after the crash and selfishly wonder how much Sterling and Remmington might be able to help our work at Amulet moving forward. As I reach out to return the pencil to the beaker, I notice the monitor, and frown when my eyes finally focus on what's written there.

> Stiles ... Page 100. Stiles ... Page 100. Stiles ... Page 100. Stiles ...

I look around the room and then back at the screen.

I grab my purse from the chair and dig until I find the small brown journal at the bottom, the one Mr. Noah slipped into my bag during our last visit to the Attic. Jillian Stiles's journal. I flip to page 100, far beyond my bookmark, and start to read. At seven o'clock, I put down the book and look around the lab again.

"Jakob is still upstairs," I say out loud. "He'll stop by to check on me if he doesn't see me by eight. I need to try."

Could Stiles be right?

The coatrack just inside the door holds a lab coat for every member of the team. I grab two of them and spread one out on the floor. I roll the other one into a ball and place it just above the collar of the first, and then I stretch out on top of them and stare at the ceiling, using the balled-up coat as a pillow. *Not as comfy as a yoga mat,* I think, *but it'll do.* My heart races. I send a text to Maeve and Aaron and tell them that I love them—just in case this doesn't go as planned.

As it turns out, Jillian Stiles was apparently a fan of Bard too. According to her journal, she'd gotten hold of his notebooks, maybe the same way I'd gotten my hands on hers? It doesn't matter. The only thing that matters is that I know a secret, and I'm exactly the right person to give it a try. I close my eyes, still afraid of what meditation might bring, but I know there's no other way. I do my best to relax, let my breathing slow, and invite them in.

Jillian called them "Umbra," Latin for shadows, and she apparently spent a good deal of time with them in the Baird. My ears begin to ring. A throbbing pain starts above my left eye. I think of the shadows at Gram Marie's and the terror I felt as a child when they got too close. The little-girl part of me wants to stop, but Nadia the scientist can't. With each breath, I force my heartbeat to slow. The right side of my face grows cold.

Something wants me to look in that direction, but I can't make myself do it. Something's definitely there.

The pressure builds in my chest, and breathing becomes difficult. That old sense of panic kicks in. I try to sit up, try to halt the cascade, but it's too late. I no longer have control. I see them looking at me through the glass of the cellar door. The only part of my body that I can move is my eyes.

In the corner of the lab, near the incubator, I see the door to the back room ease open.

"Just a draft," I hear Gram Marie say. "Grandma's old house is just drafty. Don't worry."

I breathe slowly as the door slides open even more, and two shadows emerge. *No glass between us this time.* I close my eyes, concentrate on the jacket under my head, and focus on my shoulder blades and how they press against the tile floor.

"Don't do this, Nadia." It's Remmington's voice now. "Not yet. It's too soon. You're not ready."

I feel the shadows standing next to me, as if I'm lying in the sun and they're blocking its warmth. Coldness seeps in like a shot of Novocain, tingling until all sensation is completely gone. My heart should be racing, but it isn't. I feel nothing in my chest, no sound in my ears. I no longer feel the tile beneath me. It's as if I'm floating. Then I hear the sharp crack.

When I open my eyes, the throbbing pain is gone. I sit up and look around. The room is a blinding white. There's absolutely no noise. Then I hear footsteps behind me.

"Well, well, well," the voice says. "Look who's here."

I turn to find Sterling standing there. He looks no different than he did before. He's dressed in a fleece and jeans. His dark beard and hair are speckled with gray. "This is a very strange place. It's definitely going to take a little getting used to, but I think I'll like it here. There's a lot to learn."

Cats are circling his legs, and I decide I've seen enough of them. They're getting old. To my surprise, though, when I try to remove them from the dream, I can't.

Sterling laughs. "Nice try, but this isn't a dream, Nadia." He holds up his arms as if to display the white space around us. "This is it, the end of the road. The grand finale. I think your father said the cats are how you've seen the shades before, is that right? That's probably why they're here. I've been talking with him a lot actually. He's been a huge help with my orientation, if you want to call it that. Evelyn too. It's amazing how much they've been able to tell me in such a short amount of time, although I'm not quite sure that time follows the same rules here. That's something I'll have to figure out. I do, however, think the team of Sterling, Remmington, and Bard might just find a way to open some doors for Amulet. I think both sides have some serious work to do." He puts his hands in his pockets. "But enough about me, why are you here? I didn't expect to see you so soon—at least not on this level."

"What do you mean? You're the one who led me here with your note on the monitor."

He gives me a confused look. "My note on the monitor says to look at the printer," he says. "I was trying to have you type something for me, but you were taking forever poking at the keys with that damn pencil eraser, so I gave up and wrote the note myself. I saw you look at the screen, thought you saw my message, but then the next thing I knew, you were balling up that lab coat and lying on the floor. I had no idea what you were trying to do. Then I saw the shadows, and I knew you were in trouble. This isn't where you want to be, Nadia. This isn't the second level; this is the third. I think someone's played a trick on you."

"But you typed 'Stiles ... Page 100' over and over again."

He shakes his head. "That wasn't me. Maybe next time you should listen to your dad and Rowan when they tell you not to dabble in things you're only just learning. Didn't you think it a bit fishy when they directed you to Stiles's notebook and not Bard's? They know you have them both. They know Bard got it right. Stiles didn't. It's how she died."

I look at him, stunned, thinking of Maeve, Aaron, and Rowan, all at home waiting for me. *My prediction wasn't wrong after all. What was I thinking? Why couldn't I just leave it well enough alone?*

Sterling points to a space behind me. "Luckily, you have Jakob. It looks like he's on his way back down to the lab right now. Maybe he can fix your little mistake." He looks at his watch. "If you do manage to get back to the lab, do me a favor and check the printer. You should find two sheets of paper there: one for Sophia and one for you."

A green light starts to fill the void around us.

"Do you think it was the Dark Ones that sent that message? Remmington told me they have the ability to stop the living."

Before he can answer, I feel two hands grab my shoulders. They begin shaking me. I hear a thick Scottish accent yelling for help. I turn to my right and see myself on the floor of the lab, Jakob leaning over me, his hands on my shoulders. My eyes are open, but my expression is blank. I understand Jakob's terror. It looks like I'm dead.

"Nadia, talk to me!" Jakob slaps my cheek. "Jesus, come on!" He grabs my chin and wriggles it. "Please! Tell me you can hear me." He begins CPR.

I take a step closer, and as I do, Jakob wheels around and looks directly at me, the me who's watching him from the other side of the lab.

"Quit playing around, Nadia, and get the hell back in here!" he screams, pointing at my body.

As I sink back into consciousness, I feel pain flare behind my eyes. My skin, previously cold, is now on fire. When I grab Jakob's hand, he lets out a huge gasp of air and rolls onto his back beside me, arms out to his sides.

"For heaven's sake! What were you thinking?" He stares at the ceiling and pulls in a deep breath. "Don't you ever, ever, ever scare me like that again! Do you hear me?" He rolls his head in my direction. "What are you trying to do? Send me off to where you just were with no return ticket? You're damn lucky it's only my knees that are going bad. Thank God I still have a strong ticker."

I get up and run to the printer without so much as an apology. Two sheets of paper sit in the tray. I pick them up and read them. "You're right. It is a good thing you still have a strong ticker." I hold the first paper out to him.

He sits up on the floor, takes the piece of paper from me, and reads the sentence out loud. "I'm sorry for being so difficult?" He looks up at me, a confused look on his face.

"It's from Sterling."

Jakob laughs. "Yeah, right, and I'm the pope," he says. "This is *not* from Sterling. He's never said he's sorry for anything. Someone's playing a trick on you."

"Someone did play a trick on me, but I'll tell you about that later. These are both from Sterling. I just talked to him. This one's for Sophia."

Jakob takes a minute to read it, his brow furrowed. "Well, I'll be. These *are* from him. That old bastard. I knew my sister liked him for a reason."

I grab Jakob's hand and help him to his feet.

He dusts off his pants and pulls me into a hug. "Don't get me wrong, what you just did took guts, but that doesn't mean it was OK—or that you should ever do it again. You can tell me all about it later, but maybe after a few drinks, eh? For right now though, let's just get out of here and get home. You made me promise I wouldn't let you stay beyond eight, and it's already a little past."

As we make our way down the west wing corridor, I thread an arm through his. "Why didn't you ever talk about Evelyn around Sterling?"

He shrugs. "Force of habit, I guess. It used to upset him. He took her death pretty hard—and what happened with Einstein didn't help. My sister's coma was induced by a stroke as well. She was also placed on life support. When Sterling had to make that decision a second time, I'm sure it brought back a flood of memories. The first time was bad enough."

We pass the Christmas tree near Erma's desk, navigate the revolving door, and step outside. It's quiet, and the snow looks beautiful in the moonlight.

"Rowan and I actually spoke with Evelyn when she was in the coma," Jakob says as we walk to my car. "Evelyn told us she wanted Sterling to turn off the machines, that she didn't want to return to a body if it was less than functional." Jakob paused. "Do you know how hard it was to explain that conversation to Sterling?"

"I can't even imagine."

"As soon as Sterling agreed to pull life support, he immediately regretted it. He blamed me and Rowan, didn't talk to me for quite some time and never forgave her. Sophia pleaded with him to make amends with me, and eventually, he did, once he realized I was hurting too." Jakob stops in front of my car and kicks at a chunk of ice. "You know the rest of the story."

"So, Sterling never talked about Evelyn either?"

"Sterling hardened after her death. He never mentioned her name, never talked about old times. It was his only way to cope, I think, and it's a shame because she could see it all. Our loved ones rely on us to share our memories once they pass. Keeping them alive in conversation keeps them alive in spirit. When Sterling saw that last experiment, I think he realized he hadn't been doing that—and I think that hurt him more than anything else." Jakob gives me a hug. "Go home. Go have a nice dinner with your girl. Rest your mind for a bit. Let the dust settle. I'll talk to you soon."

At home, I find Rowan and Maeve in the library, both stretched out on the rug, my journals scattered around them as if they've been sharing a few old stories. Aaron is parked in one of the leather chairs, the dogs at his feet and Ares in his lap. There's a fire going in the fireplace.

Maeve rolls onto her back and glares up at me. "No more texts like that," she says. "It's great to hear that you love me and all, but until I know you're safe and sound, don't ever scare me like that again."

"Deal," I say as I bend down to give her a hug, thanking my lucky stars that Jakob came back to the lab to find me.

CHAPTER 43

The Present
Age Forty-One
Saturday

We arrive at the arboretum for Sterling's memorial service at eleven o'clock in the morning. The temperature is mild, warm enough for a thin sweater. Most of the snow is gone, leaving only wet pavement behind. The sky is a brilliant blue.

Inside the conservatory, I sign the guest book, and watch as Maeve and Aaron do the same. Just beyond it, an urn sits on a white marble pillar tucked among a massive display of amaryllis and paperwhites.

"Evelyn and Jorg's favorite flowers," says a woman in line behind us. "They used to fill the entire house with them at Christmas. They loved coming here."

Maeve wraps an arm around me as we follow a path lined with poinsettias to join the others. Folding chairs are arranged in neat rows on a square of grass that's been planted in the center of the huge room. The glass ceiling above us is nearly three stories high, the walls covered with climbing vines.

When the service is over, Maeve and I join Xavier and his great-grandmother near a display of tropical plants. She's a broad woman, very tall like him, and given her age, I'm amazed at how well she moves and speaks. He introduces her to us as Nana May, and we chat for quite some time.

Rowan eventually joins us. Of course, she and May hit it off immediately, so when I spot Sophia and Jakob just ahead in the Orchid

Room, I don't feel bad excusing myself. They stand shoulder to shoulder, admiring one of my favorites, a small unassuming *Paphiopedilum* with mottled leaves and short flower spikes.

Jakob sees me coming. "Ah, there you are," he says.

He pulls me into a hug, and Sophia does the same. Her perfume clings to my sweater, and I recognize it immediately. Anais Anais, one of Gram Marie's favorites. It's why I love the smell of jasmine. I think of what Remmington said about soulmates in my dream, and I immediately wonder if Sophia might be one piece of Gram Marie's puzzle.

"Thank you for coming," Sophia says. "I know my father could be a challenge sometimes, but he actually really enjoyed working with you. He talked about you a lot."

"Your father and I had our moments," I say, smiling, "but overall, I think we got along pretty well."

"Oh, that reminds me." Jakob digs into the breast pocket of his suit jacket. "I almost forgot to give this to you." He hands Sophia a folded sheet of paper.

"What's this?" As she reads, a smile spreads across her face. "Where did you get it?"

Jakob lets me explain.

Sophia listens and then says, "You know, I graduate soon. I'd love to join the team if you'd have me. We can figure this out, especially if we're able to approach the problem from both sides."

I look at Jakob. "What do you think? Proceeding without a Sterling in the lab just doesn't seem right—if you ask me."

Sophia smiles as she waves to an older couple headed in our direction. "I should probably go say hi, but let's make a plan soon, OK?"

Jakob watches her go, and my heart aches for him, but not as much as it would if we didn't know what we know already. The loss of two parents at such a young age is an awful tragedy, but knowing that you haven't truly lost them must make it a little less painful. Plus, I know that Sophia is in good hands, surrounded by Jakob and our entire team.

I take Jakob's arm and lead him over to where Maeve is standing with Rowan and Aaron.

"Xavier and May had to go," Rowan explains. "Her feet were getting tired, poor thing. Xavier said he'd see you tomorrow, though, and May said we're all invited to her hundredth birthday party—so she'll see us then."

"What do you say we head over to the house for coffee?" I ask. "Sit on the patio? Take advantage of this mild winter weather?"

Rowan grabs Aaron's hand and smiles up at him. "We were actually planning a walk in your garden already, weren't we, Aaron?"

Perfect, I think. *They can walk in the garden while I tend to something else.*

CHAPTER 44

The Present
Age Forty-One
Saturday

Back at the Baird, we gather on the patio. The chairs have been put away for the winter, but Aaron pulls a few out of the garden shed and arranges them around the table. He helps Maeve set up her favorite lounge chair in the grass.

I make a pot of coffee, and Maeve serves the remainder of the chocolate cake she baked the day before.

We sit at the wrought iron table in the sun, watching as it melts what's left of the snow. The sky seems an even brighter blue now that the clouds have cleared.

Once we've finished our coffee, Maeve says, "I'm gonna go get my book."

She returns a few minutes later and curls up on the lounge chair, a blanket over her shoulders, the book propped up against her thighs. The dogs settle in around her.

Rowan and I clear the table, and when we're done, Rowan hands Aaron the photo album he left in her shop years before.

He flips through it, and tears roll down his cheeks. When he stops to look up at Rowan, she points to the wall enclosing the rose garden. She's promised him a reading.

They start down the path, and once they're out of sight, I run a hand over Maeve's hair.

She looks up at me and smiles. She knows what I mean to do.

302

From the studio, I grab Jillian Stiles's old easel and the palette. I tuck a few tubes of her oil paints into a box, along with a fresh jar of turpentine, and carry it all out onto the patio. The last thing I need is still in the attic.

The old stairs are narrow and steep, and they creak under my feet. At the top, I turn left and continue along the open path that Aaron and I cleared when we were up here last. In the far corner, next to an old cheval mirror, I see what I've come for. One last blank canvas is propped against the wall.

I carry it down to the second floor and use my hip to nudge the attic door closed behind me. The attic is drafty, so the door slams shut with a bang. In the kitchen, I stop at the island to grab another cup of coffee. Through the bay window, I see Maeve nestled in her lounge chair. She turns a page. I look at the box of art supplies on the table and realize I've forgotten something, the jar of palette knives. I want to use as many of Jillian's things as I can.

When I turn the corner at the top of the stairs, I'm surprised to find the attic door open. I clearly remember shutting it. I poke my head into the stairwell, feeling for a draft, and then I step back out into the hallway.

Be careful what you wish for, I think.

Yes, I've decided to summon a shade, to see one up close on my own, one that doesn't just look like a shadow. I can't have Xavier seeing them when I can't. It's time to tackle my fear once and for all. I don't want to see it here, though, not while I'm alone. I prefer the idea of seeing one outside on the patio—with Maeve close by.

I peer up the stairwell.

Maybe where I see them isn't my choice, I think as I creep up the stairs.

When I reach the last step and see the woman standing at the other end of the attic, my throat tightens. I can't even scream. It takes a few seconds to realize that the woman is only my reflection in the mirror.

I look up at the rafters and laugh. "Jesus, Nadia," I say, shaking my head. "Pull it together. Either you want to see them—or you don't. You need to make up your damn mind."

I do want to see them, just not here.

I quickly grab the jar of palette knives and practically fly back down to the second-floor hallway. I used to do this as a kid at Gram Marie's, convinced that someone was right behind me ready to grab my ankles. I slam the door closed, probably much harder than I should.

When I carry everything outside onto the patio, Maeve is still reading on the lounge and doesn't even seem to notice that I'm back. I set up the easel so it faces the house. Ares is perched on the outside ledge of the bay window, licking a paw. I arrange the paints and palette in front of me and throw a damp rag over the arm of the chair.

No painting from memory this time. No looking at notes jotted in a journal. Today, I'll paint what I see in real time.

"Good luck," I hear Maeve say quietly as I close my eyes.

I imagine my father at the beach, his favorite place. I think of him standing in the waves, looking out at the water, the sun on his back. I call to him and let him turn to face me. It's a trick Rowan taught me to get a spirit's attention, to call them to you. As I start to paint Ares, he remains perfectly still, watching me with those green eyes, his whiskers catching the sun. As I place a small dot of white on his right pupil, the sun's reflection, his head turns toward the window. I see the movement too, through the glass, inside the kitchen. Something tall.

Ares leaps down from the window ledge and jumps up onto the patio chair across from me. He looks back toward the house, and before I can stop him, he's up on the table and across it, his feet tracking over the palette filled with paint.

"Have you lost your mind?" I say, grabbing hold of him. "You're not allowed up here."

Maeve chuckles as I grab the rag and try to wipe off his paws.

"He's been acting strange all day," she says. "Just this morning—"

I look at her, wondering why she's stopped midsentence, and she points toward the house.

"Turn around," she says. "Tell me you see him."

"Who?" I ask, turning to look. The bay window is empty. I look down the cobblestone path toward the driveway, thinking maybe someone has pulled in.

"Right in front of you." Maeve whispers, as if trying not to draw too much attention to what she sees, like when you see a beautiful bird but don't want to move for fear you'll frighten it away.

My ears start to ring. The left side of my face feels hot. I look to where Maeve is pointing and see nothing at first, but then, there he is. My father, Remmington, is sitting in the chair across from me, suntanned, his bald spot tinted a deep brown.

"And them too?" Maeve points toward the garden.

I turn, hoping to find Gram Marie, thinking maybe Remmington was wrong, that she's fine. Instead of Gram Marie, I find Evelyn. She's sitting on the stone wall, just like she was when Remmington brought her to the house in my dream. Only this time, Sterling is at her side. They're talking, like they don't even know we're here.

Remmington reaches his hand toward the cat, and Ares sniffs at the air just above his palm. Quake's head is turned in that direction too, but he doesn't growl—as if he knows this particular shade is allowed to be here. The other two dogs are fast asleep in the grass, oblivious.

"I think it's time to paint," Remmington says.

An old woman I don't recognize slides into the seat next to me. She helps me choose the colors, pushing them toward me with wrinkled fingers. Jillian, I presume. As I begin to paint, I feel a set of hands come to rest on my shoulders.

"Beautiful," Rowan says. "You're getting pretty damn good at this."

She and Aaron are back from their walk.

"Third time's a charm," I say, and as soon as it's out of my mouth, the smell of jasmine fills the air. I turn and search the yard, but the person I hope to find isn't there.

Rowan gives my shoulders a squeeze. "I smell it too. Don't worry. We'll keep working on that one—and we'll figure it out. You have my word."

EPILOGUE

From the Journal of Nadia King
One year later

> It came as a whisper ...
> Open your eyes.
> What do you see?
> Now close them, and make yourself believe me when I
> tell you there is so much *more*.
> Now open your eyes. Has anything changed?
> Your answer should be ... everything.

When Remmington first wrote this for me, I didn't know what he meant by it. Clearly, he was referring to my dreams, to what I allowed myself to see in them, but not see in real life. It's the common thread that has woven its way through my life over the years. I haven't yet figured out if all of the shadows were real, or if they were just something my mind cooked up due to lack of sleep. I just know that I'm sleeping better now, and I don't see them anymore. Then again, maybe that's just because I see them as more than just shadows these days.

Maybe those I used to call the Dark Ones, Jillian's Umbra, are just biding their time, waiting to see how much prodding we do at Amulet. We're certainly making progress, and why wouldn't we be with so many on the other side now?

Sophia has joined the team at Amulet, and over the past few weeks, we've added another tool to our toolbox, another ingenious invention by Brannigan, a set of probes that can stimulate the cells of the CT. Using these, we think we might be able to train CT cells to pick up on a range of signals.

Aaron has volunteered to be our guinea pig. The first time he wore the helmet, he showed no CT activity. Now, after several rounds of treatment with the probes, he's pushing 50 percent red every time.

I've canceled my work with Jakob in the sleep lab, deciding that I don't need his help anymore. I've been doing my own reading and have learned some fascinating things. I guess I never realized that REM sleep helps us consolidate our thoughts, helps us make sense of the things our minds don't fully grasp while we're awake.

Remmington and I talk nearly every day. Turns out I didn't need my dad's journals after all. Having him here to share the stories in person is so much better.

I'm not sure if Lydia still sees Remmington in her dreams. We primarily stick to business when we talk these days. My second novel, like the first, is selling like wildfire. I give the royalties to Aaron and let him do whatever he wants with the Baird. He's as happy as a clam these days. Sometimes when I pass the carriage house, I see him on the porch with Lilly, Katelyn, and Anne. He can't see them yet, but he knows they're there. I give him a few months. By then, he'll be up to speed. I'm not working on any new novels right now—even though Lydia keeps asking for one. We have far too much to do in the lab. I want to focus, and I want time to enjoy my new company.

Paul and Mary are now running Sterling's other lab. The new chimp is doing fine. Her CT signal is strong. Given that Einstein and Zena seemed to know how to communicate across the levels, I have a pretty good hunch that they both have something to do with the new girl's speedy progress. That discovery will come in time. As for souls being recycled, redistributed, and divided, I'm still working on that one too. The idea fascinates me.

I've finished reading the rest of Jillian's journal. To use Aaron's words, she's an interesting bird, that one. She pops in frequently, as well, and she isn't afraid to offer her opinions while I'm painting, especially if she thinks I haven't gotten a color right. She sometimes even guides my brush when she's feeling extra pushy.

A map she drew on page 90 turned out to be something of a treasure hunt. I followed her instructions to the back of the attic this morning, saw the loose floorboard, and pulled it up. Underneath were four journals, bound together with a piece of twine. The symbols on the front of each are identical to the one on her painting journal. This is why I recognized it. I don't know how she got them, but the journals belong to Sir Anthony Bard. Mr. Noah is going to lose his mind when I tell him about these. I can't tell anyone just yet, though. This is my secret, and Remmington's, for now. I want to try a few things first.

As for Xavier, he and I have been spending a lot of time together. Rowan was right. I would have been silly to let this one go.

> Birth is not a beginning; death is not an end. There is existence without limitation; there is continuity without a starting point.
> —Chuang Tzu, Chinese mystic

And finally, another favorite saying of my mother's when I was searching for something and couldn't see it, even though it was right under my nose:

> If it was a snake, it woulda bit ya.
> —Sandra King

CPSIA information can be obtained
at www.ICGtesting.com
Printed in the USA
BVHW040706300822
645633BV00022B/37